DEADRISE

A Ben Blackshaw Novel

by

Robert Blake Whitehill

TELEMACHUS PRESS

CALAVERAS
MEDIA

DEADRISE

Cover Designed by Brian Boucher/Barsoom Design
With Photographs by Michael C. Wootton

Cover Art:
Copyright © Calaveras Media
Photography Copyright © Calaveras Media

Published by Telemachus Press, LLC
http://www.telemachuspress.com
In Association with Calaveras Media
http://www.calaverasmedia.com

Visit the author website:
http://www.robertblakewhitehill.com

ISBN: 978-1-938701-38-2 (eBook)
ISBN: 978-1-938701-39-9 (Paperback)

Version 2012.09.04

Printed in the United States of America

10 9 8 7 6 5 4 3 2 1

To my family

CONTENTS

Dedication

While writing *Deadrise*, I had the privilege of working with a fine crew of Emergency Medical Technicians who serve on the Montclair Ambulance Unit (www.MVAU.org). They stand watch at all hours, ready to aid the infirm, the troubled, and the broken patients who are likely experiencing the worst ten minutes of their entire lives. These stalwart heroes include Mavis Oklahoma Amoakohene, Matt Antolino, Colin Bloody Baker, Justin Banasz, Rescue Mary Berghoefer, Sgt. Tuna Berghoefer, Robert Bertoli, Kris The Beav Bevacqua, Benjamin J. Campos, Deputy Chief Frank Carlo, Michelle Carlo, Richard Chang and the Rescue Gang, Greelensky Charles, Sean Coffey Like the Drink But Spelled Differently, Michael Bigfoot Craig, Brett Davis, Chris DeAngelis, Vincent DeRosa, William Fitzpatrick, Deana Flynn, Elise Fournier, Lt. Aaron Avi Friedman, Ariana Goodman, Steve Goodman, Adam Gubar, Matt Guth, Sean Happy Meal Graham, Brack Healy, Brian Heff Heffernan, Deborah Herr, Sara Herr, Jim High, Jr., Jim High, Sr., Jonathan Doogie Hirsh, Rennie Jacob, Drew Johnson, Renee Karain, Corey Keepers, Dan Kosciuszko, Anastasia Lambert, Nick The Saint Lindstedt, Aaron Cheeks Lowe, Elisa MacLean, Sgt. Julie Fireball Martin, Tim Thanks for the Bagel McLoughlin, Alejandra Menendez, Paul Middlemiss, Michael Minnicozzi, Andy Montick, Tim T-Pain Peterson, Stacy Hayes Przybylinski, Ron Roberts, Mark Rossi, Lisa Schneider, Jeanne Scott, Joe Sente, Chief Jamie Simpson, Sue Simpson, Jim Skiba, Denise Smyth, Don Stapp, Sam Sutherlin, Jason Swayze, Justin Thompson, Kelley Tierney, Jeanine Troisi, and Erica Wolfe.

The steadfast men and women named here, many of whom served on the pile in New York City on September 11th, 2001, or who have served us bravely and with great sacrifice in the military, are supported by a dedicated board of directors, a crack team of Advanced Life Support medics, and our area emergency department doctors, nurses, and staff. Officers of the Montclair Police Department and firefighters of the Montclair Fire Department are always eager to lend a helping hand with our toughest cases. Together, they make the life-or-death difference on a 911 call in our town. I have witnessed miracles with them.

Special Acknowledgments

My mother, Cecily Sharp-Whitehill, is a poet and an elegant editor. My father, Joseph Whitehill, was an award-winning short story writer and novelist. They showed me what a writer's daily life looks like.

My bride, Mary Whitehill, is a profoundly astute reader. I have learned in the course of creating *Deadrise* that anything hanging up Mary's read of a draft needs prompt and certain attention, no argument. Ignoring her just means hearing the same notes from somebody else later on. She is ever my saving grace. My young son, Beau, is keenly attuned to the perfect moment to take a break from work to play with trains.

Eloise Johnson taught me to read, the gift of a lifetime. My fiction writing was further honed by teachers Josh Schmidt and Tom Woodward at Westtown School, Professor Dominic le Poer Power of the British and European Studies Group London, Professor Robert Butman at Haverford College, and Robert McKee.

Undertaking *Deadrise* was suggested by my dear friend Matthew Bialer, of Sanford J. Greenberger and Associates. His cogent ideas of style along the way helped transform me from writer to author. Good friends (and excellent agents) are like lifeguards who strongly suggest not swimming in riptides of one's own making.

Jason Sitzes, director of the Writers Workshop Retreat, dug deeply into the manuscript and emerged with a wealth of fresh schemes and new approaches to old problems in the work. Jason is an editor who helps fill a tale with color and texture by encouraging you to write deeply into all the corners of every room in the story.

Readers of first drafts are visionaries, like Detroit engineers who can squint at a mound of pig-iron and see a Cadillac. Among these kind souls are Sarah Davies, Barbara Mackie Franklin, Andrea Shane, and Diane Wilder. Their detailed notes were simply crucial.

Wayne Grant Hon Lawson was my most generous guide on Smith Island. He helped bring the people of Smith and Tangier to life, with delightful, winding stories and astounding introductions.

Tom Crouch was the first (and last) person I met who dived for Chesapeake oysters instead of dredging or tonging them up. It must have been a cold business for him, but it was inspiring for me.

There is an actual Michael Craig, and he does have a company called Pemstar (www.Pemstar.biz). Craig can work pretty much all the miracles in reality that his fictional avatar does in *Deadrise*. It's rather scary.

For a Quaker and an Emergency Medical Technician concerned with the preservation of human life, Adam Gubar is extremely knowledgeable about the hardware of life's undoing. He has been a tremendous help in matters of shooting iron, and an interested friend through the whole journey. Any errors having to do with arms and the strategies and tactics associated with their use in this story are mine alone.

Bill Jarblum, a fine feature film producer and storyteller, made some far-reaching observations about *Deadrise* late in the game, but just in time.

Suzanne Dorf Hall was kind enough to drop everything and cast her eagle eye over the manuscript, asking great questions, and making sure it looks like I can spell.

Rusty Shelton, of Shelton Interactive LLC, along with Allison Bright, Amber McGinty, Beth Gwazdosky, Richard Ricondo, William Ruff, Andrea Sanchez, Susan Savkov, Katie Schnack, Shelby Sledge, Jeremy Strom, and Nick Welp built me a beautiful website, got the word out about *Deadrise* in a heroic PR campaign, and made sure when social media mavens and bloggers pointed a mic at me, I didn't make too big a fool of myself.

Kate Knapp and Marissa Madill at Smith Publicity have also been instrumental in helping *Deadrise* find its audience. Writing is solitary and difficult. Authorship is a team effort, and while this is also no easy thing, it is a genuine pleasure to undertake the job with great people like these.

Mike Wootton is a truly gifted photographer who somehow managed to prevent the ruination of beautiful pictures of Smith Island at moments when I lurched into frame.

Brian Boucher/Barsoom Design created wonderful cover artwork for *Deadrise*, undoing that tired adage, and proving we *do* judge a book by its cover. Thank you, Brian, for being so dogged in getting it right long after I was happy.

Corinda DeVingo, proprietor of Beans, in Montclair, supplies the high-test coffee that any writer needs to carry on. There is no such thing as writer's block when one is hopped up on her Writer's Blend.

Samantha Codling stokes the oven fires at The Pie Store in Montclair, New Jersey. Her Lucullan sweet and savory creations keep body and soul together when the muse is upon you and there is no time for home cooking.

Karl Guthrie is a great legal scholar, as well as a peerless attorney. I am filled with confidence when I chat with him before any important move.

My life-crew. I thank each and every one of them from my heart and soul.

RBW
27 July 2012
Chestertown, Maryland

DEADRISE

A Ben Blackshaw Novel

PART I
HOMECOMING

CHAPTER 1

BEN BLACKSHAW DIVED the Chesapeake Bay for oysters, not corpses. November's chill stripped off any hope of comfort by a few more degrees each day. The silt, churned up from the late season hurricane dubbed *Odette* in a crackle of the World Meteorological Organization's creativity, clouded his view. It was tough to fill the plastic milk crate tied to his deadrise workboat bobbing fifteen feet above. Another oyster reef might have better pickings. He checked his watch. Not the best news. There was barely time to surface, move the boat God knows how far, and get back on the bottom to a fresh rock before dark.

Air flowed to Ben via the hose from *Miss Dotsy*'s compressor, which ended in a cracked second-hand, second-stage regulator he clamped in his teeth. The air churned through this old equipment tasted as if it had first passed over a swamp before arriving in his mouth. Such a crude rig might have earned a Gallic sneer from the Speedo-and-beanie set on Cousteau's *Calypso*, but it put Ben hands-on to his catch. That's what he wanted. Tonging oysters from the surface, or even dredging them, was working blind and too damn slow. Oyster seasons were getting shorter as the bay's pollution killed off shellfish stocks. Ben needed to earn. There was somebody special. Ben had plans.

Until that macabre discovery, the silt was clearing much too slowly. Ben passed his time grubbing and groping in the chilly dark as he often did, humming *Plastic Houses* by Chester River Runoff, the one bluegrass band he genuinely admired. The lyrics railed against malignant suburban sprawl, and

spoke eloquently to Ben's humor, which was as foul as the weather threatened to become with the new storm, named *Polly*, freshening in the south.
The times, it seemed, were leaving Ben behind with little hope of catching
up, even if he wished to.

Then, out of nowhere, a rogue current shoved Ben, and sluiced the
suspended sediment away as if drawing back a curtain. And there he was. A
dead man. Obviously a drowner, kneeling near the edge of the oyster rock.
Toes mired in the mud as if in final prayer. The prayer had gone
unanswered, like a collect call home from a kid who's mooched off his folks
one time too many.

The dead man's longish white hair floated in a halo. It was bedizened
with small spottail shiners, and a lone mummichog far from its shoreline
school; all darting in and out of the gently waving locks. What Ben could
see of the cadaver's face was blanched, puffed. It was down here only a few
days at most. Water and its denizens break a body down fast and ugly.
Ashes to ashes, flesh to fish-food.

A late season blue crab dined on an outstretched hand. Spatulate crab
legs and the dead man's finger bones all beckoned to Ben. *Come closer.*

Ben had seen dead bodies before, battle trauma mostly. More men
than he cared to remember had died by his own hand. A proud nation
thanked him for every target terminated. That was in another country. A
dead soldier in a foreign desert was a damn sight different from a bloated
sailor's body in home waters. A drowner spasmed the bitter tang of bile
into the back of Ben's throat. They were a common enough tragedy here.
Usually drunken boaters in summertime, but there were others from closer.
Not for the first time, Ben considered the irony. On Smith Island where he
was born, raised, and made his home, many watermen eked out a living on
the Chesapeake, but could not swim a stroke in it.

Whatever Ben's deeper feelings on the human condition, this deader
was less a tragedy than he was an interruption to his work. The legal hassles
of revealing a body to the proper authorities would cost him precious time
on the bottom over the next few hours and days. Ben was torn. He checked
his watch again, glanced into the nearly empty milk crate. He should have
gotten out of the water ten minutes back and avoided all this. He could still
abandon the corpse and its ensnaring problems, and get topside to hunt

more plentiful oysters elsewhere. The day's catch was altogether too light, and too late. It would not even cover gas. Surface and earn, or take a moment more to quash a growing curiosity. Ben still wondered if he knew the man.

With the air hose trailing behind, Ben paddled and slogged across the bottom toward the remains like *Diver Dan,* that leadfooted 60's TV hard-hat he'd caught in reruns as a kid. With every step, his leaky old wetsuit traded the warmer water next to his body for a chilly, brackish slurry. Ben knew exactly what a winning NFL coach went through when the ice chest was dumped over his head. Ben had no hot locker room shower close by, and he certainly had no cheering fans. Early hypothermia was Ben's constant pal down here, and it was always trying to kill him.

A collapsed airman's Mae West life-vest floated around the body's neck, obscuring much of the face. Worked for Ben. Though it billowed slightly, Ben still recognized the dead man's coat as an old green Army field jacket. Not uncommon gear among Smith Island's war vets. There was something weird about it. A spark of familiarity flashed through Ben's cold-wracked mind. His synapses fired, but the timing was off, like an old jalopy engine in need of its spring tune-up. Maybe this was a friend of his. Possibly a neighbor. God forbid, not a relative. There were few enough of those. Then, beyond the corpse's shoulder, Ben saw the wreck.

More trudging, and Ben stood in a low whirl of silt by the bow of a beautiful Nantucket Lance. *Finders keepers.* It was about twenty-five feet long, and way fancier than his own *Miss Dotsy.*

Ben's ancient boat had classic sweeping Chesapeake lines laid up out of marine plywood. She was powered by a humble Atomic Four engine that belched smoke, rattled, and snarled, and though loud and dirty, it was as reliable as a Timex. Throttle wide open, *Miss Dotsy* could do only ten knots at best. That's with a following sea.

This fiberglass water rocket lying before him on the bottom had a center console, and three big Mercury 225 Pro XS engines slung off the transom. Far too much power for such a small boat. This baby would shit'n-git, flying over the water with a hydroplane's kiss and spank, barely under control at full throttle. It was not really a racer. It was a hauler, a modern-day rumrunner.

That point was driven home when he saw some kind of cargo tied down under a tarp with canvas web strapping. With his old dive knife, Ben slashed a strap, untucked the tarp's corner and raised it. The water silted out again. Took a few moments to clear. He saw a bunch of stacked footlockers. Or ammo boxes? Ben could not be sure in this poor light. Whatever, it was salvage now. His salvage. *Losers weepers.* Maybe there was some old estate silver in the boxes. Or at least some interesting junk that some collector might covet at the Crumpton auction.

He aimed his dive light at the closest box. The bolt, the lid hinges, the usual points of vulnerability were all internal. That was strange, but okay. Maybe the boxes themselves could fetch a price. He probed the lock with the tip of his knife. No joy. The keyhole was really a flat slot. Ben twisted the blade hard. It snapped in half with a cracking ping. *Damn.* A new knife would be expensive, another setback in trying to save up. Maybe something in his kitchen drawer would fit the sheath.

As Ben pulled the broken end of the knife from the lock, a recollection suddenly wraithed into his mind. Mental gears began to grate, to scream, and then mesh and hum.

Like the dead man, the boat was also vaguely familiar. Though Ben was sure he had never actually seen this craft before, he had heard something like it described on many long winter nights as one man's ideal. A pleasure boat, yes, but with speed enough to outrun a Natural Resources Police patrol. It was not a workboat. Not for lawful work anyway. It was a poor waterman's fantasy. Not quite practical, but certainly modest next to the mega-yachts of the rich and diminutively hung.

Yes, Ben noted the vaunted Raymarine radome perched high on its pylon. And there was the latest generation Garmin GPS. And independent fuel lines, tanks, separators, and batteries for each engine. *Check.* Extreme-duty Lenco trim tab. *Present.* Many other custom details, redundancies, and failsafes Ben recalled hearing about lay foundered right there in front of him.

The man who had spoken so wistfully of this perfect go-fast boat had vanished fifteen years ago. Ben felt sick with horror. He had not recognized the decomposing face, but he had zeroed-in on the dead man's fantasy-come-true.

Galvanized, now oblivious to fatigue and cold, Ben roiled his way back to the gently davening corpse. Swallowing a gag at the thought of contact with the sodden dead, Ben grabbed the field jacket's lapel. He read the faded name stenciled on the strip of cloth sewn above the right chest pocket. Not the right name.

Ben knew this man. Felt it, but he had no proof. Frustrated, he clawed the wallet from the jacket's inner pocket. As his flashlight batteries weakened, the small writing on the driver license faded in and out. He shook the flashlight hard. The beam brightened for a moment. The name on the license was wrong, too; and it was different from the name on the jacket. Tom Chase. An alias, maybe? Ben was collecting more questions than answers. Far more questions than oysters.

It was the license photograph that caught Ben's breath. Bubbles stopped rising from his regulator as his neck muscles cinched down like a noose. He angled his failing dive light on the picture to be sure. The entire world swam before his eyes. He closed the wallet, pulled the Mae West down, fully revealing the cadaver's face. One dead eye was being consumed by the bay's marine marauders. Now it was just a dark half-lidded socket. The other eye, the right one, gazed out at him bright and implacable. Ben thought he saw the telltale scar running brow to cheek across that eye.

So much time had passed. Too many questions and truths would now have to go unspoken forever. This was not how things were supposed to end. Ulysses, the warrior, had almost made it home after so long away. All at once Ben felt the cold again. His body ached with sadness, and he heard the death rattle of hope in his heart. From a soul-deep anguish, all that sifted into Ben's frozen mind was a boy's greeting from long ago. "Afternoon, Pap."

CHAPTER 2

MAYNARD CHALK HAD her number cold, and hated her with a febrile passion. With superhuman effort he suppressed the urge to cut her throat right there on the plane. Folks behind the scenes, including her aides and a handful of journalists, knew Senator Lily Morgan, (R) Wisconsin, was anything but the sweet grandmother she appeared to be. Her white hair yanked back into a wispy bun, her matronly curves, and pink Mrs. Claus cheeks belied a ruthless nature equaled by very few outside cage-fighting circles. The Senator's small coterie of likeminded sociopaths included Chalk, who was lolling in the wide leather seat beside her. He soothed himself. He had to be back in Washington as quickly as possible. Might as well hitch a free ride on the Senator's private Bombardier Challenger 605.

Chalk was Senator Morgan's factotum, but only for a little while longer. The real price of the flight was letting her roast his personal chestnuts on an open fire. She was pissed about something, and this was another of her annoying, secret meetings with Chalk. To be endured. A genuine time-suck. According to their discreet protocol, he had boarded her jet in Milwaukee long before she arrived at the field, lest the press glimpse them together. On the other end of the flight to D.C., Chalk would have to wait on the darkened chilly plane until the Senator's limo and any reporters had been gone from the airport a full hour. What happened between take-off and landing was usually sheer hell for Chalk. Senator Morgan called them *pep talks*.

The distinguished lady from Wisconsin hissed, "Word's getting around you've lost your edge. That something's wrong on this operation. Is everything going my way? Spit it out. I want a *sit-rep*. Isn't that what you whacked-out Vietnam *grumps* call it?"

Chalk would never see fifty again, and right now he was feeling every one of his years times ten. He had helped the Senator get into local, then national office lo these many years ago by queering critical precinct returns. Black Ops were his main business, after all. Thanks to Chalk, the Senator now held enough key committee seats to work cloakroom Iran/Contra type deals every day of the week. In return for his help, she cut him in. Gigs like this were Chalk's meat and potatoes since his soul-curdling tours in Southeast Asia as an operative with Air America.

Among many other global clients, he had provided ironclad deniability to seven United States Presidents. He quietly handled all the treasonous patch-jobs that kept any modern ship of state afloat. Next to Chalk's outfit, the mercenary soldiers of Winedark Inc. were inept pansies.

Chalk unclenched his jaw, jerry-built a smile, and slapped it on the front of his head. "I think you mean *grunts*. And everything to do with this gig is on time, on target and on message. Who the hell's saying there's a problem?"

Lily Morgan looked at Chalk hard with her bright, twinkling eyes. Then she reached into her quilted knitting bag. Chalk suppressed the urge to lean away. He half expected her to draw a gun or a viper from the satchel. Instead, she removed a gaily-decorated cookie tin, opened it, and offered him a chocolate chip. "I know how much you like these."

Fit and robust as he was, Chalk patted his small tummy roll and waved off the treats. "Thanks, I'm good. Trying to work off the ol' flabdomen." He suspected there was a dash of cyanide in the recipe until Lily ate one herself. "Now who the hell is telling you damnable and salacious lies about my operation?"

Chewing, she poked a cookie at him, scattering crumbs. "Never you mind who said what, Maynard. This job has to be perfect. It's a matter of national security, and profoundly affects the health of our economy well beyond the current administration—"

"Blah-blah-blah." Chalk rolled his eyes. "Save it for your next pancake prayer breakfast. But lay off the Mrs. Butterworth, eh? For God's sake, your ass is already due for its own zip code."

Lily lowered her voice. "Listen up, fuckstick. If this job goes south, I am in deep trouble. Which means your life won't be worth a tinker's damn. Both interested parties must be very happy when you're done brokering the deal. Everybody has to receive exactly what they're paying for, and no skimming. Get me?"

"Sure, I got you like the clap. Can't this damn bird go any faster? I have actual business to take care of."

Chalk was so sick of this old bag. Jibes aside, she really was getting too big for her bloomers. Her biggest mistake was forgetting he could read her like a comic book. She was getting greedy, starting to resent handing over his rightful cut when it was due. Knowing her, she might have placed a mole inside his shell company, *Right Way Moving and Storage*, with instructions to make this operation his last.

Though this mission was troubled, Senator Morgan's eagerness to rub it in was the only tell he needed to prove, at least to himself, she was responsible for the problem. There was no way Grandma Lily could know there was a breakdown unless she had personally tossed a monkey wrench into the works. He would watch his back more carefully. Chalk did not give a damn about charges of paranoia directed against him. He already knew he suffered from it. He had the diagnosis and the prescriptions to prove it. In no small part, paranoia kept him alive. Sometimes it wasn't all in his mind, either. While they were farting around up here in the wild blue yonder, matters on the ground really were going to hell. He could barely sit still.

Chalk's trusted delivery man, Tom Chase, had recently disappeared with some very important cargo. Chalk had received no word from Chase in the last twenty-two hours. Reporting in every six hours was *Right Way's* prescribed check-in interval during a mission. If the mule in question did not contact Chalk tonight at six sharp, just four hours and twelve minutes off, things would get heated. They would get damn heated indeed.

Chalk grinned wide and cocky at Senator Morgan. "Everything's peachy, Lil. I've never let you or Uncle Sam down before."

The lady from Wisconsin smiled back. She enjoyed twitting Chalk. He hated her so much for this he balled his fists white, but he pressed them hard into his lap to keep from lashing a fatal karate chop at her gullet.

Half closing her eyes, she purred, "We've got forty minutes before we land at Dulles." Pulling out a small lace hanky that was more air than thread, she dabbed cookie crumbs from the corners of her mouth, brushed more crumbs off her broad bosom, then hooked her thumb toward the sleeping quarters at the back of the jet. "Feeling lucky?"

Chalk groaned inside. No, she did not want sex, thank God, at least not from him. In addition to the bed, the aft compartment held an elegant metal chess board arrayed in ivory pieces secured with small magnets in case of turbulence or unsportsmanlike fits of pique. In his boyhood, Chalk was a ranking chess genius. The Senator, on the other hand, was a haphazard latecomer to the game with no sense of strategy, nor any inkling of tactics. She might as well have been removing Chalk's pieces from the board by fillips from her middle finger as by any talent. Yet Chalk had brought her to checkmate only once, in their first game years ago. He'd done it in five moves.

The win resulted in such howls of protest from the Senator that they had brought the plane's first officer sprinting back through the compartment door with his pistol drawn, and a wide-eyed look that feared assassination had taken place at Flight Level 43. Senator Morgan did not speak to Chalk for the rest of that flight, nor did she did return Chalk's calls for the next two weeks during her sulk; and in the interim they had lost out on several lucrative deals.

Now, Chalk made a point of losing every game, attributing his early success to beginner's luck. She was conceited enough to believe she was outsmarting him ever since. Unwilling to roll over completely, Chalk forced her to work for every win as much as her feeble skills allowed.

For some reason, the Senator's near stochastic way of playing was getting even worse, if that were possible. It was more and more difficult for Chalk to prolong their games, let alone throw them. He would never risk spanking her again for fear of another ridiculous outburst, another expensive silence. As he followed her back through the seats to the chess board, he mused that in working with the Senator, there were too damn many ways to get screwed.

CHAPTER 3

STAY COOL. GET in the airlock. Focus. Ben coached himself over and over in a numbing mantra of delay and denial that he had used hundreds of times on long sniper missions. How could his mind encompass the enormity of what he had just discovered? He would think about it, deal with it, later.

Then the mantras failed him, and the facts hit home in his gut like point-blank bullets. This was his father. Missing for so long, and so close to home, to reunion. Why the hell did Ben have to be the one to find him? And if this wreck and the drowned remains were only a few days old, where had his father been for the other fifteen years, presumed—what exactly— dead? Alive, but uncaring?

Pulling out more old tools from his days in the service, Ben mentally smashed this heavy slab of news into smaller fragments. Then he swept them behind a thick inner wall where a hundred other dead faces waited for resurrection and justice. With his mind freshly cleared and tightly tuned, he went to work.

Ben already knew the boxes with their space-age locks and metal skins would resist ordinary prying and bashing. Maybe he would lug them to his house to cut them open with his welding rig. *Lord, no. That would draw too many questions.*

Now that was something odd. Ben could not pinpoint the moment he decided this was night work. 'Til now he had been a truthful and forth- coming man in all matters. To his surprise, this dark choice had come naturally, subconsciously. Perhaps it was his Smith Island heritage rearing up like a long-dormant gene. His people's DNA was not only ready for hard work in honest sunlight, but was also steeled for bloody twilight jobs. This wreck and everything to do with it was for the shadows. He confirmed the decision. Without a doubt this matter was best handled away from prying eyes. Ben's own certainty disturbed him. This path involved denying Pap the final rites he was due. *No rush on that now. Worry about it later.*

There had to be a key to these boxes. Ben rifled the pockets of the dead man's field jacket. Just a nameless body, he told himself. Ben was simply gathering intel. Seeking assets. Nothing more than he had ever done in the service of his country. He found no key. There was something heavy weighing down the coat's large side pocket, but Ben did not pull it out. He knew what he was looking for. He focused on hunting up the key.

He carefully patted the pants' slash pockets, then lifted the flaps to the mid-thigh cargo pockets. Loose change, a small penknife. Where was that key? Not sure if he were girding himself for nausea, remorse, or both, Ben pushed the May West aside and reached beneath the shirt collar. He avoided looking at the face again. Felt a simple chain. Dog-tags? He lifted the chain over the head of the—thing. The *not*-Pap. The *not*-human. Not one, but two gray, flat metal plates dangled from the chain. They were as wide as a credit card, and as thick. They were several inches longer than the average MasterCard. There were no letters, nor any numbers. Just random-looking grooves and holes milled into both sides.

Without another look at the body, Ben slogged back to the wreck. More ice water leaked down his back to complement the chill in his heart. He pulled up the corner of the tarp he had freed before. More silt churned. Another infuriating wait for clearer water. He tried the first key. There was a scraping and ringing sound, metal on metal. The lock did not yield. Ben turned the key over. Slid it in again. Still nothing happened. His curiosity boiled. What the hell had Richard Willem Blackshaw died to bring home?

At that thought, Ben suddenly looked around him for his mother, Ida-Beth. He had good reason to believe she too might be close by. There was no sign of her. Thank God, and just as well. Ben wanted to remember her the way she was when he last saw her alive years ago, not decaying down here like his father.

Ben's cold, stiff fingers fumbled as he tried the second key. Nothing budged. He flipped it over, and nervously scraped it around the opening before lining it up square and sticking it in again. Finally, he heard the dull pergaddus clank and thud of a deadbolt springing open. He heaved back the heavy lid with both hands.

Even on the floor of the Chesapeake, with the sun hidden above fifteen feet of turbid water and a scudding layer of gray cloud, there was absolutely no mistaking the radiant gleam. Ben's eyes widened. He reached out. *Oh my blessing!* The box was jammed with gold.

CHAPTER 4

BEN SHUT THE lid as if someone might have seen. Silt whirled. Feeling foolish, his heart pounding, he lifted the lid again. Both magnificent and unreal, but there it was. With the broken end of his knife, he easily etched a thin line in the soft surface of one of the big gold bars. That is when he noticed a faint image cast into each piece. It looked like a roughly sketched, lopsided smiley face. As if the cheery seventies icon had suffered a stroke. If this were the minter's mark, it was the strangest and crudest Ben could imagine.

Ben pried one of the luminous slabs out of the close-fitting box. Over twenty pounds, he reckoned. He had no idea what it was worth, but he knew it was a fortune. Then his mind shuddered to a halt like a heavy-duty pick-up truck on a washboard dirt road. This was just one bar. Just one bar from just one box. He stared at the full cargo. A quick count. Two boxes deep, times two boxes wide, by five boxes laid end to end along the boat's keel. Twenty boxes, and all of them could be filled like this one. *Not possible!*

Ben's skin puckered. Lizards raced on sharp dry claws up his spine. He would know this feeling again when the boxes were all inventoried, and their contents were laid bare. Among the containers, like little children's coffins, that he had yet to open, one held cargo more cursed than gold. The malignant freight in this box did not have the usual TV movie spray of colored wires in it. No black electrical tape, nor blasting caps, nor even a cell phone trigger. The plans for this engine of mayhem started with the periodic table of the elements. Unlike its conventional cousins, the isotopic bastard article would never tick unless a Geiger counter was placed within range. Ben did not know any of this yet.

He dropped the bar and the wallet in the progging bag where he stowed interesting finds from the Chesapeake. The bag was tied to the front of his dive belt. The extra weight dragged his hips forward and down. Taking the regulator out of his mouth for a moment, Ben dropped the key chain around his neck. He stepped onto the gunwale of the sunken speedboat, and pushed off for the surface toward *Miss Dotsy*.

Fatigue conspired with the gold's extra weight to make the short swim feel like breast-stroking up Niagara Falls. The keys clinked together on his chest. Before Ben's head even broke the surface, his hand groped desperately for *Miss Dotsy*'s washboards. A vise clamped down on Ben's arm just above the elbow. With a force that nearly dislocated his shoulder, he was snatched out of the water and landed on *Miss Dotsy*'s deck like a gaffed marlin. This was Knocker Ellis's idea of lending the helping hand.

Upon releasing Ben, Knocker Ellis Hogan's cabled sinews and bone-hard muscles relaxed beneath his deep brown skin. Ben had long accepted that Ellis could handle bushel baskets for hours every day as if they weighed nothing, despite his being somewhere north of sixty. Ben barely hid his surprise that Ellis could manhandle him with equal ease. Not for the first time, Ben scanned Knocker Ellis's dark eyes for more clues to who his oyster culler really was. As ever, he could read nothing behind Ellis's impassive face, which seemed carefully arranged to guard a lifetime of wounds.

Knocker Ellis was Richard Blackshaw's sole crew and culler for over a decade. When Ben's father disappeared, Ben took charge of *Miss Dotsy*. It was natural and unquestioned that Knocker Ellis should ship out with her new captain. For a moment, it felt more real to Ben, more poignant, knowing Ellis's former boss, rather than Ben's own father, lay dead just feet below *Miss Dotsy*'s keel.

After his unceremonious boarding, Ben spat out the regulator and peeled off the mask. He recalled how his culler earned his handle, and decided to take care over the next few minutes. Ellis said he was named after his grandfather. As a small boy, Ellis said his gramps drudged for pennies as a knocker, cleaning out the blue crabs' broad top shells so they could be repacked with fresh-picked lump crabmeat for restaurants. It was one of the jobs a black boy was permitted in his day. In Ellis's case, Knocker had as much to do with his honored forebear as with his murderous southpaw uppercut. It could hammer a man flat on his ass, or so Ben heard told.

Knocker Ellis turned off the compressor, faked the air hose down into a neat coil, and hauled in the milk crate. Ellis looked askance at the half-empty basket, but said nothing. Nor did he mention the strange keys dangling from around Ben's neck. This was his way. He quickly culled the few oysters just below regulation size, and dropped them back over the side. Then cast his eye up at the clouds announcing the outer bands of *Polly*, the next weather system come to drown them. He always kept a weather eye for the squalls, or flaws, that could make up so quickly on the bay. With Ben closely sizing the oysters on the bottom, most of Ellis's work revolved around tending the air compressor and the boat's Atomic Four.

Ben tried to appear relaxed. What to tell this man, if anything? He would have to say something, at least to explain the poor catch. Ben reached into his canvas tote and pulled out a small block of pine he was shaping into a mallard chick. He studied it closely before taking up the razor honed carving knife. For some reason, the last chick he'd created came out with a dopey grin more reminiscent of a Disney character than anything natural. Ellis watched him.

Without taking his eyes off the wooden chick Ben lied, "Leg cramped up on me."

Knocker Ellis turned his back and with a calloused bare hand checked the searing oil dipstick of the Atomic Four engine. It was rare for him to open his mouth. His posture alone said *no sale*.

Ben knew there was no way to avoid filling Ellis in. By rights, he was as much entitled to a share of salvage as he was due a share of the oyster catch. Ben never cheated a friend, but what was Ellis to him exactly? Ben's father had trusted Knocker Ellis implicitly. That was fifteen years ago. As Ben was learning, a lot can happen in fifteen seconds to change a man's life, let alone fifteen years. Ben shaved a tissue-thin curl of wood from the duck's bill. The flake spun away on the freshening breeze.

To Ben, this gold was a final bequest from his father. Of course, Ben understood that had likely not been his father's to give, but possession was nine tenths of the law. The question remained, for whom was the gift really intended? Just for Ben? For everyone on Smith? Perhaps bringing home this fortune was payback on a hundred years of hard losses that Ben's family and neighbors had endured. In 1900, the Lacey Act, an early law in a frenzy of well-intended conservation efforts, forbade his great-great-grandfathers from selling waterfowl across state lines. When the Act slowed neither the appetite for, nor the harvest of, ducks and geese, in 1910 their big-bore fowling guns were confiscated by the government because they were still too effective. Where once the Islanders had provided enough waterfowl for tables up and down the eastern seaboard, now they were limited to little more than subsistence hunting with smaller-gauge shotguns. As if not satisfied, in 1954, the U.S. Fish and Wildlife Service swallowed his people's prime hunting marshes to the north into the Martin National Wildlife Refuge, turning good men into poachers if lean times forced them stray onto their old grounds. Today, more than forty-five hundred acres were off limits to island gunners, starting within sight of their own front doors. When water pollution and disease from farm runoff and overbuilding condos around the Chesapeake's shores killed the fish, blue crab, oyster and clam stocks, making vast deoxygenated dead zones in the bay where nothing could live, it was Ben and his people who had to shorten their work seasons to allow the fisheries to survive. Again, they were blamed for being too efficient in their harvest work. Forget that in every war of the twentieth century, Ben's relations had gone to soldier, fought, bled, and died for a government that seemed determined to starve them. Ben himself had served with distinction.

Two more strokes of Ben's knife along the wooden duck's bill. It was closer to the right shape, yet still wrong somehow. No. Ben decided he would not offer this gold back to whoever had it before his father. Not while it might ease some of the suffering on Smith and Tangier. Certainly not while Ben's father lay drowned just a few feet below. Not while Ben was still breathing.

Another knife stroke. The duck's bill was still not right. Ben realized why he was putting off telling Ellis about his finds. As long as Ben remained the only one who knew where Dick Blackshaw's body lay, he had a grim intimacy with his father in death that was long missing between them in life. Tell someone else Dick Blackshaw is dead, speak the words to just one other person, and suddenly the remote truth becomes real. It's official; you're an orphan.

Lonesome George, a half-tame great blue heron, soared in on broad wings and claimed his I'm-king-of-the-world! post on *Miss Dotsy*'s bow. The wily majestic creature knew Ben and Knocker Ellis as soft touches. He cadged daily for a handout in the shape of a freshly shucked oyster. Ellis took one from the meager catch. He knifed it open in an instant, flicked the quivering flesh forward. Lonesome George snatched it out of mid-air, jerked his head twice to position the bite in his beak, and swallowed. Despite a scraping honk, a twitch of his crest plumes, and a pleading yellow eye, Ellis gave the flying sponger no more.

Ben steeled himself. Broached it. "Some problems down there."

Knocker Ellis nodded to himself. Seemed to have expected this. The big man shrank with an odd melancholy, but waited for Ben to say more.

"The storm. It wrecked a boat. Down there by that oyster rock. A Nantucket Lance. Nice one."

Knocker Ellis considered this. "'Tuckets don't sink." Those three words coming from Ellis made the longwinded Fidel Castro seem mute.

Ben struggled to get over the surprise of hearing Ellis say so much. And Ellis was right. How had Ben missed it? All the print and TV ads for the Nantucket Lance boasted its closed cell flotation chambers. The manufacturer would mercilessly Skil-saw the hull into small sections on a lake, but every chunk remained afloat. The ads were astounding, and certainly persuasive. Yet here was an unsinkable boat sitting squarely on the Chesapeake's bottom. For that matter, what was a man in a perfectly good life vest doing in the mud with that boat? Maybe the vest was not perfectly good after all. Ben would check it on the next dive.

Ben set that last question aside. "I know what I saw." Rather than reveal his loss, he addressed the gain. He said it sideways, in the Smith Island way. "There was none-too-much cargo."

Knocker Ellis eyed him. "That so? How big a boat?"

"Twenty-five feet. Center console. Triple 250 Mercs. She'd fetch a price."

Knocker Ellis communed with his inner calculator for a moment. "Must be close on fifty-five hundred pounds of cargo." He shook his head and smiled small, as if in admiration of something Ben could not understand.

Ben asked, "You want to unpack that a little? Maybe cut the inscrutable all-knowing Powerboat Show guru stuff?"

Ellis simply said, "Swamp capacity."

Ben was annoyed. "I'm talking about a sunken boat that shouldn't sink, and you're talking about a bayou census, as near as I can figure out." Ellis's look said it all. Ben felt like a rookie sailor.

Ellis spoke as if reciting common knowledge, "The swamp capacity of a twenty-five-foot, center console Nantucket Lance is five thousand five hundred pounds. She won't sink unless cargo, gear, passengers, fuel, and water in her cockpit sum up more than that. As a for-instance, I figure *Miss Dotsy*'s capacity is a couple-two-three hundred pounds more than the Lance, just because of her size."

That explained the boat, but not Knocker Ellis's ready erudition on it.

Anticipating Ben's question, Ellis said, "I wanted to get myself a Lance if I could ever afford to retire. So I read up." Ellis nodded toward the stack of bushel baskets that Ben had yet to fill. "I have to say retirement seems pretty far off, with you quitting work to cramp and carve and yammer and whatnot."

Silent for weeks at a time, now Knocker Ellis was voluble, sharp, and a wise-ass. Ben realized he did not know this man at all. Had his father? The thought brought Ben around.

He said, "Maybe the gold watch isn't so far away."

Ellis looked interested. "How so?"

Ben said, "I'll get to that, but you need to know something else, first." Ben looked off toward the western horizon behind the clouds, not wanting to meet Ellis's eyes. "Captain went down with the ship."

Knocker Ellis relapsed into a this-is-bad-business silence. One slow, deep breath. A second. "Anybody you know?"

Ben's hands tensed. The knife jerked deep. The wooden duck's little bill snapped off. Ben and Ellis stared at the maimed carving. Ben flipped it over the side, and watched it bob away on the swells. He admitted, "You knew him longer than I did."

Ellis shook his head slowly. Was that the confirmation of a suspicion, or a fear that something had gone wrong? Ben was not sure.

Ellis looked Ben in the eye. "You Blackshaws got a hellafied manner of doing things. You think it's your father? After all this time off island?"

"Like I said, it's a recent wreck. Storm got him."

Knocker Ellis pressed. "You sure you recognized him? After fifteen years gone, a few days on the bottom?"

"The body, the face, yes it's all a mess. But there's an Army jacket. He liked those. The name on it is wrong. The driver's license had a completely different name, too. No surprise there. He'd have changed his go-by long ago. Maybe more than once. The license picture? That's plain as day. It's Pap. Older, but no mistake. Here, see for yourself."

Ben pulled the wallet out of his progging bag, and passed the license to Ellis.

Ellis squinted at it at arm's length. His shoulders bowed like a great weight had been lowered on them. "Sorry, Ben. Was a good man."

"Suppose so. While he was around." Anger flashed in Knocker Ellis's eyes as Ben took the license back.

Knocker Ellis reached for the radio just inside *Miss Dotsy*'s small cuddy cabin. He tuned to channel 16, the frequency monitored by the Marine Police.

Ben removed the gold slab from the progging bag, and placed it on the engine box with a thump.

With his back to Ben, Ellis picked up the microphone. "We best get on with this. Call it in. Damn storm's coming round again."

"Knocker Ellis. We have to talk."

Ben failed to hide the strain in his voice. Ellis turned, saw the hunk of bullion, narrowed his eyes. "Gee, Ben. What about?"

First things first. Ben said, "Turn the radio off."

Ellis complied. He even unplugged the power cord from the back of the transceiver. He understood that a stuck mic could provide hours of amusement for other watermen listening in on the common frequency. Loose chat on the air had even revealed the location of long-secret oyster rocks. This was a time for much greater care with every word.

Ellis tilted his head toward the gold bar. "That would be the cargo you mentioned?"

Ben nodded. Knocker Ellis approached the engine box. Stroked the gold slowly with a gnarled finger. When he smiled, it looked like his golden eyetooth was communing with the bar, signaling to and fro with lustrous rays about wealth and misery.

Ellis cleared his throat. "More of these below?"

Ben nodded again. "I count twenty boxes. Six bars across, and two deep in each box."

"Mercy. Indeed we are picking high cotton." Knocker Ellis went to his Deep Blue place again and crunched the numbers. He said, "Two hundred forty bars. A lot of gold, if every box has gold in it. And here's a stamp. Four-zero-zero o-z-t."

Ben mused aloud. "Okay, that's probably Troy ounces."

Ellis continued the math. And the lecture. "A Troy pound is twelve ounces. A Scottish Troy pound is sixteen Troy ounces. That's if you go by the Incorporation of Goldsmiths, City of Edinburgh, late seventeenth century. Four hundred divided by sixteen is an even twenty-five pounds Imperial. This is an old measure. Old gold. What about that stamp? Like a grinning face, but a little sideways."

Ben stared at his culler. "You're awful well-informed, Ellis. But don't tell me. You were reading up on investment commodities for—"

"For retirement. Yes, Ben. As a hedge against hard times." Knocker Ellis replied evenly, but the warning for Ben not to dig further was plain.

"Seeing as how you're on a roll, care to hazard a guess about the value of a Troy ounce of gold, say, at the close of yesterday's market?"

Ellis scratched his head. "Don't know. If I had to guess—"

Ben crossed his arms. "Oh, please do."

"It'd come in round seventeen hundred thirty-two spondulicks, U.S. Been rising quick of late, though not as quick as silver or palladium. Still, it's a decent hedge when the stock market's soft and shot through with cowards and cheats. China and India are the big gold markets, but for jewelry mostly. Since it takes a few years to bring new gold mines in, demand is going to outpace supply for a while before there's price stabilization, let alone a downward correction. But don't quote me."

Ben picked up the gold bar and spoke quietly. "This little thing is worth six hundred ninety-three *thousand* dollars?"

Knocker Ellis smiled. "Give or take. And you think there's a few more bars still down there?"

"Yes, I'd say quite a few. What's going on here, Ellis? Every word you say has a half-dozen more behind it. Care to enlighten me?"

Ellis's turn to look toward the horizon. "I'd say we have problems. And with all due respect, we have a dead man, too."

"He'll keep."

Ellis's eyebrows twitched up a millimeter in what was for him a display of profound surprise. "Could get in some deep trouble if we keep quiet, Ben. Fines. Take your license away. The law says—"

Ben's voice was firm. His eyes, clear. "The law is not aboard right now. I'm suspending oyster season early this year."

Ellis looked back at the bar of gold and smiled just a little. "Aye-aye, Captain Blackshaw."

Ben was sure Knocker Ellis knew much more than he was saying. At the moment, his culler's sudden loquacity was the least of today's surprises. Ben felt completely surrounded by secrets the way the bay's water could press in cold and hard on all sides. Go too deep, and it would crush the life out of a man.

CHAPTER 5

THE OLD, ISOLATED frame house outside St. Mary's City, Maryland was dark as a pharaoh's tomb. Clouds kept any moonlight from the windows. Power to the lone floodlight mounted in the old oak tree outside was cut at the breaker box. Chalk was in his element on this kind of sortie. He hated time with the Senator. She was an old dog with no new tricks. Where surgical applications of mayhem invigorated Chalk, making nice with the Senator from Wisconsin cost him a little piece of his dark soul every time. Even so, business was business. He put the afternoon's flight behind him.

Of course, Tom Chase, Chalk's runaway mule, had not seen fit to check in at six o'clock. Time for waiting was over. The time to act had come.

Chalk positioned his agents inside and around the house. Like an infestation of spiders poised in an attic for the arrival of a single fly, they were waiting for a woman named Nelly Vickers.

Tom Chase had squired Miss Vickers to the *Right Way Moving & Storage* holiday party the year before. Though she had not exactly Xeroxed her ass on the company copier, she was tipsy, bubbly, and Chalk had noted her. He chatted her up and filed a few particulars away. Tom Chase was still new to the company then. Still a closed book. Nelly, a toned fox in her forties, had known little enough about her date. Like Maynard Chalk, she had only recently met him.

Tonight, Chalk leveraged some research time from a gaggle of intel geeks based in Quantico. They tracked Vickers to her house in this desolate wood. At the moment she had the unfortunate distinction of being Chalk's only lead. His only peep-hole into a personal life Chase had completely sequestered from work. Perhaps she had gotten to know Chase a little better since the party. Perhaps Chalk could help her remember something if she were stone cold sober, stripped, and zip-tied to the metal legs of her Formica kitchen table. *Worth a shot, right?*

Chalk reclined on a butt-sprung BarcaLounger in the sepulchral living room. When he put on his night vision goggles he would have a clear view of the front door. Deep tire ruts, and women's size seven shoeprints in the dirt outside told him this was the way she would enter. Not through the side door to the kitchen.

He swirled a tumbler filled with Balblair 38-year-old scotch poured from his own flask. He sipped, and flicked his tongue around, bathing it in far off Highland honey. When this was all over, he might crack open that bottle of The Macallan 60-Year-Old he was saving for special. He did not give a damn for its deco Lalique bottle, or its twenty-thousand-dollar sticker. After handling this disaster, he would need something that truly announced *recompense* in a sweet smoky liquid language he and very few others spoke.

His Glock 21 lay on a side table, a round in the chamber. There might be a small oil stain from the pistol on her copy of *Chesapeake Bay Magazine*. That did not matter. Her subscription was about to be cancelled.

In the dark, Chalk contemplated the chain of stupidities that had brought him to this house. He was just as upset with his newer man, Bill Slagget, as he was with his tried-and-true lieutenant, Simon Clynch. Both henchmen crouched behind furniture nearby. *What the hell was a hench, anyway?* Regardless, Chalk hoped they were uncomfortable. Charlie-horsed. Mostly, Chalk was furious with himself. He should never have trusted Tom Chase with such an important courier job alone.

In his heart, Chalk knew this crisis was his own fault. It might put an end to everything, including his life, even if Senator Morgan was not already gunning for him.

For this job, Simon Clynch should have worked with Tom Chase. That had not come about as planned. Clynch fell deathly ill from food poisoning contracted at a usually safe sushi joint they liked off DuPont Circle in D.C. Clynch bitched that at the peak of the illness, he could shit through the eye of a needle at fifty paces. Likewise, Bill Slagget was pinned down on the porcelain with talking-gun squirts during the critical time when this mission came in to *Right Way*.

Chalk had weathered the bacteria with some nausea but no loosening of his cast-iron gut. He could have sortied with Tom Chase personally, and should have. Against his better judgment he had chosen not to. He'd stayed home. It had been Chalk's birthday after all. He preferred to spend that special evening according to custom. With his favorite prostitute, Phoebe DeLyte.

When he thought of his odd relationships with Senator Lily Morgan and Phoebe DeLyte, Chalk felt a little like Robin Hood; *robbing the bitch to give to the whore*. This year as ever, Phoebe had earned her money, delivered like Venus herself, happily banging Chalk into a drooling catatonic state by morning. Now Chalk was paying for this lapse of judgment. *Christ on a stick!* Perhaps he would crucify Tom Chase when they caught up to him.

Dar Gavin, one of Chalk's men posted at the mouth of Vickers's long lane, gave Chalk the heads-up through a radio earpiece. "'98 Grand Cherokee. Red. Plates match. Female driver. Flying solo."

Chalk replied into his TASC II headset. "Received."

He quaffed the last of the scotch, put up the flask, and levered the BarcaLounger upright. Then he donned his Generation Six night vision goggles. The world went from shadow to glinting hues of tourmaline. He holstered his pistol. Patted his barn coat's pockets. Pruning shears: in place. Pliers. Butane lighter. Three retractable box cutters. Dental floss to stem arterial bleeds. The items were all there where he stowed them on such occasions. He called these things his manicure kit. He snaked the fingers of his right hand through the rings of a well-worn set of brass knuckles. He was more than ready for the interview. He was eager. *Time's a-wasting.*

He stage whispered to Slagget and Clynch. "Party time, boys."

The two men fidgeted. The Jeep pulled up in front of the house. Only one car door slammed in the dark. A brief unladylike curse about the apparent power failure. A bright, narrow-beam LED flashlight flicked on outside. A key scratched at the lock then slid in. Nelly Vickers pushed the door open and stepped inside.

Chalk two-stepped his black leather brogans and khaki slacks into the circle of light her flashlight carved on the floor. He whispered, "Hola, chica."

She yanked the light up, taking in Chalk, gasping with horror. She shifted her weight backward, but too late. His brass knuckles smashed hard into the side of her head. Nelly Vickers went down as if crushed beneath a plummeting Steinway concert grand. No problem. When the interview began, she'd be alert and oriented times four. And she'd know Chalk was dead serious.

CHAPTER 6

WITH THE WEATHER going to hell again, Ben and Knocker Ellis made decisions. First they swore secrecy. Word to anyone else could travel fast, and they needed time to get this situation under control.

They needed to behave the same tonight as they had at the end of a thousand other days. The rising swells would drive the fleet of homebound oyster boats too close to their current anchorage. The cases would have to stay hidden on the bottom. Wait until later to bring them up. No one in his right mind oystered after dark anyway, even in clear weather. That was regarded as taking unfair advantage in Smith Island's hardscrabble culture. It was late in the season for pleasure boaters, but there was a slim chance a few shiver-me-timbers storm-chaser types might be out poking death with bowsprit and pulpit.

Ben went down to the bottom one last time. He pulled the corpse by the coat collar over to the wreck. He belayed it there by the ankle with the cargo strap.

Then they took the catch in to Crisfield on the Eastern Shore. Fortunately, the weather alone explained why all the watermen, including Ben, were shy of their usual numbers.

Ben dropped Knocker Ellis at the pier by his small place on Smith Island. Ellis had the dubious distinction of being the only black man living on the tiny archipelago. He had moved there from Crisfield on the main soon after Ben's father disappeared. It made sense. It simplified their work.

They agreed to meet again later that night. Ben pointed *Miss Dotsy* for home.

Tonight, with so much to think about, Ben was disturbed to see another boat moored at his own pier. *Of all the damn luck.* It was a Natural Resources Police boat. Ben knew it on sight. In crabbing season, it picketed the Maryland-Virginia state line to keep the Maryland watermen and the Virginians working in their own duly licensed fisheries. Tonight, it seemed the patrol boat's pilot, Natural Resources Police Corporal Bryce, had business with Ben. Business that would not wait.

Ben moored *Miss Dotsy* and made a trudging, exhausted walk up to his front door through a yard that still glimmered with standing water from the last storm. He got none of his usual satisfaction from the collection of abstract wildlife sculptures he welded from found objects. Plenty of tourists had offered him money for his metal backyard menagerie. Money he always turned down despite being all but strapped.

A New York bond trader had bird-dogged Ben's more realistic efforts at the Sunfest in Ocean City. He'd tried to commission a full size Canada goose in brass with all the detail Ben could put on it. The trader had even offered to secure a Soho gallery through friends for a show of his work. Ben had nodded politely. Listened with less than half an ear. Let the offer go untried much to the disgust of friends who thought him stupid to pass up such a chance. Didn't his friends, themselves watermen, understand it was oyster season?

Ben's front door was unlocked as always. He went inside. No one lay in ambush in the tar-dark parlor. He stashed the bar of gold under the cushion of his old couch. He tucked the key cards into a drawer of the small secretary. Ginger, his Chesapeake Bay Retriever, thumped her tail softly on the floor three times, then went back to sleep. Though she and her ancestors would eagerly haul in downed fowl until they nearly died of exhaustion in the water, she was a sweet, but useless watchdog where Corporal Bryce was concerned.

Ben lived in a saltbox, a tall narrow house with barely room to turn around upstairs or down. It was from upstairs that Ben heard the noise. Somewhere near his bedroom, like a burglar rustling. Like clothing pulled from his bureau and dropped on the floor. A ransacking in progress?

Knowing he had to face the music before he could return to work, he quietly climbed the stairs to see what Officer Bryce was into. So far there was
no evidence from the wreck lying around to get him in Dutch with the law.
No way Bryce could know.

Ben stepped over the second stair tread, and then skipped the sixth as
well. They both squeaked, as did the seventh tread if he put his foot down
on the right side. Ben placed his foot down softly to the left. He had no
idea why he bothered to play the game. Bryce had certainly heard Ben's
noisy deadrise come in. Had heard him entering through the front door.
Corporal Bryce knew he was on his way.

Ben reached the top of the stairs. Moved across the small hallway
toward the bedroom door. He was deadly silent, but blind in the dark. Ben
heard a quick breeze of motion. Suddenly, Bryce slammed into him from
behind, gripping Ben's chest and shoulders, teeth digging into his neck. He
was driven forward through the door and onto his bed. Ben gave a quick
judo twist of his hips and shoulders, and suddenly he was on top of Bryce.
Bryce let out a woof of breath as Ben came down hard with all his weight.

Bryce grunted, "Damn boy! You're smelling kinda brackish, aren't
you?"

Ben could feel Corporal Bryce undulating stark naked beneath him.
She tore at his work shirt. Buttons flew, click-clacking all over the floor. He
was not embarrassed about not having showered. She loved the not-quite
salty scent of the Chesapeake's waters that he brought home on his skin. It
worked magic on her. She would be the last to claim that a day patrolling on
her boat left her daisy fresh. Ben tasted the salt on her neck. Inhaled the
aroma of skin that had long been out in rough autumn weather. She was
working on Ben's clothes from below like a rank peeler, a female blue crab
under the protection of her Jimmy, eager to double.

He had known this woman his entire life. LuAnna was a few grades
behind him nearly all the way through school until he quit. He was held
back one year and then another because earning money took precedence
over the three Rs. After that, they were the only two students in their entire
class. Families with children moved off island to the main even then. There
was a prison opening up on the Eastern Shore. Many crabbers and their
wives abandoned a life of doing without on the open bay to earn a more

certain living behind razor wire. Some captained tugs in the port of
Baltimore or as far away as the Great Lakes. The families promised to
return to Smith once they were back on their feet, but they never did.

LuAnna worked Ben out of his Dickies, kissing him hungrily. He
helped himself to her warm nakedness. She finally tore Ben's clothing free.
It had been more than a week since they had last held each other this way.
They thrashed and grappled like it was Judgment Day and they were hell-
bound without the least desire for mercy.

Ben was always struck by LuAnna's fierce physical way of loving him.
She was like an athlete. Subtle in her grace, with a champion's adroitness. At
other times, she was explosive with the beginner's raw, fearless ardor.

Soon they rested in each other's arms. Ben felt a sense of true belonging here with LuAnna, and nowhere else. He was a quieter sort of man.
This cut him off from an island population that was itself disconnected
from most of America, but he did not mind. Many tourists strolling the narrow paths during the summer season thought his reserve belied stupidity,
venality, or worse: inbred foolishness. Even among Ben's own people, diving for his oysters instead of hand-tonging, or using pneumatic patent
tongs, seemed like cheating, and set him apart. Though diving was obviously more efficient, Ben endured what the Islanders called nominy, Smith
Island slang for a low regard of eccentrics who would not, or could not, live
by traditional rules. He knew they would all feel differently if they spent five
minutes grubbing on the gloomy bay bottom with him in the cold. Ben was
not money-hungry, but any hard-won financial advantage from diving was
quickly socked away against the day when LuAnna would be his bride.

For LuAnna, a Smith Island girl born and raised, her defection to work
for the Natural Resources Police was a treachery mean as the Kaiser, as her
neighbors said of their quislings. She had finally moved off to the Eastern
Shore and lived alone while Ben served in Gulf War One; there had been
too much pressure placed on her by well-meaning neighbors to forget the
unconventional Ben Blackshaw, and hitch to a more regular Island man.

While LuAnna dozed, Ben gazed on this remarkable woman. The last
loom of day had long died in the west window. The early-rising moon
fought through storm clouds in the window facing east. There was just
enough light to see Officer Bryce was built lean. It was a wonder her slim

hips held up a gunbelt. This is not to say she was not blessed topside. Adding to her beauty, she stood tall and straight, with none of the shame-hooked slump of a buxom girl raised in a small town with its fair share of lonely men. When not peacefully sleeping, her eyes were the brightest blue in the world. Eyes that flashed from a face that favored her mother. They had both lost their parents. At least LuAnna could visit her folks' graves; they lay side by side on dry land in the burial ground of the Tylerton Methodist Church.

Though in her early thirties, years of Chesapeake sun had already made the corners of her eyes crinkle when she smiled, the way she was smiling just then. She had quietly awakened and was watching him contemplate her.

She murmured, "I believe you knocked my jingle-bean clean off."

Ben smiled. "I've missed you."

She stretched, then curled around him more closely. "Me too. But if I didn't know better, I'd say you were chewing on something besides me."

Ben said nothing about the feelings that his day of revelation had unleashed; the great wealth just within his reach, the loss of his father, and with that, losing the chance at a reunion with him. With his father accounted for, he also wondered where his mother had been all these years, and where she might be now. Answering one question prompted this other, and uncovered another deep well of pain.

Rather than lie, Ben told LuAnna another, older truth. "I'm thinking I don't know what you see in this man. I don't understand how in all my life of bad luck you came to be here."

Her smile broadened. "You don't want me thinking too much about that. I might not come up with a good answer." She lightly kissed his lips to show she was teasing. "But I can tell you. It's a mix of familiarity, stupidity and love. And a profound appreciation of what you do with that beautiful unit of yours. Not that you're a bad kisser. Not that your smile doesn't melt me to a puddle. And thank God you didn't get short-changed in the chin department like a lot of boys on this island."

"A close thing. My chin was nearly knocked off fighting over you."

Chivalry tickled LuAnna. "When did you ever fight over me?"

"In the Martin Wildlife Refuge across the way there was this old billy goat with a crush on you—" In truth, Ben never pissed a circle around

LuAnna. He did not have to. LuAnna smiled and bit him on the arm. What followed was her special brand of police brutality. Ben fully enjoyed it.

They drew in humid air redolent of hard-worked bodies from the sea. Ben wanted to allay LuAnna's all-too-perceptive suspicion that things were not right with him. Though he loved her and wished to soothe her, he really needed her to leave. The storm was chopping Tangier Sound between Smith Island and the Eastern Shore, but her patrol boat could handle it. And she would want to go eventually. LuAnna still preferred waking in her own place before a tour. They reserved true overnights for the weekends she did not work.

Ben turned onto his side. Looked her in the eye and asked as he had a so many times before, "LuAnna Bonnie Bryce, will you let me be your husband? Will you let me be daddy to your babies, and pop-pop to theirs?"

LuAnna smiled at him but then looked away. She frowned and said, "You know I'm thinking about it. You know that don't you, Ben? You're my Number One Jimmy-crab. I'm your one true Sally-crab. Honestly, I don't hear your heart in it this time."

Ben stayed quiet. Despite his own secrets, he was certain LuAnna was hiding something, too. She was usually forthright. Curious as he was about her pensive mien, he still had to put her off, and ease her out the door.

The moon rose farther behind troubled clouds, and LuAnna rose with it to put on her uniform. She gave him a sidelong glance as she leaned forward to cup her full breasts in the bra. "Ben Blackshaw, there's something on your mind."

"Plenty of oysters today," he disclosed, in the sideways Smith Island syntax. "Storm silted them over. Killing them. Speeding up what the farm run-off's been doing for years."

He wanted to tell her the rest of the truth. His native honesty demanded it. His love for her compelled it. The least secret between them blacked his heart with shadows until it was expressed. Yet he did not mention his dead father lying on the bottom of the bay. He said nothing of the sunken boat full of gold. The further she climbed into her uniform, the more she covered his own precious LuAnna with everyone's Corporal Bryce. With a pang, Ben remembered what he loved about LuAnna most: he could confide in her. Tonight he felt he could trust her only with his better self. She was an honest woman, and an officer duty-bound to a fault. The lawful thing to do did not jibe with Ben's gut instinct, which was issuing darker commands.

Though LuAnna seemed weighed down by her own thoughts, she still consoled her waterman. "You know what you're doing down there. Tomorrow will be better."

She did not sound so sure. Tomorrow was a long way off. The only thing certain was that when he kissed LuAnna good-bye at the pier, his night's work was just beginning.

CHAPTER 7

MAYNARD CHALK SETTLED slowly into his desk chair at the *Right Way* office. He unfolded a knife and scraped blood from beneath his fingernails before it dried. No Nytrile examining gloves for Chalk. He kicked his interviews old school. The chat with Nelly Vickers, his missing employee's sweetie, had cost four precious hours; practically every minute a complete waste of time. Turned out Vickers had hardly known a thing about Tom Chase. They broke up a few months after the *Right Way* holiday party with her feeling suspicious of her beau, but none the wiser. Chalk knew this, but had gone ahead with chatting her up on the off-chance she'd heard something more.

It turns out she had. Now it was time for Chalk to shift his resources in gear and let out the clutch. Folding his knife away, he fished his encrypted cell phone from a breast pocket. He pressed a button. He gave the person on the other end the Vickers address. He said it once and hung up. Everything would be handled. None of Ms. Vickers's neighbors would smell a funny odor at the door in three days' time. Would not have to call the St. Mary's City Police Department to ask for a well-being check on her. The police would not have a splashy crime scene to deal with. In about six hours, the house would be just like Chalk, Slagget, and Clynch had found it. It would be as if Nelly Vickers had never come home. She never would again.

Just before the end of her life's final chapter, predictably entitled *Why Me?*, Vickers offered only a single piece of intel for their trouble. Once, when Tom Chase showered at her house, his cellular phone had buzzed in the pocket of his coat which was then lying on her couch. Curious about other women who might be in his life, Vickers picked up without saying anything. A low rough voice, maybe with a southern accent, perhaps a black man, had asked for someone other than the man now rinsing off in the shower. The caller had followed the full name with a jocular "you-son-of-a-bitch," as if they had not spoken in some while, but the renewed acquaintance was welcome. When Nelly Vickers remained silent, the caller immediately hung up. A wrong number? She did not tell Chase about it. Did not want him to think she was snooping. He must have figured out she invaded his privacy. He broke up with her the next day.

With Chalk's cruel encouragement, Vickers even remembered the name the caller had asked for. Of course she had not volunteered this information at once. It had come out a piece at a time, much the same way as her appendages went bye-bye during their interview. Maynard Chalk put the *gator* in interrogator.

Having gleaned this one name, Chalk assured himself that Vickers's death was not entirely senseless. Unfortunately, it had taken none of the edge off his unbearable desire to find Tom Chase and fix him. Whatever Chase's many faults and offenses, including an abject lack of company loyalty, Chalk would take a lesson from his new nemesis: Chase did not mix pussy with business.

With the clean-up call placed, and his fingernails tidied, Chalk slathered a dollop of Purell on his hands and rubbed them briskly as if they were cold. Then he bellied up to his computer. Who was the man Vickers had dimed? Though now he could finally deploy his immense technical resources, the first clue had come as the result of a vigorous beat-down on a living, breathing witness. He stayed true to one of his core ideals of the Millennium: talk before tech.

Chalk did not log onto the World Wide Web most mortals use, with spam, pop-ups, the stroke sites, and the endless offers of penis-extending Levitran weight-loss wonder pills. This was Black Widow, a cyber galaxy that only seven men in the entire world could travel with impunity. The President of the United States did not know Black Widow existed.

On a lonely dead-end street in Quantico, an entire building dropped twenty floors below ground level. That was Black Widow's lair. It was populated wall to wall with computer geniuses, not all of whom were pim-pled, obese, mouth-breathing, asocial, compulsive masturbators, with skid marks in their Fruit of the Looms. This warren of geeks rocked day and night, hacking any site in the world to which Chalk did not already have access. Their efforts were compartmentalized so no one in the cube farm had the full picture. Their results were aggregated and collated into a whole. Black Widow was a network of front doors jimmied, fire-walls breached, and electronic sentinels co-opted to betray their designers and owners. Every database lay open and bare to Chalk with no legal warrant required. The Web of the common man was like a harem of crippled virgins helpless against his priapic despoiling. With Black Widow, Chalk could slither into anyone's bedroom window over sills of fractured code.

Chalk shedded everything he could find. Cracking into police, jail, and prison records told him a good deal about his employee. Shambling Tom Chase had been an ordinary yobbo up to a point. He seemed like a garden variety punk, a skell always looking to better his sorry lot in the easiest way possible; often getting himself pinched by the local po-po for his efforts. In the drawer of humanity there were a few sharp knives. Tom Chase was a trusty wooden spoon.

Then Chalk delved deeper in the cyber shadows and looked up the name Vickers had let tumble in extremis: This bastard was a real eye-opener, a damn revelation. Had Chalk known this was the real man behind Tom Chase, the weasel would have been tortured to death for the affront of even applying for a job with *Right Way*. This was the usual fate of any shyster with the balls to come sniffing around for a quick sting. It was clever. Chalk had to hand it to him. Blackshaw had sheep-dipped himself, covering his actual identity the way soldiers got their identities wiped from the records when they were loaned out to the CIA for special missions.

The name Chase was more than just an alias. It was also a bad pun. So be it, thought Chalk. The chase is on. Like the Royal Canadian Mounted Police, Chalk always got his man; but unlike the Canuckistani cops to the north, he slowly and painfully slaughtered him.

Chalk researched the name Vickers revealed. Plenty of Black Widow hits on the guy. The man was from right next door in Maryland. Chalk ran the name against the picture on file at the Maryland Department of Motor

Vehicles and confirmed it. The comrade Chalk knew as Tom Chase stared back at him from the screen.

At a signal from their boss, Simon Clynch and Bill Slagget sat down. They were both tall, muscular men dressed in a fresh change of casual clothing after the Nelly Vickers mess, reeking of dueling colognes. Chalk angled the monitor toward them. Clynch took hold of the mouse, left-clicked, right-clicked, scrolled up, and scrolled down. Then, as one they sat back in their chairs.

Clynch shook his head. "He got us, Mr. Chalk. He left a legit-looking paper trail three years old. Brilliant. Picks up the identity of a guy who tripped on acid and dropped out at an ashram in Upstate New York. Pretty smart. The alias's owner is still alive, but he's totally off the grid. The identity is viable."

Slagget chimed in. "Right. So no flags go up when the Social Security number gets back in play after a time-out. The real Chase, the yogi, he even had a decent military record. Which we always like. Our grifter just kept on walking the walk with the stolen identity. Now we know our guy isn't Tom Chase. He's Richard Willem Blackshaw."

Chalk regarded his lieutenants and spoke dangerously low. "Take over. Get me everything you can dig up on this shitbird."

CHAPTER 8

BEN GOT TO work before the wake of LuAnna's boat disappeared round the bend in his creek. He retrieved the treasure box keys from the house. He could not help checking the gold bar in the couch. He even stroked it once before letting the cushion flop back into place. At his pier, he refueled the air compressor engine, which ran off a separate tank from *Miss Dotsy*'s Atomic Four.

Then he ducked into his crab shanty for other necessities. The shanty was built out over his stream, and supported by posts driven into the bottom. In summer, the shanty housed shallow shedding tanks that held blue crabs until that perfect moment in their molt. Then, when their shells were at their most supple, and the meat was mouth-watering, Ben would fish up the soft-shell delicacies, pack them on ice, and take them to market with the rest of his hard-shell catch.

Off season, the shanty served more as a shed. Ben collected eighty feet of extra line, two shovels, four more plastic milk crates, and his older dive light which had fresh batteries. Then he cast off and cruised over to Knocker Ellis's place.

Ellis could have walked the several footbridges connecting his small property to Ben's. He waited at home because it was a roundabout half-mile trek across the intervening hummocks and islets, and he did not want to run into LuAnna. Ellis could see Ben's pier and her boat from his second-floor window. Also, Ellis did not want to run into any of his neighbors at that hour. He was usually snug in bed by now, and anyone sighting him

would remember, and might become curious. Though he was almost sure
the white community had finally, if grudgingly, accepted his presence after a
decade and a half, Ben sensed the proverbial dark and stormy night was no
time for Ellis to test race relations.

Outside the confines of the streams, guts, and watery thoroughfares of
Smith Island, the bay banked into short steep waves with scattered whitecaps. The wind was fluky around the compass, at times gusting to twenty
knots. Only now and then did rain mix with the spray coming over *Miss
Dotsy*'s bow. The weather was bad, could get much worse, but was holding.
As they cruised, Ellis bent lengths of line to the milk crates. Then he
inspected the air compressor, its seals, the motor, the exhaust, the air hose
and regulator.

Knocker Ellis asked, "Miss LuAnna okay?"

Ben nipped this in the bud. "She's fine. And no, I didn't tell her about
it. Not any of it."

"Seemed like you were slingin' her the dirty pound for quite a while
this evening. No pillow talk?"

Ben countered. "Did you keep things quiet? No late night calls to ex-
girlfriends bragging they should've stuck with you?" It was spiteful to rub
Ellis's nose in his solitary life, but now Ben was angry.

"Who would I tell? My cat?"

"You got a cat?"

Ellis spat, "Exactly."

Ben concentrated on navigation, and took slow, deep breaths. Before
heading in to sell their catch that evening, he had taken mental bearings on
several cellular towers on shore. A blight on the landscape by day, the towers were useful at night. When their lights lined up properly, *Miss Dotsy*
would be over the oyster rock, the wreck, the gold, and the body once
again. Ben and Ellis reverted to their customary silence. The trip took just
over half an hour. When the alignment of lights was perfect, Ben lowered
the anchor. He dragged on the cold wetsuit. Knocker Ellis started the air
compressor.

Before Ben dropped over the side, Ellis patted him on the shoulder.
"Good luck." Ben nodded acknowledgment.

Then Ellis said, "What about the keys?"

Ben pointed to his chest.

Ellis held out his hand. "It's Joe Chilly. Diving at night can be danger-ous. Especially alone."

Catching Ellis's point, but not liking the implications, or the tone, Ben handed off the keys to Ellis. "No sitting on my air hose." Ben slipped into the inky bay.

Ben loathed diving at night. To him, the murk was full of dark eyes and saw-toothed maws gaping just beyond his flashlight's beam. His fear was not unfounded. Sometimes sharks made their way into the Chesapeake with a long ocean of hunger behind them. Ben dared a shark to bite him. All it would get was a mouthful of gristle and fear. He played the beam around. Still silted, but shining the light down his own body length as a yardstick, he figured visibility was a tolerable four feet.

After a few moments descending into the dark void, his rubber boots sank into the bottom. No boat in sight. He was sure of his bearings. Maybe storm surge shifted it. The wreck was gone, and all the problems with it. Now he could go home, collapse into sleep, or grieving. He had not wanted to leave a buoy to mark the site that afternoon on the slim chance someone got curious. Times were tough, and the oystering hard. Right now not put-ting out a buoy seemed either overly cautious, or a blessing in disguise.

Ben shifted a step backward. Something tapped him on the shoulder. He swung completely around during the beat his heart skipped. The mon-ster had come for him. His father's corpse tethered to the boat did nothing to calm the Black Watch Pipe and Drum tattoo hammering in his chest.

The corpse, once known as Pap, still had the vague outline of a human being. After a few days in the water it was otherwise unrecognizable. Scraps of meat. Clumps of hair. Soup bones and tattered clothes. The eye that first glared at Ben that afternoon still blazed with uncorrupted clarity. Before he quit high school, Ben had read Poe's *The Telltale Heart*. Despite the title, he remembered it was an old man's cold staring *eye* that drove the narrator to kill.

Ben was not sure what impelled him, but he reached out and touched the dead man's eye. Very strange. It was hard, calcified. Unable to rein in the bizarre urge, he dug around the orb. The eye popped out of the socket in a small puff of thick blood. It was smaller than a golf ball, and oddly rough like pumice. Cupping the front of the bony sphere was a smooth portion, perfectly rendered with an iris, a pupil, and a white delicately riven with uncanny naturalness by thin red blood vessels. It stared at him from his gloved palm. Then he understood. This was a prosthetic eye to replace the one Pap had lost in the knife fight. The fight that had spurred his father to flee Smith Island.

Ben dropped the ghoulish memento into his progging bag. Emotion-tight bulkhead doors that had momentarily been pried open in his mind slammed shut again. Back to business.

First thing, move this body out of the way. Ben untied the canvas strap holding the cadaver's foot to the boat. That's when he brushed against something solid in the coat's side pocket. The unyielding weight he had noted before. Now he had a good idea what it was. He opened the pocket. A two foot American eel curled out, slipping into the darkness.

After making sure the pocket was not serving as a hidey-hole for some other sea creature, Ben reached in and pulled out a gold bar. It lit up the water when his flashlight beam struck it. He turned and placed it in the nearest milk crate. When he turned back, the body had disappeared. It was gone, like a phantom. Ben played the light around in a full circle. Nothing but silt.

Then he raised the light. Like an undersea resurrection, Ben's father floated toward the surface, now just disembodied pants disappearing into the murk above. Ben reached up, grabbed at a shoe, snagged it, and yanked downward. The decayed foot disarticulated at the ankle. The shoe and foot came off in his hand.

He gripped the pants leg more gently and eased the body back down. It was like wrangling a ghastly helium balloon. Ben removed the tarp from the cargo and wrapped the body, as well as the loose foot, in it. Then he wound several lengths of the canvas strap around the impromptu shroud, lashing the entire parcel to the bow of the Nantucket Lance. It was a hasty piece of work. A few quick tugs assured Ben the body was secure for now.

Standing in the wreck where the footing was firm, Ben grabbed one of the metal boxes, and tried to lift it into a milk crate. The thing barely budged. He strained. Spinal disks compressed into Smuckers preserves. Using every ounce of strength, he gradually slid one box off the top of the stack. It fell in slow motion, smashing into the crate. One down. Nineteen to go.

It took two hours. Ben loaded boxes into the five tethered milk crates. Then he surfaced and helped Knocker Ellis haul them aboard. They lined the boxes along *Miss Dotsy*'s keel to keep her in trim. They repeated the process four more times while the weather deteriorated. *Miss Dotsy* squatted in the waves under the new weight.

Ben was worn-out. Nearly killed by the cold. Knocker Ellis passed him rags heated on the air compressor motor. Ben stuffed them in his armpits and near his groin to warm his icy core. A damn long day in Nordic waters.

Ellis took the keys from around his neck. "Let's see what we have."

He picked a box and went through the routine of finding the right key. Ben crept closer along the rolling deck. The lock clanked. Ben put his hand on the lid but hesitated.

Ellis got impatient. "This is no time for speeches."

Ben looked at Ellis and said, "Not to contradict, I think this'll make you view the world very differently." Then he opened the watertight lid.

Disappointment mixed with confusion. It showed on their faces as they looked down into the metal box. It was not filled with gold. There was some kind of control panel with buttons, gauges, and a small depression as big around as a quarter.

At first it was a complete mystery to the tired men. The device appeared simple enough. Ben noticed the writing. Delicate swirls beneath the gauges, labeling the buttons. Not English. From his time in the Gulf, he knew it to be Arabic. He had no idea what it said.

The box beeped three times, loud enough to make them look around for a passing waterman who might overhear. A digital readout lit up, with 24:00:00 showing on a screen no bigger than a travel alarm clock. The numbers quickly changed to 23:59:59 and counted backwards second by second.

Ben muttered, "Whoops."

Knocker Ellis shook his head. "What in God's name have you done?"

Ben examined one of the box's internal hinges. "Trigger. Open the box and it starts. Maybe it shuts down when you close it."

Ellis said, "Like a heavy metal music box? Doubt it. I don't want to be in the neighborhood when that timer reaches zero. Let's toss that fish back."

Ben wished it were so simple. "So it blows underwater? This isn't a conventional bomb. Look at the shielding in the box. Lead, to help smuggle it across a border. The writing is in Arabic, but that gauge there is an American made Geiger counter. You don't need that for C-4 or TNT. This box can kill every living thing for miles. Then what? There's plenty I have to live with. I won't have that on my conscience."

"Run it out to the Atlantic, then dump."

"Same problem. Everything we catch in summer and fall spends the winter out there in the ocean. In twenty-four hours, we could never get it far enough away to be safe."

"So we bury it." Knocker Ellis was clutching at straws.

"On top of our freshwater aquifer. No. For now, we have to keep this thing, and figure out how to stop it. Do, or die trying."

Ben closed the box, and pushed his annoyance with Ellis aside. It was the thin edge of a wedge between the two men. He could not afford to let resentment and stress mix with a greedy sense of entitlement. That would destroy the already fragile trust they needed for this venture.

Just as Ben was mentally factoring a bomb into the day's equation, an unholy thump thundered from *Miss Dotsy*'s keel. The deck shook and heeled beneath them with a loud scrape and bang as if Vulcan's forge had relocated to Davy Jones' Locker. Ben and Ellis gaped wide-eyed, grabbing for handholds as the Nantucket Lance reared bow-first out of the water like a breeching nuclear sub in a Navy recruiting film. The body on the bow flopped halfway out of the tarp.

Ben pegged it. "Damn! We're idiots."

Ellis confirmed it. "We can't kill nothing, and won't nothing die. Either it's haints, or we took all the ballast out of her. She pulled out of the mud. Damn thing's come back on us like herpes."

Ben thought for a moment. He reached out with the boat hook to pull the spectral wreck alongside *Miss Dotsy*. "We'll never be able to hide it. Not from anyone who really wants it. We absolutely have to cover our tracks."

There was only one thing to do. They tied the speedboat to *Miss Dotsy*. They rewound the body in the tarp, and secured it.

Ben said, "We have to substitute the weight of the gold with rocks."

Ellis said, "Who's we?"

Ben knew what Ellis meant. Ben would have to dive to find the rocks. There was no other air rig aboard for Ellis to use to help. It was the least evil of two terrible choices. Ben could dive, search the bottom for rocks, and then he and Ellis could haul them up to the surface to place in the Nantucket Lance. Or they could sink the boat, and Ben could dive and find the necessary rocks, and place them directly in the Lance on the bottom, eliminating the need to haul the rocks topside. Time dictated taking the second course of action. The low fuel supply for the air compressor made it a necessity.

There was only one way to sink that unsinkable boat. The same way it had gone down the first time. With all the zeal of death-camp slaves, they transferred the gold back into the Nantucket Lance. Box by ponderous box. Then they used their combined bodyweights to hold one gunwale down before the mounting waves. Finally the boat swamped and sank from sight. For the second time. Now, if any boater should happen by in the middle of the night, the Lance, the body, and the gold would already be back on the bottom out of sight, and Ben and Ellis would have much less explaining to do.

Ellis said, "Maybe we should leave it there."

Ben glared at his culler. "Maybe you should ease off the crack."

"If I had some crack I wouldn't feel so damn tired."

Knocker Ellis bent a safety line to Ben's weight belt. For the third time in a day, Ben pulled on his wetsuit and rolled over the side into the frigid water. The Nantucket Lance settled upright, but without the tarp and straps, the boxes had shifted into a heap on the way down.

In order to safely remove the gold without the speedboat resurfacing, Ben shunted rocks, boulders, and even oyster shells into the Lance, filling the cockpit in around the cargo. It took over an hour and a half of trudging and hauling through bottom mud that gripped at his legs like deep molasses.

When Ben thought he had loaded in enough rock ballast, they worked like automatons to bring up the gold again. Their backs screamed. Shoulders ached. Their hands cramped into frozen talons.

Two boxes before ending the final dive, Ben thought he felt the wreck shift beneath him. Was it still too light? If the boat rose again, their double shift to hide it would be for nothing. Somebody would trace it, and then come looking; come hunting.

He scavenged more rocks; was running out of them. Soon he had to trudge farther from the wreck to locate stones and somehow find his way back. The silt he was kicking up made him lose the wreck more than once, so he tethered himself to it with extra line, leaving enough scope to hunt ever more rocks. When had he not been hauling rocks in the dark cold water? When had he ever been warm and dry? These were not memories, not fantasies, but delusions he could not trust in his exhaustion.

Suddenly, Ben felt three tugs on the safety line. The signal. The compressor was about to run out of its oil and gas mix. Ben carried on. He had to be sure this time. He lunged for more rocks.

Ben sucked a half-gulp of air, then nothing. His cheeks, and the skin at the base of his throat drew in with every unrealized breath. The compressor had quit. Its hum was fuel-starved into silence. Ben wrenched the next to last box into a milk crate. The rope to the final crate was the old original cordage, not the new. It had served many weeks of hauling oysters, and was frayed from rubbing over *Miss Dotsy*'s shell-embedded washboards. With the stubbed blade of his knife, Ben slashed out the ruined rope, and retied the ends with two half-hitches. His lungs burned. His vision tunneled and dimmed to dusky gray in the black water. He grabbed the last heavy box with both hands.

And the world went dark.

Ben woke on the deck of *Miss Dotsy*, more dead mackerel than living man. Ellis puffed from the exertion of reeling Ben in. After a moment, he rose and hauled up the last crate by himself. By some miracle of dogged willpower, Ben had heaved the final gold box into the milk crate before completely blacking out.

Finally, they were back where they'd been hours earlier in the night, with two rows of boxes laid over the keel. They waited a few minutes to be sure the unsinkable boat and its captain did not make another appearance. Soon they were satisfied. The Lance was down for now if not for good.

At a nod from Ben, Ellis started the Atomic Four. Ben weighed and stowed the thirty-five pound CQR plow anchor. Ellis shifted into forward. The gearbox roared like an old coffee mill grinding gravel.

Ellis said, "That damn Tucket must've pranged *Miss Dotsy*'s shaft when it struck her from below."

Ben advised the obvious. "Then take her slow."

Even with a bomb counting down the seconds just three feet away, there was nothing else they could do.

CHAPTER 9

BEFORE HIS FATEFUL birthday decision, Chalk and *Right Way Moving & Storage* were commissioned by Senator Morgan to act as go-between brokers on yet another in a long line of clandestine jobs. They drew this kind of gig from Senator Morgan all the time, but never so luscious.

This one was unique because it was the Senator's own idea, start to finish. She had a hare-brained scheme that the terrorist enemies of capital "F" Freedom could be brought down by suddenly giving them *too much* power, *too much* wealth. They would collapse under the weight of their own corruption. Or so she believed. She had her reasons.

Right Way was to deliver a large sum of gold to a radical terrorist group in exchange for a set of plans, or so the Senator told Chalk. That was simple. Then *Right Way* was to deliver these plans to a second faction of extremists who had supplied the gold in the first place. *Easy-peasy.*

True to form, Chalk had kept his own team members ignorant of the nature of the engagement. They liked it that way. The less they knew, the less they could tell, and the longer they would live. Since Richard Willem Blackshaw, formerly Tom Chase, had hauled more than two and a half tons of gold, Chalk surmised that the blueprints the gold was buying were of great importance, but he could only guess about them until Doomsday.

The delivery was supposed to take place two days from now. That's when Chalk figured the sellers would realize something was wrong. First, a polite inquiry would be made. When Chalk came up empty-handed, all hell would break loose. Word would quickly reach the buyers of the blueprints that the gold was missing. As the man in the middle, Chalk could reasonably anticipate not one but *two* very unhappy customers gunning for him not long after forty-eight hours into his very dim future. Of course that harpy, Senator Lily Morgan, would be raining hellfire down on his ass all the while. No wonder. It was the biggest deal they'd ever done together.

This was a new situation for Chalk. *Right Way* always delivered, and never failed. He rarely worried about contingency plans. True, shit sometimes happened. Once, when one of his mules was flying a computer chip for a missile guidance system, his Piper Aztec had crashed in the Mojave Desert. Chalk arrived on the scene within two hours, and found his deliveryman's remains. Then Chalk went to work with a proctologist's finesse. It was this personal touch that allowed him to retrieve the pricey component from where it was hidden within several layers of Trojan condom latex, ribbed.

Rescuers, the FAA, and the NTSB had been cleverly delayed by Chalk's operatives who set up a dummy aircraft Emergency Locator Transmitter signal one hundred miles south of the actual crash site. The authorities never knew that Chalk had gotten there first. That was years ago. An accident. Smooth sailing since then. Accidents, after all, might happen to anybody, but no one intentionally fucked with *Right Way*. Not like this.

Would such a hands-on technique salvage this crisis? Chalk fantasized, wondering if Blackshaw had accidentally crashed his truck. Maybe he was lying dead, crushed under the gold in some arroyo in New Mexico. He should have been somewhere near Albuquerque at the time he fell silent.

That prompted another question in Chalk's mind. If Blackshaw was ripping off *Right Way*, why didn't he make up false progress reports to buy time? He could have claimed to be anywhere, the way Donald Crowhurst, that round-the-world yacht racer back in the 1960s, had falsified his position reports by radio while he did circles in the South Atlantic. Why didn't Dick Blackshaw do something like that? Chalk was baffled.

He did not have any telemetry markers on the gold. Some random boob could LoJack his Chevy Nova, and the cops could find the piece of crap in ten minutes by satellite if anybody bothered to steal it. Chalk had decided not to put a transponder on two and a half tons of gold. As he saw it, the problem is this: if he could track it, so could somebody else. And the shipment was so big. It was so heavy. And Chalk was such a notorious pluperfect badass! Who'd dare mess with his shit? Someone very close to home apparently. In retrospect, skipping telemetry was another gross oversight. Really no excuse. Verged on hubris.

Chalk addressed his team in the office. "Friends, unless we move mighty rapido, it's likely we're all going to be killed before the week is out. Yes, I predict we are going to have some very unhappy customers."

"Not necessarily. I'm no profiler," said Slagget, "But after some further research, I got a sense of the man. He's still looking for his place at home, like everybody."

Chalk was nonplused. "That is pure steaming bullshit buzzing with bluebottle flies. If you had a *sense of the man*, as you put it, we wouldn't be having this conversation!"

Chalk never tolerated bloviated homilies from uppity contract killers.

Slagget plowed ahead. "We have a better sense of the *real* man now."

Chalk eyed Slagget. "I'm all ears."

Clynch jumped in. Chalk liked that. Clynch was trying to buff up some of his former luster and avoid being plugged by his short-fused chief. He said, "Let's review what we know. His name is Richard Willem Blackshaw. He was born on Tangier Island, Virginia. Not too far from here out in the middle of the Chesapeake Bay. But he was raised on Smith Island, Maryland, across the state line a little north."

Chalk assembled his features into the well-known What's-It-To-Me? face.

Clynch deferred to the new guy, muttering, "Bill here has some more thoughts on all this."

Chalk transferred his gaze back to Slagget. "This is worse than a local newscast. You going to throw in a lead about the bad weather? Maybe a pie-eating contest, or a story about a lost kitty-cat finding its way home from Guadalajara back to D.C.?"

Slagget sat up straighter and said, "Dick Blackshaw, a.k.a. Tom Chase, comes from a pretty isolated place in the world. I know it's not too far from D.C. as the crow flies, but the people there speak differently, live different. They fish, hunt, oyster, clam, crab, what have you. Even had a tortoise-meat industry for a while. But mostly seafood. And waterfowl. Smith and Tangier both have several small hamlets each, but they're populated by pretty tough individuals. Mostly poor, devout, hardworking, downwardly mobile no-nonsense types just trying to hang on."

Chalk was only an eyebrow spasm away from downsizing his operation through cold-blooded homicide.

Slagget picked up his pace. "So this Richard Willem Blackshaw, he's normal enough as a kid. Some run-ins with the cops on the mainland now and then. Nothing serious until he comes back from Vietnam. By then he's a mess. A Post Traumatic Stress Disorder poster child. Tries to fit in. Marries a local girl. They have a son who still lives there on Smith Island.

"Dick tries his best to work on the water like everybody else on the island, but he's a time bomb. Violent. Unpredictable temper. Flashbacks, and the thousand-yard stare. Booze. Drugs, maybe. The whole nine. Doesn't belong at home anymore. He's gonzo. Freaks out, and disappears. Reconnects with a few other throwbacks at the VA hospital. That's all happening fifteen years ago. Uses old buddies or some VA contacts to help him drop out, maybe. Becomes a mercenary renting out to the highest bidder."

Chalk asked, "How did this dipshit in wolf's clothing come into my employ? And where is he now?"

Something about this whole *Islands in the Stream* angle was ringing a bell for Chalk. A Chesapeake sanction. Long ago. A buddy of his had been detailed to delete an operative who knew too much about something or other, and was threatening to peach on some Poobahs upstairs. Chalk remembered that his pal might have managed to kill somebody, but he was pulled off the gig before taking out the designated target. Fifteen years ago. That's about the time Dick Blackshaw dropped out of sight. Chalk would have to dig into some fairly dusty files to figure out why it all sounded so familiar. A hell of a thing if the operative who got away back then was this same jackass. What were the odds of that? Starting to look pretty good apparently. He'd put Black Widow on the case.

Slagget wrapped it up. "Despite some intel training, Special Ops, Dick Blackshaw has been a screw-up all his life since 'Nam."

Chalk held up a hand again. Slowly shook his head. "No. It's Vietnam to those of you who didn't have the honor to serve there. *Viet*. Nam. Not

'Nam. You were still crapping your nappies when I was up to my eyes in blood, muck, shit, and gooks. Say it right. And you say it with respect."

Behind his smokescreen, the gung-ho patriotismo, Chalk had no trouble omitting that he'd coined his first million in Vietnam running smack to the States in his dead buddies' coffins. Sometimes inside the bodies themselves if they were intact enough. Once, early in his career, he'd failed to intercept a shipment stateside, and five kilos of dope had been cremated by the grieving family along with their loved one's body. Arriving too late to stop the cremation became one of the few times in life Chalk could remember openly weeping. The dead soldier's family was quite touched.

Slagget looked abashed. "Since then, Dick Blackshaw's been living dangerously; non-stop brink-of-death as a mercenary, with short breaks for drinking and whoring until his pay ran out. Angola, Chechnya, Afghanistan, Columbia, Bolivia, Somalia. If I have him pegged, at some point a few years ago, he smartens up. Doesn't want to retire with a bullet as pension. He gets to thinking."

Chalk mused, mollified for the moment. "You think this uber-wanker ripped us off so he could be The Man, and go home to get his long-overdue redneck ticker-tape parade?"

Slagget glanced at Clynch before saying, "Yes, Mr. Chalk. I do."

Chalk thought for a moment more, tossed off the last of his scotch.

"Saddle up, compadres. We're going to Smith Island. Get us some oysters. See if Dick-Willikers is available for a little confab. Short of that we'll brace his son. See what he knows. We need to shut this down quick. We have two days until everybody starts technical climbing up our rectums. By then we gotta have the gold and the blueprints, and make everybody happy. Screw this up and we are dead, plain and simple. Pronto dead."

CHAPTER 10

DARK WATER ROILED on a dark night. Whitecaps appeared as if ether-born in the howling distance. *Miss Dotsy* wallowed under two and a half tons of cargo she was never built to carry. She plowed through the waves instead of gliding over them. With just one rogue broadsider, she would ship too much water and join the Nantucket Lance on the bottom.

Ellis had the helm. Ben kept watch on the cargo lest it shift. He also kept an eye out for other boats. None so far.

Ellis said. "Daylight in three hours. You have a plan?"

Ben hesitated to divulge too much to Knocker Ellis. The culler was a closed book. The ultimate unknown quantity. Ben had never asked Ellis to talk about Dick Blackshaw, and Ellis had never volunteered. He was not the type to yarn about the past over a beer. He damn sure wasn't a gossip. It felt as though Ellis had known the corpse was Dick Blackshaw before Ben told him so. And working that particular oyster rock on that particular day had been Knocker Ellis's suggestion. Ellis had too many secrets. For now, Ben told Ellis only where they were headed, and no more. "Deep Banks Island."

Ellis involuntarily wrinkled his nose at the thought of their destination.

Ben smiled weakly. "Yep. The heron rookery there stinks to high heaven. Decades of guano. Nobody but bird watchers go there this time of year. And not in this weather. Not until the Christmas count."

Ellis set a course to the north. He eyed the cargo. "We have at least three rhinoceri that we're not talking about sitting in the corner."

Ben had to yell over the engine and the wind. "Which one first? The full count of the gold? Your split? The bomb? Reckon we can safely call it a bomb."

Ellis smiled. "How come we're taking that damn gizmo along with us to Deep Banks Island? I thought you liked Nature, you being the big waterman, the fancy wildlife artiste and whatnot. Way I see it? There won't be any split besides atoms with that bomb on this boat."

Already exhausted, Ben spoke through clenched teeth. "Ellis, I'm working on it."

Deep Banks Island lay north of the Martin Wildlife Refuge, which itself formed the northern landmass of the Smith Island archipelago. Ben navigated through a convoluted snarl of guts and streams into the heart of the island. With *Miss Dotsy* so weighed down, she could barely penetrate the smaller, shallower waterways as far as Ben wanted. Finally, he saw what looked like a dead sapling jammed in the mud directly off *Miss Dotsy*'s port beam. With almost all forward motion halted and her wheel churning up mud plumes in the water by the stern, *Miss Dotsy* was essentially aground. He cut the Atomic Four.

They sat still for a moment with the engine silent. Listening, letting their ears get used to the darkness, and their eyes to the silence. Hunters understood the need to allow all the senses recalibrate after a change in the immediate environment. The engine clicked and pinged as it cooled. Otherwise, they heard nothing but marsh and wind. The scratch of reed stalks against each other. In the distance, the ratching call of a heron waking. The stench of the rookery, pungent with ammonia, made their eyes water.

The tiny stream threading through the reeds off to the left was the on-ramp of a poacher's highway running through many of the protected islands in the Chesapeake. Though wildlife sanctuaries were off limits to all hunters, Smith Islanders looked askance at banishment from their ancestral stalking grounds. Just below the surface of the water at low tide, a series of planks led into ponds and meadows where geese and ducks rested, perfectly set up for both the silent attack, and the poacher's quick retreat. Without knowledge of this system of planks, staked-out Natural Resources Police were always mired to a halt, and rarely made an arrest in here.

His strength draining away from the long night, and sensing the early physical signs of Hell Week back in Coronado, Ben stepped over the side. "That tree marks the way in."

They carried the first box between them, sliding their feet along the slimy planks inches at a time. Ben and Ellis soon disappeared in among the reeds, the skunk cabbage, dying lizard's tail and joe-pye weed growing on all sides. Under immense stress from their combined weight, the old planks bowed and rocked with each step. They nearly toppled over more than once.

Slowly they emerged from the marshy land into a hollow sheltered by a loose stand of pines. They lowered the box onto sandy soil mixed with guano. The heron rookery stench was overwhelming. They hated to breathe, despite being badly winded. Every molecule of air was weapons-grade, and would have had doughboys reaching for gas-masks in the trenches of Ypres. Above them, more than a hundred herons stirred, squawked, and canted their sleek plumed heads for a view of the visitors.

"Only nineteen to go." Ellis the optimist. "This's some kind of stank."

As if on cue, Lonesome George glided down to a landing on his thin legs.

Ben said, "Supervisor's here."

Lonesome George watched them grunt through the labor, probably wondering when his oyster alms would appear.

They blotted kerchiefs at their watering eyes. Back again to *Miss Dotsy*. Hauling the second box of gold, Ellis's foot slipped off the hogged top of the sunken board. He did not let go of the box. Its weight pile-drove his leg deep into the mud and pinned him. Ben was almost dragged off the board after him, but held on tight. Ben slowly pulled the box back onto the plank. Planting his feet on the slippery board, he hooked his arms under Ellis's shoulders, bear-hugging his chest. It took precious minutes of heaving to lever Ellis's leg out of the ooze. From sheer main strength it came free with a wet sucking sound.

Ellis rasped, "Thanks."

"Protecting our investment."

"Mistook you for a Christian."

"That so?"

"Maybe I mistook you for a friend."

Ben did not answer. Until he knew more about Ellis's involvement in all this, there was no room for loftier sentiments.

Gasping and retching from the stench, they slogged the plankway seventeen more times. The distance from the boat to the rookery hollow seemed to grow ever longer. Normal-length sentences between the men were compressed down into quick phrases under the weight of gold.

Ben said, "Rhinoceri."

"The split. The money." Ellis led first with this box, but walked backward to keep a better grip on it.

Ben knew this was coming. "What you figure?"

Knocker Ellis gasped one word. "Half."

Ben said, "The way I figure—"

Ellis put in more. "You figure this, Ben. I'm taking half the risk. Breaking my back here for half of a dead man's dream."

Ben took a few more steps, waited to be sure Ellis had finished. Then he nodded. "I was saying, the way I figure—half's good."

Ellis eyed his partner. Shook his head. "Should have asked for more."

"No. Very bad idea."

"Who knows? Your old man might've been bringing the whole lot of it to me."

Ben asked, "Is that what he told you?"

Ellis said nothing more.

The last box was lighter than the others, but not by much. It contained the bomb. They put it down by the others. Ellis gave Ben a What now? glance.

Ben shrugged. "It's a pirate's treasure. What else? We bury it."

CHAPTER 11

BILL SLAGGET WAS driving. Simon Clynch was riding bitch in the second row of the van with some pinch hitters, new guys Chalk had brought up from his farm team. For one, nobody really liked The Kid. He was probably in his twenties, but his mug was a deceptive downy baby-face. Chalk thought The Kid had skipped the piss-and-vinegar dressing on his psychotic salad. Gone straight into rabies-and-battery-acid. Chalk never saw someone more interested in mindless homicide. A complete tool. No brains. Just a dog to cut loose in the hopes it tore a chunk out of the right person.

On the other side of The Kid sat Tug Parnell. Parnell was a little steadier than The Kid, but only a little. An untreated case of adolescent acne had left him horribly scarred. One look from him could frighten tame horses and make kind children stare. Even dermabrasion wouldn't help unless performed with a belt sander. He was calculating, a cooler head, and therefore more useful to Chalk than The Kid.

Dar Gavin, another veteran of the Vickers interview and many other sorties, rode the third bench with bags of gear that overflowed from the cargo area at the dead rear of the van.

Chalk was thumbing a file he'd printed from his last probe on Black Widow. And there it was. The sanction he recalled his buddy whining about a decade and a half ago. It had in fact been ordered against Dick Blackshaw. Sadly, the primary target had escaped once, and then a second time, never to be found again. That failure was costing Chalk big. An unknown woman had been unconfirmed collateral damage in the sanction. Now Dick Blackshaw was back. If this theft was about revenge, Chalk had a good idea who the woman must be.

Chalk's cell phone blared. For this caller, the ringtone was Vera Lynn's rendition of *We'll Meet Again*. It was the end theme of Kubrick's *Dr. Strangelove*. Strangely indeed, the song was part of an old BBC collection of soothing ditties to boost British morale after a nuclear attack. Chalk liked irony as much as the next guy.

Chalk felt Slagget's glance from the driver's seat. Incoming calls on the boss's mobile were rare.

Chalk flipped the phone open. "I told you never to call me here."

Senator Lily Morgan wheezed into the other end. "It's your cell phone, you tit! How am I supposed to know where *here* is?"

Chalk kept his voice low. "Who came down with comedy cancer tonight? Kinda late even for you, isn't it?"

"Haven't slept since the Carter administration. Just checking in. Level with me. How bad is it?"

Chalk was certain she knew he was stuck between a shit and a sweat on this detail, and she was loving every minute of it. She was definitely behind this mess, rooting for his demise.

Chalk rolled his eyes. "The hand-off won't be for two more days!"

The Senator said, "I just have a bad feeling about this. The terrorism alert level just hiked up to burnt sienna or some damn thing. They're picking up a lot of suspicious chatter on the wires. You sure we're good?"

"Take a chill-pill, Lil. Don't forget, *Right Way Moving and Storage* prides itself on being part of the problem, not the solution."

"Call me when you know something." The Senator rang off.

Slagget was antsy. "Everything okay?"

To Chalk, such an inquiry was akin to questioning his authority, his control, his very penile dimensions. This time Chalk was quiet. Slagget, a recent hire, might be another of Senator Morgan's moles, as Tom Chase almost certainly was. That is, unless his mule was lying dead in a ravine somewhere in the Jemez Mountains. Before Chalk could craft a reply, the phone sounded again. The ringtone: Steve Martin's *King Tut*.

"For the sake of our Lord Jesus H. Christ of the Andes!" Chalk pulled out the phone again. After a quick double-check of the caller ID, he focused like a viper stalking a sleeping mouse. "Here we go, boys."

He fixed a smile on his face to radiate world harmony and bonhomie across the airwaves. He answered, "Yusef, you old camel-fucker, how the hell are you?"

Yusef was an independent operative currently working for the terrorist faction selling the plans. The folks expecting the gold in two days. Though Chalk and Yusef went back many years together, through many unsavory missions, this was no time for Chalk to let on there was a hiccup.

"Maynard Chalk, you dog-raping son of a whore, I'm fine. Just fine. *For now.*"

The last phrase told Chalk that something was up. Something might have shattered the two-day window he needed to track Blackshaw, secure the gold, and complete the transaction as if nothing had gone wrong. Yusef was being unusually cagey.

Chalk had no time for finesse. "Why just for now? You coming down with a cold or something?"

"Possible lead poisoning, if you follow me."

Chalk's exasperation was not entirely a sham. "Is somebody besides me about to put a bullet in your empty noggin? We both know that'd leave you unimpaired. You do your best thinking with that uncircumcised heathen shvanse of yours. Remember Spring Break in Bangkok in '86?"

Yusef dropped his guarded manner at the recollection. "*Maynard Gone Wild.* I remember. Listen, your guy Tom Chase? He made the delivery. Two days back. Sorry I didn't get to you before. My people are loving your people."

Waves of relief and amazement swept over Chalk. Surprised as he was that Dick Blackshaw had come through after all, he did his best to mask it with Yusef. He succumbed part way to his excitement and gave a geeky thumbs-up to Slagget indicating all was well.

He blustered, "You bloody-fucking-lice-covered-turd-burgling-son-of-a-two-bit-clapped-up-one-legged-Gorgon-faced marsupial! You should have told me! Dammit, that's why you do business with me, because we communicate! Oh what the hell. On time or early, it's all good."

Again Yusef said, "For now."

Chalk fugued back and forth between the joy of his recent reprieve, and complete confusion. Yusef was still not happy about something.

Chalk said, "Don't be such a droopy-drawers. You got the stuff."

Then Yusef said, "The gold appears to be here, as you say. So until my principals know what I know, everything's fine."

"What do you know that the rest of us don't? This line is encrypted, Yusef. Even if they bugged your end, this whole conversation is scrambled. So spit it out. You said the gold is there. It is what it is. Shiny. Heavy. Mysteriously warm to the touch. Luminously yellow in hue. It don't mean a thing if it ain't got that bling. You have enough of that crap to fill every cavity in every tooth in the Kush a hundred thousand times over."

"No argument from me, Maynard. I'm calling to tell you that some-body, maybe the other side, maybe one of your people, played a sharp game. It's going to come out. You trust Tom Chase?"

Chalk bristled. "What the hell do you mean?"

"Something seemed wrong with him. For a guy who was four days early, he was in a lather to get moving. I signed off on the delivery, turned the purchased item over to him as agreed. It started bothering me. So I checked the gold."

Chalk's vertebrae turned to stacked ice cubes. "And?"

Yusef continued, "First one box, then the next. I checked them all. Two bars were missing."

Chalk said, "Holy hell, man I always negotiate a lagniappe for you. So my courier got a little greedy. Two missing bars still means a full shipment. Are you pissed you didn't get your bonus? You know I'll make it up to you. Is that all that's got your ass in a pucker?"

Yusef said, "No. The remaining bars aren't gold. They're soft, heavy, yellow in hue, as you put it. The entire shipment is lead. Gold-plated lead. I scraped it with my pocket knife. Under the thinnest coating of gold was a layer of what must be nickel. Beneath that, a thin layer of copper. Under that, lots and lots of worthless lead. Nothing more. It probably took less than the two missing bars of the real gold to finish-plate all the dummies. Honestly, it was a beautiful job, but it's one ape-dick huge problem for me."

"Jesus Effing Christ!" bellowed Chalk.

Yusef continued, "If it's your mule, he's fucked both of us sideways and dry. I'm planning to disappear, Maynard. Before my principals discover what's happened. Since I signed off on the delivery, they're going to blame me. Hunt me down. Murder me, but only after they torture my wife and children to death in front of me. And then they're going to serve you up like flank steak to their pit bulls. If I were you, I'd get out of Dodge for a while. Like for the rest of your life. These people won't forget this sort of thing. You saved my life once, Maynard. I just returned the favor. As of now, we're even."

Chalk agreed, "This is damn serious. Damn serious. What the hell kind of plans did all that gold buy, anyway? It was for some kind of weapon, right? A nuke missile?"

Yusef was quiet for a moment. "A nuke, yes. But Maynard, you honestly think someone would pay all that money for plans a fourth grader could download off the Internet? No. Your guy Tom Chase received a full-scale working model."

With that, Yusef rang off.

An astonished Maynard Chalk sized things up. If Dick Blackshaw had indeed returned home with all the spoils of his double-cross, then Smith Island, an eight-thousand-acre sandbar in the middle of the Chesapeake Bay, was now a nuclear power. Somewhere out there within seventy miles of Washington, D.C. was a crazy redneck toting a suitcase full of New World Order.

CHAPTER 12

ELLIS RETRIEVED THE shovels from *Miss Dotsy*'s forepeak. Before they buried the boxes in a shallow pit, they checked the contents of each one. Now they knew. One box containing a weapon of mass destruction that could annihilate all life in a dozen zip codes, and would do so in a hair more than twenty-two hours. Nineteen boxes full of gold. There were empty slots in one box for three bars. Ben had brought one bar up, and it lay in his saltbox, stashed in the couch. He had found a second bar in his father's coat pocket, but had placed it back in its box. Two bars were apparently missing. They did the math.

Ellis said, "You ready for this? At a seventeen hundred dollars a Troy ounce, with four hundred ounces to the bar, and twelve bars to the box, it looks like each box here but the short one is worth 8.16 million."

Ben blinked a few times in disbelief as he continued the incredible arithmetic. "Times nineteen boxes, minus two bars at four hundred troy ounces each. Ellis, that's nigh on 154 million." Ben shook his head slowly. "A million here; a million there. Pretty soon you're talking about real money."

Ellis smiled. "Time's the thing we don't get enough of. The presence of a certain bomb brings my point home, in case you missed it. And pretty soon, somebody with a lot of juice is going to come looking for it. What do you think they'll do when they find us?"

Despite the pressure bearing down on them, they listened for a moment to the wind rattling cold reeds and branches. A desolate sound.

These were men whose combined net worth that morning had amounted to four paltry figures. That, plus a quick nod toward their good character, was all they possessed.

And character was stretching thin to breaking. Fatigue and shock were working them over from within. Though decent men, they were not immune to the ancient deficits of humankind. The gold infected them. It polluted them both with a toxic brew of greed, fear, doubt, and mistrust. Strewing the last pine needles and dead leaves over the pit as camouflage, they each realized that now they were the only two men in the entire world who knew where this fortune lay buried. It only needed one death-blow from either of them, and a little more spadework for a grave. With that, the chance for betrayal disappeared.

And the survivor's fortune doubled.

Tonight, Ben was also nagged by a feeling that there were far too many loose ends. Ellis was not coming clean. In the service, Ben had trusted his superiors enough to believe that when he was ordered to take down a target, it was for the right reasons, and no questions need be asked. Out here on Deep Banks Island, that wasn't good enough. Ben hated working in the dark in every regard.

What happened next was inevitable. Sensing the moment of truth, Knocker Ellis's grip tightened on the weathered shank of the shovel. Ben felt the pressure of the broken knife he had tucked into his belt. Felt those few ounces of steel calling to him louder than tons of gold.

Ben whipped the knife out in an instant, its three remaining inches still razor sharp. He lunged, slashing the blade in a feint toward Ellis's eyes. Ellis jerked back, started raising the shovel. Still moving, Ben beat it aside, wrapped his empty hand around the haft, pulled himself hard and fast straight at Ellis. With a twist, he cocked his right leg for a shattering side-kick at Ellis's knee. He eschewed the fancy whirling aerial work of chopsaki movies. To blind, cripple, and kill, Ben kept it low, plain, explosive, and effective.

Ellis was not as quick, but he turned away just enough. Tried to save his knee by deflecting the kick off thigh muscle.

Just what Ben wanted. Ellis off balance. Instead of kicking, Ben stepped in tight behind Ellis on the foot he'd coiled, and hip-dropped the culler hard on the ground. The knife was at Ellis's throat a split second later.

"Why'd you put us on that oyster rock? That particular one. Tell me!"

Ellis answered with deliberate care. "Because that's where your father said we should be."

Ben was shaken. Knew in his bones it was the truth. "You were expecting him. He tells you he's coming in—" *But not me.*

Ben left the disturbing conclusion unspoken, but he could see Ellis understood. Worse than finding his father dead, was discovering that he'd been dead to his father. A cipher son. Hell of a thing, learning that the pit Ben had tumbled into that day had a trap door waiting at the bottom.

Knocker Ellis spoke again. Without fear, and with patience. His surprise at Ben's blunt force attack was ebbing. "I got this from him. The mail. Couple weeks back. Now take it easy."

Ellis slowly reached into his pocket, and pulled out a yellow handheld marine GPS. He pressed the start-up button. The screen came to life. Ellis pressed two more keys, turned it toward Ben.

"There. How he remembered that rock I don't know, but that was the place. I suppose it was always lucky for us back in the day. Your pappy logged it in this GPS as a waypoint. When the storm kept everybody ashore, I thought sure he'd stay in port, too. No way anybody could make it through, but he did. He went out in that damn mess. He was always a stickler for time tables."

For a moment, Ben's grip on the knife faltered. "You should have told me. My God, we left him out there. We could have gone out and brought him home alive."

Ellis suddenly wrenched himself around in a bruising blur of hands, elbows and knees. Now Ben's knife lay three feet away. Ellis pinioned him. Immobilized him in a headlock.

Ellis hissed in Ben's ear, "You want to shave a black man, you go with the grain or we bump-up something awful. Now listen to me, boy. Everything your father did was for you. Even the leaving. He'd earned the undivided attention of some very bad men. He was drawing heavy fire. He had to go. Staying would have put you all in danger."

Ben's world was turning gray with flares of red and green. Lack of oxygen from the choke hold was only half the trouble. He gasped, "He was protecting me. So why come back?"

Ellis released Ben, who rolled away massaging his throat. His vision cleared like the silted bay, and Ellis had more truth for him.

Standing, Ellis dusted grit and bird scat off his pants. "You just counted why he came back. A hundred fifty-some million reasons. And now you're old enough to stand on your own two feet. To help. You were a kid when he went. A liability. Leaving you out of it until the last minute kept you safe. Now I'm betting you're in deeper than you know. Happy?"

Ben reached over to retrieve his stub of a diving knife, and put it away. Ellis put his foot on it. "Not 'til we finish our friendly talk."

Ben's neck veins pounded. He was surprised and pissed at being bested by one old man, and abandoned by another. Kept in the dark by both until he'd nearly killed a friend. Ben quickly realized this wouldn't work. The blood in their eyes nearly spilled on the ground with nothing to show for it. Their well-upholstered future, far surpassing the brightest hopes of ordinary men, would have been wiped out. Ben sat heavily on a hummock of grass.

Squatting loose-limbed like a man half his age, Knocker Ellis asked, "First, 'fess up. Why'd you join the Army? And spare me all the stars and stripes stuff. Tell me the truth. You truly wanted to be a soldier man?"

Ben wondered why he owed any explanation to Ellis in trade for news of his father. Not wanting another fight, he decided to cough up an answer. More than one bomb was still ticking in the hollow.

"No. Pap disappeared down a rabbit hole. For him, the mouth of that hole was a letter from the draft board. For me, it was a recruiting office. I had to follow him, even if I didn't find him. I needed to figure out what became more important to him than being home."

Ellis said, "Believe me when I say there was nothing more precious to him than that. Now tell me. First things first. What exactly did you do for Uncle Sam? You've kept mum about that since you got home."

Ben's mouth curled into a rueful grin. "What do you guess? Raised on the water. Raised a hunter. Stalking the mesh. S.E.A.L.s."

Ellis nodded. "Sure. Makes sense. And I assume you did okay over there in Coronado? And afterward? Still did good?"

Ben tried to answer without picturing any of the faces of his targets. They were peering at him over that wall he had built in his mind. Now the wasted souls were reaching for him over the broken glass he had embedded in granite capstones. Suddenly, the faces of his own fallen comrades were mixing in with the enemy dead. How could they ever stand together, breath the same air, dare to look at him with anything like reproach? There were two faces in particular that haunted Ben. On his final mission, he was detailed to eliminate a general in the Iraqi Republican Guard. The man was on leave at his home in Mosul. No problem. Ben made housecalls.

After a week of observing the target, Ben was ready. The moment had come to finish the mission. He aimed through a bathroom window and took the shot. The bullet flew true, snipping the general's cervical spine between shoulder and the base of his skull. Should have been the end of it. The target was terminated. The bullet flew on.

Though deformed and fragmented, Al Jazeera reported that pieces of the spent round passed through an inner passage in the house, killing the target's wife. She was pregnant. While the general's death was old news after two days, Al Jazeera replayed footage of the wife's funeral procession for weeks; big coffin, little coffin. An unending TV procession that never seemed to reach the cemetery.

That woman's face was the most hate-filled visage among all the ghosts infecting Ben's mind. The unborn child, both casualty of war and murder victim, had no face at all. Soon after, Ben bailed out of the Army when his Expiration of Time and Service date came up. He hadn't lifted a gun in anger since then. The tragedy consumed him every day. Was he worthy of a child of his own after what had happened?

It did not matter that later intel revealed the woman was executed after the fact on Saddam Hussein's orders, just for the propaganda value. The damage was done. Ben was through as an American sniper.

Suddenly, the faces of fallen comrades and vanquished enemy who haunted Ben's heart seemed to drift apart, making just enough room among their ranks for one more soul. Ben knew they were making room for him.

To mask his flayed emotions, Ben answered Ellis, sticking to the sniper's motto. "How'd I do? One shot, one kill. Except for the last mission. The target. His wife got hit. She was pregnant. One shot, three kills."

Ellis nodded. "Rough luck for certain. Now, your pappy was a sniper, too. I think you knew that? No? He started out that way, at least. He was highly effective in Vietnam. Later, they took all his records down off the boards at Sniper School down to Fort Benning. Made him disappear. Dickie-Will became their dirty little secret."

A choking envy gripped Ben's chest. "He told you all about it, I guess."

"He didn't have to tell me a thing, Ben. I was Dick Blackshaw's spotter for Five. Motherfuckin'. Tours." Ellis tossed off a mock salute. "So I'm a dab hand with the shooting iron myself, as if I need to tell you. You best bear that in mind."

Ben reeled. The dead men in his skull pressed their shoulders hard against the inner wall. It shuddered. A more eerie legacy than all the gold was this inheritance of lethal stealth. It was a rare operator who killed after leaving the service. Yet in two straight generations of the Blackshaw line, the hunter's prowess had somehow been perverted to the work of murder. That's how a sniper's mission was viewed by regular soldiers on all sides, even his own. There was no random blizzard of machine gun fire to assuage a sensitive soldier's conscience. No faceless targets to placate the sniper's guilt. No guesses; only certainty as to whose round had done the deadly work. A sniper knew the man he was killing, intimately. Or the woman.

So Ben was truly his father's hawk-eyed son. This was a link beyond flesh, beyond DNA. It seemed they shared the spirit of Smith Island's darker history. Ben had hoped it would be different. He had wished that his own infernal path had been anomalous, and not the fulfillment of a curse passed down to him. Now Ben knew he could look to himself for clues to understanding Pap. The path to his father, to his ancestry on Smith Island, lay within himself. It was a long, dark, corpse-strewn alley of the soul. Though perhaps unrighteous to some, the sniper's way was not for weaklings. So Ben also saw Ellis in a new light, with grudging respect. And with a clip full of questions that would have to wait for now, perhaps forever.

Ellis returned from an inward visitation with his own demons. He went on. "That life got to your father, Ben. Got to him bad. After the war it was *one shot, one pill.* The shot was rye. The pill, Valium. Or 'ludes.

"Then you were born. Thank God he pulled up before he crashed, but he'd seen too much. Even your coming along couldn't rub out Vietnam. He couldn't forget. See, we'd been offered a whole slew of volunteer details that were technically off the books. Made a little extra cash to send home. The thing of it is, these gigs weren't stamped by LBJ. Bobby Strange was behind them."

"Bobby Strange?"

"That would be Robert S. McNamara. Might have heard of him. Secretary of Defense back in the day? He didn't always like to pussyfoot with the enemy like Johnson did. Maybe we didn't add up to the punch of one of his B-52s, but hell yes we could do our thing. Bobby Strange knew it. We were part of his Flexible Response and Limited Warfare philosophy. After the war, our immediate superiors, the ones without Bobby Strange's high-level immunity, they got worried your Pap would get chatty about some of the gigs we drew. They were right. Dick had a conscience eating at his insides like he'd swallowed a school of live piranha. He wanted to get the truth out. They tried to bribe him, but he wasn't in it for the bucks, and that terrified the spooks. So they came for him that night fifteen years back. And when they did that? I guess that pissed your daddy off some."

"Why didn't they come for you?"

Ellis smiled. "I was already dead. Killed In Action. Body Not Recovered. Man, I had to git ghost! Your father saw the trouble rolling down on us the first time when we were still in Vietnam. Our immediate bosses, low-level C.I.A. spooklets, they were afraid of what we knew, because of what we'd done. Because of what they'd ordered us to do. So on our last mission together your father sent me hightailing over the border into Laos. Reported I was killed. I damn near was, too. Took a long time, but I made it back here. Through Thailand. Burma. Working my passage on old freighters and scows. A few soldiers came home that way. Once I got here, well who'd notice one more negro poaching in the mesh?

"The thing about islands? You can see folks coming from a long way off. Your father was okay for a while after his discharge. He'd stashed a few incriminating files that he thought would keep your family safe from our old bosses. Time passed like I said, and the bastards got scared. Seems nobody can leave off investigating that damn war, and by now the spooklets have wives and kids and plenty to lose. Fifteen years ago, some of those boys panicked. Guys like us who took the unofficial jobs during the war were getting killed stateside. Right here! Like a clean-up operation. They came for your father to do some housekeeping."

For Ben this was only half the story. "All this talk about Pap. What about my mother? She's been gone just as long. Left that same night. Did he give you any word about her while he was dropping lines in the mail to you?"

Clearly, it was easier for Ellis to talk about his old partner. His old captain. But Ida-Beth Blackshaw was the real mystery in this. The innocent bystander swept up in an invisible twister of lies and fear.

He said, "No, Ben. I only had that letter, and one postcard before it about ten years back. Dick didn't mention her either time. I can tell you this. Before they left, she was in danger, too. They figured your pap talked to her, right enough. Remember a couple months before they went? That car wreck they had out by Mardela Springs, on the main? A Friday night. Late. How do you recall it?"

Ben cast his mind back. "Too much party in Easton, they said. On the way home. Got lost. A fog. Rolled the old truck into a ditch. They both got banged up, and Mom came home from the hospital with hardware. Some steel pins screwed into her left arm. She showed me x-rays. She framed one and hung it on the wall."

Ellis shook his head. "Remember what I told you. Dick had cleaned up by then. He had turned himself around, and they were both stone cold sober that night. It wasn't an accident, Ben. Two operators in the car, and it walloped into them three times hard before they went over the culvert. Wasn't a ditch. It was a deep stream. The killers had picked the spot. Sweet little kill zone. That was the first attempt.

"Take it forward, now. A couple months later. The night Dick took off? Somebody came at him in the dark with a knife. Cut his face. Dick put him down. They were there, Ben. Right on Smith Island. They had never dared come there before.

"So Dick left first to dig up some weapons he'd stashed over to the Martin refuge. Ida, she hung back a couple hours to pack a few things. More food. Blankets, she said. Maybe they thought they were going to lay low in the mesh for a time, not run for good. Just a few days, or maybe a week. Me, I don't think Ida stayed back for supplies. I think it was for you. To rest her heart that you were okay. You were a teenager by then. Maybe somehow she knew it was good-bye."

Another image returned to Ben from that final harried night as a family. "You were at our house when they left. Why didn't you go, too?"

"Hell, Ben. I owe your father my life. He'd put me in the clear reporting me KIA on our last mission. Believe me, I wanted to repay him, and ride shotgun. He didn't want me to go. I'd offered, and he refused outright. The fact is, he told me to stay. Wanted me to look after things here."

So Ellis was a lying coward. Ben was furious now. "You were his spotter! You should have stuck with him, watched his back like he did for you. What's the hell's so important that he left you here?"

Knocker Ellis said nothing. Then it struck Ben. He flushed with shame. "Me. He wanted you to look after me. Overwatch mission."

Ellis said, "Overwatch? That's rich. I call it babysitting. When your folks didn't come back right away I went out to the mesh. To an old duck blind in the refuge. By the south pond. Near that big oak. I see you know the one I mean. The blind's all but rotted away now. That's where they were going to meet up. I got there and the blind was empty. Like they'd never been there. I thought maybe they'd covered their tracks and split to parts elsewhere for more elbow room. Regardless, I moved out here from Crisfield the next week. First free black man living on Smith Island in quite a while. I kept my word to your father. Of course, down the road you went off to war, but you were old enough to make your own decisions by then."

Ben made another decision now. He smiled bleakly at Ellis, but did not reach for the knife again. Put his hand out instead. After a moment Ellis relaxed, and returned half a smile along with his hand. They shook. Ellis passed him the snapped blade.

The fatal moment receded. The sun was rising. This was new work. A new partnership. It would take two, at least two, to accomplish what lay before them.

The way one could sense a wild beast lurking in a dark room, Ben knew that in the corners of both their minds a single thought festered: the partnership could always be dissolved once the heavy lifting was done. Knocker Ellis may have said his piece, but it felt too pat to Ben. He was not going to let his guard down for a second. They walked out of the marsh toward *Miss Dotsy.*

Ben said, "We need to stop that bomb. Take it apart. There's something about it. I can't put my finger on it, but I have a feeling there's a way we can do it."

Ellis chuckled without smiling. "That's rich. Twenty hours to Armageddon, and you've got a feeling."

CHAPTER 13

CHALK SAT QUIETLY as the van crossed the eastbound span of the William Preston Lane Jr. Memorial Bridge to the Eastern Shore. Cold, black Chesapeake water lay at the bottom of the hundred foot drop below the roadbed. He wondered how long it would take to fall that far. *Hold it!* Things weren't that bad. Not by a long shot. Even so, Chalk had a fair idea why he was taking things so hard. He rummaged in his satchel. He found four prescription bottles, one labeled risperidone, another clozapine. And two more bottles for trifluoperazine, and lithium; potent antipsychotic drugs for schizophrenia. The kicker? All four bottles were empty. And they'd been empty for at least a week. He wondered if there was a pharmacy on Smith Island where he could get refills, then dismissed the idea of even looking for it. For a long while, the drugs had left him feeling blunted, foggy. He wanted the crisp thinking he got when not under their influence. So what if noncompliance with his prescriptions made him mean, unpredictable, and a bit more psychedelic than the average doper.

Though the mission was not something to kill himself over, it was an undeniable mess. Not to mention, instead of losing a set of plans along with the gold, he had lost an actual nuke. Worse, he had allowed all of it to be stolen by this jerkwater skell, Dick Blackshaw.

Chalk also assumed Senator Morgan was laying for him, and not in the nice way. For all that grandmotherly manner, Lily Morgan was a diabolical, if lunatic, strategist. Ma Kettle was really more like Ma Barker, and she was gunning for him. But he could definitely get through this. He'd survived worse.

Lily. What a gal. When she couldn't sleep, she did not sit up watching television, snarfing bon-bons. She read voraciously. Chalk admired this in her. She studied the methods of her nation's terrorist enemies, including every battle report from Afghanistan, Iraq, and clandestine ops in Iran. She often regaled Chalk, launching rambling lectures on world politics. She had the balls to tell him all about wars in which he had fought, and even about wars he had personally started.

Now Chalk had to think back. He was sure that somewhere in all her yapping lay the key to extricating himself from this current untidiness. He wished he had listened more closely to her polemics instead of letting his mind drift. In these so-called debriefings, the Senator told him terrorists were engaged in something called 4GW, or Fourth Generation Warfare.

He remembered her saying, "4GW is all about fighting us, but by mixing it up in a way we're clueless to understand. Also called Asymmetrical Warfare. They use politics, media, disinformation, suicide bombings, feints, IEDs, and car bombs. Coalition forces get suckered into 'U' shaped ambushes in streets and alleys in urban fighting, and that was a Japanese tactic in World War II! Our learning curve is flat, like a damn prairie! Insurgents are winning skirmishes at the same time they haul ass away from the Coalition! Think of that! It's low. It's cowardly."

Thinking at the time it was all a tempest in a teapot, Chalk had enjoyed watching her get worked up over her topic. Yes, Senator Morgan could get good and mad. "I mean, us good guys are too damn slow to catch on!"

Personally, Chalk didn't mind this intel deficit at all, because it kept military brass from tumbling to his lucrative cross-border side ventures.

Lily continued, "We're losing because we fight by an outdated gentleman's rulebook. Maynard, I'm telling you, the bottom-up control of the insurgency makes their attacks seem nearly random to our top-down Coalition leadership. In 4GW, what you see is never what you get."

The same might be said of Senator Morgan, thought Chalk. This was all old news to him. Still, he believed something in her words could lead him out of his current straits. "Here's where you come in, Maynard. Remember how Charlie Wilson stuck it to the Russians in Afghanistan? A

Congressman! Well, I'm a Senator, and I'm going to take it to the militant Islamists the world over. And you're going to help me do it."

Like much of Senator Morgan's peak activity, her eureka moment had come late one night. Not only did Lily read a great deal, she was also an avid gardener. It was not unheard of for her to abandon Chalk in her Washington office to tend prize-winning flowers in the walled garden of her townhouse. Anything that grew, blossomed or ripened was fascinating to her. Despite her name, roses were the Senator's particular pleasure. The variety called Floribunda Morgana Le Fey had been nurtured in her greenhouse and named after her in 1987.

Chalk turned his mind back to another meeting on a damp night in her Madison home a few months before when the Senate was in recess. The talk over the chess board had already stretched for hours. He was sick of hearing about her latest grandiose satori. He dutifully pretended to be interested whenever this particular bee started buzzing in her bonnet. It was so stormy she'd stayed indoors rather than flounce out to tend her Wisconsin bed of roses; instead she fetched a book from her bowed-down shelves, one of her lovingly thumbed old horticulture volumes in which she discovered a reference to the theory of Brownian Motion.

As Chalk recalled from her prating, a long-dead kindred shrubophile, Robert Brown by name, observed bits of pollen knocking around in a drop of water under his microscope back in 1827. Senator Morgan had babbled, sounding downright fixated, saying, "At first Brown thought the pollen itself was alive. Later, when scientists saw that dust behaved the same way as pollen, they realized the unequal forces of water molecules themselves were bonking into the pollen, shoving it every which-way."

Chalk shook his head at the memory. Lily didn't care about the subsequent mathematical equations attempting to predict the pollen's motion in water. To her, it mattered only that such theorems existed. She had no idea how inaccurate they were beyond microscopic scales of time and space. For his part, Chalk didn't care to disabuse her of all her New Age pseudoscientific nonsense. Why burst her bubble? It was of no consequence to him at the time if her train of thought derailed.

In retrospect, another long-overdue win at chess and the Senator's raging tantrum might have been preferable to falling in with her insane plot.

To Chalk's surprise, some of her maunderings had made sense in the moment. Tonight, driving on the bridge, they rang in his ears like a Siren beckoning his ship to founder.

When his attention had wandered, she said, "Hear me out, Maynard. The decentralized terrorist leadership makes all the shootings, kidnappings, and bombings appear random. Now think about it like Brown would, but on a macro scale. The terrorist attacks are the tiny water molecules successfully whamming into our much larger Coalition pollen. With me so far?"

"Pollen. Terrorists."

"Exactly. Well, I am going to introduce a couple of high-energy water molecules of my own into the mix."

Chalk had lost the thread of her theory, as he hoped to lose the chess game. Lily had yet to notice she could have him in check in only two more moves. He moaned, "Oh dear God, speak English."

"Hang in there. If I add the corrupting forces of untold riches, coupled with the sudden realization of near divine power over life and death, if I give them all that, and all at once, it will screw them up completely! Their thing is privation, and making do, low-tech, but high concept. This is like plate tectonics on their usual playing field. It'll fry their wiring. If I can't get in the terrorist's face, I will get in his head. Really fuck him up."

No problem for a Senator with her enormous slush funds for gray and black ops.

A few nights later, after she had won another chess game, she said, "Fort Knox."

This time, Chalk perked up and listened like she was Scheherazade herself. "Fort Knox? Do tell."

"You know I go over my General Accounting Office reports and audits with a fine-tooth comb. So there's this old supplemental audit, GAO-66-406Z. Inside that, way at the back, there's a reference in Appendix XIV:viiq to something called Extra-Reserve Materiel. I figure anything *extra* in Fort Knox is bound to be interesting." Ever the gardener, Lily kept digging.

Twenty-seven documents later she found an actual inventory. At odd times in history, the fort's Extra Reserve Materiel turned out to be well-known items like the Declaration of Independence, the U.S. Constitution, the Articles of Confederation, Lincoln's Gettysburg address, and parts of a Gutenberg Bible. The Magna Carta was once placed there. All that was a great big magna whatever to the Senator.

Eyes agleam, she said, "Listen to this. Extra-Reserve Materiel is also made up of large caches of gold listed under a special heading: Form at Acquisition. That's international payments in foreign coin and bullion for tariffs, arms, and gold held in trust from countries that over time have simply ceased to exist. Now get this, Form at Acquisition also lists gold captured in war or on exploratory Lewis and Clark-type expeditions."

Chalk was impressed. He was usually not so interested in gold himself. It was bulky and heavy. It was hard to hide, and one could not simply wire gold around the world. He would like it fine, once it was converted. He preferred less unwieldy commodities, currencies that could be reduced to electrons and binary code and beamed into numbered accounts off shore. The problem with gold is that eventually a trader always wants to lay hands on it. To grope it. And that's where it gets sticky.

The Senator explained that foreign specie was sometimes melted into coin bars slightly less pure than bullion mined and minted in America. But since the United States had beaucoup gold of its own, these caches were not always cast into the standard shape for U.S. Reserve ingots; those measured seven inches by three and 5/8 inches by one and 3/4 inches. Like a mason's brick. But thinner. This was perfect for the Senator. "This Form at Acquisition stuff is gold alright, but it's technically *off* the books. I mean, how tasty! My favorite!"

She still had Chalk's ear. "This is where it gets really interesting, kiddo! There's this old cache that was liberated from Peru in the mid-nineteenth century by a crackpot Scottish-American fortune hunter. MacRath Ruthven. After robbing those Indians blind, Ruthven barely gets back to the States alive, and he stores the gold in a Richmond Hill warehouse in Georgia. Then guess what?"

"What, Lil'? Tell me what."

"The Civil War, that's what! The Confederates commandeer the warehouse for use as an ammo dump, and the Ruthven Consignment, as it was later known, gets shoved to the back wall behind barrels of powder and stacks of round shot.

"Now, even though Ruthven was a loyal southerner, he kept quiet about the gold. Hoped to retire very comfortably. No such luck. He took the secret of the gold to his grave at the second battle of Fort McAllister in 1863. All other records of the gold? Burned with the rest of Atlanta! Picture the Lost Ark getting stashed in a big warehouse at the end of that Spielberg movie."

This might be important to Chalk. Lily Morgan had a good point. Treasure did not have to be buried to vanish. It could simply be forgotten in plain sight. War, which was itself the child of amnesia, had helped orphan the Ruthven Consignment. Only for a time.

The Senator's filibuster continued. "So when General Sherman's outriders discovered the cache during his Savannah Campaign, it was taken into government custody. Eventually it was delivered to Fort Knox when the vault was finished in 1936. There it's sat all this while, until now!"

Chalk could not believe it. "What have you done, Lily?"

The Senator lowered her voice. "I called a few old friends, and I got it! Government appropriation for diplomatic operations, or some such bullshit. Maynard, with my committees and security clearances, the GAO boys aren't *allowed* to tell me no. It's positively un-American! Now here's the best part. I got the entire Ruthven Consignment at the Reserve's 1934 statutory price of thirty-five dollars an ounce. The GAO never revalued the hoard in any of their subsequent audits. Forgot all about it! And they can't reassess it now without getting taken out to the woodshed for their mistake. So you and I will simply make it go away. It's a total win-win." She was beaming. If Lily loved anything as much as roses, it was a bargain.

Chalk said, "Nice work. That's the gold. You mentioned hawking plans or something? You got them stashed at Fort Knox?"

She leveled a meaningful look at him. "Kid stuff. For a man of your talents."

Morgan later told Chalk that her operatives had reached out to radicalized nuclear engineers in Turkey. Istanbul is the equivalent of Radio Shack for black market fissile materials. Highly enriched uranium, usually swiped from former Soviet silos and centrifuges, could be got for a price. When the geeks there came through with the plans that could specifically accommodate actual stolen material, the lady from Wisconsin was financed,

supplied, and ready to follow her idols, Joan of Arc and Boudicca, into battle. Into her own Holy War.

Soon she was flogging her new assets in the terrorist market the way a
divorced mother of five shows off her new breast implants at the town
pool. Discreetly, but not too discreetly, promoting their availability to the
right customer. Within weeks she had found the perfect extremist patsies.
Chalk brokered a sale of the plans, and their purchase using the gold,
between two opposing factions; the Iranian Shi'a Sons of Allah, and the
Iraqi Sunni Martyrs of the Caliph. Now he knew she'd switched a real nuke
for the blueprints they had discussed.

At the time, he admired that Lily was working both ends. This kind of
chaos was bound to shake loose some serious money along the way, and he
was just the man to scoop it up. Lily was a piece of work. Chalk smiled as
he idly watched the lights of a lone freighter heading up the Chesapeake to
Baltimore. His agents contacted only one side at a time. Neither faction
realized that in the initial negotiations, his own operatives stood in for the
real militants across the table. The warm-ups were handled anonymously,
with coded signs and countersigns. Senator Morgan and Chalk counted on
the Islamist tunnel vision, and they weren't disappointed. The hapless fun-
damentalists were tent-pole erect for this amazing deal. Blind to its magnificent improbability.

Men. Lily expected as much, telling Chalk, "I read a study about
copulating rats. The horny male rat absolutely can't be distracted from his
goal of getting off. Not even by the sight of crumbled cheddar. But when a
horny girl-rat gets a whiff of cheese, don't you know she starts thinking
fondue."

Senator Morgan believed that for men, particularly the impoverished,
poorly educated, biddable-yet-fanatical, terrorist demographic, the gold and
the weapon of mass destruction were more potent than sex. She would
inspire a powerful destabilizing fundamentalist yearning, even in the heart
of the most clinically depressed vest bomber smack-zonked on a dirt floor
in Basra dreaming of his virgins. Terrorists would turn on each other like
hammerheads in a feeding frenzy.

At first it seemed that it didn't matter to Lily which low-rent radical
cell suddenly gained ruinous millions and The Bomb. After all, how many

lottery winners keeled over from drug overdoses within weeks of their supposed stroke of luck? The chaos had to start somewhere.

During their last chess match in the back of her jet, Lily went a bit
gonzo even for her. As a gardener, Lily saw plenty of butterflies. Along with
Brownian Motion, she ate up the far-reaching concept of the Butterfly
Effect.

She had waved a cookie at him, scattering crumbs across the chess
board. "Think about it. The innocuous single wingbeat of a butterfly might
result in something huge, like a tornado, a continent away. Swear to God,
the confounding panic of a do-it-yourself weapon and a fortune will whip
through Al Qaeda like a tsunami in a sea of sand. Chaos used to be the terrorist's pal. Now it's his enemy."

Tonight, crossing the Chesapeake, which was turning out to be Chalk's
personal Rubicon, it torqued his nuts to realize she was secretly planning to
ruin him with this business at the same time. Chalk gazed south down the
bay. Somewhere out there lay Smith Island, where he hoped to find the
gold, the bomb, and Dick Blackshaw. If the Senator got her way, Chalk
would also dig his own grave. But not if he had something to say about it.
Where it mattered, Chalk always got the last word.

He recalled the wistful look in Lily Morgan's eye before she stepped
off the plane. He thought she was lying to him yet again, so Chalk had simply pretended to be downcast when she broke the news of the terminal
diagnosis her doctors had given her: Variant Creutzfeld-Jakob disease.

Soon after landing from yet another ride in the Senator's jet, his
sources confirmed she actually was dying. At least it explained the Senator's
weird behavior of late, the worsening insomnia, the slight muscle spasms,
her pretentious geopolitical ideations. Once again, chaos was playing into
Chalk's hands. Yet, it was far worse, far more ridiculous than that. Based on
what the doctors had told her, it might be prions, and not atoms that would
exterminate human life on earth. Over the decades, when the Senator fer-
tilized her beloved roses, she always used the best bone meal made from
ground-up cattle. She had no way to know that some of the donor steers
were sick with Bovine Spongiform Encephalopathy. She had inhaled plenty
of the bone meal dust year in and year out. After a long incubation, the
BSE had horribly warped Lily's judgment, slowly turning her frontal lobes

to Swiss cheese, right where her impulse control was precariously housed. If the great Chicago fire was started by Mrs. O'Leary's cow, it was truly ironic that the holocaust of World War Three would be ignited by a mad cow sitting in the United States Senate.

The quirk of fate made Chalk laugh out loud as the van crossed onto Kent Island, the bay bridges' landfall on the Eastern Shore. From the driver's seat, Slagget threw another worried glance at his boss, but understandably said nothing.

That was it! His decision was made. Chalk would take no more anti-psychotic meds. He must pit crazy against crazy to live through this fight. Since he was already capable of anything, he was moving into uncharted territory that was downright otherworldly, making a quantum leap of chaos deep inside his mind, and thence into his reality. *Eat your heart out, Tim Leary!*

CHAPTER 14

THE SUN WAS just coming up over Smith Island somewhere behind the storm clouds. LuAnna strode through the door of the saltbox decked in full uniform and foul weather gear. Ben's haggard look of surprise set her back. A tired Knocker Ellis was also there, and he likewise was not killing himself to bid her welcome.

She said, "Sorry boys. Didn't know it was Testicle Tuesday. Call me when you're letting girls back in the treehouse." She turned to go.

Knocker Ellis smiled wearily, stood. "Please, Officer LuAnna, I was just heading home." He reached for his foul weather jacket.

LuAnna's turn to be surprised. "No oystering? Good. I'm glad you're not going out in that mess. Supposed to blow up a lot worse."

Ben winced at her euphemism and said, "And *Miss Dotsy*'s gearbox is wortenoggled. Lose her engine in this kind of chop, and she might turn to and broach. Can't afford to give Sea Tow any business."

Ellis shot Ben a look, and left.

LuAnna kissed Ben on the mouth. He tried to turn away before she leaned closer still and flicked his neck with her tongue. He knew she was not feeling frisky. It was her informal forensic analysis of his scents and flavors, like a wife sniffing for a mistress's perfume, or scanning for stripper-glitter on her man's clothing, but more intimate. Without looking at him, she busied herself at the kitchen counter pulling a pot of coffee together.

Ben already knew what she tasted on him. Sweat and dirt, but with a soft middle note of sex, and an unassuming yet perky tidewater finish. She probably had enough confidence to figure he'd frothed up the shag-whiff with her. At the very least, she would know he had not showered this morning. By this time, he was usually off-gassing the manly, but okay-for-women-too, scent of Irish Spring soap.

She handed Ben a cup of coffee. Before he could take the mug, LuAnna absently pulled it back just out of his reach. Ben reflexively opened his hand to grasp. *Got him.* She saw his red, raw blisters. Very hard manual labor. Not the usual state of a man diving the bay in gloves. Not the hands he'd clutched and caressed her with just last night. She gave him the cup.

Ben watched LuAnna make a conscious decision not to cross-examine him. He was relieved, but realized this was a stay of execution, not a pardon.

She said, "I've been thinking."

"I thought I smelled smoke. What about?"

"What are you always asking?"

"To leave me some hot water after your shower."

"Funny man. Seriously."

Ben caught her tone, and quit busting her chops. He eased ahead slowly, not sure of his depth. "Okay. Every time I see you, I ask you, 'LuAnna Bonnie Bryce, would you please let me be your husband?'"

"And daddy to my babies?"

"Yes. Every last one of them." The soul-annihilating cold in Ben's bones began to thaw. "Are you thinking—"

LuAnna gave Ben a hard smearing kiss. "That's exactly what I'm thinking. Yes, Benjamin Blackshaw. I'm telling you, *yes.*"

Ben rose, hugged her tightly. All thoughts of bombs and gold and his dead father vanished from his mind. This was the only wealth he had ever truly sought, and now he had it. "I love you, LuAnna."

"I'm all about loving you, Ben. Now, there're some things we really need to talk about."

Ben smiled again. "Absolutely. When's your lease up in Crisfield? We can bring anything you want from there to here. Have to get rid of some of this crap. That old mattress, for one. It's so uncomfortable I'm pretty sure it was passed down direct from the Inquisition. And Reverend Mosby. Have to call him. We have to set a date. When are you thinking? Maybe May or June next year?"

LuAnna waited until Ben's sweet flood of logistical prating ebbed.

She said, "Sooner than June. Sooner than May."

He said, "Why not May? Mosby's got the Thanksgiving service, and the Christmas Pageant on his brain. And there's Lent and Easter yet. Go easy on the poor man. We'll get to it now we've decided."

She said, "We need to move the date up smartly if we don't want folks to talk. I bet they will anyway if we come at it so suddenly. Before Thanksgiving would be the best."

Ben was puzzled. "This is the only wedding you're ever going to get. Are you saying you don't want to plan it to death, with the showers, and bachelorette orgies?"

She shook her head. "No. I don't. You know I hate all that claptrap." She looked vexed, said, "Ben, here you are running around all night wearing yourself to a frazzle, and you're about to be a daddy."

Without another word, she took her coffee mug to the parlor.

Instead of displaying the least happiness, Ben defended himself. "I told you I'd be daddy to your babies, and pop-pop to theirs. I promised you. It's all I want."

Now LuAnna was truly annoyed. "Are you listening to me? Put it like this, Ben. You get to keep your promise a little earlier than expected."

Ben followed LuAnna into the parlor. She sensed the primeval thrill rising in his chest. "Hold it. You're pregnant."

LuAnna beamed ear to ear. She said, "One of your spats got cultch in my poor defenseless suzy, and that's all she wrote."

LuAnna sat on the couch. "Ow! Damn! What in God's name—"

Before Ben could stop her, LuAnna was on her feet yanking the cushion back. There it was. She froze, staring. Then she reached out and touched the slab to be sure it was real. Ben's couch was always good for a little loose change now and then, but this was ridiculous.

She looked at Ben for an explanation. "Seems you have a few surprises of your own."

Ben gave LuAnna his best smile. "You found your wedding gift before I had a chance to wrap it."

PART II
INTERLOPERS

CHAPTER 15

IT WAS A simple matter for Maynard Chalk and company to ditch the van and steal a workboat in Crisfield. People around there were trusting, and marina security was nonexistent. He wanted to reach Smith Island before dawn. Crossing ten miles of Tangier Sound turned out to be the problem. The craft they'd grabbed started sinking the minute they put out. There was no way to know that the boat's plywood hull had been smashed too often against the stump of an old sunken piling during the storm. The automatic bilge pump kept up with the influx of water while the boat was in its protected slip, but only just. Once out in the sound, the wringing action of the chop sprung the boat's seams. Then the bilge pump shorted out. Despite valiant efforts at bailing, the vessel sank ever deeper into the water as they went.

Chalk's trusted lieutenant Simon Clynch was proving useless. He was completely green, and seasick. Annoyance became anger when Clynch committed the ultimate landlubber's sin, puking to windward and lightly shellacking his squaddies with a mist of vomit. Almost an hour later, a very pissed-off Chalk abandoned the boat, leaving it struck hard on a sandbar a hundred yards from shore. They waded onto the Smith Island beach with his team, their gear held aloft out of the wet.

Hiram and Charlene Harris, a sweet couple in their sixties, were surprised to find so many late-season lodgers on the stoop of their bed & breakfast, in spite of the weather, too. And so early in the day. Even before the first scheduled boat from Crisfield. The Harrises were happy to have the windfall business. Soggy trousers and boots were understandable in such weather. The Harrises graciously overlooked the lack of reservations, and made the strangers welcome. This was a mistake.

Chalk kicked off his questioning of these natives with some rope, duct tape ligatures, and a box cutter.

After an hour or two in Chalk's hands, he secretly liked to think a quick death was something worth begging for. If the victim had nothing to offer. Or especially if, as in the case of the Harrises, the subjects plain refused to talk.

During the bloody proceedings, Chalk held forth for the benefit of his men. "You know, back in Rwanda during the genocide, a Tutsi with about thirty bucks still had options, even if he was about to get himself killed. See, he could pay the Hutu who was about to hack him to bits to finish the job with a gun instead of the standard issue machete. Yep. Woe betide the Tutsi short of cash, or the Hutu without a gat. The ol' snickersnee is a hard way to die, and those Hutu bastards did not take Diner's Club. Way I see it? Even up to the brink of the void, there're deals to be made."

Chalk was tempted to finish Hiram when he thought the waterman's last fragment of comprehension was shattered. He decided against. Keep him alive for now. He might rebound and get chatty in a little while.

Chalk glanced at Dar Gavin who amused himself with an incoherent Charlene. Chalk slashed a finger vaguely along the line of his collarbone and said, "Hurry up and do her."

Gavin sighed. He zipped up his pants, rolled Charlene onto her back, and shot her in the chest.

Chalk sensed that Hiram and Charlene had salient information, but they refused to sing no matter what. Nellie Vickers, while in extremis, had even tried making up bullshit about Dick Blackshaw just to save herself.

Coercive interview techniques often resulted in false intel. No problem. Chalk had his reliable gut instinct and Black Widow to help sift facts from desperate verge-of-death offerings. The Harrises were so pig-headed that, against all reason, they had refused to dime Dick Blackshaw out, even though he had lived for years within a mile of where they were dying by inches.

In the end, feeling like a jackass, Chalk resorted to the phone book; an actual paper phone book, to get the Blackshaw address. He'd hoped for more. So much more. *Who are these damn people?* He wanted to get to know them, to get a sense of what made them tick. If everyone on Smith Island was this tough, he was in deep trouble.

CHAPTER 16

"A WEDDING PRESENT?" This stopped LuAnna, but only for a moment. "Ben, it's wonderful. Where did you get this?"

Ben knew the best lie fell as close to the truth as possible. Once again, it hardly occurred to him that he should not lie. There was an alien character working within him. He started backpedaling his integrity down a steep moral scree, and the footing was treacherous. "Found it oystering a few days back."

She said, "That's a lot of precious metal there. Got to be worth something. I wonder who—"

"That's *salvage*. Free and clear to the finder." Marriage. A baby. Gold. Ben cut her off a little too sharply for the happiness that was due the moment.

Confused and stung, LuAnna threw on her hat and slicker. She stepped out the back door. Walked toward the path leading to the Smith Island hamlet of Ewell. Ben found her standing at the edge of the small yard under the gray sky. The wind whipped her hair around her face.

LuAnna sensed his approach, pressed. "Where?"

"I told you. Out by a rock I was working."

"And you don't think somebody's looking for it?"

"Apparently you were."

Ben was already done in by fatigue. Now LuAnna's ramped-up suspicion made him viciously bad-tempered. He took a breath, and tried to mend his tone. "I found it off Fishbone Island."

LuAnna took this in. "To the north from Fishbone? The west?"

Ben fumbled. "Easterly, I suppose. I was on a good rock of oysters Pap and Ellis used to work, and there it was."

LuAnna shook her head. "A good rock? I thought the oystering was poorly. And this was just laying down there on the bottom."

"That's the smart of it. It sure wasn't floating." Ben tried to laugh, but the bogus mirth died young.

LuAnna glanced back at his saltbox. Soon to be their saltbox. "Does Knocker Ellis know about it?"

Ben said, "He was aboard when I brought it up."

LuAnna pressed. "I see. So this is his salvage, too. It's not something just for me, just from you. It's from the both of you. And good old Ellis isn't looking for a piece?"

Ben's mind was a tangle of anger, guilt, grief, and confusion. He'd fought ruthless killers in his time, but there was no opponent in the world so fiercely combative as his own conscience. Or LuAnna when she had something difficult to grapple.

He mumbled, "I worked something out with him."

She asked, "Okay. But what do you figure on doing with it?"

"It's yours. Do with it as you please."

LuAnna jabbed, "Maybe you could melt it down and cast a duck out of it. Probably all it's good for, unless you want a doorstop worth more than the whole house."

"I told you before we talked the rapture off it. It was going to be an engagement present for you."

"You said wedding present."

"What I said was, 'present for you'! And now you've jumped ugly on me, which I think is unappreciative."

LuAnna hackled. "Run that by again?"

Jesus. Ben felt like a complete idiot. No wonder he never lied. He totally sucked at it. But honest as he was, the truth still felt too dangerous to share with LuAnna, especially when she was acting like this. Whipsawing emotions tore at his better nature.

He snapped out, "You heard me. Unappreciative of this, I don't know—gift that's come to us. Unappreciative of my giving you the best piece of good fortune in all my life. You picked a great time to put your skepticals on, woman."

Woman? LuAnna surprised Ben, as well as herself, by hugging him. Speechless, it was all she could do.

Ben was wretched to have destroyed what should have been their most joyous moment together so far. He was sorrier still to lie. For Ben, it was a morning full of gold, and other cheerless happenings.

LuAnna kissed Ben on the cheek, then lightly on the lips. "You're tired. You look awful. See to that gearbox later. Get to bed and don't stir, okay? Leave those oysters alone for the day."

"I will." That was another lie to his fiancé. "I love you, LuAnna." At least he knew this was the truth.

As she often did when they argued, she gave his wedding tackle a lewd caress to show all was well, if not yet perfect between them. Then she walked around the saltbox to the water side. She was already unmoored and starting the engines by the time Ben rounded the house. LuAnna backed the boat off the pier, spun the wheel, shifted, eased the throttles, and moved down the creek toward the bay. She uttered nothing more. Cast no fond farewell glance or wave over her shoulder before disappearing around the bend though she must have sensed he was watching. He always watched 'til she was out of sight. Ben waited there until her wake rippled in among the shoreline reeds and the creek ran smooth.

A scrappy old bantam waterman, Lorton Dyze, approached Ben before he reached his front door. "You two tiffin'?"

Ben said, "Just got engaged. I think."

"Condolences. She's a fine woman. Damn pity about that badge of her'n."

Dyze was a throwback to the Island's old days. He led the Smith Island Council, a loose gathering of weighty men who ran things in lieu of a formal elected body. Dyze had a face like a dried apple. On the rare occasions he removed his cap, his pale bald head was speckled with liver spots like the egg of a great flightless bird.

Ben knew only a matter of considerable import would lure Dyze down off his porch. Other than church on Sunday, and the occasional walk along the shore, he sat stationed in his rocker outside in all weather but a blizzard.

Since retiring from crabbing eleven years back, Dyze had been convinced he was dying. To Dyze's consternation, his life had stretched well into the new millennium, and showed no signs of ending.

Dyze held out some envelopes to Ben. "Stopped by the post office. Thought I'd save ye a trip to your box."

With Dyze's bum hip, this errand took him a long half-journey from his place on the other end of the island. Dyze never fetched for anybody. It was always the other way around.

"Thanks." Ben accepted the envelopes. They promised little more than catalogues and bills he could not pay.

Dyze said, "Maybe ye'll stop around later."

Ben knew this was not an invitation. It was a summons. "Anything on your mind, Lorton?"

"That depends. Anything on your'n?"

Ben hedged. "*Miss Dotsy*'s gearbox's is going like a champ. Ran her ashore."

Dyze snorted softly, shook his head. Studied Ben for a second. "Her gearbox, is it? A gearbox? Who are ye, Benjamin Blackshaw?"

Ben thought this was oblique stuff, even for an old man who'd enjoyed the bully pulpit of the dying for better than a decade. Ben said nothing. Waited the old man out. He knew something, but was standing pat until Ben confided first. Lorton Dyze was a hunter, as patient as granite, but he was no sniper.

Beyond the reeds on the beach, Ben saw a familiar eleven-year-old boy, Kyle Brody. He was ditching school to skim the sand with a metal detector, sweeping it back and forth to see what Hurricane Odette had left him. Ben felt a kindred spirit with this kid. Innovating on the old ways. He hoped Kyle found something special as he progged around the shore.

No, Lorton Dyze could not outlast a hardened sniper. He gave up, hocked out a gobbet of green snot in disgust, turned, and limped down the path toward the beach. When his hip was not killing him, he too enjoyed a leisurely progue for flotsam, jetsam, peace, and quiet. Or whatever might wash up on the beach. Over his shoulder he said, "Say ye get curious. Come on around. Hear?"

"If I do." Ben headed back toward the saltbox. The little old man hitched his way through the reeds.

Ben let him go without another word. Something weird and momentous was happening on Smith Island, but it still lay outside his understanding. His father's appalling homecoming, Knocker Ellis's secrets, the gold, the weapon, and Lorton Dyze's meddlesome curiosity were signs of a great change at work all around him. Not to mention LuAnna and their child. Something on the island was stirring, quickening. And then there was this storm circling around everything; pure wrath of God stuff.

Ben had good reason to cast a jaundiced eye at Lorton Dyze. The residents of Smith and Tangier Islands had not always been God-fearing Methodists. Their ancestors had crossed the Atlantic hundreds of years before from Cornwall in England. *Pirates of Penzance* was not just the catchy title of a Gilbert and Sullivan comic opera. The barren Cornish coast, including Fowey, St. Keverne, Helford, and of course, the eponymous Penzance, was known to harbor a particularly wicked brand of corsair. The western waters of England had been plagued by pirates since the fifteenth century.

When the Cornish sailors settled in the Chesapeake Bay, they brought along their ancient attitude toward home waters. Proprietary, and predatory. During the American Revolution, King George III offered letters of marque to any Smith or Tangier Island captain willing to privateer, harass, take, burn or destroy the shipping of the fractious colonies. Sporadic raiding, kidnapping, and even enslavement continued long after the Revolution ended. For a good while, Ben's people were Smith and Tangier Islanders first, Americans second. Some never forgot this more insular loyalty, especially when income taxes were due and owing.

Ben wondered if this sense of drowning in a riptide of intrigue might be nothing more than sheer exhaustion working on him. No wiser, Ben dragged himself inside.

CHAPTER 17

NEITHER THE YOUNG brawler nor the gimpy old coot noticed Maynard Chalk watching with his men a hundred yards up the path to the little town of Ewell. Chalk's eels were taking a post-havoc constitutional around the island, studying the lay of the place. That lady cop seemed so upset that she'd also missed the interlopers before she shoved off. But Chalk had seen her. Now she was definitely on his screen.

Chalk was riveted in place there on the path. That tall guy in his thirties. The build was the same. The Paul Bunyan shoulders. The clean-and-jerk power-lifter thighs. This one even had the same striding gait as the traitorous Richard Willem Blackshaw. Chalk felt like the ornithologist who gets the GISS, or General Impression Size and Shape, of a tiny bird, and can identify it on the wing from a hundred yards away. He just knew. Like father, like son. That guy had to be Dick Blackshaw's brat. And that lady cop might prove useful in getting the brat's attention.

Chalk's cell phone rang. The funky bounce of the *King Tut* ringtone. Chalk answered, and heard puffing on the other end of the line. It sounded like an obscene phone caller who measured his freak in breaths per minute. Or like someone running.

"Maynard. They know!" It was Yusef, of course. Not at his best.

"How do you mean, Yoos?"

"They know. They *know!*" There was a series of rapid popping sounds in the background. Then the line, rather like Yusef himself, Chalk imagined, went dead.

The hod of bricks descended toward Chalk's head. He stashed his phone, hissed his orders. He detailed a squad made up of Simon Clynch, Dar Gavin, and Tug Parnell to double-time back to the Harrises'. They were to verify that Hiram's thirty-foot deadrise, the *Palestrina*, was seaworthy. If the damn thing would stay afloat for at least a couple of hours, those boys had to get back on the water fast to run a very special errand.

Bill Slagget and The Kid accompanied Chalk down the path toward Ben's saltbox. Chalk's shoulders rounded and tensed with anger. His fists balled and flexed. He was ready to throw down.

CHAPTER 18

BEN TOSSED THE mail onto the little table in his cramped vesti-
bule. A few of the slick catalogues slid over the edge, slapped onto the
floor. Ginger rose and padded over to Ben. Nuzzled the fallen mail. Ben
assumed Ginger was seduced by a paper perfume sample. He believed the
smellum-goodums tantalized her with an exotic break from the hot-dead-
fish-at-low-tide aromas she was used to snuffling up around the island.

Ginger picked up an aromatic free-standing insert, and was about to
retreat to her cedar-chip cushion. Ben noticed the envelope sticking out.
Handwritten address. The dog gave up the tug-of-war with her master
when she realized the fragrant ads were hers to keep if she would only turn
the unscented envelope loose.

Ben read the postmark through Ginger's slobber. St. Mary's City,
Maryland. It was dated four days ago, right before the hurricane blew
through. Ben tore it open, and removed a page ripped from a legal tablet.

Dear Ben,

*It's been awhile. I hope you will let me make it up to you.
It had to be. Maybe my coming back home won't be so bad
for you and our neighbors on Smith and Tangier.*

*Truth to tell it's been hard just staying alive all these
years. I had to bide my time. Watch for the right chance.*

The right moment. It's here now. It is definitely here. Future's bright. It'll put a smile on your face.

There's been at least one big surprise along the way. He's a necessary evil, I guess. Has a keen eye, and that's very important to get things started. I'll put up with him for now. If somebody gives you a funny look, pay attention, especially if you're reading this and we haven't met up yet.

Give my best to Knocker Ellis. The weather's trying to shit the bed. Got to get a move on. See you soon.

Pap

Ben reread it to confirm his first stark impressions. One, this was no real apology. Two, it was a lame-ass rationalization for abandoning his kid. The classic A-Man's-Gotta-Do defense. Three: a vague announcement he was coming back, but not when. Not much good now. A few lungfuls of water too late. Four: there was a hinted promise of better times ahead woven in among the business about the bright future with the smile. Obviously meant to be the gold. The end that justified the means. Five: the unexpected person involved. Probably Knocker Ellis. A partner Dick Blackshaw needed, but was reluctant to entangle in this business.

How had Lorton Dyze known about this letter? Had the postmistress tipped him? More than likely. Dyze had taken pains to bring the letter to him.

All in all, Ben judged the letter useless. Not the least bit informative. No solace whatsoever. Soon after the letter went in the mail, Pap went into the drink. This single page was more like the last will and testament of a grand larcenist, who was also a paternal wash-out.

Someone pounded on the front door. Five times hard like there was an Amber Alert and Ben was the closest registered pedophile. *Now what?*

Ben stashed the letter under the couch cushion with the gold bar. Quick glance out the window. Three guys. Strangers from off. Fit, tense, and amped. Ben knew that look. Killers. But how bold? Only one way to find out. Ben opened the door.

CHAPTER 19

CHALK KNEW IN an instant he hated this guy with a passion. The young man at the door reminded Chalk too much of Tom Chase/Dick Blackshaw. It was a limbic, animal response. The same way a person would want to toss gasoline on a hornet's nest after a savage stinging, Chalk wanted to gun this punk down where he stood. Eradicate the ilk of Dick Blackshaw from the face of the earth. He was becoming less and less surprised at losing his cool this way. Too long since his last round of meds. Despite Chalk's outward calm, this shit-heel twerp managed to bring out the young pistolero in him.

Chalk appraised him further. Tried to look beyond his initial reaction. There was definitely a wild look about this cuss.

He said, "Hi. I'm Maynard Chalk." Chalk put out his hand to press the flesh.

The guy at the door did likewise, and gripped. To Chalk, it felt like he'd jammed his mitt into a Peterbilt crankcase running flat out. The hick owned Chalk's hand for a moment too long, but not as though he was trying to macho it up. It was as if their clasped hands made a serial port. The redneck was docking, downloading, and processing critical information through palm and phalanges. In a word, Chalk felt scanned.

The other folks on this island ghetto looked like the Joads, only cleaned up, slightly better fed, well-meaning, and used to doing without. This cracker seemed plain fierce, with a killer's lean build. Suddenly, Chalk wished he'd let Black Widow run a deep background check on Dick Blackshaw's son. Too late for that.

Ben released Chalk's hand. "Ben Blackshaw."

Chalk brightened. "Really? Hot stuff! I'm looking for my old friend Richard. Must be your dad, right?"

Ben said, "I'm sorry, Mr. Chalk. You missed him."

"Did I now?" Chalk cheered up a little more.

Then Ben said, "Yeah. He was just here, ten—fifteen years ago."

A smart-aleck. Chalk's ire grew, but he worked, really worked hard to contain it. "I see. Any idea where I could find him?"

Ben shook his head. "He's not the stay-in-touch type."

Chalk was getting nowhere. Again with this redneck omerta, the cracker code of silence.

Chalk wanted a man on Ben's flank, or better, to his rear. As planned, The Kid, who had been shifting back and forth on his feet in a classic pee-pee paso doble, said, "'Scuse me. Could I please use your bathroom? I gotta go real bad."

"Since you said please." Ben stood aside so The Kid could step through the door.

Chalk and Slagget took a step to follow. Ben suddenly banged the door shut in their faces. A big, old-sounding lock clanked home.

Chalk barked, "What the hell!"

Inside, it sounded like the house was getting demolished. Furniture tumbled and splintered. Something fragile shattered. A dog growled and barked. Then more breakage. And then nothing.

Slagget slammed his shoulder against the door, but the old timber and iron held. "Shit!" He clutched his aching shoulder.

Ben spoke through the door. Low and even. "I think your friend had a little accident."

Slagget reached under his windbreaker for a gun, but Chalk waved him back.

Chalk shouted, "Dammit, Ben! How about some of that Southern hospitality?"

Ben said, "Maryland's a border state. Hospital's a good idea for your boy."

Chalk fumed. "Did you kill him?"

"No, but it's early."

"Well I don't give a fuck! Go ahead! *Do* him! But you better tell me where your father is or I'll—"

Suddenly, The Kid screamed. Loud, high and piercing. The howl was full of so-*this*-is-the-Abyss horror. As quickly as it started, it stopped. Choked off. Then Chalk heard a window open in a nearby house. They were attracting attention. The situation was deteriorating.

"Or you'll what, exactly?" Ben spoke slowly. "Mr. Chalk—Maynard, you don't have time to huff and puff on my stoop all day. You know it. I know it. Will you take a friendly suggestion?"

The neighbor's door opened, and a man stepped out on his front porch. He cradled an old Remington twelve gauge in his arms.

In a blur of black and amber fur, a German shepherd shot out the neighbor's door and sprinted to the property's edge nearest Chalk. The dog did not cross out of the neighbor's lot. Nor did he sit on his haunches like he was content to just watch. He growled at Chalk and Slagget, and bristled. Coiled for his master's order.

The neighbor studied Chalk. Rumbled to the dog, "Easy goes it, Adolf. Just sit tight."

Chalk spoke softly to Ben through the door, "Suggest away, you dead fuck."

"Leave. Now. Whatever you want with my father is over and done. Definitely not worth what it's going to cost you."

"Found something, did you, boy?"

Ben said, "Maybe I did. And maybe it's already counting down."

Chalk bridled. This situation was completely out of control. "For Christ's sake, punk, you truly don't know who you're dealing with."

The Kid screamed again, excruciating pain. Even Chalk, who was not easily shocked, felt his balls tuck and scrunch up.

Ben said, "That makes two of us. But this noisy fellow in here? He's got a pretty good idea what's what."

The neighbor jacked a shell into the shotgun's chamber. Leaned on his door frame, watching. Just taking everything in. Adolf paced to and fro at the property line, doing a good impression of a starved wolf clocking a fawn.

Chalk and Slagget assessed their position. Then Chalk glanced out into the bay. In the storm's haze, he thought he discerned black smoke rising from someplace out on the water.

Chalk smiled. "Okay, Ben Blackshaw. Appreciate the advice. I'll toddle along. For now."

Chalk stepped off the stoop, but then turned back. "Hey Kid! If you're not dead, you're fired! Sloppy pissant."

Then Chalk and Slagget made a quick tactical withdrawal up the path.

As they went, Chalk patted his belly and said, "Let's see what Mrs. Harris has in her fridge. I declare, I could eat the ass out of a dead cat."

CHAPTER 20

SOON AFTER CHALK and Slagget left, Orville Hurley, Ben's neighbor, stopped by the saltbox with his dog to see that everything was okay. Hurley believed, as many Smith Islanders did, that since they had no police force, folks had to look out for each other. Lacking a well-regulated militia, Hurley was a self-appointed irregular. Hurley was not put out that Ben didn't invite him in for coffee. Hurley didn't pry about all the screaming. Ben was not bothered that Hurley still carried a shotgun with him.

To Ben, things seemed a little too cozy on Smith Island, what with Lorton Dyze personally delivering his mail, and Hurley dropping around armed to the teeth to check up. Why was no one saying exactly what was on his mind, or asking what was going on? It felt to Ben like everybody was aware of this crisis, but no one would speak about it. No one wanted to break the spell. All in a day's work, apparently.

Ben's call to Knocker Ellis's home phone went unanswered. Not good. Where was he? Maybe trusting him was a mistake, and he was out on Deep Banks Island hiding the gold somewhere else. Ellis was full of surprises, like a piñata stuffed with grenades, pins pulled, zero candy. For the moment, Ben had to compartmentalize his misgivings before they grew into crippling obsessions.

Through his door he heard Chalk tell the other sidekick they were going back to Hiram and Charlene's place. Ben's blood chilled at that. He had to follow them. The Harrises were good people, like the guardian aunt and uncle he never had. Ben could not stroll up the path in plain sight. He was too busted up from subduing The Kid, and too careful for a frontal assault. He'd make it a sniper's stalk, if he could.

Some of Ben's left ribs ached like hell. If he inhaled too deeply, they stabbed him like tenpenny nails driven deep by John Henry's sledge-hammer. Opening his shirt, he saw the red, black and blue mottled bruise, but no flailing bones, like a total break. Broad as his palm. Already swelling. In hand-to-hand training, Ben had been taught his ribs were the babies. His upraised forearms and fists, the baby-sitters. Ben was rusty. During the scuffle, The Kid managed to thrust a knee hard into Ben's floating ribs. Definitely shaken baby syndrome. If The Kid succeeded in working in another good shot, Ben would've been gargling blood from a punctured lung.

Once again, he dragged on his clammy wetsuit, favoring his ribs where he could. To don the close-fitting neoprene required agonizing contortions. On the upside, there would be streams and guts to swim on the route he was planning. Maybe the frigid water would numb the pain. With the zipper snugged-up under his chin, he found the wetsuit acted like a half-decent tape job, stabilizing his smashed-up flank.

To make this stalk unseen, Ben would need more than a wetsuit. He pulled out his homemade reed-patterned ghillie suit. In the best of sniper tradition, the enormous baggy pants, jacket, and hood were festooned with ragged strips of burlap to break up his profile, and conceal him from game when he hunted. Head to toe, the rig was streak-dyed with marsh tans and browns to help him blend in with the lower vegetation of his boggy surroundings.

Next he took a sturdy old bread knife from the kitchen drawer. Slipped it into a belt at the small of his back. The handle was carved like a braided loaf. It would make a decent grip even when wet. Chalk's men were waiting for him. This was not a problem. Ben could bring them a good fight with just a knife. Part of him was looking forward to it.

At the back of the downstairs coat closet, Ben pushed a wooden panel aside. He took out a waterproof bag containing his straight-body Leica Televid 62 spotting scope. He'd toned down the scope's original silver trim for field work with blotches of Krylon OD, Desert, and Travertine Tan. There were cheaper scopes, but none better for Ben. To a man who stayed alive by seeing more, farther, and better than the enemy, the expense was worth it. He stuffed a waterproof blowout kit in the right thigh patch pocket of the suit. He hoped he would not need it to treat a trauma, but he never patrolled without one.

Ben regretted that he had not stashed the gold bar in the closet from the beginning, but he hid it there now. If he did not make it home, at least LuAnna, who until today shared in all his secrets, would know where to look.

Ben checked on The Kid in the next room. Still unconscious from the choke hold Ben had crooked around the intruder's muscled throat. He wondered if his prisoner had suffered brain damage from lack of oxygen. He decided it was fifty-fifty whether that would hurt or help The Kid's charming personality.

He tugged the ropes binding The Kid hard and tight to an old oak chair. Ben did not give a damn if his hostage's circulation suffered to the point of requiring amputation. Then he laid the chair on its back. Now The Kid could not knock it over, make noise, and draw a kindly neighbor in to offer help and get killed for his trouble. Last, he duct-taped a sock in The Kid's mouth. Ben wondered if The Kid was allergic to Ginger. His nose might congest. He could suffocate. And that would be a damn shame, Ben felt. Just awful. Then the pretty-boy operative might miss his debut at the Angola prison farm as the human pin-cushion. Ben left Ginger growling low into The Kid's face.

After scanning out all his ground-floor windows, Ben descended the stoop. He halted there, and did something unprecedented in his entire life. He locked his front door upon leaving.

Outside, the wind blew fifteen knots, gusting to thirty. Ben crept to the reeds at the water's edge, glancing now and then down at his chest in case a red laser sighting dot appeared there; a gunman taking a center of body mass shot. If he did notice such a dot, he would try to dive for cover. With a well-trained shooter drawing a bead, very likely it would be the last thing he did.

He made it in one piece, no extra ventilation in his ghillie suit, no fresh holes in his head. Chalk had left no one behind to clip Ben. He was likely covering a smaller perimeter closer to the Harris place.

Ben vegged-up the ghillie with cut reeds. Wove them quickly into the suit's loose mesh. A few practiced swipes of chilling mud on his face, and Ben dissolved into the wetlands.

He didn't have to go too slowly at the beginning of his stalk. The grasses and other growth were high and waving like mad in the wind. The scrape and rattle of the cattails covered the sound of his movements. If anyone had been there to listen. Underfoot, the mud was laced through with bulrush roots which made it spongy. He had just shy of half a mile to patrol in.

Ben rose out of the first stream, frozen to the bone despite the wetsuit. His ribs throbbed as if Ron Bushy was pounding out the drum solo of Iron Butterfly's In-A-Gadda-da-Vida; the nineteen minute fifty-one second live version.

In the sodden ghillie rig he looked like a bedraggled scarecrow. Here, the band of reeds narrowed to just fifty feet. Beach on one side, and crabgrass yards on the other. Anyone looking out a second-floor window would still have trouble noticing the downpress and parting of the reeds as he slithered through. Just in case, Ben slowed his approach.

At the second gut, he stepped down into the water and touched the old plank submerged there. His head low, Ben eased along the secret wooden network. It was a more roundabout route this way, but he could stand a little straighter, could make better time.

Finally, Ben arrived within one hundred yards of the Harris place. His ribs pounded. He sat leaning at the back of the neighbor's old tool shed. When he caught his breath, he slid in through the shed's rear window. Prayed the rotting sill would hold his weight. The pain in his flank was all-consuming. His eyes adjusted to the dark. Cobwebs. Old paint cans. Curled Venetian blinds. A yellowed computer monitor with a shattered screen. *People* magazines dating from the years when nobody knew who shot J.R.. The stench of a wild animal den.

He took the Televid out of its waterproof pouch. Uncovered the mil-dot reticle. Aiming it through the shed's front window, he started his survey of the Harris place, using the first wheel on top of the scope body for coarse focusing. Then the second wheel to refine the picture until it was eagle sharp. No one in sight outdoors. Chalk seemed to know his business.

If Ben were still in the service, this would be the time he'd pull out a small sketch kit and draw the terrain before him, with all the ranges from his hide to the enemy positions filled in. Many of his former superiors still had his sketches and range cards framed on their office walls, such was their functional beauty. Few understood that a sniper's skill in the stalk was more often exploited for penetration deep behind enemy lines to gather intelligence, rather than for the spot, the shot, and the kill.

Ben's stillness was nearly perfect as he made a very slow sweep, collapsing each sector of fire before him one by one. Depending on how Chalk put together his team, there was every possibility of a counter-sniper out there waiting for him to toll in close. Chalk had abandoned The Kid too easily. He was cocky. Sure of his resources. No doubt he was trying to draw Ben out.

He studied shadows, bushes, and trees for bumps that did not seem right. Scanned for glints of light on lenses, rings, wristwatches. Listened for brave talk and laughter on the wind. Tested the breeze for scents of smoke, sweat, gun oil, gunpowder, and blood. Still nothing. There was no sign of Chalk, or his friend. Worse, there was no sign of Hiram or Charlene Harris. No warm aromas of food that usually came from her kitchen, especially when she had guests.

Ben zeroed in on the house. Windows were the obvious vantage points, but not the only ones. If the interior lights were off, a man could perch four or five feet back from a window in shadows like a ghost, and pour down death from there unseen. Once Ben eliminated all the obvious hides for a watcher, he began looking where he would have chosen to wait, the less apparent, out-of-the-ordinary places. The roof line was clean. He scanned for any small crack knocked in the shingles, or attic wall, possibly a new gun loophole. There was nothing strange except the quiet.

As always happened to him on a stalk, Ben was momentarily struck by a false sense of security. No one was really standing guard. As if Chalk were not dangerous. Ben had just kidnapped and beaten the bejesus out of a complete stranger based on an intuitive sense probably corrupted by fatigue's paranoia. In a place behind his navel and an inch or two below, the gnawing buzz known as bubble guts joined the pain in his flank. After ten more minutes, when nothing in front of him had been stirred by anything but wind, Ben got a new sensation. He was too late.

He stowed the Televid in its pouch. Slipped out the back window of the shed. His ribs were deadly. Still, he inched away flat on his belly. Kept the shed between himself and the Harris place.

Bracing once again for the cold, Ben slid into another small gut. It was only about two feet deep. Maybe three feet wide. No catwalk planks in this one. With only his nose and right eye above the water, Ben appeared to be a raft of detritus drifting slowly along. He was freezing. He was exhausted.

Something made a noise around the next curve. Ben held completely still. A rare river otter, thirty inches long, probably male, with brown fur and dark round eyes, lazily slew-tailed down the stream within four feet of where Ben lay. Ben stopped breathing. He was not worried about upsetting the playful creature. He did not want to startle it into giving away his position. Ben closed his eyes to prevent the animal from keying into facial features amongst his ghillie thatch and muddy war paint. The otter passed Ben without glimpsing him. When it was out of hearing around the downstream bend, Ben resumed his skull drag toward his target. After fifty feet, the gut joined with a stream.

Ben turned northeast into the stream. Pulled himself along the bottom, letting the incoming tide help. Stayed hard against the shore closest to the Harris house. He made his way thirty yards like this until he was underneath Hiram's crab shanty, which jutted over the stream on stilts. Shoulders howling, ribs baying, Ben pulled himself up into the shanty through the trap door.

He slowed his breathing and took stock. He had noticed Hiram's boat, the *Palestrina*, was out. So was his smaller outboard skiff. Unless Hiram had the skiff in tow abaft the *Palestrina*, Chalk was probably in one of the boats. Who was left inside?

The feeling of having come too late pressed in on Ben once more. He still could not rush. So far he had stalked within fifteen feet of the house's corner. It had taken nearly forty minutes, a heartbeat compared to some missions. Another scan. This time with his naked eye. He saw nothing. Not even a lookout at the window. He must have missed something. At this point, a fatal bullet might be his only clue he had been seen.

He took off the ghillie suit. Kept the wetsuit on. Drew the knife. A final scan all round. He edged the crab shanty's door open. No one fired at him. Ben sprinted to the nearest corner of the house. Hugged it. Waited for sign or sound he'd been detected. Still no alarms.

Now, the pain in Ben's ribs made him want to rush against all his training. At the back of his mind lay a constant awareness of the bomb. He reminded himself over and over again that if he went slow, he would live long enough to think up a solution to handle the invaders and their toy. Act with haste now, and he might be killed along with two of his lifelong friends.

Creeping below the first-floor windows, Ben went to the waterside door of the house. Turned the knob. Not locked. It never was. Never needed to be until today. He listened. Still heard nothing. Then he eased the door open. A quick look into the tiny foyer and beyond, into the living room.

The Harris place looked like a slaughterhouse.

Abandoning all thought for his safety, Ben pushed into his friends' living room. The walls, once a plain, clean white, were now hook-stroked with blood like a de Kooning fresco. Where was Hiram? Where was Charlene?

Then Ben heard footsteps upstairs. A man on the second floor yawned, contented as if just rising from sleep. As if he were a guest coming down for his morning coffee.

Ben stood in a daze of his own for a second, unable to reconcile the man's ease with the horror of the living room. Ben moved swiftly and silently to the wall by the foot of the stairwell. He saw feet, then legs descending, reflected in the glass of a painting hung at the bottom of the stair. Another self-satisfied yawn. Apparently the guy had Goldilocksed his way through the upstairs bedrooms until he found a mattress that was just right. Then, as in the fairytale, he woke up and met the bear.

When the drowsy intruder was four steps from the bottom, Ben reached blind around the corner and grabbed a fistful of shirtfront. He yanked with all his might, rattling his own ribs like Lincoln Logs. The man gave a yelp of surprise, and crashed headfirst into the wall. The picture glass shattered. He bounced stunned into a broken heap on the floor. Ben dropped onto his back, both knees driving out all breath. Since the man's left hand was pinned beneath his body, Ben controlled the right arm, attacking the thumb, levering it hard up between the scapulae. Ben pulled out a wallet and flipped it open. The license read Tug Parnell.

Ben got in low to Tug's ear. "Chalk. Where?"

"Fuck you!"

Ben slowly torqued the thumb hoping Tug would talk; wrenched it back well past misery into agony. It made a soft snap, like a carrot just a few days past crisp. Tug Parnell cried out. There was a demon on his back and he knew he was dead.

CHAPTER 21

LUANNA SLOWLY WOKE. The rush of pain from body parts she was formerly unaware of overwhelmed her. She could only open her left eye through the swelling. She lay naked against a wall on a wood floor coated with chipped gray paint. The acrid smell of wild animals weighted the air. Wan light strayed in through small windows. She could not tell if the floor's tilt was real, or symptomatic of a concussion and inner ear trauma. Smoke from an oil fire wafted up from her uniform.

There were sounds of wind and high water bashing all around. She thought she could feel the floor shudder with each wave. There was something familiar about the place. She could not clear her mind of pain enough to draw the line between sensation and recollection.

She knew she was hurt. She trembled. Maybe bleeding out. That's what the chills could mean after the drubbing she had obviously taken. Her Death entree would come with a convulsion appetizer.

How long ago had it happened? Hours? Days? She had no idea. She had been on her way to Crisfield from Ben's place. Saw the smoke to the west. Hard to tell what was going on in that wind. Maneuvering closer, she thought she'd even seen a lick of orange flame. A boat burning out in the storm. She powered out to investigate. The boat dead in the water. A fire near the engine box. She knew the vessel well. Not just a boater in distress. A friend. Hiram Harris's *Palestrina*. Nearly broaching in the rising waves.

As she drew closer from upwind, she saw Hiram leaning against the wheel. Inert. She'd tried to radio for help, but the storm was making static of everything.

In the immortal words of Hooper in Spielberg's *Jaws*, this was definitely *not a boating accident*. Then she saw the muzzle of the automatic pistol aimed at her face from the shadows of the cuddy cabin.

Now, on the floor of this tilted world, she heard footsteps. No, two pairs of boots thundering down a metal staircase, resonating through her aching skull. She could not move to see who or what was coming next.

A voice. "Why'd you mess her up like that?"

Another voice. "Just business. She put up a fight."

"Maybe. But Chalk wants to chat with her before we snuff her boyfriend. Between you and me, I think the Old Man's scared of him."

"Doubt it. Call it a healthy respect. That man's never afraid. He'll kill them all over there, pick the nicest house, and set up shop for a while to unwind. You're right. We better leave this one for now. She's Chalk's."

A shoe connected with LuAnna's hip. Rolled her onto her back. She blacked out, drowning under a wave of pain.

LuAnna woke again, sensed she was alone. Could not remember anything more, except that she was pregnant. Or had been. *Was she still?* She ran her tongue around a few broken teeth. Touched her damaged face. Wondered if Ben would still find her attractive.

Wondered if he would find her at all.

CHAPTER 22

OTHER THAN EARNING a slew of expletives, Ben got nowhere with the intruder. A quick frisk, but no gun, and no knife. All Ben knew was the man's name, but he did not use it. He was in no mood to strike up the warm fuzzy rapport that often yielded useful information. There was no time for clever cat-and-mouse badinage.

Even in defeat, Tug Parnell did not capitulate. There was no hint of remorse. No germ of conscience to help Tug see the light, see his error, and come to Jesus. Ben recognized the look in Tug's face. It was not that this jackal was simply inured to mayhem, or even business-like about it. Busted up as he was, Tug was *proud*. Proud of his day's work. Proud of his claim to a little piece of hell on earth. For Tug, this was not a necessary evil, not a means to an end. It was a calling. Ben felt his pulse shoot up. A detached part of his brain witnessed his vision iris down into a killing focus, and become an etched telescopic gun sight, its optics tinted blood red. Instead of a gun, Ben reached for his knife.

Then something behind him moved. A soft thump. Ben looked, but the living room remained empty, foul and silent as death.

That's when Tug tried to squirm away.

Ben walloped him down with a double-fisted hammer. Tug was either out cold or faking. No time to figure out which. One of Tug's feet was still cocked on the bottom step.

Ben stood, stepped across another line within himself, and stamped down hard. Tug screamed again. So he had been playing possum. Now he was cursing Ben's ancestry, dooming his descendants, and suggesting acts that defied even the limber anatomy of a Cirque du Soleil performer. So be it. With that bad leg, at least ol' Tug wouldn't be sneaking up behind anybody today.

Ben went through the living room into the small den. Found a 9mm Beretta on an end table by the loveseat. Probably Tug's. No sign of Charlene.

The soft thump again. Ben could not pinpoint its origin behind the windy creaks and shudders of the old house, and Tug's curses. He grabbed the Beretta, flipped off the safety. There was already a round in the chamber. He cleared the hallway. Next stop: the laundry room. Nobody was there either.

It had been a few minutes since Tug screamed, and no one had come to help him, so Ben sped things up. Shouted into the emptiness. "Hello!"

Then Ben noticed the small pool of blood spreading from under the laundry closet door. Standing well to one side, Ben opened the door an inch. A pale white hand on the floor caught the light. He opened the door.

There was Charlene, stuffed in next to the wicker laundry hamper. She sat fetal on her haunches. A small bullet entry wound in her chest, powder burn tattooing meant close range. Charlene's eyes were open, full of terror. Glazed with tears. She was looking up at Ben, panting. Not recognizing him. She looked like Satan's chew-toy.

"Charlene! It's me, Ben Blackshaw. Your neighbor, Ben."

Charlene's face eased. She blinked slowly. Tears flowed into the wrinkles of her haggard face. Ben kneeled beside her. Carefully leaning her forward, he confirmed there was no gaping exit wound in her back.

Tug Parnell laughed, and spewed filth from the next room. He encouraged Ben to admire a job well done, and to take a turn with Charlene himself.

Ignoring Tug, Ben gently uncurled Charlene from the confined space so she could lie flat. He inverted the laundry basket, elevated her feet with it. Thready pulse. Charlene's breathing was shallow, labored. Close to agonal. Ben pulled his blowout kit from his leg pocket and dressed the wound. He grabbed towels from the closet shelves above, pressed one over the trauma dressing. For her other hurts, Ben felt helpless to care for her.

He could only grab more towels. And finally a blanket from the top shelf to cover her.

"Hang on for me, Charlene. I'm going to your phone, okay? You need a hospital. I'll get a helo out here."

The State Police flew Medevac for all of Maryland. Trooper Four out of Salisbury could scramble a Dauphin helicopter with paramedics to the Smith Island pad at one hundred sixty-five knots; under twenty minutes. Charlene could be in Peninsula Medical Center in less than an hour, if shock did not claim her first.

She slowly edged her feeble hand onto Ben's hand. Her voice no more than a whisper. Ben had trouble understanding her. She slurred like a deaf woman. "No damn good. Stay."

"I'll come right back, I swear. You need help, ma'am."

Charlene frowned. Moved her head, *no*. "Hiram. Using him. The boat. Coming for you. And LuAnna. No point."

"I'll find him for you." Ben was lying and Charlene knew it. Hiram had to be dead. And Chalk somehow knew about LuAnna, and was looking for her. Like a troika of wild horses, rage, horror, and pain dragged him in three directions at once. If Chalk could do this to Hiram and Charlene, how would he use LuAnna?

Charlene squeezed Ben's hand weakly. Her face showed enormous effort and a hurt from down in her soul. "No calls. No doctor. No police. You do this. You, Ben. No police. S'what your father wanted. You sort this out. You can do it. I know. For us all."

Ben was stunned. Charlene had somehow heard about his father's return. Even she knew that something linked to Dick Blackshaw was simmering on Smith Island.

Ben's duty as a human demanded he get Charlene help. As her friend, things were not so clear. Her wish, her selfless dying wish was that he carry on without regard for her. He'd seen this kind of courage in mortally wounded soldiers. She was sacrificing any hope of survival. For what? *For us all*, she had said.

Charlene gave Ben a sick smile. "Goddamn picaroon." Her face relaxed. Her breathing deepened, slowed. Two minutes later Ben could find no trace of her pulse. Not the least warmth of breath. In that time he had found the two house phones, upstairs and down. Both smashed to pieces.

He gently closed her eyes.

CHAPTER 23

HELL, IT WAS already midmorning. Maynard Chalk scanned the Chesapeake toward Smith Island. He could not see it. The storm and the distance obscured his view. Even though he was standing at the top of the fifty-two-foot Point No Point Lighthouse, visibility was down to a quarter mile, and often much less.

Looking directly downward, he saw the Natural Resources Police patrol boat moored to the lighthouse's foundation, which was a circular iron caisson. Hiram Harris's *Palestrina* was also tied there. She showed smoke damage from the decoy oil fire set in an old washtub on the afterdeck.

Hiram Harris was no longer aboard.

Hiram's skiff also surged beside the *Palestrina*. Chalk and Bill Slagget had almost drowned crossing to the lighthouse in that little outboard, but by God they had dodged the bay's mounting growlers like salty old sailors and made it!

The lighthouse's rusty caisson was footed on the Chesapeake bottom at a depth of twenty-two feet. A two-story brick octagon design, measuring eleven feet on a side, topped the caisson. Capping the brick octagon was a wood frame watch room with four dormers and a mansard roof. The two-foot-high, fourth-order, Fresnel lens surmounted all. It was housed in the glass cupola with a grab rail ringing its outside deck. The entire structure canted to the southeast like its cousin in Pisa from a century of Chesapeake ice flows.

Chalk's people thought he was a genuine madman because of the ferocity with which he conducted his business. They did not realize that wreaking this kind of havoc in the lives of human beings, until this gig anyway, required a sanitary mind. A mind free of clutter. A mind focused like this lighthouse lens, manifold of crystalline contours, yet concerted of purpose.

Chalk had heard all the mustache twirling cuckoo-bird claptrap. Others said he was not a mad genius, just a blowhard whacker with a lucky streak a mile wide. They also said his luck wouldn't hold forever. In fact, there was growing evidence that his good fortune, like his antipsychotic pills, had already run out, but he would not cave. *Not by a long shot.* Even though this mission was screwed up as a football bat, he would get through this in great shape. He always did. His growing instability was the linchpin of staying agile.

Chalk's phone skirled a bagpipe riff from *Scotland the Brave*. He had switched it over to a cloaked satellite network. The cellular coverage out in the Chesapeake was anemic.

This call was welcome. Chalk was suffering from a news blackout. He had no idea what the clients were actually doing right now. Yusef was sleeping with his forebears, so he was useless for further intel.

Chalk answered. "Go."

A weary man spoke up on the other end of the line. "Mr. Chalk. Everything good?"

Chalk's contact on his B-Team was Farron MacDonald. MacDonald knew how to send a storm of bullets downrange. Deft work was not his long suit unless he was on a surfboard.

"Sit-rep." Chalk had no time for shit-chat with this stoner. News was all he wanted.

MacDonald got to it. "Pura vida, my man. Okay, so late last night we located the pilot of an airplane chartered by our boy, Chase." MacDonald let the news sink in.

Chalk shook his head in admiration. Of course. Dick Blackshaw had bought time for electroplating the lead dummies by using a plane instead of a truck to move more than two tons of gold, and get to his rendezvous early. So simple.

"And? What else? Spit it!"

MacDonald was making Chalk work for his news. That meant Chalk was losing MacDonald's respect. The employee sensed his boss was in a tight spot and was enjoying making him wriggle. Chalk would tune him up properly when he got through this. Smug little MacPrick. And God damn Dick Blackshaw for good measure.

"The pilot's been detained," said MacDonald.

"How many hours?" Chalk knew how Farron MacDonald's interrogations worked. He could assess the likelihood of getting useful intel just from the amount of time his agent had his hands on the flyboy.

"Two hours. We really just got rolling."

"Two bloody hours? You're slipping, Farron. Is this guy a merc? Is he Company? What makes him so tough?"

"He was in a mondo bad way when we recovered him."

"I don't follow."

To hear better, Chalk climbed down out of the wind-whistling cupola into the watch room below where Slagget, Clynch and Gavin slouched and smoked.

MacDonald explained. "What I mean is, we weren't the first to chat with him. Somebody else is, like, interested in what he knows. Really interested."

Chalk's blood thinned a little. This was the first actual sign of the parties of the first and second part: the clients in the deal. Somehow, they already knew the deal was FUBAR, and they weren't waiting around for him to fix it. They hadn't even called to reason with him. Things were much worse than he imagined. Senator Morgan had probably ratted him out, and said he'd gone rogue with no intent to follow through brokering the exchange. It's how he would have played it. That'd just about guarantee he would be collateral damage in this deal.

Chalk turned his back to the men and went *sotto voce*. "What the hell are you talking about?"

"What I'm saying is, when we tracked this guy down he was in custody of another group. In a motel room in Wilkes-Barre."

Fucking Wilkes-Barre? Chalk could not believe this. The clients were out ahead of *Right Way*. How much they knew now was anybody's guess. He asked, "How'd that go down?"

MacDonald tried to sound chagrined, but his pleasure beamed across the connection. "Things got a little wet, no lie. We dressed out like Homeland Security on an interdiction assignment. Turns out the other folks had been working on the pilot for a while already. But hey, we shook 'em loose before they snuffed him. So that's cool, right?"

"Tally me bananas."

"Yeah. Not so hot there. Baker's gone. A round in the neck."

Damn neck wounds. Never good.

MacDonald was still talking. "Oh, and Duncan took one in the foot. Should have seen him hopping around bleeding like an idiot. It was super-fuckinggay. He'll make it through fine, but no way he's coming back to work all gimped up."

"The other side. Cuantos?"

"We figure there were nine to start. Down to six or seven now. Maybe a couple walking wounded."

"Okay, but where'd they go? The other guys."

"They boogied into the woods behind the motel. I think they had wheels stashed there. Like an escape route. Real pros. Could be anywhere. Like I said, still no way to know what they got out of the pilot. Maybe nada."

On the contrary, Chalk now had to assume that the clients could show up at any moment. And they'd be packing serious firepower. He had to get left of this situation ASAP. Good thing he had cleared most of his team off Smith Island proper. Tug Parnell was still at the Harris's to watch in case Blackshaw's brat showed. Chalk briefly debated going back for him. *To hell with Parnell!* LuAnna was the key.

Now they were bunkered in a hundred-year-old lighthouse adobed in gull guano. Waves shook the tower as if it might fall into the soup any second. At least there were no marsh monkeys with shotguns loitering for a chance to bust a load of double-ought up his butt-crack.

Chalk ordered, "I want that pilot singing, and I mean yesterday."

"Right. Cool. Thing is, Mr. Chalk, we've spent the last two hours trying to keep Sky Captain alive and out of the World of Tomorrow. The work the others did on him was real crude. I think they were seriously cranking on him around the time we got there. Dialed up the heat way bad. Then there was our rescue. Mister Pilot was collateral in that. Not good. Bad scenics."

"You plugged the pilot? The pilot we need to talk to?" Chalk was going white with anger.

"Super sorry. Yeah, like I said, the whole thing went down wet and dirty, sir. Could've been anybody's bullet. Da fuh-shiznit was flying righteous."

"Prognosis?"

MacDonald said, "See, that's the problem. It's abdominal. Entrance, lower left quadrant. Of course the round tumbled and fragmented inside him. A piece exited through the top of his right shoulder. You believe that? We got him in a safe house and we're doing everything we can. Truth is, he's leaking like a sieve inside. We've got large-bore lines pumping Ringer's like crazy."

"For Christ's sake! He going to live?"

"Long enough. My word on that."

"Dammit, Farron! You make him sing pretty."

"Aye-aye, sir. Roger wilco."

A thought struck Chalk. He had to ask. "Are you damn certain that Tom Chase wasn't there? Got any surplus dead white guys laying around?"

"Except for Baker, no. Both enemy stiffs are Arab ethnics. One of them called for his ma-bird in Shirazi Farsi by the sound of it. And no, dude, he kicked before we could squeeze him. I know me and the whole B-team have a jinormous order of regret about that one."

Chalk would not be placated with anybody's regret just now. "Work the hell out of that pilot. I want every scrap of intel in his brain even if you have to hold a séance. You hear me?"

"We're on it, Your Chalkness."

Chalk thought for a moment. *Farsi. Iranians. The ones trying to buy the bomb.* "Say, Farron?"

"Mr. B?"

"About Duncan. That foot of his. You say he's permanently benched?"

"Never rumba again, sir."

"Too bad. Okay, Farron I want you to retire Duncan. Pension him off. Understood?"

"Copy that, Mr. Chalk. See to it personally. Peace out."

Chalk hung up. That's the last thing he needed: a spavined warhorse padding his disability payments by writing a tell-all bestseller about his glory days with *Right Way Moving & Storage*.

He turned back to Slagget, Clynch and Gavin. "Great news, boys. Seems that a pilot who flew the shit for Blackshaw has been located. We'll have some intel out of him soon."

"The clients?" Clynch, seasick as he was, understood the stakes.

Chalk confided, "They are very, very busy."

Dar Gavin kvetched, "More than I can say for *us*." Though he was not a rookie, Gavin was always virulently eager to wag his pecker in a firefight.

Chalk counseled, "Dar, there's an old saying. 'Sit patiently by the river, and the body of your enemy will float by.' Be the river, Dar Gavin. Be the motherfucking river. Now, if Dickie Blackshaw told that pilot anything, and the clients compromised the pilot, we can expect things to hot-up around Smith Island in the very near future. Before we head out, let's step downstairs and check on our little lady. See if she's awake. See what she's got to say for herself."

CHAPTER 24

BEN PLACED CHARLENE on the double bed in a downstairs guestroom and draped her head to toe beneath a counterpane. It was all he could do for her.

After fastening Tug's hands behind his back with a clothesline, Ben hogtied his wrists and his ankles together. He cinched hard on the bad leg with no remorse. Ben suspected the agony he was inflicting crossed from binding into the darker realm of torture. He also knew this thrust him down into the moral crevasse right next to Chalk and the rest of that crew.

To Ben, trussing Tug like an animal, even with a crepitus fracture, felt like coddling him. Given the invaders' treatment of Hiram and Charlene, Ben could just as easily jump on Tug's neck with both feet. He found a bloodstained roll of duct tape, and quickly encased Tug's head in a sticky silver hood leaving only his nostrils exposed.

Before Ben left the charnel house, he looked for anyone on the path. The house was isolated from all three Smith Island hamlets. No one was lying in wait for him.

Ben exfiltrated straight for his saltbox. The entire way, there was no one abroad to remark on a local man double-timing down the path in a wetsuit, and toting a rolled up ghillie rig under his arm. It seemed the neighbors were staying indoors, out of the wind and rain, or out of trouble. Just another day in paradise. Ben's eyes scanned right and left, looking for further sign of murderers. Now, all of Smith Island was no longer his home. It was a battlefield. He assessed its vantages and weaknesses like a general. He saw nothing of the enemy.

Ben's saltbox was another story. The door was wide open. The Kid was gone. The shattered kindling that had recently been the stout oak chair lay festooned in the ligatures that Ben had used to bind his captive. Ben examined the chair. Nothing other than feral brute force could have destroyed it. The Kid was powerful. And savage.

Ginger, Ben's dog of seven years, and raised from a pup, lay dead. Her skull split, caved with a leg of the chair. Fresh blood on the floor, and more blood staining Ginger's jowls showed she had given noble account of herself before being struck down.

Ben shrouded his second body in fifteen minutes with a throw blanket from the back of the couch. Charlene Harris had crocheted it for him as a Christmas gift years ago.

He tried LuAnna's home line, and her cellular phone. No answer at either number. He left quick messages. Maybe Chalk had seen LuAnna outside his place that morning. He remembered she had copped a feel and kissed him. LuAnna's affection for him made her a target. And their child as well. Because he had lied about where the gold came from, she had no idea of the menace looming to pounce her. For the moment, he reminded himself her patrol boat could outrun anything Chalk had stolen from Hiram Harris.

He tore through the house looking for The Kid, praying to find him. He had not hung out for a rematch. Perhaps he was making new friends among Ben's neighbors. Ben hoped they were better prepared than the Harrises.

Ben ransacked his crab shanty for what he needed, and jumped aboard *Miss Dotsy*. He did not go forward to open the cuddy cabin.

With no visible enemy on whom to vent his fury, and no way to find LuAnna, Ben had to deal with the bomb before it killed everything and everyone that mattered to him. He had to defuse or destroy it. There was less than half a day left until it exploded. He thought he knew how to handle the thing, but he was not sure. On the run back from the Harris home, his father's letter suddenly became clear. Perhaps those stupid empty sentiments concealed a vital clue. On the other hand, if he were reading too much between his father's lines, Smith Island would soon become the first chapter in the history of the Apocalypse.

Miss Dotsy's gearbox rattled and thumped, but she moved. As he pointed her down the stream, Ben got a new take on the old conservationist's anti-erosion sign posted on the shore: **YOU ARE RESPONSIBLE FOR YOUR WAKE**.

Yes, it was suicide going into eight-foot waves with *Miss Dotsy*'s damaged drivetrain, but he had no choice. Macabre as it was, that sign on shore gave him the seed of an idea.

The ride back to Deep Banks Island was rough. Unburdened by the gold, *Miss Dotsy* rode over the waves well enough, but she surfed fast down their backs to auger her bow deep into the troughs. He kept trying to raise LuAnna on the radio, but got no reply. The hurricane had played hell with cellular towers, but the wireless companies had gotten most of them back in service as soon as the storm blew through. That did not explain why LuAnna was not answering her radio. Scanning the police and emergency channels, Ben heard no indication that her dispatcher had missed her. That was a good sign. Then he remembered LuAnna's eleven-to-seven tour ended that morning. No one but Ben wondered where she was.

He continued to listen for distress calls on the radio, but heard none. Ben felt like a monster. He did not know where LuAnna was, so he could not help her if she needed it. Since he could not help her, his cold soldier's heart tried to set the matter of her well-being aside, to compartmentalize. He confirmed within himself that for now, he had picked the next right objective out of a grab-bag packed full of shitty options. Maybe LuAnna was safe and sleeping at home.

Ben steered into the maze of guts leading to the planks and the hollow below the heron rookery. The water calmed. Pushing farther inland, now the wind carried reeds and branches whipping past him.

He stopped *Miss Dotsy* next to the sapling marker. He set the CQR anchor on shore in case the baby gale backed to the east and blew straight down the gut. He took a shovel with him through the plank-lined channel in the reeds. He glanced up as he approached the hollow. The herons were hunkered low in their nests.

The wind obliterated nearly all sound but itself, yet for a man of Ben's checkered and bloody past, there was no mistaking the hornet buzzing past his ear. A high-velocity bullet.

Ben ducked low and turned just in time to see a man stalking up behind him, almost invisible in the reeds. The man collapsed backward. Ben was strangely aware of nearby cattails that seemed airbrushed to a Dallas-in-Autumn shade of Zapruder pink.

Ben crept to the body. A gunshot wound in the face made recognition difficult. The cranium was completely evacuated leaving the usual canoe of a front to back headshot. There were adhesive tape marks at the elbows and wrists. Deep canine bites on the right leg confirmed his suspicion. Ginger went down fighting. Here lay the psychopath once known as The Kid.

Ben looked back toward the hollow, then into the rookery. There, high up, a strange shape detached itself from Lonesome George's penthouse nest near the trunk of the tree. Not a bird at all. It rolled over the branch on which the nest lay. Dangled down from a line for a moment like a giant, hairy spider. The spider fast-roped down until it gently touched down on the ground. It stood upright on two feet, and became Knocker Ellis. He wore a ghillie suit thatched mostly with bare branches like his nest hide. He carried an M40A3 rifle with a custom-milled, Inconel alloy, baffled noise suppressor. It was scoped with an ATN 2-6X68DNS 3A daytime eyepiece.

Ben said, "Fancy meeting you here."

Ellis said, "Had to check the trap."

Ben smiled. "For a man killed forty years ago, you seem to have all the latest toys."

Knocker Ellis smiled back. "What? This old thing? Fell off a truck a few months back. Right after it was house-tuned in Quantico. Couple boxes of match ammo tumbled out along with it. You're not the only man with friends in low places."

Ben nodded, but inside, he was even more suspicious of Ellis. Only two hundred M40 sniper rifles had ever been made, in-house, by the Marine Corps itself. And they were all accounted for, supposedly. Did this quiet man have the kind of juice to get one of these guns for himself? Could Ellis have acquired it through Dick and his connections, or worse, through

Chalk? Ben said, "A little close, that shot. With the elevation and this wind?"

Ellis said, "A hundred six yards? Kid stuff."

"Speaking of, how'd you know he was a baddy?"

"How you figure I wasn't aiming for you and missed? And that was rhetorical. I never miss. Fact is, from up there I saw this cat climb out of *Miss Dotsy*'s cuddy not a New York minute after you started patrolling in."

Knocker Ellis bent next to the body. The head wound was draining from gravity, not a heartbeat. Blood in the muddy stream turned to thick liquid rust. Ellis reached under the corpse, picked up a knife.

Ben's sense of vulnerability morphed into outrage. "My own goddamn Ginsu!"

"Cuts through bone and frozen food. It would do a number on a penny, too. Not to mention your fool neck."

Ben had forgotten the gallows humor of war, dark jokes that helped discharge gigavolts of nerve-lightning built up from days of unrelieved mortal jeopardy.

Ben said, "They came to my place. A guy named Chalk. And this one. And another. I sequestered this one. Thought I had. He broke loose. They called him Kid."

Knocker Ellis was not happy. "Wait, *Chalk*, you say?"

Ben looked closely at Ellis. "You know the name?"

Ellis covered, "No. Not at all. Just not sure I heard you right. Unusual name. Ben, you know what that visit was, don't you? They were peeping things out with you. And now they know you've got skills."

"I was supposed to give them a cup of tea? Ellis, they killed the Harrises to get to Pap and the gold. Tortured them."

Ellis was quiet as he frisked the body. Then he said, "Good people. Always said hello."

"I found Charlene. She was still alive. In a closet. They—you don't want to know what they did with her. I found another one of their men. So that's four we know about. This one's dead. The one at the Harrises'—"

Ellis said, "Tell me you greased him."

"Not exactly."

Ellis was angry. "You saw firsthand what they do. They're like cockroaches! They can run round for a week with their heads snapped off. Ben, I'm not sure there's a place for mercy in all this. You're not going pacifist on me, are you?"

Ben hesitated. "I mean you no judgment, but I'm not in the service anymore. Killing somebody here in civilian life, that's the last house on the block for me."

Ellis looked offended. "Oh. You're welcome." Ellis opened his hand. "If that's the last house on the block, you better file a change of address before Maynard looks you up again."

Ellis held a GPS. The one he had received from Dick Blackshaw. The one he had used to guide Ben to the oyster rock where they found Richard Willem Blackshaw dead with his treasure. Its screen glowed bright in the storm's twilight. Ellis asked, "How'd the bastard get this?"

"Hell!" Ben closed his eyes, disgusted with himself. "I left it forward in the cuddy."

Ellis checked the GPS closely. "Now it's got Deep Banks Island logged in as a way point." Ellis scrounged in among the reeds. After a moment he found something else lying next to a clotting patch of scalp. "And this is The Kid's?" Knocker Ellis held out a blood-smeared satellite phone. "Guessing from the gray matter and hair, it wasn't in his hip pocket at the time of death."

Ben took the gory phone, and pressed a few buttons to bring up a call history. "He was talking on it four minutes ago."

"Roughly when I notched him up."

Ben was angry. "How do I know that phone was ever on this guy? Maybe you palmed it, smeared it just now. Maybe four minutes ago it was you up in that hide having a chat with somebody. See Ellis, I never said the guy's name was Maynard. Just Chalk. In all the mess, I forgot his first name altogether till you reminded me."

Ellis looked pissed. Upset enough that Ben might have hit close to home with his suspicions. Ellis opened the bolt of the rifle. A shell ejected. He closed the bolt, sliding another round home in the breach, and policed his brass. "You want to say that again? Not sure I heard you over this wind."

Ben said, "You heard me plain." He knew he should have frisked The Kid before going to Hiram's and Charlene's. Maybe he'd have found a phone. Maybe he would have known The Kid had no phone at all. And he should have checked *Miss Dotsy*'s cuddy cabin when he discovered The Kid had broken free. Ellis was right about one thing. Ben was going soft in peacetime, and it was killing people he cared about. He was certain of Ellis's loyalty. Almost. "If the phone's not yours, that Kid might have tipped Chalk."

Ellis relaxed, shrugged. "Maybe. Or he might have been sucking on my full metal jacket when the call went through. Hard to talk without a brainstem and whatnot. Can't say for sure. Let's assume Chalk knows about this spot and his mind is going like a gerbil on a wheel. Don't want to seem indelicate, but did Charlene Harris tell you anything?"

"Yes, but she was so badly hurt. Shocky."

Ellis's face clouded with disgust. "Understood. What did she say?"

Ben thought back to what seemed a hundred years ago, remembered Charlene's wounded body, and her stalwart heart in the face of death. He regrouped.

"She didn't want help. No doctor. No police. Said I should take care of this myself. Called me a picaroon. Before that she said LuAnna and I were in trouble. But she said there was nothing we could do."

Ellis stopped him, "Hold it. After all that cheerleading, she said quit?"

"Right. No. Not exactly. She was dying. She knew it. What she said exactly was, there's *no point.*"

Ellis and Ben stood in the rain and wind, thinking. Reviewing facts and stirring in their impressions.

Then something rose into Ben's mind out of the horror of the last two hours. A spark of meaning in the madness. He said, "It was the laundry closet. Where they put her. You know, a louvered door. Slatted."

Ellis said, "I know what *louvered* means. You think she heard them talking?"

Ben sorted a little more. "They thought she was dead, or as good as dead. It's possible."

Ellis smiled. "She didn't mean for you to quit."

Ben nodded. He got it. "She meant Point No Point. Where they're bivouacked."

Ellis said, "The lighthouse. Right. See, now that's the Charlene I'll remember."

"I haven't been able to raise LuAnna. Phone or radio."

Ellis asked, "How often does that happen? That you don't get her, or she doesn't get right back to you?"

"Never. Today we argued some. We're engaged, and she's pregnant."

"You lovebirds move quick. I'd surely puke if I weren't so worried."

Ben was galvanized. "Now that we've got a line on her, we're going to need a few things." He started back for *Miss Dotsy*. He stopped next to The Kid's corpse. Faced Ellis. "How'd you get here? And why?"

"My skiff's in the east gut. Figured you'd be along sometime to look in on the goods. Figured somebody might follow. What about you?"

"I think I can stop the bomb. I had a letter from Pap, and he all but gave me directions how to do it."

Ellis's eyes filled with mistrust. "You never said he wrote you."

Ben said, "Wasn't worth mentioning before now."

Ellis said, "Anything else you care to say?"

"No."

Ellis seized Ben's arm. "Then let's stop that damn bomb. Now."

Ben wrenched free of his culler's grip. "No. We still have a few hours on the timer. We need to find LuAnna. She comes before everything."

"No offense, but you sure about that?"

"Damn sure, Ellis. I don't want another word about it 'til she's safe."

Ben noticed Knocker Ellis's hands tighten on the rifle.

CHAPTER 25

THOUGH CHALK WAS talking on his sat-phone to The Kid, he still had the mental bandwidth to be pissed off at Dar Gavin. He nudged Corporal Bryce's naked form with his foot. She was unconscious, and he needed her wide awake. Gavin had been too heavy-handed in her initial capture phase. They could learn nothing from her about the Blackshaws in this unresponsive state. Since Chalk still needed her alive as leverage, that meant no more abuse. For the time being.

Holding up his phone, Chalk said, "Check out who's bucking for MVP. Hold on Kid. Read that again." Chalk whipped out a Sharpie indelible marker, and with no paper in sight, he squatted, and scrawled Lat/Long numbers directly onto LuAnna's bare hip. He always used a Sharpie. He believed his few written orders should have the permanence of law.

Chalk finished a readback of the numbers, and said, "You stay on top of them Kid! You hear?"

There was no reply. "Yo Kid! Kid?" Chalk snapped the phone shut. "Okay ladies. The Kid scrounged up a GPS, and just gave us the first solid piece of intel in three damn hours. We've got to reconnoiter another island. Slagget, Clynch and I are shipping out A-sap! Let's get ready. Asses onboard in five. Gavin, get those coordinates for us. And then you'll hold the fort here while we're gone."

Slagget and Clynch went downstairs to the lower story to collect their gear.

Gavin muttered to LuAnna's inert form, "We coulda had fun all afternoon. I admit I kinda got a case of rapies for you. But Boss wants you presentable. Such a waste. Oh well. A man can dream."

Dar Gavin looked around for a scrap of paper on which to transfer the long string of digits on LuAnna's hip. He couldn't find anything, which was too bad, but then he didn't search very hard. He drew his Smith & Wesson Extreme Ops automatic knife with its sexy, angular tanto point. Slid the lock down, and pressed the silver button. The wicked blade flipped out in an instant, the heavy spring-load jerking his hand.

Gavin leaned over LuAnna's hip. "Gee, baby. Too bad the boss writes so big. This is gonna leave a mark."

CHAPTER 26

CHALK, SLAGGET, AND Clynch set out from the Point No Point Light in Hiram's skiff. Though faster, Chalk assumed that a missing patrol boat might get the Natural Resources Police looking for it. Maybe they could even track it with some kind of transponder on board. After ransacking the twin engine boat, they reluctantly set it adrift to get lost in the stormy Chesapeake. It didn't matter. They had a damn good idea where the merchandise lay. Now they were going out to make sure, to size up the situation, and make their plan to recover it. Soon, this royal cock-up would be over and done with.

Hiram's larger *Palestrina* would have withstood the weather very well. With more than thirty feet on her waterline, her size also made her more obvious. Any boat out in this slop invited attention Chalk could not afford. So it came down to Hiram's anonymous eighteen-foot skiff, its antique Evinrude, his handheld GPS, and balls of case-hardened steel. God how he hated Dick Blackshaw for bringing him to this pass.

Chalk tried to distract Clynch from the rough weather, and his queasy belly, with shop talk. They had a frank exchange of views on the relative merits of the AN-94 Abakan, a primary assault weapon usually acquired from the obliging corpse of a Russian soldier, and the Heckler und Koch G-36, darling of the Bundeswehr.

Clynch, between poorly aimed barfs to leeward, said he preferred the light heft of the two-point-eight kilogram HK-G-36C. True to form, Chalk was infatuated with the staggering, albeit theoretical, 1,800-rounds-per-minute firing rate of the AN-94. Never mind that the standard AN-94 magazine only held thirty bullets. The prospect of a clip-voiding ejaculation of death scintillated Chalk to his deeps.

They had almost reached an agreement to disagree on hardware when a few more knots wound into the gusting wind. Their situation went from merely uncomfortable to abjectly dangerous. The overloaded little craft started shipping serious water. Chalk got busy bailing with the half Clorox bottle tied by a length of clothesline to his bench.

"Should we call it a day?" Clynch was a true berserker in a gunfight on land. He was of no value out here in the wet.

"Never say die, me hearties. Never say die! 'We've just begun to fight!'" Amazed, Chalk was John Paul Jonesing himself into a suicidal courage. Maybe there was a point to downing all those pretty pills every day.

"Clynch's making sense!" Slagget yelled over the din of engine and wind.

"Bullshit!" shouted Chalk. "Our merchandise is out there somewhere! We're this close! I can feel it!"

They pounded farther south through the waves, passing abeam of Holland Island, then rounding northeast toward their destination.

"There!" Slagget looked up from his chart. He had been wearing his night vision goggles to help him navigate through the storm's murk. Holding up the ragged, rain-rinsed flap of human skin with coordinates scrawled on it, he pointed. He waited until the skiff crested the next wave, shouted, "Yes! I think that's the place! Deep Banks Island!"

"Oh I do like the sound of that!" Chalk was feeling merry.

The day went nearly black from thick cloud cover. Chalk and Clynch donned their NVGs and passed Slagget a fresh battery pack for his.

Chalk said, "Let's take it easy. Orbit out here for a few. See who's around."

In ten minutes of watching the island, they saw nothing. Chalk steered toward the east side of Deep Banks. Everything looked dandy until they were a hundred yards out. Chalk went rigid. Bellowed, "Slagget! Clynch! Take off your damn bug-eyes! Now!"

Knowing from experience that most of Chalk's orders had kept them alive, at least so far, Clynch and Slagget yanked off their NVGs.

Clynch asked, "What is it?"

Chalk said, "Slagget, hold this course. Clynch, I want you to get down real low, and put your red-eye on that island where I'm pointing."

Sick as Clynch was, he quickly complied, raising an infrared scope.

Chalk quizzed, "What do *you* see? About two o'clock."

Without his night vision goggles, Slagget was steering blind. He bore vaguely east, confident he would not ram anything solid in the middle of Tangier Sound, for the next few moments at least. They waited for Clynch's answer. It came soon enough.

Worry hollowed Clynch's voice. "I got a big-ass inflatable boat. Color is dark. Could be tactical matte black. Six, seven, eight guys in it. It's tucked in tight to the shoreline. In the reeds. Pertinent negative: no fishing poles in sight."

Chalk was profoundly pissed. "What the hell are they doing out here?"

Clynch said, "They're watching us. Damn! They're all watching *us* with NVGs! Oh boy!" Clynch narrated like he was calling a ballgame. "Now it's all assholes and elbows over there! They've got weapons, and they don't care who sees them! They're coming right for us!"

Chalk rasped out again. "Beat to quarters, boys."

Clynch snatched up his submachine gun.

Slagget had to ask. "Maynard, who are they?"

With an unholy rage in his face, Chalk cocked his H&K MP-5K submachine gun. Slagget could barely understand Chalk as he roared out the answer they all dreaded. "My *clients!*"

As if to mock Chalk, the stormy sky lightened, laying Chalk's team bare in plain sight. The black inflatable bore down fast. There was a flicker of tiny lights at its bow. Muzzle flashes. Wood splinters flew off the skiff's gunwale where Chalk's hand had rested an instant before. Though the bullets were hitting home, the buzz of machine gun fire barely reached them through the weather. The three men of *Right Way Moving and Storage* returned fire. Loosed from such an unstable platform, their rounds flew wild.

Lucky long shots from the clients kept falling aboard the rolling skiff, blasting up a hail of painful splinters. Slagget ran the small outboard engine up to full throttle, but managed only a slight increase in speed. The black inflatable would be on them in less than a minute.

When it looked like the two boats would be slugging it out yardarm to yardarm, Chalk caught a break. A localized squall swept in and hit them with terrible force. It kicked up a microburst of wind complete with waterspout. Chalk thought he was bound for Oz until the squall dropped a heavy curtain of chilling rain. For a moment, the inflatable disappeared in the silvery gray dimness of sheeting torrents.

Chalk took advantage of the natural screen. Threw a hastily emptied gear bag into the water. Slagget caught on. More jetsam followed. They had to leave a debris field behind as though they had foundered with all hands. Even if their pursuers didn't ultimately buy the ruse, curiosity would slow them down.

Chalk grabbed the outboard, shoved the tiller over to the left, veering the skiff precariously to the right. Away from their former track. He prayed the enemy would not have the patience or smarts to stop their engine to listen for the racket of an old Evinrude in retreat.

Now, rain and spray were definitely filling the skiff faster than the stern drain could void it. Several large-caliber bullet holes had stitched the waterline, so even more of the Chesapeake flowed aboard through them. They were three men in a tub, and it was sinking.

Chalk turned to order Clynch to help bail. Clynch was slumped over in the bottom of the boat. Rain-thinned blood streamed through fingers as he clutched a wound in his gut.

CHAPTER 27

THE WEATHER DETERIORATED into a froth. Low fisted storm clouds uncurled claws of rain to rake the water. Gusting flaws whipped spume off the wave crests. *Miss Dotsy's* gearbox threatened to fail at any moment. With Ellis's coaxing, it somehow continued to turn. His outboard skiff was in tow astern for possible use as a lifeboat. Ben's ribs throbbed. He had taken ten ibuprofen at his house to little effect.

Ellis said, "So, Charlene called you a picaroon."

Ben checked the gear he'd collected at the saltbox. "Yes she did. A goddamn picaroon if I remember right."

"And a picaroon is what you Smith Island folks call a pirate."

Hell of a time for this, thought Ben. "We both know that."

"So that was high praise from an old-timer like her."

Ben did not look up from his work. "Depends on who you ask."

Ellis said, "You deny they're your people?"

"That was a long time ago. We've changed." Ben did not need a moral dialectic at this particular moment.

Ellis continued. "You went off to war. You did what you had to there."

"My duty to my country." Was Ellis *trying* to annoy him?

Ellis glared at Ben. "You kidding me? A war's been brought home to you, Ben. It's here. It's touching people you know. Killing them. And I'm not even talking about the concept of justifiable self-defense. There's legal precedent for that at least, Mr. Peacetime Civilian Man."

Ben gave a noncommittal, "I hear you."

Ellis would not let up. "I'm not sure you do. Ben, I'm not telling you to kill. Face it, your back's up against the wall. I am warning you as a friend that killing is in your blood. I'm only saying this so you don't surprise yourself and get all crippled up with guilt when it happens."

Ellis rounded *Miss Dotsy* up into the wind one mile south of the Point No Point Lighthouse. He baited Ben. "Look, if you don't think this a righteous stalk, we can still call the police on this and stand tall before the Man." Ellis balanced heading and throttle to hold *Miss Dotsy* in position.

Ben said, "And get everybody killed? Absolutely not. Who better to handle this than us? And Christ, Ellis, we already have blood on our hands. Police'd ask too damn many questions we can't answer without picking up serious jail time." Ben spat into his mask and rubbed. He pulled on an old set of U.S. Divers Rocket fins. "No. I got LuAnna into this. If she's in there, I'll get her out."

He had been wearing his wetsuit for most of the last twenty-four hours. No longer a protective sheath, it now felt like a half-molted eel skin from which he could never fully twist free.

Ellis said, "You don't even know for sure she's there. Or who's with her if she is."

Ignoring Ellis, Ben checked the large mesh bag full of home fumigation bombs. Smith Island's healthy population of feral cats sometimes led to flea infestations. One pesticide bomb per house was the usual prescription. For some reason, the wizened clerk at Rookie's dry goods store hadn't batted an eye when Ben put two entire cases on account. Ben wondered again if everyone knew something he didn't. Maybe fatigue really was making him paranoid. While under way, Ben taped the bombs together in four bundles of six cans each.

He also had a waterproof first aid kit, and a deflated life vest with a fresh CO_2 cartridge in its mechanism to blow it up in an instant. Given Chalk's treatment of the Harrises, he did not expect LuAnna to be ready to swim laps in the bay.

Ben looped a canvas sling over his shoulder. It was tethered by ten feet of line to the mesh bag. Ben said, "So we're all straight on this?"

"Squared away. Yo, Ben?"

Ben stopped, poised on the gunwale, about to roll into the water. "What?"

"Know what it costs a Smith Islander to get his ears pierced?"

"What!"

"Buccaneer." Ellis smirked. "Don't you drown, ya bad-ass picaroon."

More bewildered by Ellis's pun than amused, Ben tossed the bag in the Chesapeake and followed after it feet first.

The water was cold, and now Ben was exhausted, starved, enduring a rack of fractured ribs, and now dragging a bulky bag in tow. For this swim, he would not have the refuge of a SCUBA diver's depth to protect him from the bashing heave of the waves. He planned to let the wind and making tide carry him up the bay to the lighthouse. His main exertion would be to steer a course. His wrist compass and watch would help him dead reckon the way.

Favoring his ribs, Ben swam a labored sidestroke until the line to the mesh bag paid fully out. Then the sling snugged down across his chest. It felt like a sea anchor. Though he'd equipped himself with only the few things he would need, it was slow going. He was still making his plan of attack stroke by stroke as he went. He found a strange rhythm in the waves despite the bay's apparent chaos.

Like many children of the Chesapeake, Ben was no stranger to the light at Point No Point. Though an important aid to navigation, it had been automated for decades. It was unmanned by the Coast Guard since the early 1960s. Which meant it was a prime party and trysting site for any young guy with the four Bs: a babe, booze, a blunt, and a boat.

Getting into the lighthouse would be hard. Assuming no one witnessed Ben's approach and shot him, the rusted-out access ladder to the top of the iron caisson started six feet above mean high tide. Too high to reach, perhaps too corroded to support him if he somehow could get to it. It was for a boater, not a swimmer. There were ancient davits for holding the lighthouse keeper's tender out of the water, but they had not been rigged for many years. There was no rope to climb. There was only one other way.

Through the hatch.

The lighthouse's caisson foundation was not solid iron. It had one dogged watertight doorway, much like a passage through a submarine's bulkhead. It was originally designed to admit someone from a small boat at just above the water level.

Sadly, the foundation for the lighthouse had been inadequately prepared. Time, the gradually increasing leeward lean of the iron and brick tower, and settling into the muck, conspired with one result. The lighthouse had sunk, and the four-foot hatch had sunk with it. It became half-submerged and unusable except at spring low tides within ten years of its construction. Now, a century on, the hatch was routinely five feet under water.

When Ben was a kid, he often snorkeled down to the hatch. After repeated dives with a crowbar, he had managed to break or bend back five of the iron dogs pinning the hatch closed.

The sixth dog had always remained stubborn. Immovable. Ben had never cracked it when he was younger, and now it still blocked his only way in. Worse, today the bay was gulping a high tide at the same time a severe storm surge was rolling through. The hatch would be at its deepest ever.

Ben had a bigger problem right now. Something was wrong. When he sighted the lighthouse from the wave crests, it lay more and more to the west. Instead of swimming for minor course corrections of his drift as he had planned, Ben was forced to churn harder to cover distance. Odd currents generated by tide and weather were fighting him, and to find LuAnna, he would have to fight back. At first, swimming in for LuAnna made sense. As Ben expelled uncounted snorkels full of cold, brackish water, he was having second thoughts. His decision tree for this sortie had woodpeckers and squirrels living in it.

Cold was shutting his mind down. His arms were numb. He was moving by rote, barely looking up to check his course. After what seemed an eternity, he almost swam head first into the barnacled iron caisson.

Ben bobbed like human flotsam in the roiling eddies of the lighthouse's leeward side. There was no rhythm to this water. Waves and surges pounded in unpredictably. The dying Charlene had heard right, proving what many Hospice workers observed, that hearing was the last sense to wither as death enshrouded the human mind. Chalk and company were using the lighthouse as a shelter from which to stage their operation. To Ben's left lay Hiram Harris's *Palestrina*.

Ben was tempted to pull himself aboard the boat, curl up and rest in her cabin. The mission would not allow this. God willing, LuAnna might be nearby. With a less kindly God, she would also be in need. Ben dared not tread water too close to the lighthouse. The waves would rasp him up and down the barnacled caisson flaying him to bloody shreds like a giant grater.

He hung on the side of the *Palestrina* more like a butchered slab of pork than a knight in shining armor. He was not sure he had strength for what was next; the longer Ben waited, the weaker he felt. Over and over since yesterday morning he believed his reserves were completely tapped out. Then he would reach deeper within himself one more time and find just a little bit more strength to go on. Now he had nothing left. Breathing was hard labor, his flexing diaphragm bashed his ribs. Every kick to tread water, every heartbeat left him closer to total systemic failure. LuAnna was up there. He felt it. He had to press on until he finished this, or died trying.

Mustering himself, Ben unzipped the wetsuit jacket. Pulled out the short crowbar he had stowed there. He let go of the *Palestrina*'s gunwale, and sank into dark gray water. It was suddenly quiet now, out of the wind. A few kicks, and the barnacled caisson loomed out of the darkness before him.

Treading water, he scanned its curved wall. No hatch. He thought he had pegged exactly where it was positioned, ten feet counterclockwise from the metal ladder. There was nothing. He surfaced. Gulped for air. Down again. Had barnacles completely covered the hatch since he was last here?

After searching nearly a quarter of the caisson's circumference, Ben turned back toward the *Palestrina.* Then it hit him. This was not just a spring tide. It was a perigean tide. Extra high, with the new moon at its closest to earth. With the storm surge stacking the water even higher in the bay, Ben had not dived deep enough. He had wasted precious time and strength. He was running out of both.

Back where he started, Ben bent at the waist, and jackknifed for the bottom. He stayed close to the caisson, but still found nothing. All the air burned out of his lungs fast. And then he saw it, a full fifteen feet below. There, occulted in that zone where the marine gray-greens rotted to blackness, lay the hatch. Its corners were rounded off by swaying dead algae, barnacles, and weeds.

Ben tore at the slimy vegetation. At the hatch's bottom right-hand corner he found the one dog he had failed to wrench open when he was there years before. Before the war, and before the faces behind the wall in his skull. Before his father had come home in a sodden, gilded fatal triumph.

He slipped the crowbar between the dog and the jam, planted his feet on the hatchway sill. And he pulled. With all his heart and might he pulled. No movement. The dog did not budge. He shredded his fingers clawing his way up the barnacled caisson wall back to the surface, back to air.

Ben sounded again after three deep breaths. He replaced the crowbar, but tried a different angle. He coiled his body and hauled hard. No movement. Then in his mind's eye, he saw a gravestone with LuAnna's name. And then her face joined the many others in his head. The ones he had killed. The silent accusers. She stood with them. With all his strength Ben pulled on the crowbar one last time. His ears rang. He tasted blood. Muscles and tendons sheared in his shoulders, back, and legs. He was close to blacking out, and Ellis wasn't there to reel him back into the world.

Ben's left foot, which was planted on the hatch itself, pushed inward an inch. The movement was so small that if the hinges had not complained out loud, he would not have been sure he had made any progress. He quickly jammed both feet on the hatch, grabbed the side of the opening, and pulled straight out as if yanking the very caisson apart. The hatch swung grudgingly open nearly two feet now. Though faint from lack of oxygen, Ben did not rush back to the surface. His lungs ached, his diaphragm spasmed to open his throat, to inhale something, anything; even if all he got was bay water. Ben swam into the caisson's dark maw.

CHAPTER 28

CHALK LOVED GOD, but he didn't believe in Him. Rather, Chalk reveled in the enormous cost that religion in general, and a supreme deity in particular, exacted from humankind. All the senseless killing on both sides to protect a divine being that supposedly could look out for Himself just fine. It stoked his heart, and filled his bank accounts. Right now, some of the fallout of religious fanaticism was settling too close to home.

Slagget pulled a semi-conscious Clynch into the middle of the boat. Then he performed a rapid trauma exam worthy of any 68-Whiskey combat medic. Entry wound, but no exit. That surprised Chalk. Maybe the round had come through the skiff's side and lost some energy before Clynch caught it. It meant Clynch had a bullet knocking around in his large intes-tines. Slagget stuffed a QuikClot sponge into the wound, and put Clynch's hand over it. "Press!"

Clynch did his best. At least he held the sponge in place so the hemo-static agents could arrest the bleeding. Next, Slagget zapped Clynch with a green morphine injector pen out of their first aid kit. It was the same deliv-ery system that injects epinephrine for an allergic bee-stung patient crashing in anaphylactic shock. He pushed it hard against Clynch's thigh. A spring-loaded hypodermic needle pierced the flesh of his leg, and delivered the painkiller. Clynch howled at the new insult. Slagget looked at Chalk, shook his head.

"This is where we like it," Chalk pronounced suddenly, as if finishing a speech that he had begun in a dark, cobwebbed recess of his brain. "At the edge of chaos is where all the really amazing shit happens! Like surfing! *Be the wave, Simon Clynch!* You've come through worse than this! A gutshot man can hang on for days!"

Which, in Chalk's view, was a big problem. He met Slagget's eyes with purpose. He was assessing Slagget's loyalty to the mission versus his compassion for Clynch. Loyalty and Compassion now lay in opposite pans of a tetanus-ridden scale in Chalk's mind. Slagget stared back at Chalk, gave a nanosecond's worth of deliberation for show, and nodded to his boss. He was in.

Chalk was cryptic. "Check up front for something."

Slagget hunched low, crawled forward to the bow over Hiram's plastic duck decoys. As he groped along, he stopped to unsnarl his ankles from the lines attaching decoys to their lead anchor weights.

Chalk cooed to Clynch, "It's like my boy Fred Nietzsche always says, 'One must have chaos in oneself in order to give birth to a dancing star.' Words to live by. Have you dancing in no time! Give that dope a chance to work. Must hurt like a sum-bitch. Hey! Remember that crazy cocksucking Spetsnaz? He bit my hand 'til you cut his throat. Bit me to the bone. You bet that hurt, boyo! Remember that? Still got the scars. Stay with us, buddy. Stay with us."

Clynch could only reply between moans. "Gut hurts like fire! Fire! Whole mission's cursed!"

Sadly, Chalk never took luck into account, not for a mission, and not for a man. Performance, utility, a steady gun hand, and a clear eye to aim. And all these things right now; the few criteria for judging a soldier in Chalk's opinion. Simon Clynch was not measuring up anymore. Not even close.

CHAPTER 29

BEN SWAM BLIND into the dark well of the caisson, worked the mesh bag through the hatchway, then clawed upwards. His head broke the surface into the chamber. Foul entombed air ripped through Ben's teeth into his starved lungs. He was in the wet sub-basement of the lighthouse. The waves outside thundered against the iron.

As Ben treaded water, he bumped into something floating in the dark with him. He reached into a cargo pocket of his wetsuit for a small light. Turning it on, he found as expected that he was in a circular crypt. Like the bottom of a big water tank.

Ben swung the light. He was treading water with Hiram Harris. His friend was blanched, dead. He slumped at the surface in the life vest he kept on the *Palestrina*. The body undulated up and down in Ben's wavelets making Hiram appear to nod. Ben felt his stomach turn. Another friend gone. *What had they done to LuAnna?*

Ben tested the first dry rungs of the rusted interior ladder running down to the submerged hatch. They held, so far. He climbed up to the next hatch that gave access into the basement level above. One hard push and it rose. It was unlocked, and nobody waited to blow his brains out. That's one break, anyway.

Ben played the light across the five-hundred-gallon tanks. Four of them. Good. Still there as he remembered. He rolled over the hatch coaming onto the cement floor, and pulled the mesh bag up after him. Two of the tanks were cisterns that held the former keeper's water supply, collected from rainfall.

The other two tanks held kerosene. Fuel for the big navigation beacon. Though the light was automated and converted to electricity, the kerosene system had been preserved as a backup in case of a power failure.

Ben got to work with the two cases of aerosol bug bombs. Popped them all as fast as he could. A poisonous fog began filling the space.

Ben opened the stiff purge valves at the bottom of the kerosene tanks. Fuel gushed from the taps and ran across the cement floor. Fortunately, the hatch coaming in the floor was five inches high. There would be plenty of kerosene and volatile vapor loose in the airspace before anything overflowed into the sub-basement.

He gathered up the bag, and climbed another ladder. Pushed on the last hatch leading into the first floor. He would suffocate in the fumes if this one turned out to be locked. The hatch gave. Now he had access to the living quarters above the iron caisson. The kitchen and sitting room formed a continuous open space around the central spiral stair.

He peered around the room as best he could. The hatch itself blocked his view directly behind him. The noise of the storm covered the sounds of his invasion. No one in sight. He rose out of the floor into the brick walled space.

He lowered the hatch and saw LuAnna.

What was left of her.

Her fragile nakedness cut him to the bone. Her body bled from lacerations and scrapes. The only sign she was alive was her near convulsive shivering. A large welted bruise swelled from her forehead.

There was a terrible avulsion on her hip, as if a huge chunk of her flesh was torn out. She must have fought this bravely. Fought everything they had tried to do to her.

Her helplessness provoked a choking spasm of shame in Ben's chest. Facing facts, there was nothing he could do for her here, nor was there time for self-recrimination now. If he was going to save LuAnna, hate him as she rightfully might, she had one more ordeal to endure. It would be the worst by far.

Someone moved overhead.

Ben planned to carefully lower LuAnna with the sling and tether into *Miss Dotsy* with Ellis's help, but now there was no time. He fitted the inflatable life jacket around her, and buckled it in place. He listened.

Whoever was up there was coming down the central stair. There was no time to surprise and subdue this man as he had Tug Parnell. Ben scooped LuAnna in his arms ran through the door leading out to the deck. Without stopping, he made straight for the railing.

"Hey! You!" A man's footsteps in pursuit. Then gunshots.

Ben threw one leg over the rail, and hurled himself backward into space with LuAnna embraced in his arms, bullets flying past them.

Ben lost hold of her when they struck the water. His mask flew off his face, and he was blinded in the murk. All that was left in his hand was the rope, the mesh bag, and the plastic pull-toggle for the CO2 cartridge on LuAnna's life vest. He surfaced long enough to see a man with a gun looking down from the lighthouse deck.

Then bullets rang off the deck's rail. Ellis was covering. Chalk's man disappeared into the lighthouse firing blind over his shoulder.

Ben dived for LuAnna. The water was liquid ice. LuAnna would be dead in seconds if he couldn't find her, drag her up, get her warm. He had lost her.

He surfaced again, and saw her adrift next to the *Palestrina*. Her life vest had inflated. He swam toward her. Suddenly there was a buzz of machine gun fire from above. Ben braced for bullets to tear into him. Little geysers erupted in the water. The shooter in the lighthouse shifted his aim to something else, fired three times.

Ben had to keep LuAnna out of sight in the water. He towed her under the far side of the bow of the *Palestrina* for cover. LuAnna was still unconscious.

The gunfire ceased. Seconds passed. Ben held LuAnna close. His mind froze. He had her in his arms, but had no idea what to do next.

Miss Dotsy's bow knifed into sight over the crest of a wave. Ellis leaned over her washboards, snaffled LuAnna by the back of the life vest, and plucked her from the water. Ben grabbed a mooring cleat on *Miss Dotsy*'s stern as it careened by. He hung on, completely unable to pull himself aboard.

Again Ben felt Ellis's crushing grip on his arm, and he was back on the familiar deck. Ellis set the steering tiller for a heading away from the lighthouse, then he dragged LuAnna into the cuddy cabin, stripped off the uniform, and wrapped her in a blanket. Ben followed close crawling on all fours.

Ellis put his head out of the cabin door. "You got this shot?"

Ben said, "Hell yes. Gimme."

Instead of producing the sniper rifle, Ellis handed Ben an ancient Webley and Scott break-action signal pistol with a wood stock, vintage 1917. Ben's great-grandfather's flare gun. Not like Ben's sniper rifle by any means, but from shooting it on many Independence Days as a kid, he knew the piece as intimately as any deadly weapon.

Ben marshaled his last strength, and crouched on the heaving deck. Didn't brace himself at all. He let *Miss Dotsy* roll naturally under his feet as she had for so many years. He took aim at the nearest lighthouse window on the lower brick level, and compensated for wave and wind. "Shooter ready."

Ellis smiled. "Send it."

Pulled the trigger. A wet popping sound, a dull flash and smoky puff, and nothing else. A short round. The ammo was so old.

Ben broke the signal gun open. Plucked out the hot dud, slapped the last flare in the barrel and snapped it shut. He took aim again, now compensating with a negative lead for the distance *Miss Dotsy* had just traveled.

Ben muttered, "Shooter ready,"

From the cuddy cabin, LuAnna's voice feebly croaked, "Send it."

Ben pulled the trigger.

The gun kicked. The blazing red flare arced through the storm pretty and true, the smoke plume dissipating fast downwind. The little meteor disappeared through a thin glass window in the lighthouse.

For an instant, nothing changed. Then the flare ignited the bug-bomb aerosol. That touched off the kerosene flood in the basement.

The lighthouse disintegrated. The iron caisson acted like a mortar tube, directing all the blast force upward into the masonry and wooden frame structure. A white-orange column of flame. The lighthouse beacon flew up wildly into the clouds like an anti-aircraft searchlight. Then it winked out. A man cartwheeled in a high trajectory through the storm-wracked sky, a scarecrow burning alive.

Ben mumbled, "For Hiram and Charlene. Down payment." He yelled to Ellis, "Now let's get LuAnna home."

CHAPTER 30

CHALK HAD TO give him credit; Slagget sure moved quick. A good thing, since the leaky old skiff was still overloaded, slow as a barge, and their clients were still out there in the storm looking for blood. Slagget found what he needed in the bottom of the skiff, forward of the bow seat. Its chain was fastened on one end to a length of bristled, sun-rotted yellow nylon line. The other end was shackled to a Danforth anchor lying awash in the rising water. With flat, scapular flukes, and a straight shaft, it looked like a steel stingray on a leash.

Slagget grabbed the anchor. He hurried aft trailing the clinking chain like Jacob Marley on his Christmas Eve mission, but did not stop to untangle the duck decoys' anchor lines snagging in the rusty links.

In the stern, Chalk scanned through the rain for their pursuers in the black boat. No sign, yet. This squall could blow through any second, leaving them exposed in clearer air. First things first. He made gun fingers over Clynch's bowed head. Ever the professional even in semaphore, he pantomimed parking not one, but two bullets in Clynch's noggin. Then Chalk pointed at Slagget. Again Slagget nodded.

Chalk said, "I don't think that hit of morphine's doing the trick. Slagget, better give him another."

Slagget balked at the waste of meds. "Really?"

"I mean, fuck it a little, eh Bill? Our buddy's in pain."

The condemned tried to communicate. "Tangs, Mayn'rd. Slug'z killin' me!"

Not fast enough, thought Chalk. He blathered out more encouragement, all the while searching for any sign of the clients bearing down on them again, guns ablaze. "We got to get you in tip-top shape, Simon. Lots of work to do. Hurry up, Slagget! And make it two hits."

Slagget complied. All that dope would keep Clynch calm. Limit his struggles against the inevitable.

Clynch quickly slumped. Lost all muscle tone. He slurred, "Damn! Hurzzz!"

Chalk looked around the horizon through the blowing curtains of cold rain. He thought he saw a low shadowy boat in the distance, and snapped off three shots at it. A buzz and flicker of distant automatic weapons answered, but the shooters had no clear bearing on a target. "Not even close, pussies!" Chalk gave Clynch an appraising look, then nodded at Slagget again.

The curtain of rain returned, harder than before. Slagget drew his FNH Five-SeveN pistol. Chalk hated Slagget's choice of sidearm. It was a hobbyist's piece, with exotic ammo. Slagget had to form and load all the cartridge brass himself, and when he'd shot it all, what did you have? A two-pound bludgeon? Plus, unless you had the armor-piercing bullets, wet wool would stop the little bitty rounds cold. Chalk allowed Slagget his vanity piece because in the end, the man was a half-decent shot.

Slagget cajoled, "Easy there, Simon. Why don't you lie down a bit? Might have given you a little too much of that poppy juice, sport."

Slagget leaned Clynch's head to starboard over the water. A simple thing. The wounded man was rubbery now. Chalk slowly hiked out to port to keep the tippy skiff on an even keel.

With a round already in the chamber, Slagget cocked the gun. He positioned it in that just-behind-the-ear quadrant favored by John Wilkes Booth.

The deadly familiarity of the hammer's snick registered deep in Clynch's doped-up squash. He gave a little tremble of resistance. Asked, "Bill?"

Slagget held him down, pulled the trigger twice. Ba-pop! The wind carried the sounds away, but Chalk could still taste the acrid smoke in his mouth. Two very fast, very small rounds went into Clynch's head.

There in the storm, his enemies on all sides, and facing his worst crisis ever, Chalk couldn't help but ponder Clynch's neurology. What part of his mind contained that first twinge of fear; that realization he was about to be killed? Was the presentiment of death still synaptically fizzing around somewhere inside Clynch's head? No, Chalk decided. More likely it was now just an electrochemical yelp now eddying in the bloody waters astern.

Slagget's hand and wrist were sprayed with blowback. Blood mostly. The body twitched in his grasp. Nervous impulses with no guiding volition. Old fashioned death throes.

Chalk raised a hand. "Hold on there." He drew his gun again, and blasted a round of his own through Clynch's head. The coup de grâce it was his duty as leader to perform. The twitching stopped.

Slagget pulled the body inboard to prepare it for disposal. Chalk throttled back until there was just enough thrust to keep the boat headed into the wind. At a dead stop, they were even more vulnerable. Scouring the surrounding waters for the enemy, he said, "Hurry it up, Slagget! We've got shit to do!"

Chalk was pissed that he had to kill and dispose of one of his own men to prevent the clients from slaughtering his entire team. This was not a moral stance. It was a question of numbers, and right now he needed more able-bodied men, not fewer. He scanned the gray black waters for the clients, but with a new idea in mind. His boldest yet, he believed.

Slagget dropped the Danforth into Clynch's lap, flukes and shaft pointing up toward his bloody chin. He faked the chain in loops around Clynch's abdomen, and tied the line around the corpse. He bent on a large constrictor knot, bragging he'd learned it in summer camp when he was eight. Slagget gave the body a shake. Good and tight. Nothing even rattled.

Slagget looked at Chalk. "Would you like to say a few words?"

Chalk's brows shot up with surprise. "Fuck him."

They both reached for Clynch's ankles. Hoisted as high as they could. The body toppled into the water, and disappeared immediately.

In a surreal moment, three entangled decoys went over the side after Clynch, and swirled down into the Chesapeake's murk. It looked as if Clynch was the reincarnated Konrad Lorenz, trailed by his imprinted ducklings.

The boat throttled up faster without the anchor and Clynch's body on board. Now Chalk needed to get on shore. The firefight with those Iranian shit-birds he'd stumbled into, and barely escaped, was on reflection, exactly the skirmish he now needed to *win* and to complete this damn deal. The next meeting with them must happen on his terms. With his strength in numbers chewed down to just himself and one man, somehow he had to eliminate this new threat. There was only one way to do it as quickly as it needed to get done.

CHAPTER 31

MISS DOTSY'S RIDE back to Smith Island from the lighthouse was punishing. A stormy assault with intent to drown. Ben stayed forward in the cuddy tending to LuAnna. Knocker Ellis manned the helm.

The two men played an odd game of catch, tossing wet rags back and forth from warming on the Atomic Four, to the cabin where Ben applied them to LuAnna. Aside from bundling her up in blankets they had stowed, he was actively restoring her core temperature as best he could. LuAnna no longer looked Smurf blue from the abuse and her involuntary skinny dip. Regardless, she had clearly been the Everlast heavy bag for a man with deep-seated rage.

Between hot rags, Ben gave her a clinical assessment. There were no grossly broken bones, which did not rule out smaller fractures. No abdominal bloating or tenderness. No obsessive thirst, or pallid gums to hint at shock, hypothermia, or internal bleeding. She had radial and dorsalis pedis pulses, so her pressure was decent. Double-checking her perfusion, he pinched the tip of her index finger, and was relieved to see the nail bed return from white to pinkish-purple in under two seconds. Good capillary refill.

He dressed the gash on her hip as best he could without stitches. He prayed that what he saw was all she got, with no masked fatal complications. He said a prayer to no one in particular for the little Blackshaw inside LuAnna. Perhaps nothing more drastic than stitches, bandages, and time would do the trick. Perhaps they'd still make a family.

Ben called back to Knocker Ellis, "Thank you. For back there."

"Shucks. 'Tweren't nothing."

Ben clarified, "No, Ellis. That was one hell of a shot you made. I mean, off a moving boat. I know what it costs to kill a man."

Ellis shook his head *no*. "Credit where it's due."

Ben was cold, tired, not tracking this. "You shot the first sentry at the lighthouse."

Knocker Ellis said, "I know I touched-off that virus back at Deep Banks. The Kid, you called him. But this other guy just now? You were talking all non-lethal, like Gandhi, so I just winged that guy in the shoulder so he'd mind his manners. I didn't kill him. Credit where it's due, *Tiger*."

It sunk into Ben's slowly moving mind. He had released the kerosene. He had popped the flea bombs. Then he had pulled the signal gun's trigger, and shot the flare true. Ben had done these things. Not Ellis. Ben had killed in cold blood.

Had he only been trying to rescue LuAnna, and deny Chalk useful assets to keep him off balance and on the move? No, somewhere inside, Ben knew his enemy, this pack of mad dogs, was never going to jail for what they'd done. They would have immunity from justice under some secret protective legal clause; like a warped rendering of Ron Paul's post-9/11 Marque and Reprisal Act, which would permit God knows what off-shore perversions of American rule of law in the name of Homeland Security. What was Ben's defense? He didn't have one. Just the core imperative to save the love of his life. He wondered if that was enough.

Ellis tried to ease Ben's conscience. "Look at it like this. The lighthouse needed fumigating, right? So you killed yourself a flea." Ellis smiled.

Ben did not. This was not killing on an overseas deployment for God and country. This was civilian murder in home waters. Had he redeemed himself from what he had done in the war? No, Ben could not smile over this, despite possessing a fair measure of the well-worn coping mechanism of gallows humor. Instead, he crossed the threshold he had sworn to avoid. He entered that last dark house on the block. And with a fresh ache of remorse, he felt completely at home.

LuAnna was coming to. When Ben was sure she could swallow, he gave her warm canned chicken broth from his Thermos. He'd microwaved it in his one concession to the modern kitchen back at the saltbox. It was deliciously salty. Her mouth was raw where chipped teeth had flayed her tongue and the insides of her cheeks. She sipped anyway, the sting helping to wake her. Ben cocooned her in a third blanket.

There was a lot going unsaid between them. She offered, "I don't think they got frisky on me." As if suddenly aware of how numb she felt all over, she added, "Do you?"

Ben said, "Hard to tell. You got a good rinse in the bay. I believe you're okay. If you say you are." *God, that sounded terrible.* "Meaning I'm not a doctor." *Worse!* "Meaning I'm just glad you're alive, LuAnna. It's all that matters to me."

"Nice try. You get a 3.7 on the Nadia Comaneci Bullshit Scale. Obliged for the effort. Damn, I'm lithping. Must look like a Jack O'Lantern."

"No Hon. You're beautiful."

"Obliged again, liar. Now, how come I'm all busted up?" That was LuAnna. To the point.

Ellis yelled over the wind. "Go ahead. That girl's paid dear for the truth."

Ben told LuAnna everything. About his father's death. The gold. About Chalk. The Kid. The Harrises. Tug Parnell. The flaming human cannonball at the lighthouse. And the bomb that lay buried with the gold. He finished, confessing, "It's my fault. I didn't tell you everything from the start. That's why your guard was down. That's why this happened to you. I'm so sorry, LuAnna."

"Did you think I'd call the cops?" She put a hand over her mouth, hiding her shattered teeth as she tried not to smile.

"Something like that."

Then she surprised them both. "Okay. I'm resigning from the NRP."

Ben was taken aback. LuAnna loved her work.

She went on. "I was thinking about it before all this. I decided for sure while I was laying there wondering if I was fixin' to die."

Ben's spirit bowed again beneath a full load of penitence.

LuAnna explained. "I'm serious. I've been looking at this law I swore to uphold. How it's legal for bigshots to kill the bay with chemicals, bad soil runoff, all those condos they're building on the main, with all those toilets flushing damn near straight into the water. If you have enough money, you can buy your way out of anything. And here I am running roughshod over the little guys, some them in my own family. Cause they kept an oyster that's a quarter inch too small? Crazy. I feel like I'm waking up from a dream. Where have I been all this while?"

She fell silent. Ben stroked her hair.

LuAnna was dead serious when she said, "And now this. Well, Ben Blackshaw, I have to resign. The men who did this to me? They said their boss was going to kill us all, or maybe live on our island to see what made us tick. Even if he doesn't actually stay on, he'll leave something evil behind. So there it is. After what these jokers have done so far, quite honestly I think we have some additional killing to do."

Astonished, Ben was convinced LuAnna was gripped by fever, though her forehead did not feel hot. Had her time in Chalk's hands warped her personality? Then he remembered the burning man twisting through the sky above the blasted lighthouse. Ben had killed a human being well outside the law. LuAnna only suggested it.

She rested, trying to compass the bedlam that had descended on her world. Then, forgetting her own pain, she looked at Ben with genuine sympathy.

She reached up and touched his face. "Poor thing. You've had one hell of a day."

PART III
PICAROONS

CHAPTER 32

THERE WAS A reception committee waiting at Ben's pier. The gathering of men looked more like a quorum of ravens perching there in the gray shadows, their long, black foul weather oilies snapping in the wind and rain like pinion feathers.

Lorton Dyze stood out in front of the group in the midst of Ben's welded menagerie. As *Miss Dotsy* approached, Ben recognized more Island Councilmen. Men who worked the Chesapeake for their living. These silvered comrades might not be young, but they had strength in their backs, and a quiet manner when it came to important business after dark.

Wade Joyce was a big man who fussed over the engines of a very quick fiberglass deadrise. He had been known to volunteer the craft for after-hours hauling when needed, and when properly cut in for a share.

Sam Nuttle was a good man with a family to feed, and was not too particular about how food got on the table in tough times.

There was Tom Fox, who could see at night better than a bat. He was a wiry, smaller man as many Smith Islanders are. In a fight Ben knew Fox could eat nails and shit bullets.

Ephraim Teach was ready for rough work whenever it came along. He believed he was linked to the genealogical line of Blackbeard himself. For good or ill, that only encouraged him.

Sonny Wright knew the sunken planks and guts of every island around there better than most. It was rumored he wasn't above baiting and trapping a duck in winter if the Chesapeake looked likely to freeze, and stores were short.

In a former life Art Bailey was bested by booze. He had since sworn off alcohol completely, and stuck to his promise. Nowadays he still had to blow off a head of steam, but he managed it in more socially acceptable ways. Though he'd never played golf in his life, in times of stress he would go down to the shore with a few rounded-off rocks and an old wooden golf club he found washed up there. Ben swore Bailey could knock those stones all the way to Baltimore when a temper was on him. Not just Ben, but the entire island knew when Bailey was in a mood. He would maniacally shout, "Fore!" in his high lonesome tenor before every swing. A nod to tradition and good golfing manners.

Reverend Avery Mosby was a man who followed the Lord on Sunday, and followed the water the other six days of the week. He never shied from a righteous clash. When all was said and done, most of his flock were desperately poor, and the church needed a new roof. He would help raise money any way he could.

All these good Methodist men, these stalwart brigands, waited stock-still on the shore. Ben looked at Ellis.

Ellis said, "Took them long enough to get onto us."

Ben said, "Coming from you, that's pretty interesting. I think they've been onto us, and this whole damn business, from the start."

Ellis considered this. "You reckon?"

"I think Pap always saw this as a large-scale operation. He kept key players in the dark, probably 'til he could come back and marshal everyone up himself."

Knocker Ellis cast a withering eye over the men on shore. "Don't fancy getting in with that flock of swans."

Ben said, "Anything else I should know before we land? Anything that could save our butts in the next ten minutes?"

"Right now, I'm not sure your pappy got all his bases covered."

"I'd say you're right, given that he's dead."

Ellis tossed mooring lines to the outstretched hands on the pier. Without a word, the lines were made fast. Old tires were hung on the pilings, and shock-absorbing spring lines were added to secure *Miss Dotsy* in the mounting weather.

Ben and Ellis handed the blanket-clad LuAnna up to three women who threaded out of nowhere between the Councilmen to help. Ben briefed them on her condition.

Mary Joyce, Wade's wife, was a slip of a woman next to her massive husband. She was sharp, tough, and quick. She peeked under the dressing on LuAnna's hip. "Oh my blessing! I got a chain stitch that could close the Grand Canyon. This poor girl's gonna need it."

Redheaded Kimba Mosby, the Reverend's bride, feared God as she should, but God stepped gently around her, too. When provoked, everyone knew she caught like gas. Julie Nuttle was soft spoken, and resourceful. It was said she could feed an army out of a bare pantry with loaves, fishes, and hot goose pie. These island mothers gently whisked LuAnna into the saltbox.

Lorton Dyze turned to his tall confrere and said, "Wade. Ben says *Miss Dotsy*'s gearbox is shot."

Wade nodded. "Shot? Sounds nuked. Have her straight in no time."

As many hands helped Ben and Ellis out of *Miss Dotsy,* Wade jumped down into her cockpit with a big steel toolbox clamped under his arm.

Dyze said, "Let's get these men indoors, dry, and fed, before we send them back out again." He chuckled like he'd said something funny.

Inside, Mary Joyce brought Ben a change of clothes. She handed another set of clothes to Knocker Ellis. They were taken from his own home.

Mary said, "We took a liberty going to your place for these. Oh don't look at me like that. Everybody knows about your spare key under that conch shell in your back garden. I do hope you'll forgive us."

Ellis smiled. "It's all right, thanks. Just so you left my Hi-Fi and color TV."

Mary did not smile. She returned upstairs to LuAnna.

Ben and Ellis changed into dry clothes. Julie Nuttle already had duck soup warming on the stove. The Councilmen remained standing in their long black oilies as if they wore the robes of an ancient order. Judicial vestments signifying a forgotten code. Dripping water all over the place.

Ben waited. The storm outside made the parlor seem all the more quiet.

He said, "Quite the headcount here, gentlemen."

Lorton Dyze cleared his throat and said, "I asked you this morning: Who are you, Ben?"

Ben looked the old man dead in the eyes. "I'm Benjamin Fallon Blackshaw. Son of Ida-Beth Lilah Orne, of Smith Island, and Richard Willem Blackshaw, a man of Tangier. I'm born to this island. She's my home. I'll either die here, or die fighting for her wherever I am. Is that the pledge you wanted to hear, Lorton? Or is there some damn secret hand-shake I should know about? Maybe with a gob of spit? Or chicken blood?"

Dyze looked at his fellow Councilmen. Grinned small. "It's a start." He continued, "Let's get us all synchronated here. There's been some trouble. What can you tell us?"

Ellis obviously was not happy about this line of questioning, subtle as it was. Right now, it was not clear to him whether Chalk's open hostility, or a cozy chat with this mob of ofays was more dangerous.

Ben hedged. "Lorton, what trouble do you mean?"

Dyze got agitated. "That mess over to the Harrises'! That poor woman! Who knows where Hiram is? And here in your own house, your own dog beat down to death. That big flash out toward the No Point Light. We already got Ginger buried out back. Charlene'll be more complicated, of course. I know ye take my meaning in full. Now quit being so damn coy."

Ben said, "We have visitors here. They took LuAnna. We got her back and took the lighthouse down. Hiram's dead."

At this, the Councilmen swept off their sou'wester hats in slow dirge-time unison, uncovering bald heads and grey ones. Many pates were battles-carred like tough old stray dogs, but they were all bowed in grief.

Ben went on. "Ellis and I left the *Palestrina* there at No Point where they took her. If these bastards come around again, there's a fair chance they'll use her."

Dyze smiled approval at Ben, "I like that. Good idea leaving them with something big we'd recognize from a distance so they can't get all sneaky." Dyze spoke louder to the assembly. "Y'all heard the man. Everybody knows what the *Palestrina* looks like. Anyone aboard her is a bad'n. Shoot accordingly."

Ben said, "I left a man tied up at the Harrises'. He was party to what happened there."

Sam Nuttle smiled wickedly. "You mean a fellow with a busted-out leg, and a whole wad of duct tape on his head?"

Ben said, "That'd be him."

Nuttle shook his head. Clucked with mock sadness. "I can't confirm or deny I have a clue who you mean. If I did know, I'd say any man who was up to the Harris place ain't there n'mare. Nor could I say where he is at present, excepting he might or might not've mentioned going for a long swim. And in this flaw, too."

Ephraim Teach chimed in, "And if there was such a man, and supposing he went for that long swim, didn't he strap on his lucky engine block before he jumped over the side?"

Nuttle said, "I can't confirm nor deny it, Ephraim, though it's surely got a plausible ring."

Okay, Ben got it. Tug Parnell was dead. There were bloody hands all around, but this did nothing to assuage Ben's conscience.

He pushed for more answers. "So what's happening, Lorton? You must know. You brought me Pap's letter yourself this morning. He was coming back. Ellis knew, too."

A few disconcerted Councilmen shifted their weight and glanced at Knocker Ellis on hearing this news.

Ben went on, "As for me, I didn't have a clue about any of this until we found his boat sunk and Pap drowned sob-wet."

The Councilmen raised their sou'westers over their hearts again in honor of another fallen comrade.

Dyze took in the bad news, and said, "Your pappy was a fine man, Ben. I'm sorry."

This entire conversation was truly odd. Ben pressed, "You were in the loop too, Lorton, Weren't you." Not an inquiry. An accusation.

"Your father might have dropped me a line, yes. Said to keep my eyes peeled, but for what, he didn't say. Just to be ready. All of us. Don't take offense, Ben. Knowing old Dickie-Will, I'm sure he kept ye in the dark for your protection."

Ben felt anger rise. "I keep hearing that. I did the same with LuAnna. You see where that got her."

Dyze looked back and forth between Ben and Ellis. "That girl knows where she's from. She's no Miss Fairy Pants. Now, Ellis, what all did Dickie-Will say to ye?"

Ellis figured the truth would be safest, for the moment. "He wrote that he was coming home with something. Didn't say what, but he made me his partner in it if I could help. I said I'd do it. I owed him my life. I've been helping my friend Ben, since my friend Richard Blackshaw is dead."

"Did he come home with anything like he planned?" This from Art Bailey, the waterman golfer.

Ellis said, "I can neither confirm nor deny that, Art. Ask my new partner."

Ben got up from his chair, and reached into the hidden compartment at the back of the closet. He removed the gold bar. It was wrapped in a terry cloth towel stained from LuAnna's baking wild blueberry pies that summer. The men of the Council craned in for a better view.

Ben unswaddled the gold. The men muttered approval. There were a few rapacious growls, but Sonny Wright whooped with glee like a boy. The bullion was undeniably beautiful.

Ben said, "Gold. That's it. At a seventeen hundred dollars an ounce, it's worth six hundred ninety-three thousand dollars in a proper market."

Rapturous faces all around. Dyze stretched out his hands, and come-hithered with his knob-jointed fingers. Ben rested the bar in the old man's grasp. Dyze cooed like an old man holding his first squirming grandchild.

"How precious a thing." Dyze studied the cheerful minter's mark. "And lookee! It's smiling at me."

Ben said, "There's one problem you should know about. A big one. We don't have a lot of time to sort it out."

CHAPTER 33

CHALK FELT SURROUNDED by idiots, and beset by Senator Morgan's spies and plotters. That meant he needed more intel. With no warm bodies at hand to play with, he lobbed in a call to get a situation report from Farron MacDonald. MacDonald was still running the B-Team's operation. Maybe he still had Blackshaw's pilot on life-support after the Wilkes-Barre firefight. By now the man must have talked. Chalk dialed.

"*Redondo Surf Shop.*" MacDonald still sounded bushed after the shoot-out. Not so glad to see his boss's code name in the caller ID.

Chalk's satellite phone was fancy, advanced, but not perpetually hack-proof. Nothing was.

"Everything coming up roses in Wilkes-Barre?"

MacDonald said, "More like pushing up daisies. The pilot? He, like totally bailed. No connecting flight."

Blackshaw's pilot was dead of his wounds. Chalk was enraged. "Damn! Damn! Damn! When?"

"Not twenty minutes back. Super sorry. Did everything possible."

"I'm sure you did, Farron. Including shoot the son of a bitch full of holes in the first place. Did you get anything useful? An idea of Blackshaw's plan? The bastard's favorite color? Anything?"

MacDonald filled Chalk in. "So we pumped him full of adrenaline and epinephrine to wake him up one last time. I mean, the man got a sweet pharmaceutical-grade buzz at taxpayers' expense. Some real *Up in the Air Junior Birdman* shit! Know what I mean?"

Chalk lost all patience. "I didn't ask what you put into him. What did you get out?"

"That's the thing. He just babbled. Nothing really useful."

Chalk was slashing and burning his way through a decent swath of citizenry, and he was getting no useful information. He already had to deal with a conniving Senator who was losing her mind and might start blabbing about him any minute. Then the bloodbath in a Wilkes-Barre motel. It was all a tremendous liability and exposure for *Right Way Moving & Storage*. Clients breathing down his neck. Precious time wasted. Nothing shiny to show for it.

To be certain, Chalk asked, "You got *nothing*? What the fuck—Over."

"Zilch. Nada, compadre."

Chalk moved on. "How's by Duncan?"

MacDonald got a smirk in his voice. "Duncan *who*?"

At least MacDonald had done something right. Handled the problem of their injured squaddie with dispatch.

Despite acute frustration, Chalk rallied and issued marching orders. "Get back to the airport. You've got your multi-engine and type ratings. You fly that pilot's Casa to Frederick, Maryland. Keep outside the Washington Special Flight Rules Area. And keep your transponder off. No flight plan. Got me? Land there and hold. Nobody stands down. You get to Frederick, you and the boys sleep right on that damn plane. You piss in a bucket on that plane. You get hungry, you eat your own feces on that plane. Gobble-gobble. Wait for my orders. You copy that, troop?"

"Okay. But dude, look out the window. The hurricane system's covering the whole east coast. It's kinda below IMC minimums. Stormy and all."

A drenched and chilled Chalk shouted over the wind. "I missed that, Farron! What did you say? You want me to jot down your fucking suicide note?"

MacDonald replied quickly. "Don't sip on that Hate-orade, dude. Frederick, Maryland. Steer clear. Eat shit. Stand-by. Hela-wilco."

Chalk terminated the call. He quizzed Slagget. "That bunch in the inflatable. The clients. Where'd they put into the bay, do you think?"

Slagget considered. Yelled back, "Maybe western Maryland or Virginia? Would make for one long-ass ride across the bay in this weather. Wouldn't leave them much jizz for a fight, no matter how well-trained. Best answer: They put in from a bigger boat. Or from a landing on the Eastern Shore."

Chalk shook his head. "A mother ship? No. Takes too much time to reposition to their search area. On the upside, their appearance here shooting at anything is a damn strong commitment of resources. If it's the same bunch as Farron engaged in Wilkes-Barre, they could've driven down here since last night easy-peasy. And they got something out of that pilot. Not for nothing, they've got good faith in their intel. So I say Eastern Shore. A public landing. A boat ramp. That's what I'd do. A truck and a stolen boat trailer would be most riki-tik."

Slagget stuffed another patch of poncho in a bullet hole in the skiff's bottom. It immediately popped loose on a small geyser of water. "Damn! You think Dick Blackshaw's around here, too?"

Chalk shook his head. "I hate Blackshaw. You have to respect the snow job he put over on us. Patiently and lovingly crafted. And so far, pretty damn well-executed. I want that fucker dead."

Slagget said, "Let's not get sidetracked. Dick Blackshaw's a red herring. A weasely schmuck. No factor in the recovery effort."

Chalk said, "Bullshit. You have no idea. He put this in motion. I've got a file that says he was a missed target from a sanction fifteen years back. Dick's not some mook who found a bunch of gold in his lap and wandered off with it. He came looking for us, for paybacks against his very own government, the traitorous little shit. I hate a cliché as much as anyone, but Blackshaw's on a mission."

Slagget stuffed another patch into yet another bullet hole. "What got him so pissed?"

Chalk kept a sharp eye for the black inflatable. He said, "Let you in on a secret. Our boy Dick escaped the sanction on him, but I have a feeling someone he cared about got tagged. I have a good idea where it happened. Work with me; I'm extrapolating here. So far, his son is no lightweight, either. So don't let them fool you, Bill."

Slagget kept his mouth shut.

Chalk said, "Since we're about to sink, let's cruise closer along the Eastern Shore here. See if we can't find where the clients put in. And if we do run into them, laddy-buck, try not to shoot their damn boat full of holes. We won't get back to the lighthouse without it."

Chalk decided not to call The Kid for fear of blowing his operator's cover with a poorly timed ringtone. Chalk could rely on The Kid to touch base with news as soon as he could, he was such a bloody kiss-up.

CHAPTER 34

LORTON DYZE, THE true picaroon, shifted from contemplation of the gold bar's beauty to the task of realizing its value. Jubilant only moments before, he seemed deflated now. "I know the problem you mean, Ben. We won't get but dimes on the dollar when we try to sell it. Not through the folks we know."

Ben said, "Not exactly the issue I meant by a long shot, but LuAnna had a thought about the selling. About how to get full market value, and then some."

Knocker Ellis said, "We really don't have time for this. Shouldn't we talk about that last case?"

Sonny Wright said, "Just hold on a minute, Ellis. Ben, that's an idear I'd like to hear."

Ben knew Ellis was right. Jawing here with these men burned precious daylight, such as it was. And the twentieth case was still ticking, even though it did not make a sound. Ben had chosen to rescue LuAnna, and would never regret that. He wondered if he had saved her from Chalk only to kill her along with everyone and everything else because he had forgotten the greater good and not defused the bomb first. Did he really have a handle on how to stop it from going off? He might be rationalizing his own selfishness again. Despite the doubt, Ben sensed there was no way he and Ellis would get out of the room alive unless he proved their worth on this mission here and now.

Ben said, "Anybody remember that guy out of New York? At the Sunfest in Ocean City a few years ago. A bond trader. Noel Swerdlow. I have his card somewhere. Anyway, he thought he had an eye for art. I'm not hypocriting here, and Swerdlow might have been crazy, but he said he liked that bronze widgeon I cast up. Again, no bragging, but that bird took a blue ribbon. And Swerdlow took the bird home, cash money. Sam?"

Sam Nuttle said, "Course I remember that bird. I helped you pour her. That bronze prop we melted down didn't quite fill the mold. Didn't we throw in a dozen nails and some bolts to fatten her up?"

Ben smiled. "That we did, but don't tell Swerdlow. I never gave it a second thought, but you know what he said? He thought pieces like it would catch on in a Soho gallery if I moved up there and made a few more. If I made different birds, too. Not like that welded-up stuff in the yard. Other castings based on my carvings. So when LuAnna saw that gold with the grin this morning, the first thing she suggested was casting new pieces, but not pouring bronze."

Ephraim Teach picked up the ball and ran. "Pouring gold instead."

Sam Nuttle did a mental end-zone jig. "I gotcha. There's the value of a Troy ounce of gold which ain't too shabby. But a Blackshaw ounce, that's something else again."

"With any luck," said Ben. "That way we get at least the full value of the material, plus whatever money the artwork adds. It's a backwards way of looking at the marketing. And any such sculpture would be a gaudy thing, but I'd do my best on it. The whole thing would take a while, though."

Sonny Wright shook his head. "You'd have control over the gold the whole time. Don't know, but it sounds fishy."

Ephraim Teach scowled. "Shut up, Sonny, afore I shut you up. You doubt Ben? After all him and Dickie-Will's done by us? And Ellis, too."

Ben shrugged. "Why would I rip you off, Sonny? I never had to mention the gold in the first place. If it makes you feel better, I'll work it a little at a time. Doesn't matter to me."

Considering Ben's logic, Sonny relaxed.

While Dyze had never been a vocal detractor of Ben's eccentric artistry, the old man had often radiated silent hints of nominy whenever Ben was around. Suddenly the assembled group got a fresh view of Dyze, the Ben Blackshaw booster. He said, "Lordy go to fire, Ben, we all been wondering why ye drudge so hard on the water when ye got such a gift, but there's no telling ye nothing. You're your pappy's rock-headed boy all right. And that LuAnna don't have a headpiece on her at all."

Though not as flashy as pom-poms, hot pants and a halter top, from Dyze this counted as real encouragement in the sideways Smith Island syntax.

Art Bailey agreed. "It's an idear. We could make a fair jag of it."

Dyze said, "Ye really want to live in New York City?"

Ben smiled. "Oh *hell* no. But we'd have to lay low someplace after all this. Might as well be near the gallery as not. To mind the shop, so to speak. LuAnna and I would manage for the time it takes us to do the work. Manhattan's just an island. And we know our way around islands, doncha know."

Sam Nuttle said, "Hang on. This dog don't hunt. About these fonny boys what kilt Hiram, and Charlene, and Ginger, what was the best damn gunning dog around. They come all this way, gone to all this trouble for six hunnerd thousand? It's nothing to sneeze at, but ..."

Ellis said, "Ben, I don't think these gentlemen understand the full extent of the problem."

All eyes turned to Ben for enlightenment. "I'm on it, Ellis. Sam's right. Chalk didn't come here for a bar of gold."

Dyze smiled, scenting the truth. "Then why's he here? What's he really after?"

A voice from the stairwell. "I hope your pace-maker's up to taking this kind of news, Lorton."

It was LuAnna dressed in a spare change of clothes she kept at Ben's. Baggy khakis, and a tent-like flannel shirt. A vision in L.L. Bean. She stood at the bottom of the stair. Her forehead was bandaged. Eyes blacked, she looked Dachau gaunt with a ghostly pallor lurking just below her tan. She leaned heavily against the wall. Mary Joyce and Kimba Mosby stood close behind their beloved survivor in case she fainted. LuAnna looked at Ellis, who lowered his eyes, then at Ben. He nodded she might as well get on with it. She caught Ben's look and, like Ellis, realized that these neighbors could be as dangerous as outsiders when it came to staggering plunder.

She spoke cautiously, not yet revealing all the facts 'til she better understood the mood of the crowd. "Ben says that happy little bar was in a box. And in that box, there weren't eleven more bars just like it."

The grin stamped in the gold was now mirrored in all the faces of the Councilmen.

CHAPTER 35

CHALK WAS GLAD to have made it to land alive. The skiff was a leaking nightmare, but his hunch was paying off. He and Slagget waited, and watched, as the black inflatable skimmed across a heaving Tangier Sound to the secluded boat landing on the Eastern Shore. The crew climbed out and stood in the chilly water, positioning the bucking inflatable to winch onto the trailer behind a matte black Chevy Suburban.

At a signal from Chalk, Slagget opened fire. A staccato buzzing sawed from behind the inflatable's team, jittering the tall weeds by the landing ramp's edge. A man pitched forward across the boat, bounced off the sponson, flopped into the water and sank.

The buzzing ripped forth again. Another man's chest bloomed red. He went down. Thrashed weakly, stirring up mud. The inflatable's captain dived for the water.

"Down!" The captain's voice was shrill, shaking. "Fan out! Take cover!"

The rest of the team dived into the cold water like kids at the end of Adult Swim. Their eyes scanned wildly for the invisible enemy. They drew pistols. The leader fired a few rounds blind into the storm.

Chalk waited while the intruders lay in the water, letting the cold soften them up for what he had in mind. One man was still on dry land, stretched behind the Suburban's left rear tire with a grazed leg. A corpse from the first volley floated up out of the water next to the leader who grabbed it and pulled it close as a shield. The body had absorbed at least one round already. Why not a few more for the cause?

Interesting, thought Chalk. *Resourceful.* He spoke up. "This is going to sound corny as hell but no shit, we've got you all surrounded. You know the drill. Throw down your weapons. Drop them in the water right now. It doesn't have to get any worse than it already is."

One of the intruders, momentarily torn between homicide and a martyr's suicide, yelled, "Allahu-Akbar!" He fired two rounds into the weeds across the landing. Behind him, Slagget's shotgun barked. A hole the size of a Ruby Red opened in the intruder's back. The man rolled, lay still.

Chalk shouted, "I hope you cocksuckers habla the Inglés! *Surrounded* means you should damn well do what I say. Capisch? Anybody!"

The leader spoke softly, "Who are you?"

Chalk smiled. "A broad!" Then louder, "Baby, my name's Legion, for we are many. But you can call me Maynard. Now drop them! And I'm not talking about your knickers. At least not yet."

The woman hunkering in the cold water tried to buy time. "How do I know you won't kill us all?"

Chalk spoke again. "You don't know, sugar-tit. I could be lying. I do it all the time. For damn sure the four of you will croak from the cold there in the water if you don't drop your goddamn weapons, raise your hands, and stand up! Don't get me wrong. I can wait. Ammo's expensive. I'm already looking at serious cost overruns on this gig. Got to trim where I can. Up to you."

The woman scanned around her. Her squad-mates waited for some kind of orders, eyes darting with terror. One of her men crouched low in the water near a floating body. The dying soldier's eyes were half-open, like a man half asleep, three-quarters stoned, or ninety-nine percent status-asparagus. Chalk watched her appraise her situation, calculate her team's readiness for more fight, and the dawning realization her men were useless and helpless.

Chalk called out, "What's it going to be, sister? I got a Thermos full of black coffee here. Lot's of sugar in it, and none of that damn cheese they go for in these parts, I swear. We all want the same thing. We should talk this through. Get together. Ideate. Synergize!"

The woman shivered, said, "I can hear you well enough."

Chalk spoke again. "You got brass ones, baby, I'll give you that. What's your name?"

After a moment, "Tahereh."

Chalk said, "Tahereh. A lovely name. Goes with your very sexy voice. Are you very sexy?"

Chalk enjoyed watching the woman blush hot even as she froze to death. He went on. "Here's how I see things shaping up, Tahereh. And I'd rather not be shouting our business back and forth in public like this, but that's life I guess. Anyhoo, there's the matter of some gold."

Tahereh said, "What gold?"

Chalk paused for a moment, then spoke again. "Sorry, Tahereh. Just pouring a cup of coffee. Damn tasty if I do say so. Sweet! Sure you won't have some? It's dee-licious."

Tahereh said nothing. Her lips were turning blue. Her teeth chattered, and no amount of clenching would stop it. She said, "What gold, Maynard? What are you talking about?"

Chalk said, "Look, let's not play stupid, okay hon? You know what gold. And you know about the device for that matter. I'm guessing that's what you were buying when my delivery boy went on walkabout. Am I right, or am I right?"

She said, "Perhaps."

Chalk said, "I'll take perhaps. What I propose is we work together. We could use your manpower, no offense. We get the gold. You can have the device like you wanted. We'll go on our merry way and finalize the payment for it. This way we don't run into each other coming and going. An amicable and productive truce. Mutually beneficial in a symbiotic way we can all live with." Chalk wanted to shoot the rest of Tahereh's men to help make his case, but there would be time for that. After he made use of their backs.

Tahereh began, "How do I know …?"

Chalk interrupted. "You *don't* know! Tahereh, dammit, we went over that. The cold's getting to your brain. You're slowing down. God knows you're already too twitterpated to shoot your way out of this. You've heard the old saying: Slaughter, slaughter everywhere, and not a stop to think.

Take a moment. Consider your position. I'm telling you it's a pretty good deal. I could have killed you a long time ago."

A noise-suppressed gunshot bupped from the weeds behind Tahereh's team. The man who lay outstretched on dry land clutched the side of his head as a bullet clanged against the metal trailer. Blood coated his fingers.

Chalk said, "See what I mean? Now let's cut the bullshit. This really isn't a negotiation, sweet-cheeks. It's dictation, with me being the afore-mentioned dick. Savvy?"

The recently injured guy pulled his hand away from his head. His left ear was bleeding from a scarlet half-moon punched out of the lobe. He glared at Tahereh in silent accusation, injured pride etched on his face as clear as the notch in his ear. She did the only thing she could. She looked at her three remaining men and nodded.

She yelled, "We're coming out. Don't shoot!"

Chalk yelled back, "That's my girl! Nice and slow now. Drop the hoglegs in the water. Keep your hands up where I can see them."

They did as Chalk instructed. With their guns lying in the shallows at their feet, they slowly stood up. Muddy, and shivering. Sopping miserable, they held their hands out harmless, empty, streaming water at their sides.

CHAPTER 36

DYZE WAS ELATED at LuAnna's news. He practically bubbled. "A dirty dozen bars like this? Swagger die, that's nigh on eight million and some. Now I get it. No disrespect to Hiram or Charlene, but that's worth a killing or two!"

Dyze stopped suddenly, looking hard at LuAnna. He was remembering her badge and all it stood for.

Ben needed to shift the cross-hairs off her as quickly as possible. "LuAnna has an announcement."

As the Councilmen looked at her, she demurred. Ben could tell she was not sure which piece of news from the last twenty-four hours he meant her to share. The engagement? Their baby on the way? "You go ahead, Ben. Tell them."

Ben said, "You should all know that LuAnna has resigned from the Natural Resources Police, effective immediately. A note or a phone call soon will make it official. Meantime, you all are on notice: LuAnna Bonnie Bryce is no longer a corporal on the payroll of the Natural Resources Police. She's thrown in with us, free and clear and all the way. End of story. Anyone who has doubts can step outside with me right now for clarification."

With his newfound sense of Smith Island's bloody history, Ben knew he had probably just saved LuAnna's life for the second time in as many hours. Now she should be resting. Why was she mixing with this crew after the beat-down she'd suffered from Chalk's mob?

Lorton Dyze angled a dead-eyed smile on LuAnna. "Welcome home Honey Girl. Glad ye come to your senses. Now, how about a little coffee for us old farts to take the chill off?"

LuAnna smiled, limped into the kitchen. Mary and Kimba followed her to help. Ben bit back the urge to suggest bed was a better place for her than slinging joe for this mob. He would never embarrass her like that.

Dyze studied Ben and Ellis. "Now we come to the interesting part. How do you boys figure the split?"

Ben was quick to address this. "Half of everything belongs to Knocker Ellis Hogan. That's our deal. I'll stand by it. I gave my word."

Unhappy eyes bored into Ellis. There was a rumble of awkward throat clearing.

Dyze said slowly. "That so? All right. I suppose we can cross that bridge when we come to it."

Ben shot back, "No, Lorton. We're standing in the middle of the bridge right now. Any more conversation about the split, and you're burning that bridge. None of you knows where the gold is. And you damn well don't have a clue how to disarm the bomb."

Reverend Mosby spoke up for the first time. "Easy there, gentlemen. If Ben's given his word to Ellis, then we'll abide as if we gave it ourselves. It's our way. What in God's name do you mean about a bomb?"

Ben said, "The way it looks to me, Pap interrupted some kind of sale. Intercepted the government cheese as well as the food stamps."

The Council elders smiled and nodded at one another; *that's our boy Dickie-Will.*

Ben went on. "Gentlemen, this bomb is the real thing. Not a toy. Not dynamite wired up to a battery and an alarm clock. I'm pretty sure it's a dirty. We're talking about radiation. It's got a timer, and the timer's counting down right now to detonation when it will probably kill us all in—" Ben glanced at his dive watch. "Six hours, seventeen minutes. And yes, the bomb is sitting right on top of the gold at this very moment. Now friends, I do believe Reverend Mosby's assurances, but he doesn't speak for every one of you. Your word, gentlemen. I want your word you'll honor my promise on the split with Ellis whether I'm alive or dead."

The bomb Ben once feared was now a bargaining chip. Ellis looked stunned, wondering if this show of loyalty would protect him, or put the kiss of death on him.

LuAnna yelled from the kitchen, lapsing for a moment into the patois of her island home, "Ben, I know ye want your coffee black. Lorton Dyze, ye oughtn't take cheese, nor heavy cream n'mare, not with that bum ticker o' yar'n. Skim's more like it."

Dyze sang back, "Honey Girl, ye put that chalk water in my cup, and you'll see what happens. I ain't so old, and ye ain't so tall I can't still give ye a whuppin'. Especially with the head start them fonny boys dealt ye."

Looking around, Ben understood. The sharp-eared LuAnna had broken the tension in the room without even being present. Ben so loved that woman. He understood why she was downstairs now. As best she was able, she was backing his play.

Ben looked at each of the Council members. They all nodded, mumbled assent. It was a grudging bond they made, but it was ironclad.

Then Dyze said, "Now that we're all settled, what are ye doing with your share of it, Ben Blackshaw?"

"What's in those boxes isn't *my* share. I believe it was Pap's gift to these islands. To all of us."

No one spoke for a moment.

Reverend Mosby said, "This time around I do speak for one and all when I say that's a fine sentiment, Ben. The finest. Your pappy would be proud."

"Thank ye kindly, Ben. That's most honorable." Eyeing Ellis, Dyze needled. "Wish everybody was so community-minded. But things are what they are, and we shall be grateful for the bounty of the Lord. Ain't that right, Reverend? Be it known I personally will skull-fuck the family, livestock, and household pets of any man who raises a hand against our neighbor Knocker Ellis. And if for some tragic reason Ellis don't make it through the troubles before us, his entire share inures unto his family's use and no one else's. That's how we done it before. That's how we'll do it now."

Ellis put up a wan smile. "Thanks loads Lorton, but I don't have any family."

Dyze grinned like a gargoyle. "Oh yes ye do, Knocker Ellis. You're a-lookin' at 'em."

CHAPTER 37

CHALK FELT TAHEREH would comply in order to survive, but he still had to break her. The cold water there at the landing had only begun the process.

He said, "Now everybody take it slow, and walk up onto dry land. Everybody move to the left of the truck. Easy now. That ramp's slippery with the mud. Hold it there!"

Tahereh's team, what was left of it, stopped ankle deep in the water.

Chalk watched Tahereh scrutinize the weeds for his hiding place. He said, "Get a couple of your boys to haul those bodies out of the water up on the bank. We'll have to deal with them in a bit, once we've had our chat. And we still have you covered, so don't try pulling any back-up guns. Yours, or off those stiffs either. Savvy?"

Tahereh nodded and glared at her man with the notched ear. Chalk did not shoot him. The leg wound was only skin deep, so he was still useful. The two other men grabbed the bodies and dragged them onto the bank.

"Okay," said Chalk. "Now come on over, sweetheart, and have a cup of java. And for gosh sakes, don't take it so hard. After all, surrender just means you've joined the winning side!"

Chalk showed himself for the first time. He imagined what Tahereh saw, a man in his sixties, thinning gray hair, a slight paunch, and a face with a scar at the hairline like the relic of an aborted scalping. Her eyes stopped on his left arm just below the shoulder. The minx smiled, noting he had been winged.

Slagget rose from the weeds, carrying his HK G-36C. He also had a custom stainless Mossberg Mariner shotgun, with a folding stock and pistol grip, on a sling over his shoulder.

Chalk chuckled watching Tahereh look around for the rest of the attackers. And there it was. The realization that she and her entire team had been bested by only two men. *Beautiful. Wish I had that on camera.* Perhaps there was more to the psychological side of torture than he had thought possible. He'd never gone up against a female soldier in any sense of the phrase. This would be interesting.

Chalk told Slagget, "Pat them down. And no funny business, Tahereh. You've come a long way baby, but I'm pissed as all hell to be here so I'll still kill you if you make me. Count on it."

Slagget frisked them professionally. Collected two knives from Tahereh. One in a wrist sheath. Another taped up-side-down against her spine. Chalk was pleased that Slagget did not linger over her breasts, crotch, or buttocks. Chalk wanted all of her to himself, his rightful property as boss. Slagget finished frisking Tahereh's remaining squaddies. Eight more weapons, some sharp, some loud.

Chalk instructed, "Take a pew, dearie." He gestured toward a wobbly old picnic table in the winter-brown grass by the landing's pavement. They sat. Chalk pulled his pistol. He told Slagget, "First aid kit, if you wouldn't mind, Bill."

Slagget jogged fifty paces south to where they'd drawn Hiram's skiff into a drainage ditch for cover. He grabbed the kit and hurried back.

Tahereh fixed him with her almondine eyes. "Why kill my men if you want to work with us, Mr. Maynard?"

"Why knock down the Twin Towers just because Euro Disney sucks? See? Life's a mystery, wrapped in an enigma, stuffed in a chalupa. And Maynard's my first name, baby. It's Maynard Pilchard Chalk. Remember it. If you must know, we had to drop a few of your boys to keep things manageable. They were the convincers. To make sure that when I talked, you'd listen."

Chalk straddled the picnic table's bench facing her. Slagget kept them covered with his Heckler und Koch.

Ever the gentleman, Chalk asked Tahereh, "Would you kindly do the honors while I lay things out for you?" With some difficulty, he poured another cup of hot coffee.

Tahereh opened the first aid kit. Chalk put his hand over hers as she reached for a sharp-edged pair of medical shears to cut off the sleeves of his jacket and shirt. She looked into his pale green cobra's eyes. He shook his head. Clacked his yellow teeth together twice. With her men lying dead around her, Tahereh capitulated. Did as ordered. She bit into the bloody sleeve of the man responsible for her losses and failures. Chalk was digging this bright spot in an otherwise lousy day.

With the entrance and exit holes in the coat slightly extended by her bite, she tore the sleeve off the rest of the way. She did the same with the shirt sleeve below.

Chalk fixated on her bloodstained lips, like she was a beautiful canni-bal princess. Enormous brown eyes with thick lashes. Her ballistic vest swelled forward with natural promise. He seized a fistful of her thick black hair and drew her to him. It was not a kiss. He hungrily consumed the lower portion of her face, mauling her lips, her tongue. She shivered in his hands. Revulsion? At that moment he did not care.

One of Tahereh's men growled as the kiss endured. Slagget reminded him not to move with a small shift of his gun. Tahereh was destroyed, completely in Chalk's thrall. He wondered if any woman had ever hated him so much.

He released her, let her pull away from him. She gasped for air. He reveled in her rage, bewilderment, and the injury to her pride, so evident in her flushed cheeks and wide eyes. He said, "Get to it, chica."

She wiped her mouth, wrenching her focus back to business. She reached for a single-dose styrette of morphine.

Chalk said, "That won't be necessary."

She pulled a bottle of mercurochrome from the kit. Opened it. Chalk could see she was tempted to dash it in his eyes. She remembered the vigi-lant Slagget and his gun, poured a small amount of the liquid over her fin-gers to clean them.

Chalk resumed his pitch, "So here it is, sweets. We're all auslanders here. Have you met the locals yet? They're lean, religious, mean, freakishly tough and persistent as hell. You know the kind. You probably are the kind, except for the scrawny part. Anyway, they're not to be taken lightly. Now, you and I, we want the same thing. Better put, we want different things that are in the same place. You with me?"

In reply, Tahereh emptied the rest of the bottle of mercurochrome into his wounds. Chalk grimaced only a little as the liquid burned his raw, pierced flesh.

He continued. "I'll take that as a yes. Now be reasonable. You already spent the gold for the device. So, you're not ever getting the gold back. My reputation, and my life depend on making up for the bullshit my man got us all into with his heist. Trust me. When I see him, he's a goner."

Tahereh said, "Richard Blackshaw?"

Chalk raised his eyebrows. "So he dropped his alias with the pilot. Wow. I'm surprised. That was phenomenally stupid. Did you know he spent a couple years setting himself up as a rogue sleeper? Must have thought he was home free when he got on that plane. Regardless, kudos to you for getting to the aviator before we did. Nice work on him. He was pretty shot up when we got him off you. No matter. Here we all are."

Tahereh pulled out a fat rolled elastic bandage used for sprains from the kit. She told Chalk, "Lift your arm." He did. She inserted the flesh-toned roll into his armpit. "Lower it now, and clamp it firmly against your side."

The wounds were too high on his arm for her to manually compress the brachial artery. She could not slow the blood flow with one hand and dress the wounds at the same time. The rolled bandage would hold some pressure on the pulsing blood vessel while she worked on him. She was not gentle packing the entrance wound with QuikClot gauze.

Chalk's eyes watered as the QuikClot heated up as it merged with his blood. He asked, "How'd you get a line on that pilot, anyway? In the first place, I mean."

"I could say something to make myself appear clever, but given the present circumstances, we know that's not the case. The truth is, we received an anonymous tip."

Lily Morgan! That bitch of a whore! He'd kill her, but first he'd find out if Dick Blackshaw had approached her with this sting two years ago, or if she somehow recruited and propositioned him. "Blackshaw is so fucking dead."

Tahereh said, "I'm not interested in revenge on your courier. He betrayed you. He's your problem. You're offering us the device, and you take the gold. Is that right?"

Though another idea was wriggling into the twilight from a dank snake hole in his mind, Chalk said, "That is the sum and substance of my proposal. For the duration, we work together. Common goals and the common good. You help us move the gold, and we're cool. Then you can disappear. Go irradiate any and all parts of the countryside to your heart's content. We'll settle up with the folks who sold the whiz-bang to you, just like the brokers we are. Done and done."

Tahereh had to know. "How did you find us?"

"Didn't. One of my men tracked Blackshaw's kid to Deep Banks Island. We simply stumbled over you all. Not too many crabbers out on the water at oh-dark-sparrowfart sitting in a Zodiac using night vision goggles. And then you started shooting, you sassy vixen. Plugged one of my boys. We figured you'd launched from somewhere close to the action, and there's a finite number of landings. The Suburban with the empty boat trailer was a dead giveaway. Now, have you seen Blackshaw, or anything else interesting?"

Tahereh dressed the exit wound, which was more ragged than the entry. The round had tumbled or deformed in its brief transit through his arm. It needed more QuikClot gauze to staunch the bleeding. There was gross muscle damage, if not permanent nerve injury.

She said, "There was a younger white man, and a black man in a boat called *Miss Dotsy.* Towing a small boat. A skiff. They left Deep Banks Island not long before we first—met you."

Chalk glanced at Slagget with a wan smile. "That's Blackshaw's kid, Ben. We've got his girlfriend on ice. She's Natural Resources Police. Not much more than a park ranger with a slingshot. Nothing to worry about. In fact, I think she'll be good leverage."

Tahereh wrapped a bandage around Chalk's upper arm, securing both dressings in place. She said, "So you don't know where this boy's father is? Have you seen him at all?"

Chalk smiled broadly. "You do want a piece of that bastard, don't you. Bad as I do. That's good. I like your spirit."

She said, "On the contrary, I only want to know where he is. Richard Blackshaw has gone to a great deal of trouble for this theft. He could be trouble again. He won't give up. I wouldn't. So where is he? He's a wild card until we know."

Chalk said, "I expect he'll turn up close by. Don't think I'm not looking forward to it."

He pulled out his sat-phone and dialed Dar Gavin's mobile at the lighthouse. The line burred and burred. No answer. Radio silence from Gavin, Parnell, and The Kid. What the hell was going on? He hoped it was interference from the weather, but he sure as hell wasn't counting on it.

CHAPTER 38

LUANNA BROUGHT DYZE and Ben their coffee. A slight stagger told Ben her energies were starting to fade after the first hours of freedom. The strength she had summoned here just to stay vertical shamed and inspired him. Kimba Mosby emerged with more mugs on a tray. After years of brewing pot after pot for this august body of rogues, Kimba knew how each man preferred his cup; particularly who took a snort of hooch along with.

Dyze sipped, grinned. He said to Ben, "Honey Boy, I couldn't help but notice before ye said, 'those boxes'. Which was it? Just the one box, all for-lornsome? Or was there another? Ye can tell your old Uncle Lorton."

The old man was still sharp as a razor. Ben smiled, savored the coffee and his news. "There wasn't just the one box."

Sam Nuttle twitched. "You're giving me the epizootics! Well go on then! What're we looking at here, Ben? Two boxes? By God, maybe three?"

Ben nodded at Ellis, who paused for effect. "Nineteen boxes."

Everyone's intake of breath sounded like Leviathan's lungs filling for a transcontinental roar. All that followed was silence. All minds were turned inward, multiplying.

Ellis said. "Don't blow a fuse boys. That's one hundred fifty-four million dollars, give or take."

Dyze and the Council remained mute. Absolutely struck dumb.

Ellis smiled. "Divided by two, that is. According to our deal, all y'all's share is a respectable seventy-seven million. Remember that's market rate. Before Ben sets his hand to the stuff and wows 'em in Soho."

Dyze's hearing aid whistled as he tried to adjust it. He barked, "What was that?"

"Have mercy," Reverend Mosby whispered.

Ephraim Teach said, "Seventy-seven million, Lorton." Teach nodded at Knocker Ellis. "After taxes."

Sonny Wright said, "I don't suppose we could leave them Tangiermen out of the picture could we? They's Virginians, after all."

They all looked to Dyze. He was still Smith Island's ambassador to its nefarious past. Once he got his hearing aid under control he simply sat there, musing. No one interrupted.

When he did speak up, his first-things-first way of thinking was clear. "Virginny or no, Tangier is cut in like the old days. And Ellis gets what's due him. He'll earn every red cent. Don't forget, we still got them fonny boys to reckon with. And the bomb." Dyze pondered further, and quietly gazed up toward the Firmament.

Reverend Mosby encouraged him. "Good for you, Lorton. Calling on the Lord for help in this trying business."

Mosby got no response. Dyze, still looking upwards, seemed to have better luck. He keenly scrutinized Heaven. Then Dyze saw what he was looking for. That's when Ben realized the old man was not looking to Paradise. He was studying the ceiling.

Dyze used his cane to lever himself to his feet. The Council members parted like wake before a deadrise bow as he hitch-stepped underneath the ceiling's centermost beam. He seemed to be looking hard for something particular. Then Dyze steadied himself with a hand on Ben's shoulder. He jabbed the end of his cane at a dark oval knot in the old timber. They all heard a click. What happened next was nothing short of amazing.

The end of the big oak ceiling beam closest to the front door started descending slowly toward the floor. The other end was anchored by an invisible hinge in the ceiling. As the beam came down, there was the muffled sound of something big knocking inside the wall, like the counterweight of an old window sash, but much heavier. Finally, the free end of the beam settled on the floor with a gentle thump. Ben observed that the beam was hollow, but hollow did not mean empty.

Ben had never given this old house timber a second thought. Until this moment he had no idea what it held. The ten-inch-wide slot was lined with layers of old mattress ticking now rotted to shreds. While it lasted, the ticking had protected the biggest brute of a headache gun Ben had ever seen outside a museum.

Some would call it a punt gun. A steroidal flintlock. The barrel, welded up from sections of telescoped pipe, stretched nine feet. Seven inches around at the lock. Its fat stock was old polished curly maple. Its trigger was the size of a grizzly claw. Its hammer could drive a railroad spike; this gun kicked like a Brahma bull.

This massive blunderbuss, and many others like it, were tools of the trade for market gunners and poachers a hundred years ago. Such artillery threw shot or scrap metal by the pound. A man could mohawk fifty ducks out of the air at once. Then, tireless Chesapeake Bay Retrievers like the slaughtered Ginger, always more partner than pet, would swim out into the icy water with their webbed toes and thick oiled-wire pelts, and gather in the fallen fowl. Ducks and geese would fill barrels bound for restaurants from Baltimore to New York City. The birds were once a cash crop on the wing.

That gun was part of why the onetime Corporal LuAnna Bryce got her job. Such monstrous fowling pieces in the hands of these Island men had been all too efficient in thinning the flocks. This way of hunting started back when autumn skies went black with migrating birds. Any thunder rolling across the water in those days might have been a real storm or gunfire. In later years, the rumble might have been a munitions test at the nearby Aberdeen Proving Grounds, or hunters at work.

Ben never knew such a gun was hidden just overhead in his own home. Dyze gazed at the personal howitzer. Bent, and caressed it fondly.

He made the introductions. "Friends, meet *Barking Betty*. She's old Tully Wessel's' market gun. His people had this place long before your family, Ben. When the game wardens come a-confiscating these pieces, Tully hid the old gal good. There's a couple-two-three others like her scattered round this island yet. Swagger die, boys, doncha know she'll bark again good and loud."

CHAPTER 39

BEN'S PLAN WAS taking shape, but the disastrous consequences of failure prompted him to make one further crucial step. This meeting with the Council was bringing the full enormity of the risk down heavily upon him. He stepped into the stairwell and climbed it half-way, sitting on a step with a small semblance of privacy. He limbered up The Kid's sat-phone, and dialed a number he knew by heart.

It rang only twice on the other end before Michael Craig picked up. "What." Ben pictured Craig trying to clamp the phone between his ear and shoulder, a task made more difficult by several fused vertebrae in his neck. Craig was a giant of a man who loathed direct human contact. His size helped him avoid most conflicts. His charm helped with idiots who would attack him to prove themselves. When these failed, a prodigious strength, augmented by rage, settled matters quickly enough. But these encounters throughout his youth left him wishing for a quieter existence, which over time he had built for himself in a comfortable cabin in Vermont, far from the world.

Craig amply sustained his solitude with Pemstar, his very discreet consulting business. With proprietary and public-use software, Craig, assisted disaster relief coordinators and incident commanders handling emergency responses to storms, floods, wildfires, earthquakes, terrorist incidents, biohazards, chemical spills and salvage operations. He even provided vital sit-reps to security clients when solar flares threatened sensitive communication links in low-profile, high-stakes covert operations.

Craig also modeled and projected the effect of weather on war games as well as actual campaigns and large scale battle plans for the militaries of several governments, not all of which were recognized by the United Nations. His refusal to leave the private sector vexed generals and politicians alike around the world. Sometimes he even received calls from the personal assistants of savvy celebrities trying to plan outdoor birthday parties, weddings and other benign events. Once, a former First Lady had called to ask about the effects of certain planetary alignments on the introduction of important legislation by her husband. That's where Craig drew the line.

Craig's fees would damage the economy of a small country, but his work was so accurate that the calls poured often and from everywhere. Ben knew Crag from a job in Iraq involving a sniper mission, a sandstorm, and a smoke-belching oil rig fire. The target had gone down in the middle of an open town square, and Ben had safely exfiltrated the area along a path suggested by Craig, disappearing like a wraith into the storm and haze.

Ben asked, "You know who this is?"

Craig said, "If you're an ex-girlfriend calling to tell me you're a dude now—because twice in one month would really hurt my feelings—"

Ben smiled. "No. This is worse. You placed me yet?"

"You don't want me to say your name because you're not a hundred percent sure the line's tapped, encrypted, or both, but yeah, I know you."

Ben asked, "Can you run a scenario?"

Craig was in such demand that he always sounded on the verge of complete exhaustion. "It's what I live for."

"Say there's this storm around where I live."

Ben heard tapping on a keyboard. Craig said, "Wow. In this scenario, hypothetically, you'd be in deep shit."

"There's a device involved."

Michael Craig was quiet for a time before speaking. "Like a food processor?"

Ben said, "Okay. Sure. But it's got a timer. I think I can manage it, but the processor is going to—process."

"Definitely?"

Ben said, "No, not definitely. But in a hypothetical way that's pretty concrete."

"Oh dear God."

Ben affirmed, "Something like that. I need to know the absolute best time, after dark today, for this to happen. To keep the food from going all over the place." Ben rattled off coordinates, and talked for almost a minute about what he knew about the dirty bomb, wasting most of that time trying to cloak his subject in terms that seemed more appropriate to a cooking show.

There was another long pause while Craig input the data into his software. Then he began a disquisition about the weather, the nature of a hurricane, upper atmosphere steering currents and other factors that could ruin a picnic. He stated a time that night that was all too near for Ben's comfort when he checked his watch. Craig wrapped up saying, "The thing you need to look out for is the chimney. When you're cooking. The flue I mean. When the downdrafts come. The opposite of what you usually have in the stovepipe. Do you *see* what I mean? In the middle of it all?"

Ben knew what Craig meant. "Thanks."

"Can't you put the lid on this thing? Hypothetically? Because if you time this wrong—"

"I'm listening," Ben said.

Mike Craig sounded more tired than ever. "Forget it. If you time this wrong, it won't matter much, will it?"

Ben broke off the call. Ten minutes later, he was back on the roiling Chesapeake in Miss Dotsy with Ellis.

As Wade Joyce promised, *Miss Dotsy*'s gearbox was much quieter after his laying on of hands. On the other hand, the weather had not improved. Knocker Ellis could manage the waves so far. Large as these mammoths were, they rolled in predictably. The Chesapeake could deteriorate still further in just minutes. At least now there was none of the deadly scissoring wave action for which the bay was infamous. They didn't call it chop for nothing. Very bad for small boats.

On the way out the door Ben had noticed the mercury in his old barometer dropping faster than Jack Kevorkian's patient roster. Beyond that, he'd avoided listening to the marine weather. There was no point.

What were his options? Hunker down ashore 'til Polly, this new storm, and everything else blew over? No, he and Ellis would deal with it gust by gust. That was the only way. If they sat home and did nothing, the forecast was death one way or another.

Ellis said, "My turn to say thanks."

Ben asked, "What for?"

"You stood my ground on the split. Good lookin' out. Thanks."

Ben shook his head. "I stood for what's right. Hey, I'm no Boy Scout. I'll just sleep better."

Ellis said, "I don't know how you'll sleep. You'll definitely wake up better."

Ben smiled. "Roger that. Pissing you off is bad business. I'm still not sure who your friends are in all this."

Ellis looked uneasy. "Me neither. Dyze and them might not keep their word about my cut, what with their odd Smith Island notions of family."

A quartering wave surged under *Miss Dotsy*'s stern. Then two more waves canted and rocked her.

Ellis said, "Let's not all answer at once."

Ben said, "How do I put this? Dyze is tricky. He'll keep an oath with—neighbors."

"But I'm a horse of a different color."

"I'd hate to think it. Might be the case. Don't worry. We'll watch out. Lots to do between now and then. Lots to talk about."

With a practiced hand, Ellis eased the tiller to best traverse another wave. "Right. Suppose it's like Lorton said, we'll burn that cross when we come to it. Meantime, what about that bomb? We going to straighten that out?"

Ben said, "No. Not now. Have to let the timer get a little shorter. That's the only way I know how to trim its fuse, so to speak."

Ellis was angry. "Hold it. We have LuAnna back. You said we would take care of the bomb when she was safe. Now she's safe, so let's get to it!"

"She told me if Chalk bests us, he might want to hang out on Smith Island. So take your pick. Chalk, or the bomb? Which would you like?"

Ellis said, "He can have the island. We can afford to buy a new one. For me, I'm concentrating on not getting shot, and not getting nuked. The problem seems to be getting killed either way from listening to your fool sophistries, and not doing anything about any of it. If your Pap was Ulysses, you're Hamlet, dithering all over the damn place."

Ben said, "I need you to trust me. I think I've got the bomb figured out."

Ellis fell silent. "Okay Ben. I'll go with you on this, even though you don't seem sure of me yet. No problem. Now, we're almost sure Chalk is poking around for our gold on Deep Banks. We check there first?"

Ben smiled. "Maybe. Let's give him a jingle." He pulled out The Kid's mobile phone.

CHAPTER 40

MAYNARD CHALK, BILL Slagget, and Tahereh hung on with
death grips in her careening inflatable. The boat was designed to plane at
high speeds, not slow-tow balky loads like Hiram's outboard skiff. A ride
on Coney Island's Cyclone would have been restful in comparison. Tahereh
vomited. Chalk appreciated that she parked her cookies to leeward.

Tahereh's three surviving men all bailed the skiff astern as if their lives
depended on it, which was actually the case. If the makeshift patches on the
bullet holes did not stay put, and they gave every indication they wouldn't,
the skiff would founder with all hands. That was Chalk's promise anyway.
No reversing the inflatable's course to hunt for survivors. Or as he phrased
it, *No bobbing for Ba'athists*. Let them deal. They'd put the damn holes there
in the first place. For now the old skiff yanked and tugged at the towline
like a peevish wallowing hog.

Chalk recalled The Kid saying he'd seen Ben Blackshaw toting a
shovel. With Tahereh's team neutralized and pressed into service, they were
now going back to Deep Banks for a closer look. Chalk would like to see
Dick and his son dig up his gold, and then scratch a little deeper for their
own graves.

Chalk's phone blared a few bars of the Merry Macs playing their hit
Mairzy Doats. He answered, "Scrote-Lick! About time! Let's have it."

A panicky voice, pitched high and pressured, talking fast. "Where's
Corporal Bryce? What'd you do with her?"

Not The Kid. Chalk bellowed, "Who's this?"

The caller sounded like he was trying to keep his cool, but was failing. "You dropped by my place this morning."

"Ben Blackshaw? Son of a gun! Put The Kid on for a second."

"First answer my question! Where's Corporal Bryce? I know you've got her. Don't you?"

"Simmer down, peckernut. Maybe I do. Maybe I don't." Chalk knew he was back in control. By the sound of it, the Blackshaw whelp was about to crap his drawers with worry. "How about my property. Let's confab a little about that."

"I have the gold. And the other thing. I'll trade it all for LuAnna safe and sound."

"Oh my! A big-time wheeler-dealer! And chivalrous, too. Fair enough. You just bought yourself one slightly used officer of the law."

"If you hurt her—"

"You'll do what, marsh monkey? What the fuck will you do? Not a damn thing, that's what. Now you bring my shit out to Point No Point Lighthouse before sunset. Think you can manage that? And come alone. Do it, or your gal's gonna get to know my boys a whole lot better. Three at a time. We have an understanding?"

"No! Please don't do that!"

"Do what I say and we got no problems. And here's the kicker, you little shit. Fuck with me again, and you'll never see the girl, or your mother! I got her, too! You miss her tucking you in for prayers at bedtime? Well, I got her, and you can take that to the bank, punk!" Chalk ended the call. Not since schoolyard days had he spat out a "Yo mama" to such good effect. He smirked at Slagget and Tahereh. "You heard. Let's get back to the lighthouse and set up."

Slagget said, "We got the kid's mother? Dick Blackshaw's wife?"

Chalk grinned. "Let's say I have a pretty damn good idea where I can lay hands on her."

This was the best possible outcome. No more hunting for the gold. It was about to be delivered to him like a pizza. Soon he could murder some cracker-ass Blackshaws, get the gold to the dirty bomb vendors, make good, and get home. He would put up his feet with a stogie and a highball and think deep thoughts like they always did at the end of *Boston Legal*. It had been a long day already and it was barely half over. Something momentarily nagged at the back of his mind. *Where was The Kid?* No matter. He had written off that Hotspur hours ago.

Chalk dug his fingers into a shirt pocket beneath his poncho. Took out what looked like a grey piece of soggy parchment. He looked at the Lat/Long numbers he had jotted down on LuAnna's skin in black Sharpie. Grinning, he flicked the ragged flesh over the side.

CHAPTER 41

ELLIS STARED AT Ben as he put away The Kid's phone. "And the Oscar for Best Lying Whitecracker in a Clusterfuck goes to—"

Ben said, "Folks are predictable when they think they've got the upper hand. It's when they're desperate you have to watch out."

"Think that nickel-slick stuff will work? Maybe you've been perusing *The Art of War*?"

"*Dear Abby*. Now we don't need to know where Chalk is. We know where he's going. And he clearly doesn't know we've already got LuAnna back, or that the lighthouse is denied, so that works."

"Good enough. But, Ben?"

"What is it, Ellis?"

"Do we think we've got the upper hand now? Did we just become predictable?"

Ben's smile was grim again. "Wouldn't worry about that. Chalk said he's got my mother, too."

"That's no good. You believe him?"

Ben didn't answer for a moment. "He seems sure enough that she's not on Smith Island now. And I didn't say she was there, so that was a mistake. Dammit! As good as a confirmation. I don't know what to think. We just found Pap mixed up in this mess. Maybe she was, too."

Ellis said, "That's true. Just because your pappy didn't mention her doesn't mean she wasn't still in his life. He told her everything."

Ben asked, "You have any history with this Chalk? Know him from Vietnam, maybe? Was he there when you were?"

Ellis said nothing more.

This was hell for Ben. Not only was his father dead after years of no contact, his mother was now firmly involved. More than that, Chalk near as swore he had her captive. Through the years, Ben carefully maintained a nebulous image of Ida-Beth safe and happy somewhere, but with a tragic fairy-tale spell holding her in exile from Smith Island and her family. He carefully cleaned and checked Knocker Ellis's rifle in the cuddy cabin. If he killed Chalk now, he might sever his last link to finding his mother alive. Ben was disgusted with himself. After all, closure was for suckers. Wasn't it?

They set *Miss Dotsy* on a large, slow, circular course to the southeast of the Point No Point Lighthouse ruins. Fighting the storm exhausted them even more. At least *Miss Dotsy*'s repaired gearbox was holding, so far.

Ellis manned the helm for the first half-hour. Feet set wide, Ben propped himself against the cuddy cabin with binoculars scanning the bay as best he could. Ellis's rifle lay cleaned, inspected, dry, loaded, and secured just inside the cabin door.

CHAPTER 42

THE GPS CHALK swiped from Hiram Harris's *Palestrina* said the Point No Point Lighthouse should be in easy view by now. He remembered how damn tall it was. So imposing and phallic. Like having a big dong for a hideout. Chalk got a kick out of that. It sure beat a bat cave. Who wanted to hole up in some dank, Freudian vagina? How was that cool? Now, even when the inflatable crested the waves, he still saw absolutely nothing. It was understandable on one level. The storm sooted out the daylight with heavy rain, wind-blown spume, and thick cloud.

Slagget said, "Maybe this gale knocked the light out."

Chalk checked the GPS again. Though not really night at all, he needed to try anything to see better. "Hell. Give me the goggles, Bill."

Slagget passed Chalk the NVGs. Chalk slipped the straps onto his head and flipped the switch. The gallium arsenide photocathode sucked in the wan light, beamed it to the phosphor screen. As his eyes adjusted to the dimness, the screen transformed the dark gray water into liquid emerald.

Even this late generation of goggles still tunneled his field of vision to just forty degrees down from the usual naked-eye one hundred ninety. He swiveled his head hard to the left and right of the boat's extended rhumbline, searching. Somewhere close, he expected to see the loom of the lighthouse beacon even if heavily obscured through low cloud. Just one lousy glimmer would do.

Instead of light, a chasm of darkness rose up at him out of the water, a black wound hacked out of the squall-battered sky. Chalk reeled back like the victim of a cheap effect at a 3-D movie. "Damn!"

Chalk pulled the inflatable's motor hard to starboard, wrenching the boat over to port. The bright beacon was not there. Worse, the lighthouse's iron caisson foundation lay dead ahead not twenty feet away. Its top section was peeled outward like a gigantic rusty flower blossom with serrated petals, some bent down to Chalk's eye level. The next wave would have surfed the inflatable straight into the harrow-like wreckage of the iron wall. For once, Chalk was grateful the skiff in tow was such a heavy drag, like a sea anchor. Above the caisson, the lighthouse was gone. Just not there. A phallus cum vagina dentata.

Then Slagget pointed to wreckage in the water. "What the hell?"

Planks and shingled sections of the lighthouse's mansard roof surged in an eddy to leeward of the ruin. There, the caisson was split wide open from the top to down below the water's surface. It created a miniature harbor of calmer water within. No, the lighthouse was not like a flower here so much as the open, jagged collar of a headless court jester's motley.

Tahereh shouted. "Look! A boat!"

More improbable than the lighthouse's total destruction was the sight of the *Palestrina* still afloat, moored to the caisson's remains on a twenty foot painter. Chalk veered the inflatable toward the deadrise. On the upside, now they had three boats to use for an attack to retrieve the gold: the *Palestrina*, the inflatable, and the old outboard skiff, such as it was.

Slagget jumped from the inflatable over to the *Palestrina*, tied the painter to the big deadrise's stern cleat. Tahereh crossed next, Chalk steadying her from behind with his two big hands on her hips. Then he beckoned to Tahereh's men in the skiff to pull themselves and the leaky outboard in close with the tow line so they too could board the *Palestrina*.

Chalk turned his attention to the *Palestrina*'s cockpit. It was littered with blasted masonry from the lighthouse's destroyed middle story. Here and there a few bricks lay still cemented together. A chunk of roof dormer and its window had spun through the air and landed forward under the *Palestrina*'s hardtop. A single pane of glass remained intact.

Chalk ordered, "Clean this crap up. Pitch it overboard. What the hell happened here?"

Two of Tahereh's men, al Mubi and al Temiyat, boarded *Palestrina* from the outboard skiff. At forty-three, al Mubi was Tahereh's oldest squad member. He had fought the Soviets as a boy in Afghanistan. Al Temiyat helped al Mubi clear debris as best they could, seasick as they were. Last, Surur of the notched ear, a former Islamic literature student from Pakistan, leapt gamely from the skiff, pitching himself over the deadrise's transom. He landed hard on the deck, clutched at his ear and retched out a violent dry heave. The Simon Clynch of Tahereh's team, he was not cut out for sea duty.

Slagget said, "The whole lighthouse is stonked! Something must have set off our grenades. Maybe Gavin was horsing around. And what about the chick?"

Chalk said, "Dollars to doughnuts she's dead."

Tahereh and al Mubi started lifting the section of dormer with its remnant of glazed window frame. Suddenly they froze, eyes riveted on the debris. Something was staring back at them through the frame. A childhood monster peering through a bedroom window; a demon.

Chalk was the first to snap the hex. He staggered forward, grabbed the edge of the dormer, threw it aside. There lay a burned human body. Hair singed. Clothing charred. Flesh, medium-well. Fists up in the classic pugilistic burn posture.

Chalk said, "Jesus fucking Christ!"

Slagget said, "Not by a long shot. That's Gavin!"

Al Temiyat began shouting at Tahereh in Pashto-accented Arabic. He'd been pulling the skiff in to cleat it closer to the *Palestrina*'s stern. He pointed at the skiff's old Evinrude outboard. There was a big bullet hole in the left engine cover.

"Now what?" Chalk went aft steadying himself by holding the Palestrina's washboards. He tried to examine the skiff's engine from the deadrise. The wave action made it hard to see.

He ordered, "Slagget! Jump back in that skiff! Get the engine cover off!"

Slagget obeyed. "Somebody must've shot the thing back at the boat ramp."

Chalk wasn't buying. "No, this wasn't an accident. And besides, we hid the boat too far away and down in that ditch for it to take a hit. Anybody hear a shot just now?"

Tahereh said, "Out here? Impossible. Not over this storm."

The engine's perforated cover was barely fastened in place. A quick yank, and it came off in Slagget's hand. He shined a flashlight on the mess inside. The cable assembly was a rat's nest. The fuel line was nearly severed. The engine was ruined.

Slagget said, "Hello."

Bedded in the side of the starter coil smoldered part of a mangled bullet. Slagget used his pocket knife to pry the fragment free. He bobbled it from palm to palm while it cooled.

Slagget said, "Slug's still hot! Anybody here shooting .308 Winchesters?"

"What are you talking about?" Chalk leaned in close, took the slug from Slagget, put his flashlight on it. "That's not .308! It's M-one eighteen LR. A hundred seventy-five grain. This, my friend, is sniper spore."

Chalk looked wildly out into the storm. Tensed for the next slug to smash home. He knew he would never hear it coming. Defiant, he held the bullet up high in his fist.

He shouted at the wind, "Look at me, you damnable pop-eyed bastards! See me, and fear me, and fall down before me! You *missed!*"

CHAPTER 43

"YOU MISSED?" KNOCKER Ellis was incredulous. Tried to bury the embarrassment he felt for his captain. Ben was not his father's son after all.

Ben lowered the smoking rifle. "Head us back to Smith."

Ellis timed the turn with the waves. Hauled on the tiller. Set the course for home.

Ben stowed the rifle in *Miss Dotsy*'s cuddy cabin. "And what do you mean? That wasn't any Maggie's drawers." Ben was speaking Sniperanto, meaning the red flag raised from the pits down range, indicating a shooter had totally missed the target.

"Oh, so you really killed somebody just now? I must've not seen it. These old eyes, and whatnot."

"Okay! I hit the *N* not the *R*. I admit that." Ben looked abashed.

"Come again?"

Ben spelled. "E-V-I-N-R-U-D-E. I was aiming for the *R*. It's embarrassing. I reckon the *N* will have to do."

Now Ellis was fuming. "You risked our lives out here in this mess just to shoot up an outboard motor. And the bomb's still live? He spooked you! He messed with your head, talking about your mother."

"This was a recon sortie, Ellis. Now we know they're six strong. We've denied them an important asset. Cut their flotilla by one third. And we scared them. They won't know when the next shot's coming in, and you know that's a bad feeling. You have to trust me. I do have a plan."

Ellis was not placated. "What the hell important asset! Hiram's janky old skiff? Why not plug that inflatable's engine? Or shoot something with a trigger finger."

Ben said, "Entertaining as it might be, what I have in mind doesn't mean picking them off right now. Soon. Not now. Not if you want to sleep easy when all this is done."

Ellis negotiated *Miss Dotsy* over several waves. They were getting bigger.

He railed, "You want them to think they got the upper hand. Okay, that's one thing, but Ben, you're giving away the damn store!"

CHAPTER 44

THEY CUT HIRAM'S skiff loose back at the lighthouse with Dar Gavin's body tossed in the bottom. The storm would take care of the burial. Chalk's mind boggled that he'd been so punctilious, wasted so much time disposing of Clynch's remains. Maybe the meds had their purpose after all.

Chalk stood forward at the helm under the *Palestrina*'s hardtop. He frequently looked aft to emphasize his points. Big gestures. Tahereh was parked near Slagget on the engine box in the middle of the boat. She gazed forward at Chalk with rapt attention.

Slagget faced aft. His Five-seveN gripped in his right hand. He guarded al Mubi, and Surur with the recently pierced ear, and al Temiyat.

Al Mubi seemed to Chalk like the toughest of them. Older, and battle-hardened. Al Mubi had not let himself run to anger yet, nor despair. He was calm, though Chalk was sure the Islamist had already weighed matters and found them wanting.

Out of the corner of his eye, Chalk glimpsed Slagget as his lieutenant reached under his jacket and cupped his hand around a small knife he'd taken off the prisoners back at the boat ramp frisk. It all actually happened in the blink of an eye, but like a nightmare, it seemed to take hours, and Chalk was rooted in place unable to act in time.

Al Mubi and al Temiyat swapped looks. Very uneasy. Surur was still taken up with his own problems; nausea, a bleeding earlobe, a grazed leg, self-pity, and a dearth of handy virgins. He was not paying attention.

Casually, Slagget lobbed the knife aft toward the three men sitting cross-legged at the transom. Al Mubi and al Temiyat saw Slagget do it. Watched the knife float through the air. An easy underhand toss, as if Slagget was passing it to them.

Chalk arrested his soliloquy as the knife bounced once off the deck on its rubberized handle, and settled harmlessly in al Temiyat's lap. Al Temiyat was about to reach, but al Mubi recognized deadly bait when he saw it. He slapped his hand over al Temiyat's to keep him from grabbing the knife and giving Slagget probable cause to shoot them. The two men held still for a nanosecond starring at Slagget.

Asir Surur was not savvy. He had not seen the toss. Had only seen the blade flop into al Temiyat's lap. To Surur, the angry, wounded, gullible student, this looked like a gift from Allah. Surur went for the knife as Slagget clearly hoped he would, digging into al Temiyat's lap with the verve of a hooker doing piece-work at a Vegas bachelor party. Finally, he came up with the needle-fine tip pointing at Slagget.

Slagget waited a half a second before he raised the Five-seveN. Surur's eyes met his. Even with the knife in hand, he realized he was seated too far away to scratch Slagget with it. Al Mubi swore at his squaddie's mortal stupidity.

Slagget fired. Tahereh turned and watched in horror. Though he didn't have the knife, Al Mubi went down first because he was toughest. Slagget put the first round in his heart, and parked a second pill in the middle of his forehead. Al Mubi's head snapped backward. He collapsed on the deck and lay still.

Surur, small and quick, was close to getting on his feet with the knife stretched out toward Slagget. At this range Slagget seemed relaxed as he shot Surur in the knee. With Surur's thigh aligned with Slagget's gun barrel, the tiny, hyper-Mach round punched through his patella. Shattered the medial condyle knob of his femur's south end. Threw a tablespoon of loose change, bullet and bone, along the femur shaft. The shrapnel sieved the femoral artery like buckshot. With that kind of trauma, Surur should have bled out with respectable speed. To Slagget's astonishment, the dumb bastard kept coming.

"Allahu-Akbar!" cried Surur.

"Kumbaya," Slagget muttered as he shot out Surur's left eye. That did it. Surur flopped face down on the deck. The tip of the knife blade lay three inches from the toe of Slagget's left shoe.

Chalk yelled, "What in the holy fuck!"

Al Temiyat, who'd been sitting between his recently deceased friends, had a mix of rage and hopelessness in his eyes. Slagget paused long enough for the poor guy to think he'd been reprieved. With one look at Slagget's deadpan face, al Temiyat scrambled to stand, started alternately splaying his legs out from beneath him like a Russian folk dancer. His feet could not get a purchase on the slippery deck. Two in the heart.

That was the proof Chalk needed. This bastard Slagget was definitely Senator Morgan's other mole. That meant he had to die. Though not before he helped move the gold off the island.

Slagget stood up quickly, and backed away from Tahereh. For a moment, Chalk thought she would make some kind of stupid, butch girl-move so Slagget could complete this purge. Not this gal. She quickly put her hands up in surrender.

Covering the woman, Slagget bent low and picked up the knife. He held it up where everybody could see it. "Sorry Maynard. I guess I missed this one."

Chalk looked from Slagget to the three dead men, and finally to Tahereh. He was gauging his chances of scoring with her after this latest thinning of her ranks. It looked bad but he still had a few ideas up his sleeve.

Unable to suppress his irritation, Chalk growled, "Goddammit Slagget! This boat's only got one fucking anchor!"

CHAPTER 45

THE SALTBOX WAS a hive. Oily-cloaked men ghosted among Ben's welded menagerie in the yard while working on five very small boats.

Tom Fox pulled an old punt, or sneakboat, out of the gut where he had submerged it to let the dried-out shrunken strakes soak and swell tight. Two other sneakboats lay near the pier.

No man would fire a big headache gun like Barking Betty from his shoulder. Not unless his life insurance was paid up. In the normal course of a fowling sortie, the gun would be laid along the sneakboat's keel, its muzzle hanging over the front like an iron bowsprit, and braced against a thwart with a cushion stuffed with pine needles. The gun was coigned with wooden wedges for elevation. The sole hunter aboard used two small paddles, like a waterborne ping-pong champ, to maneuver the boat and traverse the gun left and right. In anything more than light airs, such a small, low craft would swamp. With hunter, dog, and heavy gun, its sides rose only inches above the water.

Ben stopped on the way into the house. "Tom, a day like today? Somebody's going to drown in that thing."

Fox cast an eye at the weather. Still horrendous. "Should be just fine come the time we want her. You'll see. And all them little islands around about are as good as a breakwater. They'll keep the waves plenty low enough for our doings, swagger die."

Ben said no more. He had come dangerously close to telling Tom Fox his business. As it stood, Ben felt lucky to have gotten off the water alive in a boat as large as *Miss Dotsy*.

Then he saw Wade Joyce dash a soup pot full of boiling water into two other relics from Smith Island's past. Hunter's sinkboxes. Scalding water tightened the seams in old wood more quickly than simple soaking. The sinkbox resembled a coffin with hinged wooden panels extending outward from the gunwales. Like the flaps of a cardboard box, but bigger. The panels lay undulating on the water's surface like a flexible deck to quell small waves. It was like a dry foxhole in the water where a man could lie down below the surface out of sight. Remington by his side, he would wait for his ducks to toll in range. Then the gunner could pop up out of nowhere and open fire.

Once again, Ben questioned the wisdom of using such a boat. A sinkbox showed even less freeboard than Tom Fox's punts. These boats were built for tidal pools and marsh ponds, not for today's wild Chesapeake. Ben nodded at Wade Joyce, but kept his mouth shut. He went toward the house with Ellis.

The living room was converted into an armory with Lorton Dyze bossing. He told Ben, "We quick paid a call over to the Smith Island International Maritime Museum. Picked up some odds and ends."

Ben said, "So I see." Before his last trip to the lighthouse, Ben suggested the men collect their pump guns. In addition to the three sneakboats and the two sinkboxes getting a quick and dirty refit outside, there was now a second big market gun measuring the tight space in the parlor. There was also a battery gun undergoing inspection.

In addition to concealment, the museum, with its grandiose name and its 501(c)3 tax exempt status was the Islanders' work-around for the confiscation of their old fowling pieces. Though technically decommissioned, the guns could be restored by skilled hands to working status in times of want, or menace.

As for the hunting boats, the islanders had argued long and hard with authorities that they were harmless enough on dry land without a big gun aboard. Their owners pleaded, saying they could not let antique craft once belonging to their grandparents fall to pieces in a police impound yard. This was disrespectful of venerated ancestors, and of their heritage. Nor could they bring themselves to tow the fragile vessels up some godforsaken gut and abandon them to die. Not when a museum would preserve them for posterity. They'd even tossed in expressions like *lifeways,* and *folkways* to give the proposal a real anthropological sound when making their case to the state. It had worked. An old picking house was transformed into a tiny museum. The suggested contribution for admission was fifty cents.

It helped that it was off-season and the museum was closed 'til spring. It really helped that Dyze's niece was the museum's docent.

The second market gun was built along the same lines as *Barking Betty.* Huge. It was named *Vesuvius* for its volcanic eruptions of hot metal and death. The piece was old, and might kill a gunner if the breech ever failed when he touched it off. In harder times this gun and others like it were loaded with old nails, screws, nuts, bolts, and washers instead of proper shot. A popular island legend had it that one Baltimore restaurateur closed his kitchen and opened a hardware store to sell off what his pickers took out of just one barrel of ducks *Vesuvius* knocked down.

Sam Nuttle was oiling the gun's big lock. On the coffee table lay a tompion he had carved from a Styrofoam trotline float. When greased, the plug would keep rain out of the barrel and ensure the powder stayed dry. Next to the tompion was a white plastic puck containing CCI No. Eleven Percussion Caps. The end table by the couch was loaded down by six clear plastic bags of Hornady double-ought buckshot. There would be no bird shot in the loads tonight. Double-ought was the man-killer.

To a waterman's eye, a genuine battery gun like *Chanticleer* was a thing of beauty. It had eight muzzle-loaded barrels fixed in a wood frame that fanned them out in a small arc of a circle, like the tines of a leaf rake. Instead of discharging one large linear gout of shot like a market gun, *Chanticleer*'s splayed barrels spread the shot pellets laterally across a broader area. It followed the natural traverse of the flock's attempt to escape on the wing. A sneakboat armed with a battery gun could throw its own version of a broadside like a one-man pirate sloop. Looking like an old god tuning a deadly pan-pipe, Sonny Wright meticulously cleaned Chanticleer's barrels.

Dyze pulled Ben and Ellis aside. "I called up Bob Crockett over to Tangier. Explained the situation."

Crockett was Dyze's pal and opposite number on Tangier Island's council. He was a good friend to Smith Island in times of trouble.

Dyze went on, "We figure a whirlybird would be grounded by this flaw. Not so a big aeroplane if Chalk has the sand to whistle one up for help. Bob Crockett and his boys, they'll see to that runway before too long." Dyze asked Ben, "That sit okay with you?"

This last sentence took Ben aback. Dyze was asking Ben's approval. Was Dyze passing some kind of torch to Ben? More likely he was manipulating the only two men who knew where the gold lay. Ben did not care, and was not sure he wanted any kind of leadership in this rag-tag band. He was no Captain Morgan, and this was Smith Island, not Port Royal. All he cared about was that they listened to him for the next few hours, and listened close.

Ben said, "Okay Lorton. Good idea. Did you work out a boat?"

Dyze smiled. "We got Sonny's *Busbee.*"

Ben was not thrilled. The *Busbee* was a seventy-year-old skipjack sailboat. Fifty feet long. Sloop rigged; the mast raked wickedly back. Its only engine ran the oyster dredge's windlass amidships. To move legally while dredging, it either had to be sailed, or it was shoved by a small motorboat stowed on davits when it was not in use, at the skipjack's stern. All depended on whether it was a *sailing* day, or a *power* day, as designated by landlubber state congressmen in Annapolis. Though truly majestic under sail, the *Busbee* was not what Ben was looking for at all. Not tonight.

Ben had to ask, "Wade Joyce wouldn't put in his deadrise? She's quick."

Dyze huffed, like he was secretly nostalgic for ye olde close-hauled action under full sail. "Don't need no go-fast boat for this."

"Uh, yeah we do. Right now. We need to get to Deep Banks quick as we can. If we don't deal with that bomb, we lose everything."

At this, Dyze relented. Disappointed, he reached for his rain gear. "Ellis and I'll talk to Wade." Then Dyze gave Ben a pitying look. "Ye best step upstairs. LuAnna's took a turn."

Fear clawed Ben's gut. Dyze did not need to tack on the *bless her heart* that always followed mention of the feeble-minded or desperately sick. Ben took the steep stairs three at a time. His ribs seared like a brand.

LuAnna lay on his bed more in a state of utter collapse than rest. Mary Joyce, Julie Nuttle, and Kimba Mosby applied cool rags to her head. Ben knelt, caressed her brow. She was burning up. Hypothermia one minute, raging fever the next. Her teeth chattered. She was enduring a medieval trial by ordeal, and she was innocent.

Mary Joyce said, "She had that gash in her hip. I cleaned it best I could. Sewed them good with fresh cleaned *Dyneema* fishing line. You'd figure in November that the bugs in the water wouldn't be so bad, but she got herself something nasty. Might be pneumonia, too." *Bless her heart.*

Ben noticed the bedside table was covered in white capped amber pill bottles. Looking closer he saw that each bottle had a different patient's name on the label. The women had collected all the unfinished antibiotic prescriptions from neighbors around the island for LuAnna.

Kimba Mosby said, "Don't worry, Ben. We're dosing her good. This'll break quick."

Ben stroked LuAnna's damp hair back from her face. "She needs a hospital."

Julie Nuttle shook her head. "She needs quiet. A fast ride over the sound in this chop might be too much for her. We're giving her everything she needs here, Ben. Count on that. And she's tough."

For a moment, Ben considered calling in the Medevac he had been so ready to summon for Charlene Harris. He knew Charlene was right. This business was his to finish. No authorities. As Lorton Dyze said, this weather would keep a helicopter grounded anyway.

Ben felt disingenuous even as he vented his frustration at Julie. "You don't need to tell me she's tough. Truth is, you don't want anybody from off-island interfering in this business."

The three nurses would not meet Ben's eyes.

He said, "LuAnna? Can you hear me?"

LuAnna opened her eyes. "Of course ya big bully. I'm sick, not deaf. Quit hassling the girls. I'm fine. Go do what you need to do."

Ben told the women, "She's pregnant. She needs a hospital."

Kimba Mosby, the Reverend's wife, took Ben by the elbow. Gently led him out into the small landing between the bedrooms.

She patted Ben's arm. "LuAnna's been through so much today. She'll be fine. She's young. So are you. Thing is, Ben, she's not pregnant now. Not n'mare. She didn't want us to tell you. Wanted to break it to you herself later. Right now she feels terrible. Like she let you down. Right now she needs to know you still love her."

Ben felt a small explosion in his chest. The thump of an incendiary bomb burning white-hot inside him like phosphorus. He was not angry at LuAnna. He wept inside for her. Ben's rage was for Maynard Chalk and company. They were slaughtering innocents. Not only had they marauded too close to home, they had now penetrated his heart. Lining these men up against a wall, gunning them down into an open cesspit was too good for them. Cleaving to his original plan for handling this crisis would require a Zen master's detachment and a fencer's finesse. Ben knew this fury had no place here today. It would ruin everything. Still it boiled inside him.

He sat softly on the bed next to LuAnna, and took her hand. Kissed her brow. Julie and Mary stepped out onto the landing with Kimba.

He said "It's okay, Honey."

LuAnna opened her eyes again. Shivered. She looked so small. "Did the girls feed you that bull about us being young?"

Ben nodded. "It's true. There'll be plenty time again."

"Ben, I was already loving this one. Whoever she was." Tears glistened in with the fever's sheen on her face. "Couldn't help it, coming from you like she did."

"You think she was a *she*?"

"Oh hell yes. I prayed so, anyway. Lord knows I'd need back-up in the house with you on a rampage." She caught her breath. "You still like me?"

"Always will. Any kid of ours is going to have to understand that, and get used to it. You're my A-number-one Sally crab."

"You'll accept no substitutes?"

"How could I when there aren't any? Not even close." He kissed her cheek. "You better rest up. Seeing you all sweaty and helpless is making me hot."

LuAnna laughed softly. Weak as her voice sounded, it rang inside Ben like the most beautiful music.

She squeezed his hand, whispered. "Please go kill them. For us. For *her.*"

Ben smiled down at her. "I love you, too." If she lived through this, they'd weather anything together.

CHAPTER 46

CHALK FIXED TAHEREH'S brown almondine eyes with his piggy slits. Even in the low light of the *Palestrina*'s cabin, she was a beauty. He asked, "What are your people going to use it for?"

Tahereh was quiet. Then she answered, "You still actually plan to hand it over to me?"

"Of course!" Chalk sounded righteous, like a paragon of integrity slandered. "I did want to discuss another possibility with you."

Tahereh got angry. "I'm already a dead woman! I've known men like you."

"And you lived to tell the tale, didn't you, spitfire?" Chalk was quieter, less blustery. He was going Senator Lily Morgan one better, laying out a little Fifth-Generation Warfare of his own tonight. "No. You've never known a man like me."

Tahereh sneered. "You're all alike. You all think you're special. You listen to your mothers too closely."

Again Chalk did his best to look offended. "Tahereh honey, I think you've got me all wrong. I'm suggesting an alliance. You and I working together long-term. When I hand you the dirty bomb, your folks are just going to nuke some fleabag Third World country, right? Take out an embassy full of ass-kissers? Microwave an American city? Is that the big plan? Is that all you got? Is this all we've got to look forward to, you and I? Does this have to be the end, is all I'm asking."

Tahereh all but guffawed. "You want to entertain me with a fantasy in my last hours? Go ahead. I'm curious."

Chalk spoke as if he were confiding state secrets. "In a little while, you'll have a device you can call your own. You can go set it off someplace, and have your moment in the sun. And though the history books might record the deed, the cold hard fact you have to face is that the visceral effect, the terror of that event, will quickly fade away. Sorry to break it to you, but we must face facts."

Chalk was giving it his best, but Tahereh's laughter dripped with derision. He soldiered on. "You said you'd hear me out. Listen, do you think anybody honestly gives a crap about Hiroshima? Or Nagasaki? Sure, there are some monuments here and there. Bleeding-heart liberals will point and shed a tear at Man's Inhumanity to Man when the round-number anniversaries come along. Fine. What do we know? Today those cities are booming in a whole new way. They were annihilated, but today they're making money. America did its worst, but today the Japs go to work, come home, fuck, eat, piss, shit and breathe just like they always did for thousands of years.

"Life in the grand scheme is truly a dull, meaningless existence occasionally punctuated by catastrophe that's quickly forgotten. I'm telling you, honey, that is the human condition. And we all know that eventually terror withers away."

Chalk paused, saw he was still not getting through to her, but at least she was listening. "Need a more recent example? What about Ground Zero right there in New York City? Is that sacred ground now? Hell no! Within a few short years of September 11th, it's back to being top-dollar real estate! Is that the kind of glory you're after? Because that's all you're going to get."

Tahereh remained quiet. Sensing she was becoming intrigued, Chalk continued. "I'd hate for you to throw away what we have. I like your style. Your guts. You're hot as hell, and I'm digging your chili. You're a chick running an Islamist terror cell for Christ's sake! Who has bigger balls than you, except for me? I'm saying we could be good together.

"I'm also saying that device is not a one-shot deal. It's perpetual leverage! Set it off, and it's just a blip on the EKG of human history. Instead, let's *threaten* to set it off over and over and over and over again! I know just the short-hairs we can yank to make this threat truly credible. Play it my way, and you've got the world eating out of your hand not once, but dozens of times."

Tahereh inquired, "Exactly how crazy are you?"

"I am not crazy! Sure, I've been known to drop acid socially now and then, but the fact is I'm bored! I want to put the fun back in dysfunction. I'm not a kid anymore. Been in this biz for a long time. I'm ready for a change. For some real excitement. This device? Call it a starter bomb. Keep it for us. Screw your boss mullahs. They'd sooner stone you as thank you for everything you've done so far. So instead, be a little more enterprising on our behalf. Think of the money we could make, and what we could do with it!

"Use that stinker a little differently than you planned, and you won't have knuckleheads in Spain strapping C-4 to their chests. Hell, you'll have the resources to set up bomb production lines that would put Henry Ford to shame, but not for plain-Jane, hum-drum dirties. You can make nukes! Real whiz-bangs you can *really* set off. I'm talking about serious mega-tonnage, sweetie. Do like I say, and you can trade a dirty bomb's puny Geiger counter Rice Krispies crackle for a real mushroom cloud, with a genuine shock wave roaring across the countryside roasting and flattening everything in its path."

Chalk's voice rose with passion. He realized the lack of his medication was making him rant like a 42nd Street zealot, but he didn't care. "It'll be like the 1950s all over again. Above-ground detonations! Air bursts! The nuclear winter of our discontent. Total Omega Man! Soylent Green! Planet of the Apes! 'You maniacs! You blew it up!'"

Tahereh was speechless.

Chalk wound into a raving climax. "Baby! Think of it! And you and I running the whole damn show. Mark my words. If what we achieve is ever forgotten, it's because we haven't left a single human being alive to remember. Now that, my little chickadee, is what you call *terror*."

The mad chief went on, hoping he was playing Tahereh's song. "Or do it your way. Temporarily spike the local cancer rates someplace. Oh, and you will also create yet another opportunity for the next Winedark, Halliburton, or Bechtel to swing in and suck up some no-bid government contracts. Honey, you will have helped Western running-dog capitalism more than hurt it. But hey, you go ahead. I'll see you off with a tear in my eye and a fervent hope that we might do business again someday in the future, inshallah. You stick with me, cupcake, and I swear there is nothing we can't achieve. The world will bow down before us, even as it dies."

Tahereh had one brief response. "What about him?" She nodded toward Slagget topside at the helm.

Chalk leaned in, dropped his voice, and let his lips tickle Tahereh's ear. "A foot soldier. Nothing more. Expendable, I assure you."

Whether she was buying time, or buying in, Chalk thought she was a vicious little bitch. He might, just might, be in love.

Tahereh nodded, and said, "Then tonight, you prove it. Expend him and you can count on me."

All Chalk said was, "Done and done." Not even a decent pause for the appearance of moral and ethical deliberation. Chalk knew what he wanted. And with that, a death warrant had been drawn up and signed.

Chalk should have been happy with his new ally, but an ancient enemy still had him surrounded. There was a change in the Chesapeake itself. The waves were not as big now. The wind was not as strong. Somehow, this dying storm was a more chilling harbinger of doom than a Fujita Force 5 tornado touching down in his back pocket. World dominion lay within his grasp, yet he still had to reckon with a gang of Islanders who simply did not understand fear.

CHAPTER 47

THEY CRUISED UP the west side of Smith Island in Wade Joyce's big fiberglass deadrise, which was christened the *Varina Davis* in honor of the First Lady of the Confederacy. The big market guns, sneakboats, and sinkboxes were left at home. It was not time for them yet.

Ben sensed that half the Councilmen politely concealed their surprise that he was the architect of their strategy. The other half believed it was too complicated to pull off. Everyone, Ben included, knew that even the best battle plans lasted only until first contact with the enemy. After that, anything could happen. Only educated guesses on Chalk's next moves, coupled with the Islanders' impressionistic sense of discipline, would make the outcome anything more than a crapshoot, especially if Chalk was telling the truth about Ben's mother.

Dyze had thrown in solidly behind Ben's plan. He said they could make a right good jag of it. Ben remained unsure whether Dyze's support was based on respect, or because Ben and Ellis were still the only ones who knew precisely where the gold lay. Regardless, the Council doubters followed Dyze's lead. The Monday-morning tacticians did likewise. Ben and Ellis would get the true answer as soon as the first shovel bit into Deep Banks Island.

With Dyze's blessing upon Ben, everyone settled down for the moment. It was possible they'd meet the fonny boys that very afternoon. With raffish fun, hard work, and bloodshed ahead, they all relished the bracing chill of the spray-damped air.

As they neared Deep Banks Island, Tom Fox squinted into the dim stormlight. Fox said, "I do believe that's Hiram's deadrise. Abaft at ten o'clock."

Dyze smiled. Patted Ben on the back. "Ye got them boys figured like they's a *Dick and Jane*."

Ben said, "Maybe, but we still have to see Spot run the right way."

The others stared hard over the transom through the dark afternoon. Ben and Ellis, their snipers' eyes as sharp as Tom Fox's, quickly picked the gray boat out of the gray waves astern.

Ben said, "Least they haven't sunk her yet."

"Nor run her ashore," said Ellis.

Ben asked Fox, "What's the headcount? I make it three."

Fox paused. "Looks to be two. No, I got three for sure. Might be somebody below we can't see. And they got one boat in tow. An inflatable, by the look."

Ben told Fox, "Keep them in sight. Might be a woman aboard. One of us."

Reverend Mosby asked, "Another hostage?"

Ben nodded, "Somebody we haven't seen in a while. Wade, cut on over into Little Pungers Creek when you can, please. Only three now? There were six before."

Ellis watched the *Palestrina* like a hawk. "Probably below."

Ben was puzzled. "Maybe. That cuddy cabin's not so big."

Mosby's face turned gray. "Ben, you're not thinking Ida-Beth's over there on that boat, are you? Your mother. After so long?"

"Just keep an eye out."

The Reverend whispered, "Good Lord," like he meant it.

Everyone stared at Ben. Wade Joyce throttled up. After a short reach to the north he swung the wheel to starboard. They passed by Johnson Cove. Now they rounded southeast down past Gun Barrel Point to the inlet.

Ellis noticed Sonny Wright and Sam Nuttle conferring with their heads close together. They glanced his way every now and then, and they were not smiling.

Ellis nudged Ben. "Think they're after my eighty-million-and-a-mule?"

"We'll soon see." Ben studied Sonny and Sam. Let them know he was paying attention to them. They immediately broke up their huddle.

Ellis said, "Want a word with you."

Ben nodded and led the way among the Islanders on deck, and forward into the cuddy cabin. He and Ellis sat opposite one another around the chart table. Ben waited.

Ellis said, "I knew Chalk."

Ben drew and released a slow breath the same way he did before he pulled the trigger on a mission.

Ellis went on. "In Vietnam, like you thought. I didn't just happen to make my way back here after your Pappy reported me K.I.A., Body Not Recovered. Yes, the route was the same, the steamers, the safe houses, all like I said, but I wasn't the first to come back that way. Chalk sent things home. Dope. People. He was kind of a travel agent for guys like me."

Ben said, "For deserters."

Ellis's eyes narrowed. "Watch it, Ben. Remember there was a price on my head, from my own side, because of those ex parte gigs your Pappy and I took on for God and country. My own people, your people, they put me in this position, and you'd best understand that."

Ellis waited until Ben nodded slightly and said, "I get it. You were in a position."

Mollified only slightly, Ellis went on. "Chalk had an underground railroad-type deal going. Burma to Burbank. It was my only way home. The only way for me to come back here without a trace."

Ben asked, "What did that cost?"

Ellis didn't answer right away. "My soul. My good name. A wheelbarrow full of money your dad gave me. Chalk's guys said I could go for free if I muled some dope back stateside, but I said no. Your Pap backed me on that the whole way, no questions. Told me I could make a life here on the bay, and welcome. I was in a position, Ben. I could not say no."

Ben said, "You're not from around here."

Ellis sat up straighter and said, "I am now."

Ben said, "What's your real name?"

Ellis shook his head. "Next time you're in D.C., you go to The Wall. My name's up there someplace. I won't ever say which name it is. To this day, I'm ashamed it's there alongside the real heroes. That's something I'll always have to live with. You run and tell *that*. I'm done talking."

His shoulders bowed, Ellis rose and went back on deck. Ben followed. Ellis had devils, but Ben had a few of his own. He doubted that his status as a Smith Island native was meaningful enough keep him alive and in charge of this crew over the next few hours. Would vouching for Ellis protect his friend, or draw fire on himself? Ben was sick of fighting, and figuring angles and personalities, but he was in too deep. He could not give up now. That moment for backing out had passed the instant he found his father's corpse on the bottom of the Chesapeake.

He muttered to himself, "Whisky-Whisky-Delta-Delta."

Ellis caught the reference, and smiled thin. "What Would Dick Do?"

Ben nodded.

Ellis said, "All due respect, he's not here now. You are."

Ben said nothing.

Keeping an eye on the other boat, Tom Fox said, "I still got 'em. But I don't think the fonny fools got *us*."

Ben said, "Throttle back, Wade. Let them toll in closer. A lot closer."

Tension aboard the boat coiled tight. The *Palestrina* and Chalk's crew slowly closed with the *Varina Davis*.

Ben waited until the *Palestrina*'s cuddy cabin was almost always visible over the wave crests. "Here we go now. Before we lose them. Open up!"

Everyone had been waiting for the order. Though the enormous market guns had been left ashore, no one had boarded unarmed. They all snatched up their pump-guns. The men of the Council aimed above the horizon toward the *Palestrina,* and started shooting and shucking their weapons, loosing a terrible din of rolling thunder. They hooted and yelled all the while. Hot smoking spent shells flew and spun and bounced all over the deck. Some shells hissed when they landed in the water.

Sonny Wright piped up with demonic glee. "God a-Mercy, don't mar *Palestrina*'s paint! Hiram'll haunt us 'til Kingdom Come!"

Sonny knew they were too far off for the shotfall to do any harm to Hiram's beloved boat. His quip was more a reminder to everybody that dear friends had already shed blood for this fortune. That blood would be repaid drop for drop, times ten.

Ben raised a hand after a half a minute of Remington's Symphony Number 0-0, in the key of Mud Flat Major. "Ho' up!"

Everybody ceased fire. They waited to see if their ruckus achieved what they needed.

Fox confirmed, "Yep, they hauled their wind. Watching us."

Now Chalk had to know the Smith Islanders were returning to Deep Banks Island. He also knew there was a formidable company aboard, all armed to the teeth. Ben hoped his friends had sounded like a bunch of crazy rednecks. He wanted the interlopers to stick with them all night, but not venture too close. Over the *Varina Davis*'s idling engines, all Ben could hear were the snicks, clicks, and snaps as everyone on board quietly reloaded.

"Okay. Throttle up, Wade," said Ben. "It's time we give them an eyeful of what they came for."

CHAPTER 48

CHALK'S EYES BLAZED as he stared at the distant boat. "What in the hell was that?"

It sounded like the Tet Offensive over on the deadrise from Smith Island. The wind and rain had slackened. A thick cloud cover still oppressed the daylight into funereal gloom. Chalk's crew had not yet put on their NVGs. 'Til that moment he believed he had whittled the competition down to a few moronic weaklings. Now, even more of the enemy had herded together on a boat. For a party. With guns! Blasting indiscriminately all over the place. Shot dribbling into the water around them like rain; pattering down on the *Palestrina*'s deck like black sleet.

Drunken Hooples! And now they were all bearing down on Deep Banks Island for his gold! Chalk had counted on natural greed to keep Ben Blackshaw from spreading the word, and the wealth. This evidence of collaboration and teamwork was a marked disappointment.

Slagget said, "Boy Blackshaw came back with pals."

Chalk rolled his eyes. "Thanks for the news flash. And thanks loads for snuffing half our gun hands right when we need them. We could be in there and on them like Hell's Angels if it weren't for you."

As far as Chalk could see, the deceased Simon Clynch was right. This entire gig was cursed from the jump. Snakebit. So be it. There was no way he was going to cave or quit. Not this close to success.

Slagget feigned a tug of his forelock and a scuff of his shoe. "Well gosh, a man with a knife could've done a lot of damage. But I know it's my fault. I rushed the pat-down. I screwed up. I'm sorry."

Chalk knew better. After the stunt with the mystery knife, Slagget was still on Chalk's short list for killing. Yet, as he had so recently proven, Slagget was a dead-eye with a gun. As a bleak reminder of Slagget's prowess, a black cherry tea of blood and bay water still swirled across the deck. A thicker sludge of gore made it clear where the bodies had lain until they were dumped overboard. For the time being, Chalk could not purge Slagget.

Tahereh wisely chose to overlook the slaughter of her men for her own survival. She said, "I don't believe the gold, or the device, will still be on Deep Banks by tomorrow morning."

Chalk considered this. Her thought had merit. The watermen's natural temptation would be hard to resist: to land that treasure back on Smith Island where they could keep a closer eye on it. The islanders had to realize that would draw Chalk along, too. There were women and children to think of. At least Ben Blackshaw knew that *Right Way Moving & Storage* was a serious band of cutthroats. This was going to be a long night. *Una noche Toledana*, as an old merc buddy from Madrid called those dark stakeout hours without end.

They trailed the watermen as close as they dared without drawing actual hostility. As Tahereh predicted, the Smith Islanders penetrated Deep Banks Island. They entered by the small channel that opened up to the northwest. The real problem was gauging which way they might leave. From the *Palestrina*'s charts, Chalk knew that same waterway opened out to the southeast into Tangier Sound as well. No way they could cover both leads unless they split up in the two boats, and there was no way he would do that. He wasn't sure of Tahereh alone, or how she'd get along with Slagget. And he wasn't putting Slagget on a boat by himself either. God only knows what kind of play he'd make beyond Chalk's watchful eye. He'd been pretty bold not six feet away from his boss.

Landing for reconnaissance was a possibility. Chalk did not relish the idea of stepping onto an unfamiliar shore populated by drunken, trigger-happy watermen in the dead of night. That had the hallmarks of an alternate ending to *Deliverance*. Chalk was brave, but not stupid.

He aired a concern to no one in particular, "Why didn't those lunatics go in from the other way? From the Tangier Sound side? It's farther south. Closer to Smith. More convenient. More protected from the storm."

Slagget posited, "Too shallow for that big boat? Too narrow?"

Tahereh said, "Or maybe they wanted us to see them, knowing we might come in from the lighthouse in the northwest."

Chalk gave her a look. Tahereh developed her thesis. All the while she was unable to keep from glancing at Slagget's gun hand. It was like a nervous tic she'd recently and justifiably acquired.

She said, "All the shooting just now? Would they have done it if we weren't nearby? Perhaps it was a dumbshow of some kind."

"Sure. Trying to scare us off!" Chalk's hubris did not serve him well in the Chesapeake.

Slagget said, "I'm sure they don't get out much. Maybe it's like their Cinco de Mayo or something. Redneck Independence Day. Some kind of Second Amendment hootenanny."

"Or they wanted to get our attention," Tahereh persisted.

Chalk said. "Right. So we would follow them into their territory and get our asses shot off."

Slagget went off. "How do they even know who we are? It's practically dark out here. We're too far off. No, they're sitting on a fortune, and they drank too much. Got loopy with the smoke poles, that's all. Tahereh, you know that's just what your people do whenever there's a party. Blasting your AK-47s in the air on full auto, like it's Nickel Bullet Night at the Kasbah."

"Fuck off, Slagget. My people do no such thing." Tahereh stared meaningfully at him. His Five-seveN was still snug, and still hot in its holster under his armpit.

Slagget argued, "If those knuckleheads have the balls to mess with us head-on, I'd be shocked. You don't bait somebody into an ambush by shooting off guns, is my point. It spoils the surprise. It's antithetical to the very concept."

Chalk recalled Senator Morgan blabbing about *haichi shiki*, the Japanese running ambush. *Could these marsh monkeys pull off a stunt like that? Could they even think of it?*

CHAPTER 49

THE ISLANDERS STEERED the *Varina Davis* down Little Pungers Creek, cut to port, then bore north up the gut toward the heron rookery hollow. Wade Joyce's deadrise drew more water than *Miss Dotsy*, and had broader beam. They were forced to stop well short of the shallower spot where Ben and Ellis had landed before. For this afternoon's work the extra distance to the hollow would require all the manpower they had aboard.

Ben said, "It's a fair step inland. Sam, please stand watch here in case Chalk cowboys up and gallops in. I don't expect him to, but I didn't expect any of this."

If he could not shorten the distance to the hollow, at least Sonny Wright would lead them to the nearest planked gut to make the going easier. Everyone but Sam the watchman put over the side into the wax myrtle and spartina. They toted shovels along with their shotguns. Art Bailey left his golf club aboard.

Ben and Sonny led off. Everyone followed like obedient lemmings. As the Smith Island Irregulars sloshed toward the hollow, they could hear a few herons still restless on the nests. Rumbling low. Lonesome George swooped over their heads like an airborne picket offering both challenge and greeting.

Nearly there. The acrid year-round stench of the rookery's guano committed aggravated assault on their nostrils, and made a few eyes water.

Ben signaled a halt outside the hollow's natural embankment. Ellis chuckled out loud as all Ben's little chickens stopped in their tracks and held quiet.

Ben listened to the late afternoon noises. Tried to hear any interlopers over the rainless wind. He tilted his head sideways. Peeked one eye over the low hill. Only his left eye and ear were exposed if anybody in the hollow took a shot at him. Nothing happened. It seemed that all the bogies were out in the Chesapeake on the *Palestrina*. Ben waved everyone onward. The men filed over the embankment into the hollow.

Ben pointed to Sonny Wright. Gestured to the berm where he should stand watch. Sonny dutifully trudged up the slope, and faced the water. With Sam Nuttle back guarding the *Varina Davis*, Ben's two most likely mutineers were separated for now.

Lorton Dyze looked around the hollow. Visually scouring it for disturbed earth. Ben and Ellis had covered the burial place well. The storm had scattered more debris around the site, perfecting its camouflage.

Dyze eyed Ben. Excited, he shifted his weight from one foot to the other like a small boy wanting ice cream. "Get to it, son!"

Ben rested his Remington against a tree. Poised his shovel over a spot on the ground. It took only two strokes of the spade before he heard a shotgun shell ratcheting into a chamber.

Ben turned just as a different shotgun blasted next to his ear. Herons squawked loud above, took flight in panic.

Tom Fox dropped kneeling into the dirt clutching his bleeding flank.

Reverend Mosby jacked another shell into his smoking shotgun. Pulled the trigger again. This time, a twenty-foot hip shot. Fox's chest opened in tatters of flesh, bone, and flannel.

Everyone stared at the man of God.

Mosby spoke quietly. "A born sinner. Sorry boys. He was about to throw down on Ben. And he's been dipping into the collection plate on Sundays. May God have mercy on his soul."

Ellis muttered, "Gimme that old time religion."

Mosby had just cut down a man he had grown up with. Known all his life. The other Councilmen remained impassive. Including the suspect Sonny Wright.

Aware that Ellis was also backing him, Ben moved ten paces to where Tom Fox lay. Nudging the body with his toe, Ben said, "And for those of you playing the home version of our game, Tom was standing right on top of our gold. Seriously, boys. Don't worry. There's enough to go around."

Shovels bit into blood-clotted earth. Five minutes later they had one box uncovered. Ben pulled out the flat metal key from his shirt. He wiped dirt away from the box's slot. The lock clanked as the key went home. Ben opened the lid. Everyone but Sonny Wright, who stayed at his post, gathered around.

Dyze said, "Nothing too nice about that."

It was the bomb, the timer still counting down. Two hours, fifty-six minutes, fourteen seconds 'til detonation. All the men except Ben and Ellis took a step back.

Ben said, "Can we have a minute here?"

Dyze said, "Hell, ye can have two hours and fifty-five minutes as far I'm concerned. Drop us a line when ye find work. Come on, boys."

The Councilmen trudged single file out of the hollow. They were barely halfway down the planked gut leading back to the *Varina Davis* when Ellis called to them from the brow of the embankment.

He shouted, "It's safe! Ben stopped the timer. Now let's do what we came to do."

Lorton Dyze asked, "Care to tell us how he managed that?"

Ellis shook his head. "Can't. I didn't see. God help us, for this scheme to work he'll be starting that damn thing up again pretty soon."

A grumble went through the assembly as they moved back toward the hollow.

Sonny Wright said, "Ye can't be serious. Look here, Ellis. Ye think Ben's okay upstairs?"

Dyze said, "Don't care if he's crazy as a shit-house rat. We're letting him run this one."

Art Bailey said, "None of you all got a better plan to bring in a few million this afternoon. His pap started it. The boy's bringing it home, far as I'm concerned."

Ellis nodded agreement. "Ben is Ben. Always been a little off-kilter, but he's no fool. And for now, the bomb's safe, which is a big load off my mind. So please come back and lend a hand with the gold. I'm sick of looking at it, let alone hauling it."

Sonny quipped, "When you get sick of spending it, is when I'll jump in."

Working hard, the move took an hour. Finally, Lonesome George settled on the ground as the men marched the boxes out of the hollow for the last time. He gave them a single hacking bleat as if to say farewell, and good riddance.

CHAPTER 50

AN HOUR PASSED on the *Palestrina*. Slagget said, "I think the wingnuts slipped out the other side, chief."

Chalk said, "Patience, Slagget. Be the night. Now cut that engine, pronto. Let's give a listen."

Slagget shut the motor down. With no steering way, the *Palestrina* rolled dangerously in the waves.

Despite the weather, the late afternoon held a certain beauty for Chalk. He believed there was a degree of romance woven in with the closeness of death. A few more quiet minutes passed. Then it came.

At first it was a subsonic rumble of large diesel engines, first felt in the chest like an extra heartbeat before it was heard. Chalk, Slagget and Tahereh put on night vision goggles to help them see through the twilight to the source of the thrum.

Finally, the boat emerged from the interior waterways of the island. As if to confirm their sighting, the watermen opened fire at the sky with their shotguns once again. The flashes and the din of guns competed with the lightning and thunder of the night.

Slagget muttered, "Idiots."

If Tahereh was right, the firing meant they were deadly smart. That did nothing to squelch Chalk's frustration, "Dammit! What a bunch of Hottentot retards!"

Tahereh was silent.

Chalk ordered, "Start the engine! Let's see where they're going, but for God's sake give those dipshits a wide berth."

Slagget restarted the engine. Geared the prop, ahead slow. There was every reasonable expectation that the men on the target boat would turn south toward Smith Island.

To everyone's consternation, the Smith Islanders set a course to the northwest away from their home port.

"Where the hell are they going now? The lighthouse is gone. Are they still delivering like I told them?" That was too much for a skeptic killer to believe. Chalk pulled out a chart, and examined it with a small red-lensed flashlight. He said, "There's nothing out that way now except a patch of sand called Spring Island. Shallows all around it. Tahereh. Bill. I ask you. What. The. Hell?"

Slagget said, "Beats me. Deep Banks was a good place to keep the stuff indefinitely. And Smith Island would be good too, if second best. People all over the place. The FIBUA would have favored them since it's their home turf. Whatever you may think of these jerk-offs, I guess they know their way around a shotgun, and these sand hills."

Tahereh asked, "FIBUA?"

Slagget sneered, "Princess Achmalah-Malah doesn't get Fighting In Built Up Areas. Means house to house. Dragging a recovery mission and a firefight down on their families might go against these guys' grain."

Chalk concurred. "That's what I thought. Or maybe they're like Apaches, and their squaws are the most savage of the lot. Tahereh, what's your chick-vibe on those nimrods? Give us the Margaret Mead 411."

She paused before she spoke. "I agree with you. Perhaps relocating the items together might confer a sense of wider communal ownership? We all know what an effort it must have required of Dick and Ben Blackshaw to get the items to Deep Banks Island. The bulk. The sheer weight. From wherever they got it, this was difficult work, and they did it quickly."

Chalk interrupted her. "Save us the time-and-motion studies, pussycat. What in the name of all that's holy are they doing now, in your estimation?"

She confessed, "I'm as baffled as you. For now, we're doing all we can. Follow. Wait, and see. It's what reconnoitering's all about. Gathering data. Then we interpret the intel. Then we plan. Then we execute."

Chalk gave a disgusted snort, and shook his head as he looked from her to Slagget, and back to her. Disappointed as he was, he knew Tahereh was right.

Tabling further speculation, they continued to follow the Smith Islanders north-northwest toward Spring Island. The distance was not great, but it still lay a good eight miles from any substantial landmass in all directions.

They watched through the NVGs as the deadrise landed on Spring Island, which was little more than a postage stamp of salty grit during a storm-surged spring tide. Chalk was transfixed. He gripped the boat's gunwale until his knuckles blanched, nearly spat with rage as the watermen offloaded all twenty boxes of the shipment. His shipment!

Chalk vacillated between drawing his gun, and calling Ben on The Kid's sat-phone to make a bargain for the mother. It took superhuman effort to fight both his natural inclination and the gathering psychotic storm that his meds had kept at bay for so long. He held tight, knowing he had already seeded the cancer of hope for Ben's ma-bird in the waterman's brain. No, let that tantalizing hint do its work. Let it grow its malignant tendrils. Let it eat Ben alive for now. He'd cash in that chip at just the right moment. And if it didn't turn out to be a powerful threat, it might just serve him as insurance.

There was an old building on the island that seemed to be the men's destination. After reaching the structure, they labored like a line of ants to and from the boat. At times Chalk thought he'd lost them behind the reed-covered islets that dotted the surrounding waters.

On the chart, Slagget drew in the smaller islands that weren't already depicted.

When the hauling onshore was done, Chalk observed that two fewer men reboarded the boat.

Tahereh said, "They've posted guards at the old building."

Chalk watched as the boat passed a half mile off, and finally bore south toward Smith Island.

He said, "Okay. That's it then. Spring Island is now our target. But we'll need some bodies to get this done."

He pulled out his sat-phone. Speed-dialed a number. After a moment, he said, "Farron! Wake up, you sissy-ass punk! Get your team prepped. I want you boys wheels-up at twenty hundred hours. Your destination is a little airstrip on Tangier Island. TGI on your sectional chart. And remember to stay out of the D.C. Special Flight Rules Area. I'll meet you."

He ended the call without waiting for a response. Chalk said to Slagget, "We're done here. South to Tangier Island for the pick-up. Keep your distance from those bastards."

Chalk had called in his cavalry.

CHAPTER 51

SONNY WRIGHT AND Art Bailey stood watch over the hoard on Spring Island. They would be warm enough in the ancient Barren Creek Hotel if it did not collapse in the breeze and kill them outright. The hotel was abandoned many decades before. Spring Island was once so much more than this all-but-eroded sandbar. It had once boasted its own post office, a general store, a number of homes, a small church, and a burial ground. The Chesapeake Bay's tides and winter ice floes had claimed almost all the buildings over the years, carved it down to the islet it was today. Only the hotel remained.

The rest of the men returned on the *Varina Davis* to Ben's saltbox for final preparations.

Ben went straight upstairs to LuAnna. She slept fitfully. Kimba Mosby told him the fever had broken with the passing of the storm. Kimba spoke confidently. LuAnna would be whole again in time. Ben knew Kimba was lying to keep him focused on the mission. The storm was by no means past.

LuAnna was ashen, damp. Her breathing was shallow. The sight of her like this fueled Ben's rage. He promised himself Chalk's jackals would pay in the worst conceivable ways for what they'd done. Though Ben would hate to confess it even to himself, revenge was now an integral part of his plan. That is, once the question of his mother was settled. If LuAnna's illness was an all-consuming distraction for Ben, the possibility of rescuing his mother from dangers unknown pressed him even further down. What the hell did Chalk really know? With no understanding of the true threat against his mother, Ben was hamstrung.

Looking down at LuAnna, the tortured faces of Ben's military targets reared up to haunt him again. Now there were new faces in the crowd. Chalk's fallen lackeys. Hiram Harris, and Charlene. Innocent friends stood in that mental sepulcher alongside his dead enemies. Ben finally understood. In fact, now they all knew the truth, the ghosts and Ben. His once-vaunted wartime blood-letting was just as damning as any peacetime murder. Killing then was as banal and horrific as killing now. He was no hero. He was no yeoman reaper made innocent by his medals. Yet he had to go on, no matter what lay in store for him tonight.

Dyze hollered up to Ben from downstairs. Ben kissed LuAnna, perhaps for the last time, perhaps his last kiss for anyone, and descended to the parlor. With a swift scourge of self-loathing, Ben knew there was room in the dark hollow of his soul for even more faces. All of humankind could enter there. Ben wondered what had happened to him. When had he turned? At what point had he regressed, and fallen from grace? His love for LuAnna, his terror at the thought of losing her, had dropped a junkyard electromagnet on his moral compass, twirling it like the Mad Hatter's tea-cup ride at Disney. North was south. Right was wrong. Wrong was necessary, and what's more, it was good.

Despite the insight, Ben still felt trapped. The Islanders depended on him to help see them through this bad business. For now, Ben had to stay the jagged course he'd plotted and sold to his friends. He would try to find his way home to peace, redemption, and forgiveness sometime later on. If there was a later. If there was an after.

At Lorton Dyze's suggestion, Ben stepped across the way to Orville Hurley's house, and knocked. Hurley had stood watch with his shotgun and his dog, Adolf, when Chalk first visited the saltbox.

The Councilmen had eyed Hurley to join their cabal. Tom Fox's death on Deep Banks Island left an inconvenient vacancy both in the Council's ranks, and in the plans for the night's work. Tapping Ben to make the summons ratified his own nomination to new power and status in the shadow circle. On the surface, it appeared Ben had more than made his bones. Just as well. He'd done it literally many times before, returned living human beings to eternal dust.

Hurley and Adolf met Ben at the door. Hurley quickly agreed to come aboard in every sense. Adolf padded along by his side.

Lorton Dyze confirmed by phone that Bob Crockett had done what was asked. The Tangiermen had begun to earn their share.

While the men were out on their maneuvers, Julie Nuttle and Mary Joyce had prepared a vast meal. Eggs, fried chicken, potatoes of every description, oyster fritters, and preserved fruit pies. Several of the women, including Julie, worked in the Smith Island Baking Company up the path in Ewell. She could knock out the Island's famous eight-layer chocolate cake with her eyes closed. For some of them it would be the last sweet flavor of home, of life itself, except for a final taste of gunpowder, bile, and blood.

Coffeepots were charged and emptied over and over again. No one touched liquor now. A relief from boredom, but never courage, was to be found in the stashed jugs and bottles on Smith Island. A clear head was the order of the day, and of the night to come. Ben's order. Despite the feast, Ben did not touch a morsel of food for fear he wouldn't keep it down.

Ben's throbbing ribs tormented him. Iron Butterfly's Ron Bushy had surrendered the thoracic drum kit to a poorly rehearsed high school half-time marching band. Despite the tympanic fugue, Ben refused to allow Kimba Mosby to look at his injury.

Between mouthfuls, the men stripped, cleaned, oiled and reloaded their guns. There was nervous palavering, too. Sometimes the excited chatter made no sense, was barely even English. Regardless, everyone still nodded and smiled and laughed by turns as if they had heard sage insights or hilarious jokes. Their more coherent yarns were peppered with expressions and references only a Smith Islander could fathom. These few pre-battle hours brought them all even closer as a fighting unit.

Darkness fell. Time came to set out. They loaded the *Varina Davis* with all they would need. They embarked with the sneak-boats in tow and the sinkboxes stowed on the *Varina Davis*'s stern.

Julie, Kimba, and Mary were all fair hands with a shotgun. They were reluctant to stay behind, but they still had work to do. From the mainland, they summoned a sympathetic Dr. Alan, who had long ago lost her license to practice. She was available by boat in any weather for a price. She specialized in removing bullets, stitching gashes, and staying quiet. She would wait at Ben's saltbox for casualties, her instruments, saws, needles and suture thread laid out at the ready. Maybe she could help LuAnna.

Then the women took up shotguns and old pistols and braved the storm, paying calls on a few particular neighbors. Neighbors who understood all of Smith Island's past, and who asked no questions. They were warned to take up guns and watch over their homes for the next few hours. Just in case Ben failed and death came a-knocking.

PART IV
DEAD RECKONING

CHAPTER 52

IN ADDITION TO the real possibility of death at any moment, Tahereh was suffering an existential meltdown. After recent events, she had to acknowledge that her body-and-soul investment in jihad was predicated on a false belief. The realization briefly unmanned her though she was a woman.

Born in Tehran, educated at Bryn Mawr, Tahereh had not been aware until now that deep down, her terrorist zeal for mayhem had been fueled by personal hopelessness bordering on clinical depression. It had also been coauthored by a self-consuming rage at the Hobbesian life that stretched out before her. *Solitary, poor, nasty, brutish, and short.* Neither academia, nor a career, nor having a family held any interest for her. Her soul was nurtured, not on milk, nor on Lucite tombstones of corporate deals closed, but on sheer adrenalin. After turning to her current line, she embraced a life bereft of expectations great or small, of anything other than an angry and fiery death. How could she sustain her sense of mission now if she were no longer furious? A taste of actual happiness and accomplishment from working in league with Chalk could well ruin her as a jihadi warrior.

She had lived her life as a drone hornet, ever ready to sting. And in stinging like a hornet she was also ready to bring about her own death at the same time. She had no problem with this. This was the martyr's way. On the other hand, in Chalk's nihilistic scenario, she could be the queen of drones, arbiter of a thousand martyrs' deaths. Wasn't it was always the old soldiers, the generals, who were remembered? Never the young, the brash enlisted, or the dead. *There! Now Chalk had her thinking of posterity.* She'd never cared about this kind of vanity before.

If she survived the night, if in the morning Chalk was truly beside her, and not standing triumphant over her corpse, she sensed her life would be sadly sweetened. If death came for her tonight, she could no longer be certain how she would feel in that final instant. Would she still connect with that ultimate martyr's ecstasy she had imagined for so long? No way to truly know. If nothing else, death is last-minute.

In a much less philosophical moment aboard the *Palestrina*, Tahereh was elated to watch Slagget's face fall when Chalk returned her HS2000 pistol, her seven spare clips and her Glock field knife.

Squirming with irritation, Slagget said, "Sure that's a good idea, boss?"

Chalk puffed his chest, lowered his chin, and got stern. "All my ideas are good."

Tahereh drew out the moment by inspecting the pistol's clips, sliding open the chamber, confirming that the weapon still had all sixteen rounds within.

Slagget was ill with rage. He asked, "Got a full clip?"

When she smiled and nodded a slow *yes,* he twitted her. "Keep a good count of how many shots you fire. Situations like this, I like to save a round for myself in case things go horribly wrong."

Tahereh replied, "Pragmatic to the very end, eh Bill? Please, use all the bullets you want. I promise you won't need the last one for yourself. Rely upon me." Tahereh smiled again. She refrained from pointing her finger at him and dropping the thumb hammer. He had got her meaning. For the rest of the journey, unrelieved hate outweighed lust when Slagget looked at her. This was understandable. After two firefights, a sleepless night, and a stormy day on the Chesapeake, Tahereh was not looking her cotillion best. No matter. Chalk didn't seem to care. Nor did he know she was also saving a bullet for him.

Perhaps she would be anointed the new Queen of Death after all. She recalled the Greek cheer of her alma mater, and for once took strength from it. *Anassa kata, kalo kale Ia ia ia Nike Bryn Mawr, Bryn Mawr, Bryn Mawr!* Queen, descend, I invoke you, fair one. Hail, hail, hail, victory …

CHAPTER 53

CHALK DELIGHTED IN Tahereh's exchange of barbs with Slagget. She understood Chalk's leadership tactics. He felt a team united is a team that could mutiny. She had more in common with Chalk than he thought at first. He preferred his squad to be manageably at odds. The only problem was that he might not benefit from the full power of his group's cohesive force in the breach. At least if he lost tonight's skirmish, *he* would survive.

Chalk cross-referenced between a chart of the waters around Tangier Island and the GPS. "We're getting in close to shore. We'll beach on the west side of the island. A hop, skip, and a jump to the airstrip from there."

Minutes later, Chalk drove the bow of the boat straight onto the sand through the surf. The breeze was lighter, and steady. The new moon even showed now and then as squall clouds wraithed by, like a bright sickle slashing through uncarded wool.

Slagget leapt onto the beach, and jogged inland until he found a rock for tying off the line he carried. Chalk and Tahereh toted weapons and three sets of NVGs to the low dunes. They did not put on the goggles, preferring for now to see by the hazy loom of house and street lights on Tangier.

They reached the runway, but held to its edge. It was wrapped in darkness.

Slagget licked his finger, held it up and said, "With this breeze now, they'll land south to north. We can walk up to meet them at the other end."

Chalk thought for a moment. He said, "I have a flashlight. We'll signal them. They can taxi back to us."

Tahereh asked, "How will they manage in this fog?"

Chalk said, "They have a choice of two non-precision instrument approaches. Farron, our pilot, can bring it in with NVGs. Good as they are, goggles can be kinda tricky to fly with depending on what generation they've got. In that clag up there, he might just click the transmit button a few times on the right frequency. Then that runway edge light you're about to trip over will come on with all the others. He'll see right where to put her down."

The evening grew colder. The darkness closed in around them as lights in the distant homes winked out. This left the rare street lights to cast only the faintest glow across the hillocks, rises, and dunes.

After an eternity of no more than fifteen minutes, Slagget softly said, "There. Got to be them."

Tahereh searched the sky. "I don't hear anything."

Chalk hissed, "Shut up! Listen."

Soon, they all picked the distant whine of a twin turboprop out of the closer rustle of reeds and the swish of waves rolling up the beach.

A few more moments passed. Chalk scanned the sky. "I got them. They've got all the lights on."

He pointed up at a small cluster of winking red, white, and green position lights moving in and out of cloud, as the engine sounds grew.

Chalk said, "Guess there's no reason for Farron to do a covert insertion. Nobody watching but us chickens."

They all followed the plane's path as it passed down the east side of the island.

Chalk muttered to himself, "Good boy. Stay out of that D.C. Special Flight Rules Area."

Of course, he had his own discreet squawk number he could have given MacDonald for the aircraft's transponder so he could pass through the SFRA without getting an F-16 on his wing, or a SAM up his rectum. Fine, but why should Chalk show his hand when things were going so well?

He mumbled, "I change my squawk number every week. Like my own personal Fibonacci sequence. A Chalk sequence, I guess. I Gauss. There's a Restricted Area just to the west of here, too. Navy gunnery range I think."

"Maynard, please shut up!" Tahereh was losing all patience.

"Watch it, baby." Chalk liked her spirit, but there was a limit. He chuckled. He knew she was taut as piano wire, wondering how her fate would play out in the next few minutes. He was not offended that she hadn't fully bought in to his vision of sharing world dominion. There would be time for convincing later on.

The airplane's engine sounds changed as the pilot adjusted power and altered the pitch of the props. The plane was now lined up for a long final approach to a murk-shrouded runway. A runway that none of the welcoming party had yet seen. Suddenly, the plane's landing lights blazed out in clouded beams. Farron had not donned his NVGs. He was saving the batteries for the work to come later that night. Smart move.

The strange tendrils of fog were thickening, wreathing over the ground. The mist had crept in and enveloped the entire airstrip waist-high while they'd been staring upward at the plane's approach. Chalk found it both weird and disconcerting to be so suddenly enswathed. The eerie vapor chilled his skin.

When the plane was only fifty feet above the ground, the white runway lights suddenly blinked on. Chalk watched as the pilot made minor corrections in the plane's glide slope.

It was Slagget who first signaled the catastrophe to come. "Shit. Damn!"

Chalk caught Slagget's alarm and looked where his lieutenant was pointing at the runway. The problem was invisible to the approaching pilot through the mist. Small islets of runway edge light revealed the truth only to the three confederates waiting on the ground.

The runway was a disaster area.

To Chalk, it looked like whole trees lay felled across it. And the strip's entire useable length was pocked with craters, heaps of dirt, slabs of pavement and other debris. The rusted hulk of an old truck lay spang in the middle, very Third World. All that was missing were the chickens, potbellied brats, and Sally Struthers cadging for handouts.

Chalk uttered a low, "No."

Then he dashed toward the middle of the runway directly in the plane's path. Waved his hands like a madman.

He screamed, "Go around! No! Go around! Abort! Break it off!"

Still the plane came down. Farron MacDonald was oblivious. Seen from the air in the poor weather, the runway lights created only small pools of light. They indicated the runway's position well enough, but gave no hint of its condition. The runway lights baited an invisible deathtrap luring Farron in. The plane's landing lights were not helping either. They were reflected back into the pilot's eyes by the strange obscuring ground cloud.

Roaring in frustration, Chalk crouched low as the plane's landing gear swooped over his head missing him by inches. The inevitable became grotesque reality.

The mist swirled up and away behind the plane's wingtips, twin curlicue apparitions of moisture, ghost-rats departing the doomed aircraft. The plane's nose rose up slightly as the pilot flared for touching down.

With a flash of sparks, the plane struck a mound of dirt with its left main gear. Gave a sudden lurch to the right as if shoved by a giant hand. The nose slewed left as the shriek of metal tore at Chalk's eardrums and set his teeth on edge like a thousand fingernails on a chalkboard.

The wings canted to the right. With sick fascination Chalk watched the descending wingtip gouge a furrow into the strip. Then the entire right wing wrenched free of the body. With the propeller still turning at full power, it flipped over and over, trailing a blaze of oily orange flame.

With the right wing gone, the left wing was now alone making lift, and it rose into the air levering the fuselage onto its side. The nose skewed further to the left. The right tail stabilizer tore free as it was buried in the ground.

Then the plane inverted completely. The tips of the left propeller hacked into the old runway. The left wing could not bear this new strain. It ripped free and spun away, spewing a gout of burning fuel across the plane's body, now a rolling fireball. It bounced and ricocheted down the runway from one obstruction to the next.

At last the ruptured silence of the night healed over. All movement ceased, except for the flames. Chalk was rooted in place. His trio's volition to move or speak was completely vitiated by what they'd just witnessed. Instead of reinforcements, only the soft, distant roar of burning fuel came down the runway to where they stood.

"God damn all Blackshaws!" Chalk roared, teeth flashing, nostrils flared. "God shove them all straight up the Devil's ass!"

After a moment's paralysis, Chalk began to trot toward the burning wreck. Slagget and Tahereh followed, passing among logs of driftwood, heaps of torn-up asphalt, and the craters from which the chunks had been dug. All the destruction lay fully in view before them. The thick, low fog was dissipating as if sentient, knowing its destructive work was done.

Chalk grumbled and barked as he double-timed down the field. "Bastards! They tore up their own airstrip! In case I wanted to use it! On the damn off-chance! Jesus Christ in a tutu, Dick's crazier than I thought."

Dodging amongst burning sections of the wings, Tahereh and Slagget followed Chalk. They all felt the fire's heat as they ran deeper into the debris field. The flames threw clouds of black smoke into the air. The breeze blew it back in their faces. Eyes and noses running, they got as close as they could to the fuselage. It was a blackened, battered ruin.

The rear of the plane, which had been closed off with a clamshell cargo ramp and door, was mangled. A human body lay half-in and half-out. No movement.

Then the screaming. Chalk was comfortably numb to all expressions of human suffering, but this was a new horror. It was the sound of a man regaining consciousness just in time to witness his own immolation. The desperate paean of a condemned soul departing for hell. Or worse, for oblivion. The sound took too long to end, though it lasted only moments.

The burning man's final scream faded. The flames' roar was joined by a pounding against the metal insides of the plane. It came from forward by the cockpit. As Chalk's team approached, they noticed a small door. It bowed outward from impacts from the inside.

A muffled, choking voice called, "Dammit! Open the damn door, dude!"

A moment of reason must have followed this outburst. The emergency release mechanism was tripped. The entire door popped off its hinges and fell to the ground with a clang. It was immediately followed by a human being. His black tactical suit trailed plumes of smoke. The plane was now coffin and crematorium in one.

Without a word, Slagget grabbed the smoldering man under his arm-pits, and dragged him clear of the worst heat. Chalk disappeared, wriggling inside the door from which the survivor had just leapt.

Within seconds Slagget was back at the fuselage. He yanked the semi-conscious form of a second man out of the plane as Chalk shoved from behind. This was not risking all for comrades. Not heroics. They were des-perate for more boots on the ground. More soldiers equaled a fortune.

The team's ammunition on the aircraft began to cook off in the blaze. The bangs started singly. Then they grew faster, like killer Jiffy-Pop. Bullet holes randomly pocked the sides of the fuselage, as rounds zinged and buzzed past Tahereh. That first screaming man had not gone to hell. He had left it. And Chalk was still inside.

Twice more, Chalk and Slagget rescued dazed men from the wreck. Then Chalk hurled himself out the escape hatch to the ground. Coughing like a three-pack-a-day man, he staggered over to the survivors Tahereh was treating with water from their canteens.

Chalk gasped, "No more," between coughs. He wasn't clear whether this meant there were no more survivors, or that he had enough men and was no longer willing to risk his hide.

Slagget choked out, "We gotta get clear."

There was a loud roaring noise to punctuate his suggestion. An instant later a small missile shot out the cockpit windscreen. With its guidance sys-tem damaged and locked onto nothing, it curveted wildly through the air, and splashed with a hot hiss in the Chesapeake.

Chalk complained, "Aw crap! A Stinger! Could've used that."

Two of the crash survivors could hobble away under their own steam. Of the other two, Tahereh supported one as he limped. Chalk and Slagget dragged the last man between them. They assembled behind a low mound of dirt. Round after .50 caliber round of tracer fired into the sky. Bullets spun along the ground past where they huddled.

The man they dragged was badly broiled along his legs and feet. He turned his sooty face to Chalk and said, "Sorry, chief. Kinda blew that one."

Chalk smiled like an understanding uncle. "Nonsense Farron! They say any landing you can walk away from is a good one. *Dude.*"

Then Chalk drew his pistol, shot Farron twice in the face.

Chalk continued, "Unfortunately, he wasn't walking anywhere with those burns. We gotta di-di on out of here! Anybody notice the natives aren't exactly rushing to investigate all this Guy Fawkes Day bullshit? It's a total setup, and I'm not hanging out to get my nards shot off."

He scrutinized the man Tahereh had helped to walk. "What's the story, Petunia, can *you* hump it?" The man glanced at Farron MacDonald's corpse, then back at Chalk, nodded briskly, and slapped Tahereh's helping hand away. He gave his best, "Hoowa!"

Chalk said, "Good boy. Let's boogie."

The six made their way back down the airstrip as quickly as possible toward the boat. As they went, previously sound fuel tanks in the plane's wings heated, warped, and blew. More ammo of all sizes banged and whizzed into the sky. The odor of burning meat tainted the oily air.

Chalk took in the sabotage of the airstrip as they hurried along its length. He muttered, "No doubt about it. Somebody's screwing with me. Someone who knows me a little too well. Dick and the rest of them, they're all in on it together. Not good."

Chalk assessed his three remaining survivors along the way, ready to unburden himself of any more gimps or laggards. They all made it to the *Palestrina*. With some pushing and shoving, the new men scrambled aboard much worse for wear from the last eight minutes' ordeal.

Only Tahereh seemed bucked up about the crash. It had helped her position. With the sudden reduction of Chalk's able-bodied personnel, she knew she was still needed. So she was still alive.

CHAPTER 54

WADE JOYCE GUIDED the *Varina Davis* up the Tangier Sound side of Smith Island. They would make better time that way, and avoid swamping the low punts porpoising in tow. The water was calmer than before. Still, no one relaxed. They all knew a retreating storm could wind up again for a final knockdown punch with little warning. Ben counted on it.

Everyone looked toward home as they rounded north. Though nobody said it, every man felt sure that something was going to die tonight. Even if there were no casualties, even if dawn found the treasure finally safe, Smith Island was not going to be the same. Any eyes that looked again on their home of so many generations would be seasoned by battle. Smith Island would not simply be the place where they lived. As in the old days, it would once again be a bastion they'd defended together.

For now, and in spite of the bloody work ahead, Ben savored his welcome behind the Islanders' social palisades. Tonight he was the captain of an expeditionary party; at once sailing them into a golden future, and back in time to their crimson past.

After such a violent day, Ben knew that dealings with Chalk and his men might not play out in complete accordance with Holy Scripture. Ben studied Reverend Mosby closely. Their shepherd wore a thoughtful frown as if he were reconsidering what he was about to do. Whatever his contemplations, he never stopped oiling the lock on *Barking Betty,* the mammoth market gun.

Ben took the minister's presence, not to mention his cold dispatch of Tom Fox back on Deep Banks Island, as assurance of the rightness of their cause. Mosby's actions confirmed what Ben believed, that this single band of raiders could be of two minds and two hearts. Instead of falling down before evil, they could rise up and vanquish it, still loved by the Lord though blood might stain their hands. Or so Ben hoped. The very existence of God, let alone His relevance and blessing, were not foremost in Ben's mind. Not when he thought of LuAnna, whom he truly worshipped.

Lorton Dyze watched aft over the punts. He nudged Ben. "Gonna be some fun tonight," he said.

Ben thought Dyze was just passing time, until the old man nudged him again and pointed to the south just over the horizon where Tangier Island lay. There was a glow of fire, and little lights spinning off high into the evening air. It reminded Ben of the nighttime images of Baghdad in Gulf War One, the bombs, the tracers, the flares, the mechanized death-dealing. Ben thought how funny it was that death sometimes came with a bright light, proud like a child, *look at me, here I come,* demanding notice. Personally, he was used to a less flashy kill.

Smiling, Dyze shook his head. "No idear what *that* all is."

Knocker Ellis said, "Doesn't seem warm enough for Fourth of July."

Dyze said, "I reckon it's Crockett and his Tangier boys looking after things."

Satisfied with that, the Smith Islanders turned as one, faced forward into the night.

Dyze said to Ben, "So, the two of ye gonna to get round to it someday soon?"

Ben knew Dyze was talking about LuAnna. He said, "Soon." He caught himself before he added, *if she makes it.*

An old man could be a bother, but a wise old man was a true vexation. With Dyze's question, the real prospect of losing LuAnna crashed in again on Ben. He covered, saying, "Ready to be godfather of a Blackshaw someday?"

Dyze raised his eyebrows. Ben could not determine what the next noise was at first. It sounded like something between the tick-tick-tick of a solenoid popping from a near-dead car battery and the creak of a rusty sign blowing in a Smith Island flaw. Then he realized it was Dyze shaking and holding his sides with phlegmy laughter.

Ben said, "I take that as a yes? And her father's gone. Bet she'd like you to give her away. I assume you'll be at the wedding."

"Ye set a date?"

Ben said, "No, but pretty soon."

Ben was trying to settle Dyze down before the wheezing ancient ruptured himself. Dyze's laughter died away too quickly for Ben's liking.

The old man gave Ben a small smile. "Oh, I reckon I'll be along one way or t'other, doncha know."

With that, a chill enveloped Ben. Reverend Mosby on the other hand puffed up at the prospect of a holy sacrament to redeem himself from the damnable work he had done that day, and the blood he would shed come dark.

As word of Ben's wedding went around the boat there was a new-found lightness that had nothing to do with gold. The precious metal was simply plunder to these men. A gilded adventure forged in midnight iron and fire. They all knew money came and went. Even vast sums of it meant little to men who had no fear of hard work. On the other hand, Ben and LuAnna walking the plank was a joyous nod toward tomorrow, provided the bomb and Chalk left them any shard of a future.

Ben sensed that now they had stopped being a ragged bunch of Smith Islander Irregulars. And Community was such a weak word, the parlance of barrio playground grant-proposals. This crew had coalesced as a people, like ancient Spartans forming ranks with a bond of blood running among them.

They bore north to Spring Island. Two flashes of light from the boat. Three answering flashes from shore. The signal and countersign. The coast, small as it was, lay clear ahead. Rather than shooting the watermen down as strangers with no business putting in to shore, the waiting guards emerged from the dunes to help moor the boat.

As picnic-wrapped food from the saltbox kitchen was passed to the guards, Ben detailed everyone to their places on shore for the night.

When Ben assigned the water side of the operation, they all heard, "I want me a sinkbox."

It was Lorton Dyze. This was the only command he uttered, de facto head man though he was.

Ben said, "It's barely calm enough for a low boat like that. And it'll be a long cold night. Stay aboard the *Varina Davis*. If this flaw makes up, and you take a wave—"

"Fine. I'll anchor shallow where I can stand if it comes to that." Dyze gave Ben a wicked look, and with it he warned that favoring this old man's years was a grave mistake.

Ben had sense enough to acquiesce. "All right. Wade will tow you out."

With that, Dyze picked up his scratched and dented plaid Thermos along with his pump gun. He reboarded the *Varina Davis* with a new spring in his step.

Ben deployed Reverend Mosby on the dunes near the hotel. Anybody landing from the southwest waters would be seen from up there. Broad shallows and muddy flats would protect many of the other approaches. Ben pegged Chalk for a soldier who'd want to boldly hit the shore quick and hard. Anything to avoid slogging sob wet through a hundred yards of boot-sucking mud. No slow stealthy insertions for this adversary. Not his style.

Before Reverend Mosby ascended the dunes, he cleared his throat as he did at the start of any Sunday sermon. At the familiar sound, everyone immediately stood in a loose circle and bowed their heads. Ben was impatient as he centered down for the exercise in prayer.

The preacher kept it simple. "Lord, please protect us all tonight. May we Your children be blessed and preserved from the doings of evil men who would bring sadness and ruin to us with their sinning bloodthirsty ways. And if tonight is our last night on earth and we should perish, please take us home to Your bosom where we might abide in peace everlasting. God bless us every one." With that nod to Tiny Tim Cratchit, everyone amened.

From Wade Joyce's boat at the shoreline, Dyze called out, "And God bless you, too, Brother Mosby!"

Those were the last words they'd ever hear from Lorton Dyze, though his shotgun had volumes yet to speak.

Reverend Mosby hefted his Remington, and strolled off to his post. Orville Hurley took one of the sneakboats. Though a German shepherd, Adolf boarded like a born water dog, and lay down still in the stern. Ben issued *Barking Betty* for Hurley to place down lengthwise along the keel. Man, boat, and headache gun would roar out with a quarter mile of hot-leaded hell for anyone who came asking. Hurley would get off just one big fusillade before landing the sneakboat to mop up with Adolf. If his winter supper table was any indication, he'd make the market gun's single shot count.

Ephraim Teach vaulted into the *Varina Davis* with Wade Joyce and Dyze. Ben assigned him the other sinkbox. As tough as he was, Teach was small enough to lay out flat in the bottom of the strange little floating hide. Ben also knew the man was one of the company's few who did not smoke. He would not tip his position in the water either by sparking a cigarette, or sending out acrid signals for the enemy to scent. Hitting Chalk hard before he even reached shore was essential to Ben's plan.

Sonny Wright and Sam Nuttle got the other two sneak-boats. He issued Wright the monstrous market gun, *Vesuvius*, which swallowed and belched powder and shot like a ferrous dragon. In Wright's hands, *Vesuvius* would hack a scarlet swath through most any trouble with a pulse.

Sam Nuttle got *Chanticleer*, the battery gun with the eight fanned-out barrels. That day he'd made certain every powder charge in it was fresh and dry. Wade Joyce was to tow Wright's and Nuttle's boats around to cover the approaches to the west side of Spring Island, along with Ephraim Teach. Unfortunately, the waters were deep enough there for Chalk to make a straight-in attack.

Ben positioned Hurley to the south in his sneak boat. He also sited Dyze in his sinkbox, and Wade Joyce's deadrise to help cover the southern waters where the beach lay closest to the old hotel. That building would be Chalk's objective. Soon Ben would add more bait to the structure to be sure Chalk tolled in all the way for his plan to gel.

Ben dispatched Art Bailey and Ellis to the western side of the island to stand guard on land. They'd be ready to come running if the first trouble appeared from the south as Ben expected.

Knocker Ellis hung back a moment. "You'll need your spotter on this."

Ben was grateful for the thought, but said, "We'll need our west shore covered by the best men."

Ellis clearly disagreed, but didn't argue. "Okay Ben. But listen to me. Letting Chalk live won't make an angel out of him or you. You'll never teach that one a lesson."

"Not planning to teach him a lesson, Ellis. I'm going to burn down the school."

Ellis smiled. He headed west on foot with Art Bailey, who shouldered his golf club as well as his gun.

That left just Ben, and he had work to do. First, he ran to the old Barren Creek Hotel to deal with the bomb. When he was a child, the hotel always gave him the willies. It had big windows like empty eye sockets in a weather-bleached bone face. It brought his father's corpse to mind. Anyone foolish enough to enter the place would likely die of spider or rat bites. Ben's concerns about the structural integrity of the building were worse than usual tonight. He had not risked stationing anyone inside it. The old walls would not protect a soul from incoming bullets. There was not a stick of sound wood in the entire place. *No*, he thought, *not enough to wad a musket*.

His decision to place the gold boxes upstairs effectively baited the inn as if it were a two-story crab pot. Jimmy crabs and their sooks always fled upwards when they got nervous. He hoped the invaders would act the same, though drawn by greed, instead of driven by fear.

The bomb was now located with the other treasure coffins in a second-floor front parlor overlooking the beach. Though Ben's small brigade had tromped up and down the stairs with the heavy boxes just that afternoon, he still stepped carefully. Who knew when the warped old treads would finally shatter? Just his luck it would happen tonight.

He reached the parlor safely. Though Ben had confided his methods to no one, he was now a relative expert at dealing with the bomb's timer. At least he could start it and stop it. His father's letter had held the clue. Unfortunately, he had no idea how to reset the timer back to its original count of twenty-four hours. Now, after he restarted the thing, he carefully closed its box, and hoisted it up onto the parlor's broad front windowsill. The panes of glass and mullions were long gone. Plenty of room.

He suspended the flat metal keycard to the bomb's box from a splinter in the middle of the window. It dangled there from its chain in plain sight, dully glinting as it twisted in the diminishing breeze.

In that moment, Ben thought he heard a chuckle through the walls, possibly from the attic overhead. He held still for a moment, listening, thinking of his father, and trying hard not to spook himself. Quiet; nothing more. Probably the wind blowing through loose shingles. Ben descended the rickety stairs, collected his gear.

Earlier, Ben had swapped out the rifle's ATN 2-6X68DNS 3A daytime eyepiece for the nighttime one. The scope stayed zeroed-in that way. He lurped out into the dunes, and took a position midway up a more distant rise, about five hundred yards away from the hotel. There was a higher, more advantageous hill three hundred yards closer to the hotel, but he avoided it. He eschewed the high ground, moral and actual, wherever he could, for fear of being an easy target silhouetted against the sky. If Chalk had any counter-sniper training, that preferable, higher ground closer in would be the first place they'd hunt for Ben once he opened fire. If they could still walk.

Ben switched on the sight and scanned the area. His men, for so he thought of them, were invisible. He aimed the rifle at the hotel. He spotted the dangling key in the upstairs window. Good. If he could see it from his hide, Chalk would notice it from the beach, and from farther out on the water if he had binoculars. The prep work was done. The trap was baited and set. Now it was time for the slaughter.

Ben waited, checking his watch so often he believed it had stopped. Shadowed visions of his mother raced through his mind. One moment, she was decked in the Norwegian cardigan she loved during the months containing the letter R, happily hanging laundry to dry in the saltbox yard. The next minute she was captive in a cramped, dank oubliette. Ben still had The Kid's sat-phone. He was tempted to call Chalk to bargain for the truth about her. Might be worth a couple-two-three boxes of gold to finally know. His friends would understand that. His neighbors, on the other hand, might not.

CHAPTER 55

CHALK DID NOT personally know the three new members of his unit. He knew them by repute, and by their employment files. They were dragooned out of the New Orleans office of *Right Way Moving & Storage*. Fresh as they were to major league play like this, he was sure they understood his Calvinist Puritan work ethic based on how fast he'd knackered Farron MacDonald.

Tim O'Malley was a husky man in his thirties. An Irishman and a Catholic, he was looking for a new fight now that The Troubles back home were dying down. He had bright red hair tactically shortened both for convenience and to disguise his fast-retreating hairline and incipient fighting-monk's tonsure nouveau. The luckiest of the three in the plane crash, he suffered only minor cuts and abrasions of which nobody in their line of work would think twice.

To Chalk, Hagan Pallaton seemed twitchy, wiry and mean-eyed. In a word, perfect. Though not sure of Pallaton's ethnic origins, the black hair and broad cheekbones said it all to Chalk: angry, oppressed, displaced minority with a chip on his shoulder the size of an M1A2 Abrams main battle tank. Too bad he didn't pack the same punch. Pallaton had a serious, but not crippling, gash across his left shoulder from the crash. Tahereh had already sluiced it with peroxide and slapped a five-by-nine dressing on it before the *Palestrina* was five minutes out of Tangier Island.

The third man, Abel Stein, had two badly fractured ribs that made breathing quite entertaining for him. Despite that, his eyes were clear. Like

the other two survivors, all Stein's arms and legs were still attached, functional, and not too badly braised.

Chalk was aware that none of these guys was in midseason form for
the hundred meter dash. Smoke inhalation had played hell with their lungs.
Christ, they hacked and coughed sitting still. Once in position, he figured
they could at least point, shoot, and when needed, stop a bullet meant for
him. They were certainly not a full strength strike force. Despite their defi-
ciencies, he kept them all on the roster for now.

Tahereh and Slagget were both taking care of his new gimps. Chalk
still kept a close eye on the patients in case anyone got shocky from internal
injuries and looked like he needed a swim. No one was ever safe.
Dominance through fear and disunity was the key to all Chalk's success, but
he wished he didn't have to change the lock so often.

They cruised into the night toward Spring Island. Half the reason
Chalk wanted the gold was to invite Dick Blackshaw to try and take it away
from him again. Chalk wanted to piss off that traitorous thief. Then he
wanted to kill him. This pleasurable thought warmed him on the boat ride.
He wondered when that infernal whore-whelped prick would show himself.
The things Maynard would do to him!

Slagget interrupted Chalk's sweet flow of thought. "Chief, any ideas on
how we're going to handle this?"

Chalk replied, "Pretty routine, don't you think? Put half the team in
the inflatable and pinch those bastards in between us. We'll enfilade the
living shit out of their defilade and be home in time for breakfast. That
about sums it up."

Slagget persisted. "And the teams?"

"Tahereh, me, and Pallaton in this boat. You take the hypocrite and
the Jesus-killer in the inflatable. Any questions?"

Slagget shrugged. "Timing."

Chalk pushed the chart over to Slagget and picked up the navigational
dividers as a pointer.

Chalk said, "You want it spelled out in neon, Bill? Okay. We'll stage in
the waters a half mile south of Spring Island. Tahereh, how quick is that
inflatable we're towing?"

She said, "We made thirty knots easily with a full tactical unit."

Chalk smiled at her precision. He enjoyed this quality in her. If danc-ing the birthday boff-anova with Phoebe DeLyte got him into this mess, shagging Tahereh might be the way out. She had a sharp mind. The Bryn Mawr education she'd bragged about during their chat in the cuddy cabin would tell. Always ready with the right stuff in any situation. He could love a woman like that. In his way.

Chalk said, "Fine. And this tub'll do about six knots if I try to keep her stealthy and the engine somewhat quiet. Faster, and they'll hear this old four-banger all the way to the Naval Academy. In fact, once you're in posi-tion on the west side, Bill, here's what I want. From the time we split up, plus zero-zero-one-zero minutes, my team'll go straight in through the front door from the south like D-Day. Raise the damn roof. That should give your team plenty of covering distraction. We'll be the thunder. You hit like lightning. Be the lightning, Bill. Sound good to you?"

Slagget barely nodded. "And the exfil?"

Chalk sighed. "You're getting tiresome, Bill. Really tiresome. I'll have resources come get us when the work is done. Okay by you?"

Slagget shrugged.

Tahereh said, "You expect organized resistance, don't you?"

Slagget said, "Depends on how many we're talking about. Shouldn't be more than a guard or two. They haven't probed our perimeter at all—"

Chalk snapped, "Other than blowing the crap out of a lighthouse and killing a planeload of mercs with trees and piles of dirt? No Bill. No prob-ing." Chalk was stoked for a fight, and more easily angered than usual.

Slagget said, "But they don't have clue one about what we're packing."

A wheezing Pallaton said, "Which ain't shit. Our gear burnt up in the plane."

Chalk said, "Bill, stop talking nonsense, break open our gun locker, and arm these true blue patriots. We're going to hit these marsh monkeys hard."

Slagget obeyed. They had their own back-up weapons, Clynch's guns, and leftovers from Tahereh's murdered squad. Chalk's team might be out-numbered, but they were blooded, and damn well ready for anything.

He thought it a fine thing to watch a band of soldiers get acquainted with their new girlfriends, taking them apart. Checking the action, the magazine, chamber, barrel, and sights. Testing the heft. The balance. He loved the utter concentration and engagement of all lethal faculties for a single purpose: muscle memory, but only as it pertained to the accurate, effective discharge of weaponry with hardly a conscious thought. For Chalk, beholding these young operatives quick-wire the human fighting machine within was magical, even inspiring. Forgetting all the injuries and their paltry numbers, now he felt like they were rolling down on Spring Island like old Commodore Perry steaming into Kurihama; a squadron of mighty conquerors.

Chalk got a little hard.

CHAPTER 56

WITH NIGHT VISION binoculars, Chalk watched Slagget's Zodiac dash west around the island. It looked wet and cold, but fast as Tahereh had advertised. Slagget cranked the boat hard over into a turn to the north. Then further east to meet the island's west side. Chalk estimated they were still a solid hundred meters from shore when there was tremendous flash of light from the left near Slagget's boat. A blast, like an enormous naval artillery piece, thrummed his chest like a bass drum.

Chalk's mind grappled to make sense of it. *What had he missed? A floating mine?* Maybe Slagget watched the shoreline too hard, hit a snag and blew the gas tank. The fireburst overwhelmed everyone's NVGs, nearly blinded them.

Though it took seconds, what followed the flash stretched out in slow motion. Through lightly seared retinas, Chalk saw the front of Slagget's Zodiac rip clean through from one side to the other. Between the torn sponson cells lay Abel Stein. Stein was free from worry about cracked ribs now. He didn't have any ribs at all. It looked like his entire upper abdomen and thorax had been hollowed out from one side to the other by a giant ice cream scoop.

Tim O'Malley's face, neck, and shoulder were splashed with fluids and bits. Chalk couldn't tell if it was blowback from Stein's gutting, or a nifty constellation of wounds O'Malley could call his own.

The inflatable's forward sponsons collapsed; it shunted hard to the left. Chalk saw the bow auger deep into the water, the engine still driving full bore.

Slagget couldn't reach the throttle in time to stop the boat from flipping. He was hurled to starboard and forward. The boat cartwheeled stern high.

Slagget and O'Malley cannonballed into the water. Given their brisk clip, it must have felt like hitting a cold brick wall. Slagget's goggles smashed down hard, pulped his nose before they were swept away. He sank; the full weight of arms and ballistic armor now threatening to be his death instead of his salvation. Chalk didn't see Slagget for a few long moments. With the Zodiac inverted, the outboard engine drowned, the prop stopped buzz-sawing the air. Then Slagget's head bobbed up near the ruined boat. He must have cut himself out of the heavy body armor.

In an attempt to figure out what happened, Chalk chopped the *Palestrina*'s engine so he could hear.

Over the transceiver's earpiece, he heard O'Malley in a muffled stage whisper. "Slagget! You good?"

No answer from Slagget. Might be too beat up to talk.

O'Malley thrashed in the water. Then the inflatable rocked as he grabbed on. O'Malley called again, "Slagget! I think Abe got it. Where are you? Slagget!"

Poor bastard, Chalk thought. What with the plane crash and the boating accident, this scion of Clan O'Malley was having one egregiously bad hair day.

Tahereh had no binoculars, could not see what Chalk was taking in. "What's going on? What was it?"

"A glitch, sugar-britches. A nice distraction to help us."

In the distance, O'Malley yelled, "Slagget!"

Chalk heard another voice. It could not have been Stein. He was dead.

The mystery voice yelled, "Slagget? Rhymes with faggot, doncha know!"

Like Slagget, O'Malley failed to find humor in the situation. Chalk heard O'Malley open up with the distinctive strains of his FN SCAR-H. Scarce as ammo was these days, O'Malley let fly like he owned stock in the company. Hosed down the darkness in a furious seven-hundred-twenty degree strafe. Chalk saw Slagget duck low behind the boat, less than confident O'Malley wouldn't ventilate the one thing keeping him from drowning.

Toward the end of O'Malley's burst, and with no need of the radio, Chalk heard the happy sound of a distant man screaming and cursing in profound agony. *Hit!*

Slagget shouted, "O'Malley! Fucking cool it!"

O'Malley stopped shooting. "Where are you!"

"Other side of the damn boat! I'm coming out. Safe that weapon, troop!"

Chalk watched Slagget claw around the boat to the opposite side.

Over the radio, Chalk barked, "What the fuck! Over."

Slagget was winded from the run, but answered, "Somebody hit us hard, but the mick tagged him. This boat's stonked. Come get us."

"Negative! You got your orders! Swim!"

Chalk watched Slagget and O'Malley regroup in the freezing water. They resisted powerful temptation to climb onto the fiberglass bottom of the turtled boat. With the cries of a man in grievous pain filling the night, Slagget and O'Malley started paddling toward shore.

This changed things. Chalk had not expected to stroll onto the beach like General MacArthur returning to the Philippines during the second war to end all wars. Deadly fire before he even reached shore took him up short. The Smith Islanders had brought their A-game. So what! He was ready to play. He restarted the *Palestrina's* engine.

Bill Slagget clearly stepped in some deep shit. Then Chalk saw another flash backlight the old hotel and illuminate the low clouds. Then another crump sound. A muffled explosion. Like a distant cannon. After a few long seconds, there was automatic gunfire in reply. Slagget and O'Malley doing their bit.

Then things got surreal. On his earpiece, Chalk heard a snippet of a weird nursery rhyme, "Then, cocka-doodle-do, said Little Chanticleer," followed by a fusillade of shooting, like a firing squad with a dicey concept of unison.

Over the radio, Slagget muttered, "Cock-a-doodle-do yourself, you bastard!" There was a single gunshot, followed by more shots. Slagget was softening up the shore with gunfire. *Good. Plenty of noise.* Chalk didn't have to ask him what was happening. The shooting, panting and blue-streak swearing in his headset told the story. Slagget's push-to-talk mic was stuck open for a moment. The enemy was now looking west while Chalk came in from the south under the cover of a decent diversionary feint.

Chalk looked meaningfully at Tahereh and Pallaton. Gave it his best, declaiming, "Look sharp boys and girls. We've loosed the dogs of war. The chickens are coming home to roost in the breach. And *nuts* to your kids, who'll wish they'd been here today to fight with us. Tally-fucking-ho!"

Tahereh and Pallaton looked stunned for a moment. Chalk felt it fitting. There's nothing one could really say after a barn-burner battlefield exhortation like that. So what if his crew suspected he'd lost every last aggie, steely, and shooter from his meager bag of marbles. This did not bother him. Not his fault Smith Island didn't have a drug store to renew his scrip, even if he wanted to. He was running on pharmaceutical fumes. *Crazy was good!* Crazy was unpredictable. The onset of madness gave him a wicked edge.

Chalk throttled up the *Palestrina*. A white mustache of foam curled away from her bow. Might as well make some noise. Confusion to his enemies. Chalk was on course for a glorious frontal assault with Semper Fi stamped all over it.

The next report did not roll across the island to Chalk from the north as a soft but pleasantly suggestive thrump. This was an ear-rupturing wham just to his right, practically at his elbow.

The windows around the *Palestrina*'s helm shattered into a thousand lacerating slivers. Slashed into Pallaton's armored back. Shredded Tahereh's right forearm and hand. The two wooden uprights supporting the hardtop tore away. The cabin roof collapsed on the right side. Shockwaves from the blast concussed his chest harder than a mule kick. His ears rang. The boat careered to the left. Everyone dived for cover on deck in a baling wire scrum.

After only a moment's quiet, Chalk was not ready to bet the farm they'd heard the full extent of the welcome salute. He peeked above the cockpit coaming. What he saw amazed him; an old Hobbit standing up to his knees out in the middle of the water. Standing on nothing. Chalk knew from the charts it was more than twenty feet deep there. Not a sandbar, rock, or shoal to prop the old guy up. That was weird enough. Worse still, when the wizened little man spied Chalk, he started blazing away with a shotgun.

Chalk quickly sussed the old bastard was not loading buckshot. He was blasting out pumpkin balls, big hunks of copper-hued lead the same diameter as his chokeless shotgun's bore. The heavy loads bashed through the *Palestrina*'s sides bringing razor-sharp splinters of marine plywood in with them. Though the lead was flying wide of the meat, Chalk caught needles of wood in his face. He lay back down on the deck to yank them out. Blood ran into his eyes from gashes in his forehead. And still, this relentless old water troll banged away!

Pallaton's body armor took most of the glass slivers resulting from the big gun's discharge. He quickly wrapped Tahereh's arm with QuikClot gauze. Staunched the blood flow. She cursed like a sailor. In Farsi. Any profane artistry she possessed in that language was lost on Chalk.

His face cleared of lumber, Chalk risked another look over the coaming. He glanced aft where he figured the gnome would lie given the *Palestrina*'s forward track. The homicidal dwarf had stopped shooting. *Out of ammo? No flesh and blood target?* Not hardly. Now, instead of standing knee-deep in the drink, the killer codger stood on top of the water. Balancing on the surface. Gimbaling his knees and hips in a lewd burlesque movement as wake from the *Palestrina* rolled under his feet. A cracker Messiah out for a stroll on troubled waters. Chalk was riveted.

Until the geezer spotted Chalk again and opened up. Chalk registered that the offending shotgun's magazine tube, with its dead-serious extender stretching beyond the end of the muzzle, was loaded with double-ought buckshot shells after the pumpkin balls for subsequent target practice at a distance. Chalk respected this bloody-minded coot; would've liked to go drinking with him if he weren't so hell-bent on Chalk's demolition.

Grudging respect and the Jesus shoes notwithstanding, Chalk got sick of the damn hobgoblin. Their keen-eyed attacker did not give Chalk a moment free of suppressing fire to pop up and draw a bead of his own. Chalk's only option was to huck three M-67 fragmentation grenades astern in quick succession. He held onto each grenade longer than he usually liked to, then lobbed them hard and high. He was hoping for an air-burst. Wanted to put a discouraging amount of shrapnel in the oldster's hide.

Chalk heard two blasts and a thump. He figured the thump was a grenade that'd gone off underwater. Killed some fish with any luck. Chalk was now a fury thirsting for death of any kind. He glanced back. The seas were clear of little old farts with guns. From that direction, at least.

Then someone else opened up with a shotgun from the other side. Chalk hit the deck again. He caught a glimpse of the shoreline before he dropped behind the gunwale. Using the auxiliary steering tiller on the starboard side of the boat, he blindly adjusted *Palestrina*'s course by guestimation.

A gunshot. Another pumpkin ball flew aboard. The slug twanged through one of the cables attached to the boat's rudder. Then it punched a hole in the engine box and made things in there run rough. The exhaust stack spewed black smoke, thick and choking. The good news was that the following breeze wrapped the dark pall around them like a cloak as they raced for shore. The shooter's aim wandered away. Distance and the smokescreen gave Chalk's team a moment's respite. They needed it. There were bad-ass ghouls haunting these waters, and they really wanted Chalk dead.

CHAPTER 57

THE SHOOTING STARTED later than Ben expected. With the first report, he was momentarily transported from worries about his mother back to the Persian Gulf. Maybe it was the sand on which he lay. That, and the roar and muzzle flash of big guns, and the crackling pop of smaller arms. It all signaled the start of a fresh waiting game. Searching for a target of opportunity through the scope. Wondering who among his friends still lived, who were hurt. Who were dead. He prayed that in the adrenal rush of battle, the Councilmen would obey his seemingly bizarre order that Chalk be granted safe passage into the hotel. One impulsive thought of revenge, plus a few ounces of trigger pressure, and Ben's entire plan would fail.

CHAPTER 58

THE ENGINE OF Hiram Harris's boat caught fire. Chalk, Tahereh, and Pallaton had to hustle all the way to the bow to avoid the flames. The fuel tank was badly holed by all the shooting. Leaking gas contributed to the conflagration. It was not so much a boat that grounded on the beach as a fire ship sporting three human figureheads. They jumped for it into three feet of water, and frantically splashed ashore. Chalk was pleasantly surprised that all three of them made it to the beach alive.

They ran hard until they hit the first row of dunes. Small ones. Little cover to offer. It was better than the Omaha beach they'd just crossed. They threw themselves down. Caught their breath. Some Islander ahead and to the left kept them down with sporadic harassing shotgun fire.

When the air-to-fuel mixture in the gas tank became right, the *Palestrina* exploded. Black smoke and orange flames leapt into the air. Burning debris, some of it much larger than a breadbox, rained down around them. They were pinned on the dune in the firelight.

"Up and over!" Chalk yelled.

They dashed up the sand and rolled into the trough between the first line of dunes and the next. The loom of the flames was dimmer there. They gained a shadowed shelter.

Now Chalk was impressed. The Islanders had put up a hell of a fight. He heard more gunnery to the north. More cussing from Slagget. O'Malley was quiet now. Not a good sign. Slagget had some mopping up of his own to do. Chalk had one goal tonight: murder every bumpkin who dared come at him. After that they could haul the gold in peace.

Chalk checked in with his troops. "Tahereh?"

She looked at him, eyes glazed from pain. Pallaton had swathed her hand as best he could, but she was at least a pint low.

Pallaton asked Chalk, "Hit of morphine for her?"

"Hell no! I want her wide awake, pissed off, and shooting straight."

Chalk knew Tahereh would cope. He suspected she was just glad not to be put down like a dog. That dressing would have to suffice until they choppered her to a safe trauma hospital. There, the doctors would have security clearances that let them treat black ops gunshot wounds without reporting to the local police. There were entire surgical suites in D.C. area clinics reserved for operatives from *Right Way Moving & Storage*, and like organizations.

Tahereh said, "Still have one good hand." She pulled her pistol from its holster, and waved it like she meant business.

"That's my girl. Pallaton?"

A quick assessment, the back of Pallaton's head was bloody from collecting a glass menagerie. Fortunately, his flack vest had a high collar. His neck had been protected. They could pick the slivers out of his scalp later. As with Tahereh's maiming, Chalk hoped Pallaton's injury would make him meaner.

Chalk cracked out his night vision binos again, and scanned inland at the building. He zeroed in on the windows of the first floor. Nothing. Then he focused on the upper story windows. Nothing, at first. Then he saw it. The box on the window sill, sitting there like it needed geraniums. And something shiny hanging over it. A key.

Rage overwhelmed him. He could not control it. "The bastards! My fucking gold! They're trying to piss me off!"

There was no more time for reconnaissance. Only the one Islander picket took shots with a pump-gun on the left, but more hostiles could quickly surround them. He peeled out of his poncho and coat to free his arms.

He said, "Tahereh, I want you to hold the fort here. Don't snoop around. There's no telling who's out there, and I for one don't want to plug your sweet ass by mistake. Diggity?"

She nodded and said, "The boat's gone. You better have a plan."

Chalk said, "Don't you fret about that. I've got resources. When we have what we came for, we'll get all the help we need."

She nodded again. "Your resources."

"Yes, my resources. A chopper for starters. A crackerjack medic for your boo-boo, and some strong backs to help us tote the goods."

Tahereh broke a sweat. He watched her assess her situation, her stock tanking on the Chalk Exchange.

She said, "What about me?"

Chalk rolled his eyes. "Pull up your big-girl panties. I could have killed you a long while back if that's all I meant to do. You have to relax. Have a little faith, okay? My deal with you stands. You get what you paid for if that's all you really want. And my offer of glory stands too, in case you're feeling frolicsome. Here, watch this."

Chalk dialed his sat-phone. It was answered immediately. He said, "Tora, tora, tora. I want a heavy helo on this station in one hour. Come in packing heat. Six to dust off, with cargo. That's a *heavy*. Have two 68-Whiskeys on board. We've got casualties. Copy that?" Chalk paused listening, then said, "Good. Mark my coordinates, now!"

Chalk took the phone away from his ear and pressed a button sending a signal that would, in the best of all possible worlds, illuminate the phone's location on a discreet government radar screen in Quantico, Virginia. Returning the phone to his ear he said, "You *ident* that?" He paused. Then he snapped the phone shut.

Chalk took Tahereh gently by the shoulders and said, "There. Transport and medics. Up to that moment, my operation was totally black. Off the radar, and nobody the wiser. And now everybody in creation knows where I am. I did that for you, sweetie pie. All for you."

Tahereh smiled small. That was all Chalk wanted. It was none of her business that he'd really dialed the automated Time-and-Temperature number in his home town of Scranton, Pennsylvania. He privately noted that at the tone, the time was two thirty-seven a.m., and the temperature was sixty-four degrees.

Before Tahereh could gush with girlish gratitude, Chalk let go of her shoulders and said to Pallaton, "Okay brother-man. Let's boogie! Straight in!"

To Tahereh he said, "Sugar-britches, play us a little tune called *Keep Your Heads Down Low You Jive-Ass Sister-Fucking Rednecks*. Don't know the melody? I'll play you a few bars."

Pallaton and Chalk leveled their guns and dashed straight at the front of the old building. They wove low between the dunes as far as they could, shooting all the way.

Tahereh pumped clip after clip into the hotel. Finally Chalk and Pallaton reached the edge of an open waste between the dunes and the veranda. Tahereh's covering fire was noisy enough, but it was too far back to inspire any real fear. Chalk and Pallaton crouched, then sprinted for the porch stairs like the Devil was on their tails.

That Islander with the shotgun made the dash seem like Scranton, PA; unseasonably warm. He blasted away at Chalk and Pallaton like a maniac. The slugs churned up 3-iron divots around them, but nothing went home. Yet.

CHAPTER 59

BEN TRIED TO ignore the slight tremor in his hand. His body broke a cold sweat all over. His breathing got too quick, too shallow. This was why he had left the service. Taking this shot here and now was stepping back toward the most ruinous moment of his career.

Ben made sure he had a tight weld between his cheek and the gun stock. There could be no sighting shot to check his zero. Gauging the wind speed by the bend in the reeds, and smoke from the boat fire, he compensated. Gut-guessed his height above the target, and figured the drop. Took care not to make the rookie mistake of aiming too high for a target at a lower elevation. He folded in the temperature, the humidity. Ben had done it so many times before, this was second nature to him. Ben would take the shot CCB, with a Clean Cold Barrel. He must implicitly trust Ellis's set-up of the gun. No time to change his dope in the scope. He had no choice. Hundreds of lives depended on it.

He engaged the running man, then led him slightly in a classic ambush shot. Put the vertical line of the reticle one quarter of one milliradian ahead of the target's balaclava-cloaked head. This was a full value shot, with the wind blowing in perpendicular to the beach and his line of fire. He whispered the phrase *going hot*. He emptied his mind of any thought. B.R.A.S.S. time. Breathe. Relax. Aim. Slack. Squeeze. Ben slowly drew his index finger through the trigger in a line toward his shooting eye. The rifle's kick rippled through his body, jolted his fractured ribs hard. A small swirl of sand rose as the bullet passed close over a high dune. A second later, the target's balaclava distended as if a small explosion had gone off beneath the tight fabric. The man's momentum carried him a few feet before he rag-dolled flat into the sand, face down.

And suddenly a masked face, eyes blazing with hate, joined the ranks of the other souls haunting Ben's mind. Ben returned to the business at hand. There was no time to commune with his inner specters. Ben shifted the eyepiece onto Chalk.

CHAPTER 60

CHALK HIT THE porch stairs at a thousand miles an hour. Almost at the top, he heard Pallaton grunt behind him. Then came a big caliber gunshot. This was not the usual order of things unless the shooter was actually a distant sniper. He turned without arresting his headlong rush up the steps. Pallaton was down. His balaclava a ripped gunny full of fish guts.

Chalk rolled through the open double front door, and cleared the immediate entry hall. There was a grand old staircase sweeping up the back of the hall to a second floor landing. Chalk went for it, quick, but easy. The ancient treads squeaked, threatening to collapse in a puff of termite dust at every step.

Chalk cleared the upstairs hallway. Scanning for anyone with an eye to mow him down. Nobody there. Quiet as a tomb.

And then he heard the chuckling. A man, laughing low the way a person does when he's read something funny in a book, but has nobody close by with whom to share the joke. Chalk shook his head to clear it. No, this laughter was real, not psychosis; it came from a front room. Chalk figured the box and key were in there, too. He slowly followed the sound, his gun ready.

Whatever the joke, it must have been a good one. The mirth persisted until he reached the doorway to a parlor. Chalk's first glance through the door was directed out the opposite window. He could see the burning *Palestrina* at the shore throwing orange-white clinkers into the air. The southerly breeze wafted the sparks toward the building. This was bad enough, regardless of the hebephrenic loopster waiting for him in the room.

Chalk was about to S.W.A.T. into the parlor with a classic Hollywood diving roll when the laughter suddenly stopped.

He heard a familiar voice call out, "Come on in, Maynard. The water's fine."

Chalk was speechless, but not for long. "Richard Willem Blackshaw! You goddamn thief! That you?"

"Yeah, bunky. In the flesh."

Chalk shook, insane with rage recalling the hassles of the last forty-eight hours. "Throw down your weapon, shit-heel! Now!"

"Easy boy. Don't have one to throw. Anyway, you got bigger problems than me. Way bigger."

Chalk had not yet put his head into the room. "You don't sound so good, my friend."

Dick restarted his noncommittal chuckling. "Been better."

Despite the cordial invitation, and the fact that Dick sounded off his feed, Chalk penetrated the room hard, low and fast. He needn't have bothered.

Richard Willem Blackshaw sat on the floor propped up against the back wall. He did not even look at Chalk. Instead, he placidly watched the reflection of the boat fire flickering on horse hair binding that hung down in brittle tufts from the cracked plaster ceiling. Blood drenched the fingers of both his hands where they gripped just above his pelvis.

Chalk ordered, "Put your hands up."

Dick Blackshaw smiled and said, "If I do like you say, my guts'll flop into my lap. Our chat'll be kinda short, doncha know. Reckon I caught me a round of your suppressing fire. Messed me up good. So I respectfully decline."

"Dickie, Dickie, Dick-Be-Nimble. I hope it hurts like hell," Chalk said. "Had something like that in mind for you myself. For starters."

As Chalk patted Blackshaw down, the injured man said. "Think you're gonna get all the gold back?"

"I don't think it. I know it." Then Chalk heard somebody shout "Fore!" over his radio earpiece. Not Slagget. Not O'Malley. A stranger. It sounded like somebody playing golf. Maybe it was not the transceiver at all. Maybe stress sped up the metabolism of his psych meds, and he was finally having the auditory hallucinations he feared. *So what!*

Then Chalk noticed the rest of the metal boxes. They were stacked up against the right hand wall in the shadows thrown by the fire outside. A quick count. He totted up nineteen. Those, plus the one in the window, made twenty. *Beautiful.*

Chalk grinned. "See? All here. Gotta say your boys didn't put up much of a fight."

"Maybe not, but that big problem I told you about? That's in the last box over there. In the window." Dick nodded toward the opposite wall. Chalk went to the window, careful to keep in the shadows.

Dick said, "Go ahead and open the box. It won't bite you. Leastwise, not for a minute or two."

Chalk grinned. "I have a better idea." He pulled out his sat-phone and dialed. Then he retreated from the window, and loomed over the gut-shot man. Chalk bent down and hoisted Dick to his feet. "Upsy-daisy, Dickardo. Come on!"

Blackshaw groaned. He staggered as Chalk dragged him to the window. Chalk kept his good arm around Dick's shoulders. With his free hand he held his sat-phone to the waterman's ear.

"Dickie-Boy, I want you to say howdy to a new friend of mine."

CHAPTER 61

ONE MINUTE PASSED. Two more. Ben kept the rifle sight on the Hotel's upper parlor window. The battle sounds on the west side of the island continued for a few moments. Then the guns fell silent. The *Palestrina* crackled on the beach. More bright cinders rose into the air. Drifted on the wind toward the Barren Creek Hotel.

He glanced at his watch. This was taking much too long. The timing for his entire mission was critical, and was now verging on total failure.

Suddenly Chalk appeared at the window in full view. This was wrong, not how Ben planned. Despite his hot reception on Spring Island just moments ago, now there wasn't a hint of caution in Chalk's posture. He stood upright, straight-backed and bold, without cover. He didn't even reach for the key card dangling there on its chain. Nor did he examine the box Ben had left as bait on the sill. Instead, Chalk gazed calmly out the window holding a cupped hand near his face. Ben looked closer. Chalk was dialing a phone. And smiling.

The eerie peace of the night was shattered by the sound of The Kid's mobile in Ben's pocket. The ringtone was the Misfits' *Mommy Can I Go Out and Kill Tonight*. Ben pulled out the phone.

The caller ID said Boss.

Ben answered. He held the phone to his ear. Put his eye back to the rifle sight. Aimed the sight back at the hotel window. One look confirmed the impossible. Now Chalk was not alone. He had his arm around somebody's shoulder.

The voice Ben heard on the phone was that of a dead man. A ghost. All that sifted through to Ben's pain-racked mind was a boy's greeting from long ago. He said, "Evening, Pap."

CHAPTER 62

MAKING THAT CALL had been fun for Chalk. Good old Dickie had valiantly told his brat to stand down and stay the hell away if he wanted to see his old man alive again. Now back to business.

Chalk inserted the flat metal key on the box. Flipped back the lid. Not gold. It was obviously the dirty bomb Tahereh had been hoping to purchase. And dammit! It was live. The timer read 00:06:23.

Chalk uttered the infamous last words of many a dead pilot, skydiver, and bomb squad tech. "Oh shit!"

With detonation could come total irradiation. It would be a disgusting death, writhing in Homeric agony from beta and gamma burns and global bone marrow breakdown. Not to mention the annihilating fatigue, uncontrollable puking, hair loss, and rocketing bloody diarrhea in the meantime. Yum.

In a little over six minutes Spring Island would be so contaminated you could fry an egg on the sand for years to come.

Chalk pointed his gun at Dick's forehead and clicked back the hammer. "Did you start this thing?"

Dick's odd chuckle again. And the easy smile that had suckered Chalk into a bad hire. Both a little weaker now. Dick said, "I think my boy did."

"Then, by damn he's fucked us all."

Chalk's mind reeled. After all the danger and trouble, here lay nineteen boxes full of gold and no hope of moving an ounce of it. He checked and rechecked. All the other boxes were locked. He had no idea where the second key was. Had no time to search for it.

He fired twice at one of the top row boxes. The bullets bounced off the locks ricocheting with Western movie twangs. Chalk thought better of firing a third time.

There was simply no chance to save the gold. Even one box was far too heavy to haul alone. Not even if Tahereh had two good hands. Not even if he had killed all the marsh monkeys in the surrounding fifty miles. *Goddamn! All that gold! All that money! All that power! Wasted!*

Chalk was again transfixed by the timer's countdown. His brain raced for any alternative. Some way to both live and enjoy the full bounty of this gig. No brainstorm came up. No satori, no eureka, nothing. Instead, he came to his senses fast. Chalk had not survived this long mooning over lost opportunities. To his way of thinking, there were only two things left to do. One: permanently fix Dick Blackshaw. Two: get the hell off this sand spit before he got cooked.

Chalk raised his pistol and whirled to dispatch item one. He found his path blocked by another man. Ben Blackshaw stood like a protective wall in front of his father. He was tricked out in a vegged-up ghillie suit like Swamp Thing.

Chalk marveled. Where the hell did he come from? So quick, and without a sound! Ben was not even breathing hard.

Dick lay on the floor near the window where Chalk had let him fall. He was not so far down from the wound that he couldn't recognize his own kid. "Ben! That you?"

Ben ignored his father, and fixed Chalk with a brute's feral eye. He pinioned Chalk's undivided attention with a long knife grasped in his outstretched hand.

Chalk realized the blade was already cooling a fine line along the skin of his throat. Just above a carotid artery. With every heartbeat, Chalk's flesh pulsed a half gram harder against an edge that promised surgical sharpness. Fortunately, neither Ben Blackshaw nor Maynard Chalk was prone to jitters.

Knowing the protocol in situations like this, Chalk lowered his gun to the ground. The knife in Ben's hand never wavered. Chalk waited for the twin sensations of the cold blade going in, and the warmth of his own blood flowing over his collarbone. He had experienced both a few times before, but to his complete shock, nothing bit into him now. No hot gush.

Chalk said, "A deal."

Ben shook his head once.

Chalk broke a sweat. "Hear me out. You get your ma-bird. I get off this island."

Then this madman, and Chalk knew a lunatic when he saw one, shifted the knife one millimeter. And there was the sting he awaited. Blood trickled down his neck. "You inbred fucking idiot! You started the bomb!"

Ben hissed, "If you hurt her—Where is she?"

"Slow your roll, kid. I tell you now, you'll kill me. There's a file in my coat on the beach. It tells you everything. I'll leave it for you. Otherwise you'll have my people dealing with your people out there, and somebody's going to get hurt."

"Is she alive?"

"Deal's a deal. Kill me, and my guys will shoot you down before you see word one of that file. Time's a-wasting."

Using the blade like a precision shepherd's staff, Ben pushed Chalk's neck toward the parlor door. Chalk sensed the keenness of the blade again. Realized that to stand still would oblige this wingnut to give him a field tracheotomy without benefit of anesthesia. *No gracias.* Chalk took a slow trial step toward the doorway, away from the itchy pressure of the knife edge.

Ben pressed a little harder. A little more blood flowed. Chalk knew this bastard meant business. His next step was a little longer. Catching Ben's drift, that he was encouraging the old exit-pursued-by-a-bear, Chalk took another step. At last the blade was off his throat, but Ben still held it thrust toward Chalk to discourage a curtain call.

Still watching the wild child, Chalk said, "Ricardo, don't you *dare.* Don't you dare die. I swear I'm going to look you up. We're going to complete this detail."

With that, Chalk bailed.

CHAPTER 63

BEN WATCHED FROM the window until he was sure Chalk had left the building. Heard him clatter down the stairs. After a moment, Chalk appeared outside. The snorting old warhorse galloped past his dead soldier and dashed toward the beach.

Ben took the prosthetic eye out of his pocket and fitted it iris-down into the scanner in the bomb's panel. The timer stopped counting backwards. Twenty seconds remaining. He pocketed the eye again. Only then did Ben hurry to his father's side. "I thought you were dead!"

"All gossip, that is 'til just now. Seems a round flew right through that front wall a few minutes ago. Damn termites! But you figured it out. His eyeball controlled the switch."

"Your letter. 'A keen eye? Important to get things started?' You could have spelled it out."

"Didn't know who'd read it. Had to be careful. When they saddled me with that asshole Cyclops to come along with the bomb, I almost had a fit. Hadn't planned for passengers. Technician, he called himself. Got him drunk, and he bragged that's how he controlled it, with that eye. On and off. With a coded retina scan. See son? Looks can kill. A whole lot!"

"You need a hospital." Ben's mind welled up with questions, but blood drenched the front of his father's pants and washed all other thoughts away. Ben pulled off his ghillie coat, balled it, and pressed it against his father's wound. The entire plan had failed. His father was alive after all, but hit badly. Nothing was working. Ben was crushed.

Dick went on, his voice feeble, but still full of admiration. "You found the wrecked boat. And that sidekick they sent. Out there when the storm came in, and it looked like we were going to broach? That chicken-shit Cyclops bastard had enough. So I got us to the rendezvous point, gave him a bar of gold before he tried to dog-paddle to shore. And my wallet for some folding money, 'til he could fence the gold. Told him it was his bonus payment. Priciest anchor ever, but he was my new best friend. Already knew he couldn't swim for sour apples. I slit his life vest and helped him over the side. After he went down for good, I rocked the boat 'til it swamped. Ellis okay?"

"Minding the west approach. Let me help you."

Dick Blackshaw's next sentence floored Ben. "How's your mother?"

Ben could not speak, or even think straight for a moment. Then he remembered his father's letter. It was clear that like Ben, Dick had no idea where she was.

Ben said, "I thought she was with you. She left the same night you did. I haven't seen her since. Nobody has. I thought she was with you, 'til today, when Chalk said he had her."

Richard Willem took this in. Seemed more sobered by this news than by the bullet in his gut. His mind drifted back across the years. "They tried to run us off the road once before. Busted up her arm. Docs had to put in some pins to keep it together."

"I remember. She was proud of her x-rays. They're still framed and hung on the parlor wall."

Dick grimaced, continued. "The night I left, she and I were going to meet out in the Martin refuge. At that duck blind by the south pond. At midnight."

Ben said, "She even didn't leave the house 'til then. She could never have poled over there in less than an hour, not with that arm."

Dick pieced it together. "If she did show, I was already gone. We had a boat there just in case. I should have waited, but we set up other places at later times to meet on the main. Days, and even weeks later. She never came to any of them, and I didn't dare call for fear of bringing black-ops guys back in on you. I thought she stayed behind to take care of you. We weren't supposed to be gone long. Just 'til things quieted down again. It was me they really wanted. I had to keep moving." He squeezed his eyes shut, slowly opened them, looked at his son. "I'm so sorry I didn't show myself here before, but you were doing so damn well, and I was still half-drowned from swimming to shore in this storm."

Then Dick thought a moment more, and said, "They must have got Ida-Beth. They were looking for me that night. Instead, they found her, but who knows when or where."

Dick Blackshaw wiped his eyes with a sleeve. Ben understood. He'd come close to learning firsthand about the burden of killing the one person you loved best in the entire world. And now, after fifteen long years of waiting to meet his parents again, it was all going to hell. This was no good. Ben jumped back in the zone, and zeroed-in on the one thing he could do.

He said, "Doc Alan's waiting back home. He'll tend to you. We'll get that file if Chalk left it. Wherever she is, we'll find her."

"You do that, Ben. And you give her my love. But I'm done running. I'm done in."

"I can carry you. The boys are all outside. Be here in a second."

An impatient look crossed Dick Blackshaw's face. "Why the hell did you take the gold out of Deep Banks? You had the herons working for you. Their stench would have kept everybody away."

"I'll tell you. Let's get you some help first, Pap."

"I think I'm gonna sit tight." Now Dick sounded angry. "Dammit Ben, why'd you move the gold?"

"I didn't."

His father was usually sharp, but he was badly injured and couldn't puzzle that one through alone. He looked bewildered at all the boxes stacked against the wall. Ben realized his father wanted to talk more than move toward help. Dick's eyes tightened with intense pain, though he tried to hide it. Ben continued explaining only as a compromise. Once he answered Dick's big questions, Ben hoped he could then persuade his dad to get to the doctor. The ghillie coat was already saturated. Richard Willem Blackshaw's time, with his blood, were running out.

Ben confessed, "Pap, those boxes are full of rocks and sand. Only the bomb is real."

"You're shitting me."

"I shit thee not. The herons gave me the idea."

Dick looked doubtful. "Must be going into shock. The herons?"

Suddenly Ben was the proud kid telling his dad of a coup. "Almost nobody goes out to that rookery on Deep Banks. Because of the funk, like you said. It's the same idea. Let's say I set off that bomb here on Spring Island. Let's say somebody thinks the gold is here. They'd think it was contaminated."

Dick got it. "Then nobody'd want the damn stuff! Nobody'd want to come near enough to touch it."

Ben said, "So nobody'd even look for it. Make the few folks who're interested in the gold believe they know right where it is. Based on what they know about this bomb, now the gold's worthless. Lost in plain sight. Fouled in a radioactive No Man's Land in the middle of the bay. Too dangerous to come at."

Dick smiled at his son. "That's why you let Chalk go."

"Hardest thing I've ever done in my life. But he's our messenger back to his world. If he doesn't leave that file, I can find him later."

Dick's smile went away. "Or he can find you. And the bay? Aren't we a touch casual setting off a nuke in the middle of our bread basket?"

His father was dying, but still stubborn. Ben had to make this quick. "There's a lot you don't know about me. I've had some training. I'm a sniper like you, Pap. A good one. In the Gulf, and elsewhere. I've had other work in the service along the way. My recon stalks were good. I got to leave presents behind now and then. Demolition. You remember how I like to tinker."

Dick grinned. "That I do."

"Can't help myself. So the isotopes in that box are spread by detonating a big wad of Semtex. I took three quarters of the Semtex out of the box this afternoon. Oh, she'll still go off loud and pretty, but she won't blow rads all over creation like she was designed to."

Ben paused, turned his face toward the old hearth of the parlor fireplace. A gentle breeze, still faintly redolent of creosote a hundred years after the last embers burned there, spilled out of the flue and caressed his face.

He said, "There! The eye of the storm is here. The downdraft, it'll limit the spread of the radiation. Or would have."

Dick's face twisted. He focused hard on the talk. Tried to transcend the pain. "So the yield fouls the island right enough. Keeps it hot for a while. Especially around this building. It'd be ground zero."

"Right," said Ben. "But the fallout wouldn't have gone much past the shoreline. The rain would've settled the airborne particles even more, before they spread to the water. Weakened any contamination past the island. A little anyway. Now that's enough talk. Please, Pap, let's get you some help."

Dick shook his head. "There's a problem with your plan."

It was true. Ben knew it. When he'd stopped the bomb a moment before, Ben realized with a sinking heart that he hadn't thought of everything.

Ben said, "I know."

"You still haven't set it off."

Ben was surprised that was still under discussion. He said, "I can't now. That's where I screwed up. There're only twenty seconds left on the clock if I restart it. The timing didn't work. Chalk pussied out when his other boat drew our fire. He took longer than I expected to hit the beach and open the bomb."

Dick said. "Then it's my fault, too. Chalk was chatting with me too long. But it's not too late."

Ben was certain blood loss was starving Dick's mind of oxygen. He said, "Sure it is. It'll take more time than that to get you to a doctor. No way I can start it up again. We have to get you to the boat, collect the rest of the boys, and clear off. No way we can do it now. Not even if we took care of everything first, and then I restarted the bomb, and ran like hell. We'd all be way too close when it blew."

Dick leveled a look at Ben. "Listen, son. Anybody tries to move me, I'm dead. We both know it. I'm not going anywhere."

Rising desperation tried to close off Ben's throat. "So we'll bring help to you here."

"No. This is it. Ben, I'm proud of you. Every question I ever had about who you'd become has been answered right here. Right now. The details don't matter. You've got your whole life out in front of you. And some loot to stake you. One thing: what happened to that little LuAnna Bryce? You ever figure out she was sweet on you?"

Ben was flattened. There was so much to say, and no time. "We'll be getting married soon. You need to be there for that."

Dick smiled. For a moment he could see into the future. "I will be. Not like I hoped. Getting a chance to talk with you has been a dream come true, Ben, but it's best you were on your way." Dick paused for a moment. Ben thought his father was drifting out of consciousness until he said, "Why don't you look for the living among the dead?"

Ben said, "I don't get it." In extremis, his father was now misquoting Jesus.

Dick snapped back. "Hand over that bastard's glass eye. I'll give you the time you need. You have to go now, or that fuckwit Chalk won't see the show."

"I don't even know you. I can't ditch you here."

"Yes, you can. You will. As for knowing me, Christ, Ben. I'm just a Smith Islander like you. No worse than most. Not perfect, doncha know. Made so many mistakes. For my best parts, look inside yourself. Remember that. Forget the rest, or forgive if you can. Now please, let me finish what I started. You can give me that. You're a soldier, Ben. You're my son. I won't ask again."

Ben slowly reached into his pocket. Closed his hand around the smooth cool eye for the final time, and clasped it into his father's hand.

CHAPTER 64

CHALK HARED DOWN the hotel's big staircase. Tumbled unarmed down the front steps past Pallaton's corpse. Some Islander resumed his role shotgunning holes in the dirt around Chalk's feet to keep him moving.

As Chalk ran, he braced for the final barrage that would knock him to into the next world. Between shotgun blasts he heard the thuds of his own footsteps. His stertorous breath whistled in and out of lungs long unused to such exertions.

As he hustled into the dunes he bellowed, "Don't shoot you heathen bitch! It's me! Goddammit, it's me!"

Chalk flew over the top of the last dune, his legs pinwheeled like a running broad jumper's. He knew he would pay for this tomorrow, if he had one coming.

There was Tahereh, still alive. She had her gun at the ready, her eyes wide with wonder. Headlong flight was a shocking new facet in Chalk's character. In fact, hauling ass was now at the top of Chalk's brain stem. Heedless of which arm he grabbed, he yanked Tahereh along with him.

Unlucky for her, he clamped onto her lacerated wrist. Tahereh screamed, nearly passed out from the pain. She freed her hand with a twist, but ran after him. Chalk's poncho and rain slicker lay in the sand, forgotten.

She yelled, "Maynard! Why?"

It took a stride or two to get her feet beneath her, but panic and pain helped her keep pace. Chalk kept running. Led her down toward the beach toward the west side of the island where Slagget should be.

She gasped, "What's happening?"

"Slight change of plans. Your bomb is armed and counting down! Seconds! That mutant set it off!"

"Oh shit!" Tahereh got with the program. Three more strides and she was nearly pulling Chalk off his feet. Chalk's affection for her deepened. She was one vigorous filly, gimped or not.

Chalk scanned past the burning wreck of Hiram Harris's boat for something, anything that would float. They ran on, the soft dunes miring their steps like quicksand in a nightmare.

They found O'Malley sprawled out behind the dunes, stone dead. His skull completely caved in. Chalk barked, "What in the hell?"

Next to O'Malley in the sand lay what proved on quick examination to be an old Wright & Ditson five wood with its original splice whippings. The antique golf club's value to a collector was diminished because the shaft was now broken, and its well-lofted persimmon head was freshly gunked with blood.

Chalk dropped the club and yanked Tahereh onward, by her good hand this time. He quietly hoped the murderous duffer was not waiting somewhere over the next dune to clobber him with a Big Bertha. He locked onto what looked like a small skiff hauled out on the beach about a hundred yards away. He went for it. As they got closer, Chalk saw the craft was built low and flat along the lines of Sunfish sailboats, but much smaller. All open wood. No mast, and no sail, no engine in sight. Barely big enough for two. Chalk looked down into the little cockpit. All he saw was a gargantuan gun, and a pair of ridiculously small paddles.

That's when Slagget staggered over a nearby rise, his nose streaming blood. His hand was torn and pierced by what looked like fang marks. He pumped his legs hard as he could to intercept Chalk and Tahereh at the little boat.

Slagget called, "Maynard! Hey! What's the story?"

Chalk yelled back, "We're bugging out!"

"What about the gold?" Now Slagget was moving a little faster. He'd caught the note of—not terror surely—but *intensity* in Chalk's voice.

Chalk said, "Forget it!"

Slagget stopped his tracks. "What?"

Chalk gave the essentials. "The bomb! It's running. Any second now! Where's your team?"

"You're looking at it. Damn! You call for a dust-off?"

Chalk pointed to the little boat. "That's our dust-off. No time to wait for a helo here."

"Crap!" Slagget came to terms with the situation quickly. "Okay. Screw it. Let's go." He started running toward the boat.

Chalk clarified. "Dear boy, when I said this boat is ours, I meant hers and mine. It's much too small for three. You best run along. Grab a plank or a life ring off Hiram's boat. Anything that'll float. Got to be something that hasn't burned up yet. I'll vector the helo onto me, and then we'll come scoop you up most riki-tik. Oh, and with this particular bomb? The trick is to work your way upwind. Get me? Be the wind, Bill. Be the wind."

Slagget's eyes screwed down hard into a squint. He hissed, "The Senator said you might try something like this."

Chalk erupted, "Knew it! You little shit! I knew you were Lily's punk! The fly in my pellucid ointment! The spanner in my perfectly tuned works!" Even in the low light, Chalk saw the knuckles of his gun-hand whiten.

Slagget said. "You crazy bastard, you are not dumping me here!"

Tahereh said, "That's right." She leveled her gun at Chalk. Chalk's eyes widened. After a few long seconds, she swept the sights onto Slagget. One-handed, she let off a burst at his legs. The noise echoed long after he lay cut down and helpless on the ground. The sand drank up his life. She tossed his gun out of reach, kneeled next to him. His eyes were open, but not focusing.

She said, "You're right Billy-Bob. We're not leaving you here. This is where we're burying you." Her next round went into Slagget's head.

Chalk's mouth started working again after a moment of surprise. "Hot damn, cupcake!"

Now that the overbooking of the little boat had been addressed, Chalk jettisoned its cannon. Then with their good hands, he and Tahereh dragged the wooden shell into the water past the breakers. The wind was rising again. That would make for hard going.

Chalk grabbed both of the short-handled paddles and got to work. One hand on each side of the narrow boat. The craft was tippy, and his wounded arm burned like it was freshly injured at every stroke. He nearly put them both in the drink before he got the hang of it. Managing the balance was difficult, but the boat was slippery through the water. With some care, effort, and rhythm Chalk got it moving. He steered upwind toward the southwest.

He said, "For a second there, I thought you were going to do me in."

Tahereh said, "Ridiculous. His hand was much worse than your arm. There was no possibility he could manage this boat."

He smiled, said, "You're a tough ho' to row."

She nodded. "Don't forget that."

Chalk smiled. He liked her. He really liked her.

After many minutes of hard work on the water, Tahereh shouted, "Maynard, look! The island!"

Chalk glanced over his shoulder, once more almost capsizing them.

A spark from the *Palestrina* had caught on something dry in the old hotel. Perhaps an ember had fluttered into the attic through a shattered window. A nascent holocaust now worked its way along the roofline.

Chalk said, "Something's wrong with that bomb. It was set to pop in six minutes. I'm not complaining. Could use a bonus round. But damn, can't those Turks build anything right?"

A few more moments passed. Then the eruption. The center of the hotel's second story lifted and blew out toward the dunes. Chunks of burning wood and plumes of white sparks soared into the air.

"That's more like it!" Chalk studied the fiery island for a moment. "And so begins World War Three. Damn, baby. That was gonna be *our* war."

Chalk was tired. Picturesque as the fire was, he needed to focus on matters at hand. Before he started paddling again, he took a moment to punch the panic button on his sat-phone. The real panic button this time. Chalk had failed spectacularly. He needed real help now. Soon he'd be feeling every kind of heat from upstairs. For an instant, he wondered if things were cooling off back in Scranton.

CHAPTER 65

BEN BOARDED WADE Joyce's boat alone after grabbing Chalk's abandoned jacket. The next few minutes were a blur. Wade had already recovered Reverend Mosby from the beach, as well as Ben's rifle from the dunes. They told Ben they'd seen Chalk and the woman put into the Chesapeake on a sneak-boat conveniently abandoned there by Orville Hurley. The fugitives had paddled for dear life, but not before the woman had shot another man down. Not a Smith Islander, Ben learned. Therefore the corpse was none of Ben's concern beyond the hurried scraping of a shallow grave in the dunes.

They found Lorton Dyze's sinkbox adrift, and badly holed by grenade shrapnel. No sign of the old man, call out as they might. They abandoned the low vessel. With seconds ebbing fast, they rushed on with heavy hearts.

Orville Hurley called to them from shore. Though pressed for time, he made them stop long enough to retrieve *Barking Betty* from the beach. Orville's dog, Adolf, was shot dead in the fight with Slagget and O'Malley. They took his carcass aboard, too.

Then they cut around to the west side of the island. They picked up Art Bailey, who was cradling a wounded Knocker Ellis in his arms. Ben got them aboard the *Varina Davis* as fast as possible. Ellis was clipped in the shoulder, but would live if he got help soon.

They found Sonny Wright drifting in his sneakboat with a bullet through his leg. He was swearing a blue streak. That was a good sign, except that made it harder to hear Ephraim Teach out in his sinkbox calling for them to pick him up.

Sam Nuttle lay in his sneakboat with *Chanticleer* close to shore. He had been washed a good distance down the beach. He had an in-and-out wound through his right lung. A tension pneumothorax had him gulping like a guppy out of water. The bullet had nicked an artery. He bled too much. Nuttle died before they could get him to Dr. Alan. Most of their men were accounted for, living and dead. Only Lorton Dyze was gone without a trace. Killed In Action. Body Not Recovered.

Ben ordered, "Swing around toward the beach in front of the hotel. Quick now!"

As they approached the southern shore of Spring Island, they could see the hotel fire throwing flames high into the air. Ben knew it must be an inferno in there.

He couldn't put it off any longer. He saluted the upstairs parlor window. He thought he saw a distant hand move in return salute, but couldn't be sure. Perhaps he was only seeing what he wanted to see. Ben raised Hurley's pumpgun and fired three shells into the air, the signal the boat was clear of the island. A piece of Ben died with every shot.

He said, "Wade, take us home as quick as she'll go. This boat's gotta be faster than gamma rays tonight."

Wade Joyce rolled the *Varina Davis*'s throttles forward to the stops. The boat's stern squatted for a moment as her big wheels spooled up and dug in. Then she flew forward; leapt up on a plane carving a white foaming *V* in the water toward the southeast and Smith Island.

Ben watched over the transom. He wondered if his father had held on long enough to finish the job. He waited. The men on deck exchanged worried glances. It was taking too long.

Ben snatched up his rifle and aimed at the box on the sill. It was obscured by smoke and a sheen of tears. Ben whispered, "He's already gone. He's already gone. He volunteered. He'd do it himself, but he's already gone."

Ellis wrestled up from the deck through the press of helping hands tending him. "No Ben." He twisted the rifle out of Ben's grip, and tossed it over the gunwale into the bay. "No son should ever do that. No father should ever—not for all the money in the world."

Then the bomb blew. Disintegrated the second floor parlor in a blazing rip of wood, flame and smoke. It was done.

Steadying himself with a hand on the washboards, Ben trudged forward with Chalk's coat into the cabin. A few minutes later, Reverend Mosby checked on him. Ben lay unconscious on a berth as if tossed there in a state of exhaustion. Chalk's coat lay in pieces on the cabin sole, the pockets turned inside out, the lining shredded.

Deep in Ben's mind, all the faces that had lurked for so long behind the wall departed one by one; then the wall came tumbling down.

PART V
LAZARUS & TABITHA

CHAPTER 66

THE NEXT DAY, Ben sat with LuAnna. She was more conscious than not, which gave everyone hope. The discreet Dr. Alan brought her veterinary-strength antibiotics to supplement the ones collected for her by the Island mothers. Ben kept the radio tuned quietly to WSDL 90.7 FM, the Eastern Shore's National Public Radio station. The press got hold of a story. Not the true story. Not by a long shot.

A mild-voiced male journalist said there was a terrorist attack on Spring Island using a weapon of mass destruction. The long-dreaded dirty bomb. The first-ever atomic attack on American soil.

Japan was quick with condolences and offers of support.

Within hours, no fewer than fourteen radical terror groups claimed responsibility. Three of those claimed to be Osama Bin Laden's former cell taking vengeance on the Infidel.

According to the news, Spring Island was the terrorists' hideout, but the evil-doers all fried when the bomb they were assembling detonated prematurely.

Of course there was a hero. It was reported that a senior NSA agent named Maynard Chalk had learned of the plot through his intelligence sources, but he was too late to stop the weapon. He was credited with preventing the bomb's removal from the island. The story was spun that Chalk had saved Washington D.C. from utter nuclear extinction. A dinner in his honor was slated, to be hosted by former Senator Lily Morgan, the new

President's bipartisan nominee for Secretary of the Department of Homeland Security.

Chalk remained the man for nine full news cycles. And then the Okmok Caldera erupted in Alaska, burying a C-List starlet who was there training for an upcoming reality TV show. She was entombed in her double pop-out trailer by hot ash, along with her Pomeranian, and her hairdresser. Life for everyone else went on.

After much name-calling and other assorted dudgeon on the part of politicians on both sides of the aisle, the story of the Chesapeake bombing was eventually buried, like the actress, just not as quickly.

Word of an Emergency Restricted Area was delivered to Smith Island by the Natural Resources Police: Spring Island was going to be off-limits to everybody for a very long while. Large warning signs were posted there by workers resembling olive drab Teletubbies in their shapeless MOPP NBC protective suits. If threats of radiation sickness and death were not enough, perhaps dire warnings of prosecution, heavy fines, and lengthy imprisonment would keep the curious away. If not, beefed-up Coast Guard patrols kept protesters and gawkers from exploring the new American hot zone. Only FEMA and Nuclear Regulatory Commission scientists were allowed near the island to check radiation levels, which remained locally high, and hostile to all life forms, including, but not limited to, scoundrels.

Ben was confident Chalk and his ilk would avoid the island for a good while. Long enough for Ben and company to stash the gold in parts unknown. For all Chalk could ever hope to know now, his gold was untouchable. If he got suspicious later, it would be too late.

On the home front, Bob Crockett mopped up on Tangier Island. Crockett called on Ben personally the next morning to say his boys had already secreted the pieces of the plane wreck in a boat shed, and buried the crash victims Chalk abandoned. The plane's Emergency Locator Transmitter was dismantled and dropped in the bay. It would be at least a month before harried representatives of the NTSB and the FAA would investigate the transmitter's brief signal. Inquiring on Tangier Island, they would be met with shrugs, silence, roasted goose, and fresh oysters.

The Tangiermen patched the airstrip in just a couple of days. It was easy enough to blame the runway's poor condition on the brutal storms, which did indeed rally back for Round Two over the bay before blowing out across the Eastern Shore Peninsula into the Atlantic. Soon there was no sign of the crash. The plane would be cut up into scrap later. In seasons to come, more than a few ancient deadrises would sport hull patches made of aviation-grade aluminum.

Ben regretted that a few creatures near Spring Island did succumb to radiation including some gulls, and a few fish. The island was as close to lifeless as Ben could find in the short time he concocted his ruse. The new, large Federal restricted area put a dent in the Chesapeake's fishery, but the people of Smith and Tangier Islands felt confident they now had the wherewithal to make up for losses in their annual catch.

To Ben's delight, absolutely no sign of radiation sickness ravaged Lonesome George's heron rookery on Deep Banks Island. Ben would never treat an old friend in such a shabby manner. Especially a friend who was still guarding a fortune in gold.

There were somber memorial services for Lorton Dyze, Sam Nuttle, and Charlene and Hiram Harris, with Reverend Avery Mosby presiding. There was a special service held for Richard Blackshaw as well. Ulysses had finally come home.

Crisfield's Sheriff Tilghman, a Smith Island native, proved especially helpful to the clean-up effort when three new patrol cars and a high six-figure donation to the Police Benevolent Association were promised. He and a suggestible medical examiner ensured that the causes of death of the five Smith Islanders were variously recorded as drowning, natural causes, and a lightning strike during the storm.

Knocker Ellis slowly recovered from his gunshot wound. Ben visited him in brief breaks from nursing LuAnna.

Ben still wondered where his mother was. He and Ellis talked it over one day while Ben changed his culler's dressing. "In the Barren Creek Hotel, Pap told me he waited for her. I want to believe that."

Ellis said, "Don't tell me. Let me guess. If she didn't show, they'd try to meet later someplace else. So he wouldn't get caught hanging out if she didn't think it was safe to move. Something like that?"

"Exactly. She missed that first meet. He left."

"According to their plan. Standard operating procedure. No harm, no foul, right Ben?"

Ben had to think about that one. "No. I suppose none at all. Except, we both know she did try to meet him. She left, she tried, and she never came back."

"If it's any consolation, I don't think Chalk ever had her."

Ben agreed, "But he *knew* about her. He sounded confident enough to believe he had more information about her than I did."

"Unless he was psyching you."

"Must have been a bluff."

Ellis asked the most important question. "What's it mean about your mother? That's what scares me. What's it really mean?"

Ben was quiet. "It means she made her way into a government file that Chalk could access. Which means one of Chalk's operatives must have made contact with her at some point, maybe the night she left."

"And they didn't have tea."

Ben said, "No." He finished dressing Ellis's shoulder. "My gut tells me she didn't make it."

Ellis watched his captain carefully. "You know where to look?"

Ben nodded.

CHAPTER 67

LUANNA'S INFECTION RAN its course, leaving her weak as a kitten. Despite her struggle, after a watchful few weeks, everyone was simply relieved she hadn't taken sick with Pfiesteria Human Illness Syndrome from the toxic algae blooming in parts of the Chesapeake.

To help LuAnna get her strength back, she and Ben took long walks together on the far side of the Big Thorofare, in the Martin Wildlife Refuge. LuAnna never asked how or why they kept ending up at the ruined duck blind near the south pond. Then one day, Ben brought young Kyle Brody's metal detector. Ben did not tell her why right away.

Seated at the foot of the ancient oak tree, she watched patiently as he swept it back and forth around the duck blind. The detector buzzed a few times. Ben kneeled and carefully dug up an old fork. Then a few old shotgun shell primers, their paper cartridges long rotted away.

An hour later, she looked up when the detector buzzed for what must have been the tenth time. Ben skimmed the dirt and grass away in thin layers with a garden trowel. He held up something small in his hand, brushed off the dirt, stared at it, showed LuAnna. She could just make out what it was underneath the corrosion. A button. An embossed metal button like one might find on a woman's Norwegian style cardigan.

Ben carefully scraped away the dirt in a four foot circle around where he found the button. He soon turned up something else. It was long and thin like a metal knitting needle. He quickly found two more pins near the first. Surgical grade steel. Finally, Ben knew. His hands shook. These pins had once held his mother's upper arm together, after she and his father had been run off the road into a stream.

More careful scraping and sifting. Ben found the spent bullet. It was flattened into a mushroom shape. Now Ben knew for sure. Ida-Beth Blackshaw had meant to rendezvous with her husband that night long ago, but she had been unavoidably and permanently detained.

For a moment, Ben wondered if his parents were together somewhere, the old appointment kept. It made him all the more determined never to lose LuAnna again.

Ben kneeled and looked at LuAnna. She smiled at him with both love and sorrow. Gorgeous as she was, Ben's gaze was drawn up the trunk of the tree where she sat. Someone, something, was staring at him from a knothole where a branch had long ago fallen away. He whispered, "Don't move."

Ben slowly got to his feet, approached the tree. The thing inside the knot-hole went on staring at him, unblinking.

LuAnna said, "Ben, what is it?"

Ben said, "You're not going to believe this."

LuAnna got to her feet and turned as Ben reached for the knothole and snatched at the object as if it might get away, as if it were an Easter egg that was stashed up high where only a taller child, an older child on the verge of questioning his faith, might find it. Round. White. His blood ran cold. It was a prosthetic eye. There couldn't be two of them. He was certain he had last seen it in his father's hands on Spring Island over a month ago. The night his father died. There was something etched in its surface. It looked like two dates. Ben angled the object so the light favored clearer reading. The first date was his parents' wedding day. Pappy Blackshaw's way of proving it was he who left the eye just where he knew Ben would come looking.

The second date was for Ben's and LuAnna's upcoming wedding. That had only been decided and announced in the newspaper two weeks ago. Dick had been here, and quite recently. He had survived the fire and the bomb. He was still local, because no wedding notices had been posted outside of the one in the *Crisfield-Somerset County Times*. Ben figured his father must have known more about how the bomb worked than he let on, perhaps even how to roll back the timer to give him enough margin to escape. Dick had turned back time just enough to serve his purpose.

Ben remembered that delirious question his father had asked him in their last moments together on Spring Island; Dick's corruption of Holy Scripture. 'Why don't you look for the living among the dead?' In that instant, Dick must have figured out what happened to his wife. He had come here to be certain, and wanted Ben to understand this, too. Richard Blackshaw had found his long lost Ida-Beth.

Now Ben doubted his father had been hurt as badly as he let on; wondered if he had really been shot at all. Maybe he had faked the wound and all that blood as part of the plan, just to give himself a chance to see Chalk's face one last time there in the old hotel, right at the moment of Chalk's undoing, at the start of his fall. Dick was not just a piratical survivor; he had risked his life to gloat. This entire theft was set up from the very beginning to the bitter end as revenge for his wife.

He's alive. This meant something to Ben, but in the cascade of emotions coursing through his heart, he could not be sure precisely what. *Must have stashed a getaway boat ahead of time.*

"Welcome home, Pap," he muttered, smiling. LuAnna watched him, wondering, but she asked nothing for now. Ben pocketed the eyeball.

Ben dug no farther in the ground by the dilapidated blind. He gently troweled the earth he had removed back into place. The marsh was one of his mother's favorite places in life. He felt she was home, at peace, and always had been since the moment she died. The next day Ben and LuAnna brought flowers to his mother's grave. Ben read from the Bible, and when his voice failed him, LuAnna carried on. Together, their words transformed that profane old scene into a holy place forever.

*

Paltry savings accounts and rare 401Ks on Smith and Tangier Island were raided by the careful residents to stake the next phase of the plan. Ben soon received news from New York City of the arrival of several parcels, care of a tight-lipped army buddy who lived there. One large package sent there contained an electric furnace used to fire ceramics. With a few modifications, it could melt metal. This same friend also took delivery of a few antique plumbago crucibles in various sizes. And there was a large shipment of modeling wax, as well as plaster of Paris. No one hacking and scanning the delivery services would know a foundry was being established in Soho on behalf of a Smith Islander.

With the prospect of wedding photographs looming, LuAnna went to a wiz of a dentist up in Kingstown. He had an office with picture windows overlooking the Chester River. For three days straight, LuAnna watched the languid water flow by while the dentist worked cosmetic miracles on her chipped teeth. She overnighted with Ben at the Imperial Hotel in Chestertown. When the dentist was done, LuAnna's smile was as bright and gorgeous as ever. Just in time for the big day.

Reverend Mosby met Ben and LuAnna at the saltbox one chilly January morning. After a sip of coffee, Mosby said, "My mother once explained our most sacred rites like this. 'Hatch, match, and dispatch.' It's rare we get two in the same week, for the same folks."

LuAnna was at once downcast and confused. "We're getting married, but I'm not expecting now."

Ben took her hand, and said, "Remember when you suggested I should melt that bar of gold into a widgeon mold?"

Her confusion deepened, but her cheeks colored. "Yes. I was so mad at you."

Ben said, "It was a good idea. I don't know if you heard us talking more about it downstairs the night we got you back from the lighthouse."

LuAnna's was not following, but she covered. "If I did hear you big mucky-mucks making top secret plans, I don't recall. Would you have to kill me if I did?"

Ben exchanged a glance with Reverend Mosby. Ben surprised her, saying, "Something of that nature." Ben went on, "LuAnna, that idea you tossed out is exactly what we're going to do. Turn the whole lot of that gold into small pieces of artwork, and sell them off. I need your help."

"I'm retired. A woman of leisure. Of course I'll help."

Ben eased ahead. "We won't be able to do the work here. We won't be able to market the gold under our name. Could you stand a long honeymoon?"

"I'm listening."

Ben took her other hand. "In New York City?"

LuAnna's eyes gleamed. "It's an island. Hell, it's an island with a Fifth Avenue! Who'd mind such a thing?"

"You might, when you hear what's involved."

LuAnna looked to Reverend Mosby for clarity, but he was absorbed, studying his fingernails. She said, "Sounds weird. What's up your sleeve, Ben Blackshaw?"

Ben said, "The gold seems inaccessible to Chalk and his people because of the radiation. But I take him to be the vengeful sort. The only way you and I can be safe from the likes of him is if we aren't here. If we are no longer viable targets, to the best of everybody's understanding. We need to disappear. More than disappear."

LuAnna was getting the picture. "Like a Waterman's Witness Protection Program? It's called The Marsh."

"It's a bit more serious, and for longer. That's why I asked Reverend Mosby to join us."

The Reverend pulled a pad of paper and a pen from his worn old briefcase, and rested a pair of reading glasses on his nose. He smiled. "Let's start by talking about your wedding vows. Then we'll work our way around to your eulogies."

EPILOGUE

REVEREND MOSBY SPOKE the words for Ben and LuAnna on their day. It was a beautiful wedding attended by everyone from both Smith and Tangier Islands. Knocker Ellis, with his half of all the gold, was now the single richest man around. He accepted the honor of giving LuAnna away.

Only once did Ben cast an eye around the assembled well-wishers for sign of Dick Blackshaw. Nowhere in sight. For a moment Ben wondered if Dick had become Magwitch, the criminal benefactor lurking unseen in the marsh, to his Pip. Regardless, his father had certainly delivered on the promise of great expectations. And yet it appeared he was gone again. Perhaps for now. Maybe forever. No way to tell with that one.

The joyful wedding was soon followed by tragedy. A terrible accident. The local papers said a deadrise called *Miss Dotsy* was discovered swamped near the Martin Wildlife Refuge. The occupants were missing, presumed drowned in a storm. They disappeared at the start of their wintry honeymoon cruise on the Chesapeake they both loved. Their bodies were never found. No one on Smith Island asked what possessed them to tour the Chesapeake in a small open boat in January. Yet that is how the lovely bride, Natural Resources Police Corporal LuAnna Bryce, Retired, and Ben Blackshaw, her waterman groom, were lost; vanishing together on the very same day, and in the very same flaw.

For Discussion

- What are Ben Blackshaw's most important traits? What are his ethical dilemmas?
- Is Maynard Chalk a lunatic or an overreaching genius? Does he have a personal code?
- Is LuAnna Bryce a victim or a survivor?
- Is Knocker Ellis a man of principles, or is he loyal to the Blackshaw men to a fault?
- How do the characters change, learn, or grow through the story?
- Is the Chesapeake Bay more a part of the book's setting, or does it have qualities of a character in its own right?
- What have you learned about Smith and Tangier Islands?
- How would a sudden influx of wealth affect your life? Would it have a universally positive result?
- In what ways is Smith Island a microcosm of the American Experience?

About the Author

Robert Blake Whitehill was raised in a Quaker family on Maryland's Eastern Shore. He is an experienced Chesapeake sailor, a private pilot and a contributor to Chesapeake Bay Magazine. In addition to writing for Discovery's The New Detectives, Whitehill is also an award-winning screenwriter, including an Alfred P. Sloan Foundation win at the Hamptons International Film Festival, for his feature script U.X.O. (Unexploded Ordnance). He lives with his bride and their son in New Jersey where he also serves his community as an Emergency Medical Technician. DEADRISE is Whitehill's first novel.

Find more about the author, his blog, upcoming releases, and the Chesapeake Bay at:

www.robertblakewhitehill.com

Enjoy the opening maneuvers of the next Ben Blackshaw thriller!

NITRO EXPRESS

PART 1
QUIETUS

CHAPTER 1

THE MURDER WAS spectacular. Though in the immediate after-
math, mainstream news producers and their corporate handlers steered
away from calling it an outright assassination, the devoted, some might say
rabid fans of Lucilla Calderon reacted as if a Kennedy had been slaughtered
in front of them. Compared to Calderon, the death of the short-lived
Tejano star Selena was a mere media hiccup.

Lucilla Calderon was huge. Galactic. At twenty-four, she was a
breakaway crossover success with her roots deep in Latin traditional music
with updated lyrics and funky, danceable techno arrangements. She wrote
mostly about the new struggles of *The People*, that is, anyone who was not a
multi-millionaire by age twenty. She could krump, or pop-and-lock, or
tango—depending on the need—for her dazzling music videos. Practically
her every exhalation for the last six years charted in the top five on the
major popular music rosters, with most going number one. Her fan base
spanned the globe, literally. There was an astronaut serving in low earth
orbit aboard the International Space Station, a biologist, who was known

play Calderon's tunes while working on his experiments. That story alone fizzed for several news cycles on the major networks.

Yet La Luz, or The Light, as journalists hastened to translate in spavined simile and hackneyed metaphor, was down to earth. So said her ardent fans. She was down with the brown. She represented La Raza with a wild kind of dignity that included one of Playboy Magazine's more chaste, yet best-selling pictorials in the last decade of almost anything goes.

And now she was starring in her first movie. It was called *Ganar: To Win*. Calderon played a plucky, big-hearted revolutionary leader struggling in a fictional South American island nation. Her character was a charismatic Valkyrie, like Evita, but she rose to power not through her President husband's death, but through her own initiative and integrity, uniting disparate political and socio-economic factions into an unbeatable rebel force. The picture was laced, of course, with measured applications of violence, and a love triangle with a male and a female comrade that, while deemed shocking by the more straitlaced, had endeared her to the more open-minded critics who mattered. In an unrealistic plot twist, upon winning the revolution, her character immediately holds multiparty elections deemed honest and fair by European monitors, and impeccably wins leadership of her fledgling democracy by a landslide. Luz was George Washington with all her own teeth, with no implants of any kind, if her publicist was to be believed.

Advance notices for *Ganar* in the print trades, in the blogosphere, the twitterverse of social media, and in film and television entertainment outlets all led off with breathless predictions of top honors ahead for *Ganar* at the major award ceremonies. Luz was poised to fulfill the glorious pan-media destiny tragically denied to Selena.

After a lackluster year for the film industry, the premiere night's screening at the Theatre Formerly Known as Kodak in Los Angeles guaranteed a phenomenal box office for the project in the weekend to come. The smaller Grauman's Chinese Theatre located on the same block had been considered only briefly for the occasion, but was dismissed as too small, and too reminiscent of a bygone Hollywood era dominated by the White establishment.

It was a good call. Within a half hour of the premiere's announcement, almost every one of the larger theatre's 3332 seats was booked by

Hollywood's most beautiful and most potent, both in front of, and behind the camera. Mere mortals deluged any film industry god or demigod with the most tenuous link to the production and distribution of *Ganar* with fevered demands to find a way to get them in. Even the film's lowly writers, all twenty-three of them, whether credited onscreen or not, were fielding offers of lavish gifts, drugs, cash, travel, and even sex if only they would part with, or somehow scrounge up, a single ticket.

A lucky few members of the masses got exactly what they wanted without usury. Luz Calderon had insisted that a full five hundred seats would be reserved for *The People* and bestowed upon them free of charge by a lottery on specially marked bottles and cans of the soft drink AzteKola, void where prohibited, no purchase necessary, and forget for the moment that the bubbly sweet beverage was originally created in Mexico back in the '30s by a very White immigrant from Kansas. This gesture, a slick move some cynics called it, had garnered even more delirious press for a star who already could do no wrong.

Luz Calderon's populist ways played hell with her handlers. She shunned the roided-out security details on which so many industry players insisted. Opening night at the Kodak would be no exception. Her only concession to protection from some lunatic, because only a crazy person would want to hurt La Luz, was a trio of unarmed cholo friends who had known her since kindergarten back in East Los. At Luz's insistence, these three men had been required to publicly abandon any gang affiliations before she would take them on. The press loved this. Devoured it. So tonight, Luz was on her own, and she liked it that way. There were no artificial barriers, no poser's need for distance from the very people who adored her, and whom she loved in return, each and every one. It would not matter in the end. Even if La Luz had recruited the fierce yet ragtag rebel army her character led in the movie, it would not have saved her.

This did not stop the Los Angeles Police Department from pulling extra officers onto the *Ganar* detail. Lots of them. There was the usual show of strength at the street level for several blocks around the theatre, with a loose cordon of uniforms starting at West Sunset Boulevard to the south, North La Brea to the west, Franklin Avenue to the north, and North Las Palmas to the east. There were additional uniformed officers in position on the streets closer to the theatre, but they were heavily reinforced by plain-clothes detectives pressed from the outlying Valley, Central and South bureaus so as not to irk *The People*'s starlet with an apparent police occupation of the area.

Rooftops were another matter. Every structure on the theatre's block and immediately adjacent was secured by teams of spotters and snipers. In an unusual move, Incident Command for the event was positioned on top of the theatre itself to be a less provocative element. This did not make the Incident Commander happy. She was a hands-on officer who had risen through the ranks from her start as a beat cop, but she was used to seeing practicalities bend under the weight of the whims of the rich and famous.

Though six of the twelve Aerospatiale B-2 Astar helicopters from the L.A.P.D.'s Air Support Division were aloft, they were loitering five miles away, so the area around the former Kodak would not look as though an aerial suspect pursuit was in progress during the premiere. All spotlights were on the ground, and they were pointing skyward, not the other way around. There was a ten-mile-radius Temporary Flight Restriction centered on the theatre for nearly all General Aviation aircraft. The single exception was made for five news choppers. They were more than welcome, provided their networks had filed in advance for their clearances, and they squawked discreet codes issued specifically for the event on their transponders. Luz Calderon demands, and La Luz gets. She got more than she bargained for.

As always, most of the attention around the theatre was focused on Hollywood Boulevard. Camera and color announcer towers were erected overnight by crack crews, many of whom looked like slobs, appeared never to shift out of first gear, but who got the job done right on time, the first time. The towers were tricked-out with bunting colored like the flag of the movie's revolutionary army, and populated with camera operators for wide shots of the celebrity get-in. Camera and sound crews for the tighter shots, and glamorous network talking heads roved in packs around the cordoned and carpeted gauntlet leading to the theatre's exterior proscenium entrance. A network's rank in the ratings influenced its interviewers' positions. Other crews grabbed and held less desirable spots where the elite had to pass and offer their sound bites. This was a special event for the public, but for the union workers actually making it happen, it was barely more than a drill. They had just done it for the big award ceremony in February a few weeks before. This slightly scaled-back effort coming on its heels was a piece of cake.

One hurdle for the celebrities during the get-in was trying to think up fresh ways to declare that working on *Ganar* had kept them in a constant state of emotional orgasm, that everyone involved, especially Luz, was an absolute dream to work with, and that *Ganar* was the most important project of their lives or anybody else's. Writers had been oncall for weeks perfecting seven-second mots justes for those movie deities who preferred not to work the gauntlet off the cuff. The lavish writing fees put the scribes in striking distance of buying tiaras, either the bejeweled kind, or the fiberglass variety with big twin diesels. Big openings were big business all over town.

It was getting close to curtain time. By now, most of the attending stars, directors and producers were through the chute outside, and on their way past the bars where they scooped up flutes of pre-poured Cristal champagne with the zeal of walled-out marathon runners snatching cups of water from hydration volunteers. The five hundred lottery winners were still on Hollywood Boulevard. They would enter after La Luz's arrival. She was coming in last. She understood the importance of creating anticipation, of making a grand entrance. It was her exit that everyone would remember.

Tonight La Luz looked like a queen. Eyes heavily accentuated with black mascara, lips a glossy red, with buscanovio spit curls plastered to her temples. She wore a mantilla comb in her hair, a turquoise halter top, and tight black mariachi pants with silver buttons from hip to the snug hem just below her knee. Her only nod to bling was a beautiful turquoise pendant two inches across hanging on a long silver box chain at her sternum between her small gravity-defying breasts. Luz was everyone's *ruca*, their true love.

She was homing in on the theatre in a blazing neon green lowrider, once a '58 Ford Fairlane Skyliner with the retractable hardtop. She led a procession of other heavily modified cars that hopped and bounced and danced with trunk-loads of batteries boosting 72-volt systems for the hydraulic lifters on each wheel. The car behind Luz's was blasting the movie's theme song, which she had written herself. The windows of nearby buildings pulsed in time with the bass line and threatened to send glass window panes guillotining down into the street.

La Luz's parade of lowriders had already made several laps in the streets outside the police cordon purely for the enjoyment of happy crowds of *The People*, some of whom had personal reasons for not rubbing up against the L.A.P.D. presence closer to the theatre. Crips and Bloods, as well as the Black P-Stones, Los Zetas, and Mara Salvatruchas, the MS-13, were out in their colors, but the truce that Luz had negotiated between them for the occasion seemed to be holding. She was becoming her movie character; the Great Unifier. Her revolution was well under way.

Finally it was time. The nine parade lowriders behind Luz's peeled off to stage on Sycamore Avenue outside the police cordon where she would rejoin them after the screening. There were several after-parties scheduled, and she planned to arrive at each of them with her full convoy. Luz's Skyliner continued toward the theatre, but not alone.

A gaggle of credentialed open paparazzi cars and motorcycles gunned it to fill the paved gap left by the nine lowriders. Flash units strobed the night into ten thousand instants of day. La Luz's car was not bouncing now, so that she could pull up in front of the theatre perched on the trunk, her legs draped over the center of the backseat without risk of getting launched like a rodeo bull rider. She was like a beautiful game animal driven toward the hunters by noisy beaters.

Luz's car slowed to a stop in front of the theatre. Her fans screamed adulation. Gowned and tuxedoed talking heads checked their positions and eyeballed their camera and sound crews. Ready.

Then absolute hell broke loose. The Light went out forever.

CHAPTER 2

DEAD MEN ARE supposed to rest in peace. They never tell tales. They are soon forgotten despite the deepest cuts in a headstone. Yet Ben Blackshaw, dead to the world these last four months, was strangely unnerved. This should not be. He should feel nothing like the disquiet now creeping across his skin, hackling the hairs on the nape of his neck. But the writing was on the wall, and he recognized the hand.

Winter in Greenwich Village had been cold and hard. Christmas and New Year's had passed Ben by with little more than an empty longing for people and places too far away in miles, or lost to death and time. He would have felt even worse, but his work filled every waking moment these days. He was not from around here. The distractions of carving fresh models for lost wax molds that his unusual commissions required did nothing to allay the sense that he was a stranger far behind the lines in an alien land. Though Ben was from Smith Island in the Chesapeake Bay, Manhattan was like no island he had ever known. This was nothing like home.

The spring chill clung with icy talons down in the shadows between the old factory buildings. Most of the structures in the area were long ago converted to airy or drafty spaces, depending on whether you were realtor or tenant. Now they were high-end homes and trendy minimalist office cube farms with struggling retail joints at the sidewalk level. It was so early in the day that nothing was open right now.

Ben drudged through twenty-hour days in the raw basement space of a pile that had been shunned by hungry developers because of an encumbering mass of unsettled title disputes, crippling back taxes no one wanted to pay, law-suits, glaring code violations, and zoning quandaries. An entire five-story building buried beneath paper. If he were alive, Ben would have been called a squatter. Today, he was a ghost.

Or should have been. Now, unlike the many dead he himself had killed, or seen dispatched into oblivion during Gulf War One, unlike the dead man he was supposed to be, he felt fear. That summed it up. Bubble guts. He was afraid.

According to custom, this morning he had emerged from his build-ing's concealed back alley entrance before sunrise, and walked a cautious seven blocks to an all-night Korean deli. He varied his route every day, sometimes going well out of his way for a cup of bad coffee that cream and sugar could not improve. If he felt especially homesick, he would impose the meandering pathways and streams of the Smith Island archipelago on the angular urban grid. A stroll to the Drum Point Market back on Smith led him uptown and toward the West Side. An imagined visit to the home of his friend Knocker Ellis meant heading uptown, but then east. He always broke away from the path before reaching his fancied destination. There would be no miraculous arrival at the weathered saltbox he once called home. He always wound up at the deli where no one had ever heard of putting cheese in the coffee.

Ben did not need the caffeine. He desperately wanted the fresh air, such as he could find it in New York. Fetching coffee was merely a mission. The deli, an objective. His hunter's mind, honed by years of military service, functioned more easily when there was some kind of plan underpinning his movements. The piecework of his current occupation, however rewarding, numbed his soul. Fatigue did the rest, all of it making him vulnerable to a homesickness he never felt when he served in the Gulf; and that was an unforgiving sentiment that might cause him to drop his guard and wind up, well, much closer to dead than he was already.

Someone knew he was in town, but Ben's anonymous work clothes had not betrayed him. They were dark, dyed by their maker to hide the dirt and grease of hard menial labor over many days between laundering. He zipped his coat up closer to his chin. This jacket was cheap nylon, a sub-dued navy blue. It was a shapeless, poly-filled item cloned overseas, and sold throughout Manhattan's discount stores to working men who barely got by. He had fixed the few holes, scorched from leaving it too close to his molten work, with black duct tape. He pulled his watch cap lower over his ears. Its wool and synthetic knit was likewise dark. Nothing special. No logos. Head to toe, Ben was a blank. A cipher. He blended in. He was dead to the world, but now someone was trying to bring him back to life.

On the roundabout walk home from buying the coffee, he took a sip every half block or so. Slightly tilting his head back to drink, he let his eyes case the sidewalk ahead and across the street, and the windows above. Without thinking, he filtered out the soft-treaded footfalls of his own rubber soled boots; stayed alert to sounds on the street behind him. Anything remotely close to a furtive step on his six earned an easy glance over his shoulder. The first week in town, he had worried this precaution would make him look guilty and draw attention. He quickly learned this was the Big Apple, and everyone had eyes in the back of his head.

Regardless, at this hour, few others were out, and they had bigger problems than some random guy on the move with a lousy cup of joe. Muggers were in bed after preying late into the night on those who had drunk too deeply, or gotten too high. They fed on the party kids who could not hear a quick and stealthy approach over their blasting earbuds, and on those who had survived to old age, but who were now unable to handle themselves. Ben's stride showed just enough purpose and just enough direction that, when factored with his daunting height and crappy clothes, he was not worth a mugger's trouble. That left police and desperate junkies to hassle him, and had any of those been in sight, they would be watching out for each other, not for a nobody like Ben.

He paused at the mouth of the alley leading to his door, sipped the coffee, glanced around, and peered deep into sunless holes. He let his eyes rest every few seconds as he looked not only at, but through the windows of parked cars for movement, for any sign that somebody was peering back at him from the other side. The street was clear.

The electric furnace he had turned on before he left would be plenty hot by now, drawing enough amps to spin the disk in the ancient glass-bubbled Con Edison meter like a Frisbee. Ben could start melting gold for the morning's pour right away. The electricity his work devoured was just another casualty to all the bureaucratic confusion surrounding this troubled old building. When he took up residency, Ben had tapped the trunk line with little risk anyone would report the heavy usage. No one had noticed so far, anyway. If they did, there was no clear owner to serve with a bill. Most phantoms had no money. A bigger effort to collect on utilities might have been undertaken if Con Ed knew Ben was a multi-millionaire.

Again, Ben scanned the darkened buildings around him from basement windows to rooflines. Satisfied no one was observing him with undue curiosity, he lodged the half-empty blue styrofoam cup into a poorly closed garbage bin from the building next door. Time for work. He turned and entered the alley. He passed small patches of grit-blackened snow from the last blizzard that survived in the darkness between a few broken, rotting wood pallets.

He reached the old steel door and stopped dead in his tracks. There was no knob on it, but that was not the problem. On arrival months before, Ben had torched a two-inch hole in its face on the side away from the hinges. After dirtying up a short length of steel chain, a Paclink, and a heavy duty 2170X padlock, he had threaded the chain through the hole in the door and around the steel frame where the masonry had spalled. The inconspicuous security measure, standard in such abandoned buildings, was as sound as he had left it; as sound as he always found it again on coming home. The wall was the problem. Someone had left a message there.

The black spray paint barely showed over the building's sooty grime. The figures, about three inches high, were simple enough, but they inverted his world with more violence than a well-aimed bullet. **BB2AMKIABNRMCG1300ZRIPAU**. He was certain the wall had been bare when he left for coffee. The communiqué was meant for him. Someone was rudely ignoring the fact that a dead man cannot read.

Using a stout key from his pants pocket, Ben unfastened the padlock and went inside. He rethreaded the chain, padlocking himself in the basement. The furnace had made the drafty space warmer. Out of habit, he kicked an old moving quilt against the threshold to block any cold zephyrs until Spring got serious. He sat in the dark on the single metal folding chair he had scrounged from a pile of eviction discards on the sidewalk. He had to think.

The first five figures routed the message to him personally. There was no doubt. Though he had not worn his toe tags in many years, he knew what they said by heart. Every soldier did. Reading top to bottom instead of left to right, the first figure in each line of the metal tag was B for Blackshaw, another B for Benjamin, 2, the first digit of his Social Security number, A for his blood type, and M for Methodist. Only a precious few understood this cipher agreed-on long ago. Fewer than the fingers of one of his powerful hands.

The rest of the message opened up with a little more thought. KIABNR meant killed in action, body not recovered. An expression too well known in the military family. The sender was aware he was hiding, knew where, and knew in particular that his faked death by drowning in the Chesapeake Bay months before had not yielded a corpse for burial. MCG1300Z was the call to action he could not shirk. He was needed by someone to whom he had once pledged life and limb. It was not hard to parse. McGuire Air Force Base. That's where he had to go. 1300Z was one in the afternoon Zulu time, or Coordinated Universal Time. Converting to local time in his head, Ben had to get to McGuire somehow by nine this morning. He still had no idea why, but that would be revealed in due course.

It was the RIPAU that bothered him most, even more than the call to a mysterious mission. Rest In Peace. That was plain enough. But why add that in? A message from anyone who understood this format, and who had taken the trouble to use it instead of meeting him face to face, would have earned his swift response. The sender was telling him two things. The first was that it was understood his current undertaking had his full attention. A contrived death, and a self-exile to the last place on earth he would ever wish to visit, let alone sojourn, meant big doings. How much did the sender really understand? That was made clear in the second metamessage. *Au* was the kicker. The chemical symbol for gold from the periodic table of the elements.

Somebody knew Ben's business. If the loyalty and the blood obligation demanded by the message were not enough to get Ben moving, curiosity about who was tracking him certainly did. It could be there was a loose end or two to tie off before he and his work were going to be truly secure. The message's mention of gold meant the sender could easily guess there were cubic dollars involved, and perhaps other stakeholders who were relying on him. Somebody was crawling around in his head, in his life. Whoever left this message knew he would do almost anything to avoid having to abandon his current enterprise and break from cover into the unknown.

In full, the seemingly random letters said, I know who you really are. I know where you are. You're not dead. You better be ass-on-curb at McGuire by nine. You can rest easy with your gold, and get on with your life after you help me. Fail me, and it won't be so peaceful.

There was a slim chance he was reading into the last part, the implied threat, but Ben did not take it lightly. With resignation, he turned off the furnace. The dull hum of massive electrical power surging through the heavy-duty circuitry went silent. In the new quiet, he glanced around the space. Gray morning light wandered in almost by mistake through filthy gunslit windows. A cache of stolen gold bullion lay under another moving quilt. Not a lot. About four million dollar's worth in today's market. In five minutes this same boom market would make the gold worth significantly more. The rest of it was stashed back home on Smith Island. Only small quantities were brought up to him in every shipment to minimize the risk of losing everything to theft or a raid to recapture it. Can't be too careful. The former owners of the gold had long memories, and were likely to be irritable for even longer about getting foxed.

A graceful solid gold sculpture of a swan, about ten inches high, lay waiting under another blanket for a final polish. The gold was so pure, so soft, he could have carved it with a sharp knife instead of casting it. In fact, many of the finishing details that would make the swan such a precious an expression of his vision were added in by hand. That would have to wait. The woman who was expecting this piece at the gallery down in Soho would also have to wait. The buyer, an arms dealer who lived in London's Connaught Square, would have to cool his heels, too.

Ben was not laundering money. He was converting stolen gold to cash in the only way he knew. He was transforming bullion into U.S. dollars at about 1.38 times the market rate per ounce at the time of final sale, so prized was his artistry. So far the system had worked. Thirty-six million dollars had already been realized from this gambit. The revenue had all been sent back home to Smith Island. More accurately, the sale price of every piece, less the gallery commission, was wired to a numbered account at Scotiabank in the Caymans. He and his people believed in the safety of islands. Manhattan, it was turning out, might not have been a foolproof bet.

Plans were in the works back home to lease a gallery in The Village to eliminate the present gallery commissions. The Smith Islanders could afford it now. Until recently, lean times meant many at home could barely afford to eat more than once a day. That was changing. The price of gold was rising faster than the cost of New York City real estate. Ben's slow output from his basement studio had its advantages in dollar-cost averaging.

The sender of the strange message was right. Picking up and leaving town was not something Ben wished to do, not if he ever wanted to finish his work here in Manhattan once and for all, and get home to the open skies and waters of Smith Island.

There was no question Ben would accept the summons. On the other hand, he preferred not to walk blindly into this mission. He had to pay a visit.

He left the basement, refastened the chain on the door with the lock on the outside, and carefully climbed three flights up his building's back alley fire escape. He went slowly because the metal stairs were old, and any regular step might set up a sine-wave shudder that would alert the person on whom he was dropping in, or worse, bring the whole rickety structure down on top of him.

On the third-floor landing he peered in through a small patch in a grimy pane of glass that had been wiped clear as a peephole by the occupant. She lay in there on her mattress, sound asleep. Ω was how she signed her work. Omega. Black, about twenty or so, too thin, not exactly living la vida loca in this squat, but she enjoyed the freedom to do her own thing. She slept in her baggy pants with a shredded blanket pulled up around her arms. Omega was a one-girl crew, a hardcore tagger getting *up* in the neighborhood. Lately she was expanding into an *all-city piecing* with some brilliant murals dotting the town. Ben had surreptitiously watched her work one night, noted her particular style with admiration, and kept an eye out for new efforts. In her world, she was royalty. He was sure that Omega had written the message by his door downstairs. Having seen and enjoyed her work often enough over the previous few months, he recognized her hand.

Ben worked his fingers in over the sill and slid the window upward. It moved easily enough. It had to. It was the front door into Omega's illegal crib. The interior door to the apartment was barricaded against the addicts lurking in the rest of the building. Like Ben, she shunned attention of any sort, other than through her art.

When he got the window raised about eighteen inches, a chilly draft made Omega frown, moan, and pull the blanket more closely around her. Ben noted fifty-plus cans of vibrantly colored spray paint with fat and skinny interchangeable nozzles, all meticulously cleaned and ready for the next night's work. The different hues were arranged in families on the floor, like an art school color wheel. One wall of the room was covered by a corner-to-corner mural of an underwater dream world infested with demon fish.

This was the first time Ben had seen her up close without the respirator mask over her face and a bandana protecting her hair. She was pretty, deep golden skin, with a narrow face, high freckled cheekbones, long lashes, full lips, and a little scar on the right side of her jaw. Ben slipped in through the window. He hated creeping up on her like this, dangerous as it was for them both. There was no time for better manners.

He lowered the window, picked up two spray cans, shook them hard. The mixing marbles inside rattled loud like castanets in a palsied flamenco. He barked, "Omega!"

Her eyes flew open. Ben ignored the knife she flashed out from under the blanket in defense. He was completely taken with her vivid blue eyes.

"What the fuck!" Omega sprang to her feet, stepped bravely toward him into the center of the room, the knife held out in front of her waist high and angled at his throat.

"What the hell fuck!" She was still waking up, but with sleep quickly fading from her eyes, Ben knew she could be deadly. He put the spray cans down, and held out his hands to show they were empty. The universal sign of harmless intent in a touchy situation.

Again she shouted, "What the goddamn hell!" Fear was giving way to its more common mask of anger.

Ben tried changing the subject. "You been working up some sick bombs lately. You bust a fine spray can. I'm impressed."

"That'll be the last thing you can expect to be."

"That throw-up you did outside my door. Not your best. Your heart wasn't in it. Who said to do that?"

Omega was not having it. "Get out of here while you can. Don't want your blood messing all over my space."

Ben nodded. "I've worked a fair bit in that color myself. Settle down, tell me who gave you that message, and I'll be on my way. No problems."

Omega said nothing. The knife lowered an inch.

Ben said, "I don't care about racking and mobbing. It's about that graff. Do I look like a cop? Come on, neighbor. You know me from round about. This won't come back to you. It was some tough news you left. I need to know whatever you can tell me."

Omega hesitated. "I thought he was a vig'."

Vigilantes were strangely driven older white men who scoured graffiti off of buildings wherever they found it, or painted over it in the name of order. Police regarded vigilantes who used paint as vandals, just as they did the taggers.

Ben nodded, "But he wasn't a vig'. Could you put the knife down?"

Omega said, "No. I don't think I can." The knife did not move.

"Alright. Suit yourself. Did he pay you?"

She hesitated. "Girl's gotta eat."

"No doubt. I'm going to reach into my pocket nice and easy. We good?"

She did not answer. She watched his hand slip into the right coat pocket. He withdrew it just as slowly, but she coiled tighter for trouble.

Ben opened his hand. In his palm lay a rough sawn rectangle of pure gold the size of a small box of matches.

He said, "Market value, about five thousand dollars. Don't sell it down around here. It might come back on you. Or on me. Go out to Jersey, or even to Philly. I'm not kidding. Any joint with *We Buy Gold* in the window will be glad to try to rip you off, no questions asked. I'm betting whatever you get for it is one hell of a lot more than what that guy gave you to tag my wall. Am I right about that? I mean, you said it. 'Girl's gotta eat.'"

Omega relaxed a little. "Toss that over onto my coat."

Ben hesitated. "We have an agreement?"

"White. Shorter than you by four, maybe five inches, and skinnier. Maybe six feet. But strong. Green eyes. Dark red hair. Little mole on his chin."

Ben took this in. "What did he say?"

"He said toss that gold on my coat before I cut you."

Ben gave the piece of gold an easy lob toward the coat by her bed. It shone in the air like bright little yellow comet, and made a popping sound as it dented a nest in her leather. Omega was sharp as her blade. She did not take her eyes off Ben for an instant.

She said, "He told me what I already knew. There's a guy squatting in my building. The basement. He said what you looked like, but he said you had your hair shaved high and tight."

Ben's hair was much longer now, and not exactly neat. So the message came from somebody who knew him in the service. Ben said, "Okay. The message?"

"He handed me a slip of paper with the letters and shit on it. He knew about you. He knew me, too, my work. Said that I had to put the whole thing on the wall by your door where you'd be sure to notice."

Ben said, "You could have put the paper under my door, and I never would have known it was you."

Omega shook her head. "See now, he just let me read it. Made me memorize it, and say it a hundred times, like. Then he took it back. Told me to wait 'til you went out."

"Did he seem to know what the message meant?"

Omega's eyes narrowed. "No. Matter of fact, seemed like talking to me was a big pain in his skinny white ass. Acted like he was above it, or like he wasn't happy passing along a message he couldn't read."

Ben nodded. "Like he was cut out for bigger and better. Ever seen him before?"

Omega was getting uptight again. "Oh hell yes. Seen his kind every day. But not this particular one, no."

Ben asked, "When? When did you meet him?"

The knife shook in her hand. "Four this morning, give or take."

"Can you be more specific?"

Omega bridled. "No. I must've forgot to wind my damn Rolex." She wore no watch.

Ben asked, "Where'd this all happen?"

Omega shuddered with rage, and something else. "About where you're standing. Sick to death of waking up with white men in my damn room!"

"Got it. I'm sorry. Last question, but it's important. What did he pay you to tag the wall?"

Omega said nothing, but Ben thought he saw dew in her eyes. After a moment, she yanked the ratty collar of her t-shirt down hard over her left shoulder. An ugly bruise in the shape of a handprint marred her smooth skin.

CPSIA information can be obtained at www.ICGtesting.com
Printed in the USA
LVOW131930061212

310437LV00009B/1173/P